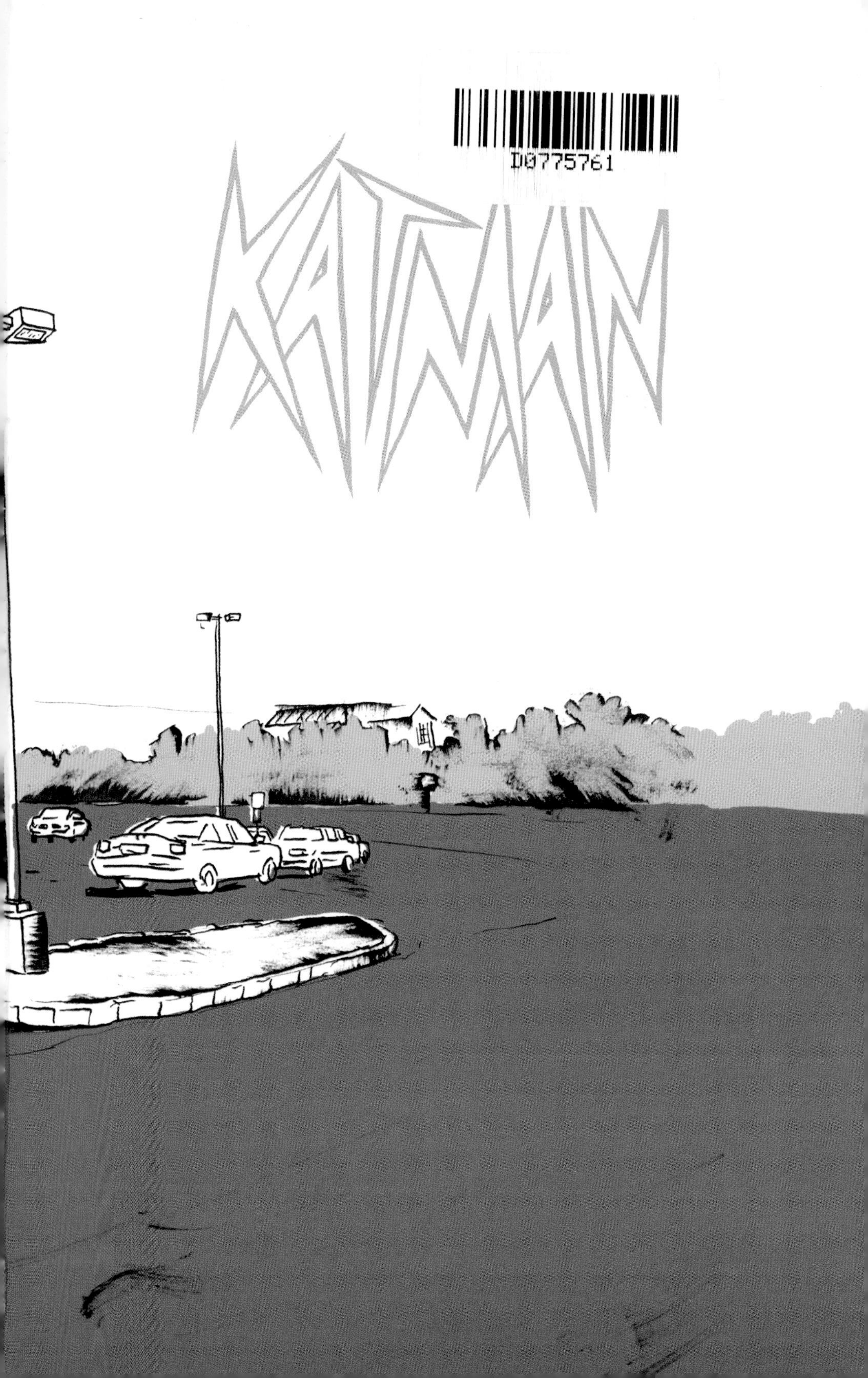
KATMAN

For Scott, the Katman of Brooklyn

Henry Holt and Company, LLC, *Publishers since 1866*
175 Fifth Avenue, New York, New York 10010
www.HenryHoltKids.com

Distributed in Canada by H. B. Fenn and Company Ltd.

Library of Congress Control Number: 2008937398

ISBN-13: 978-0-8050-8285-2
ISBN-10: 0-8050-8285-9

First Edition—2009
Printed in China on acid-free paper. ∞

1 3 5 7 9 10 8 6 4 2

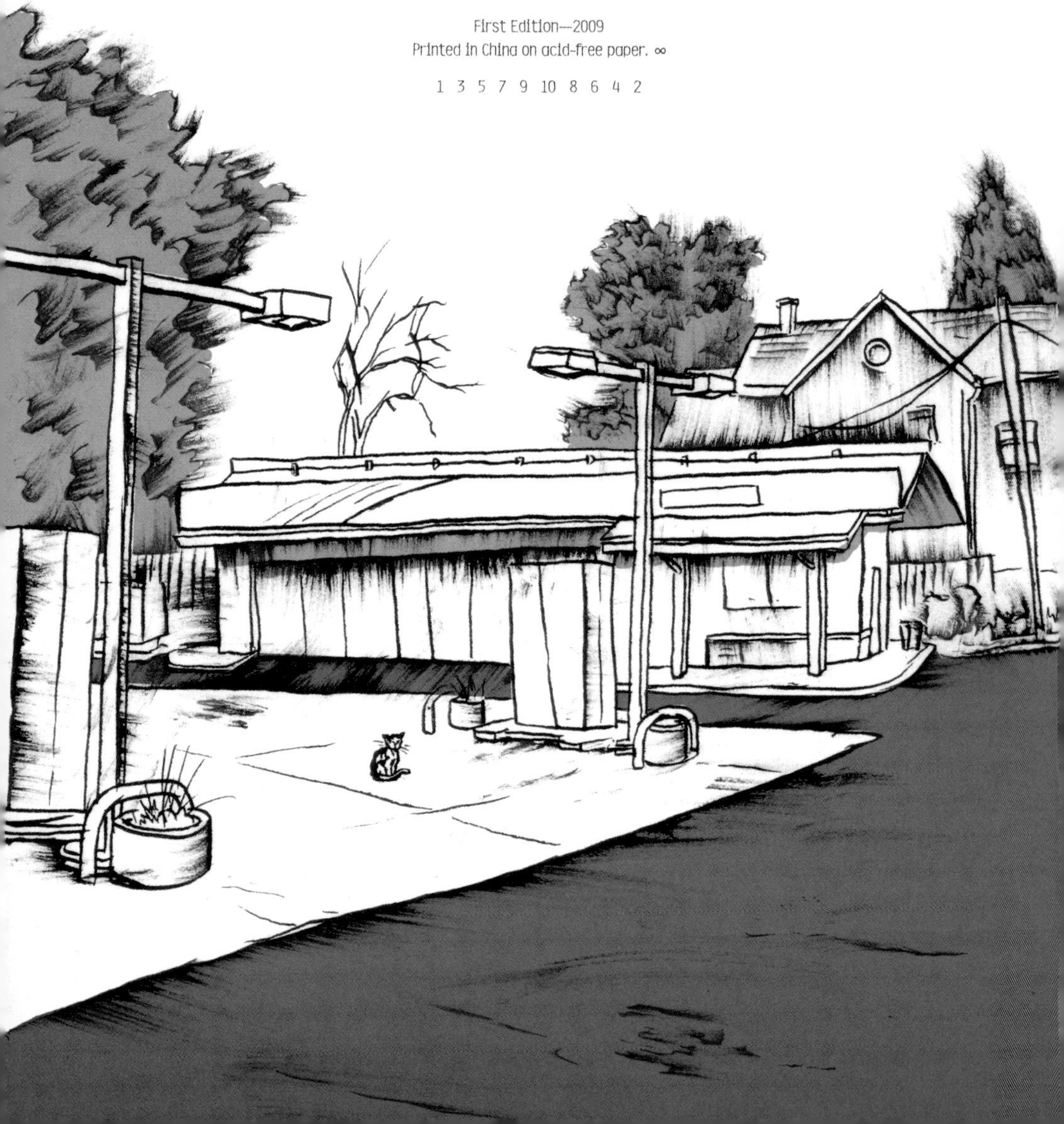

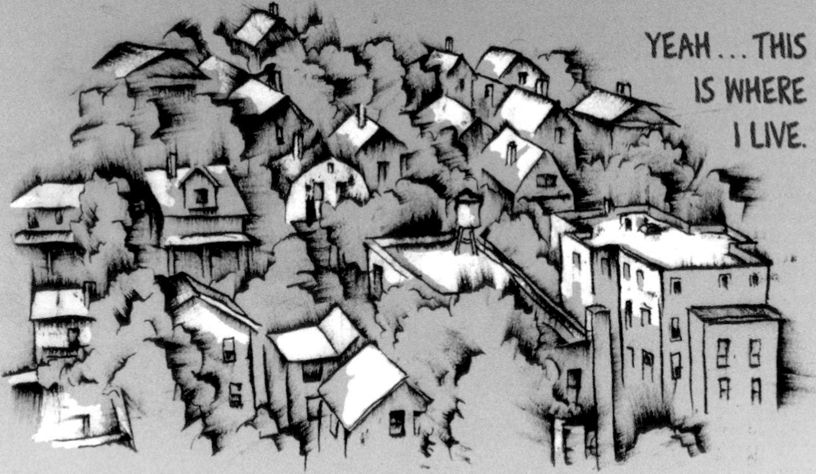
YEAH... THIS IS WHERE I LIVE.

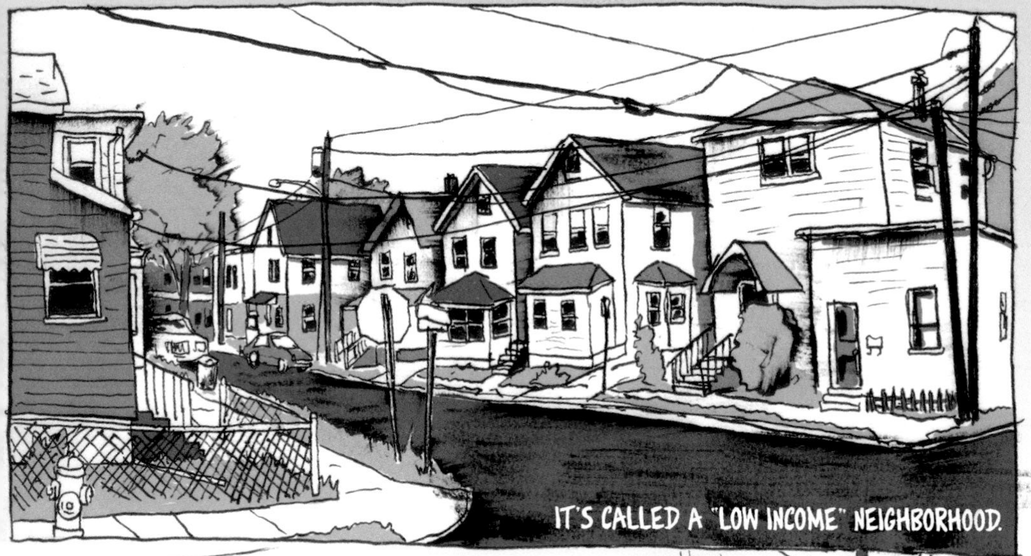
IT'S CALLED A "LOW INCOME" NEIGHBORHOOD.

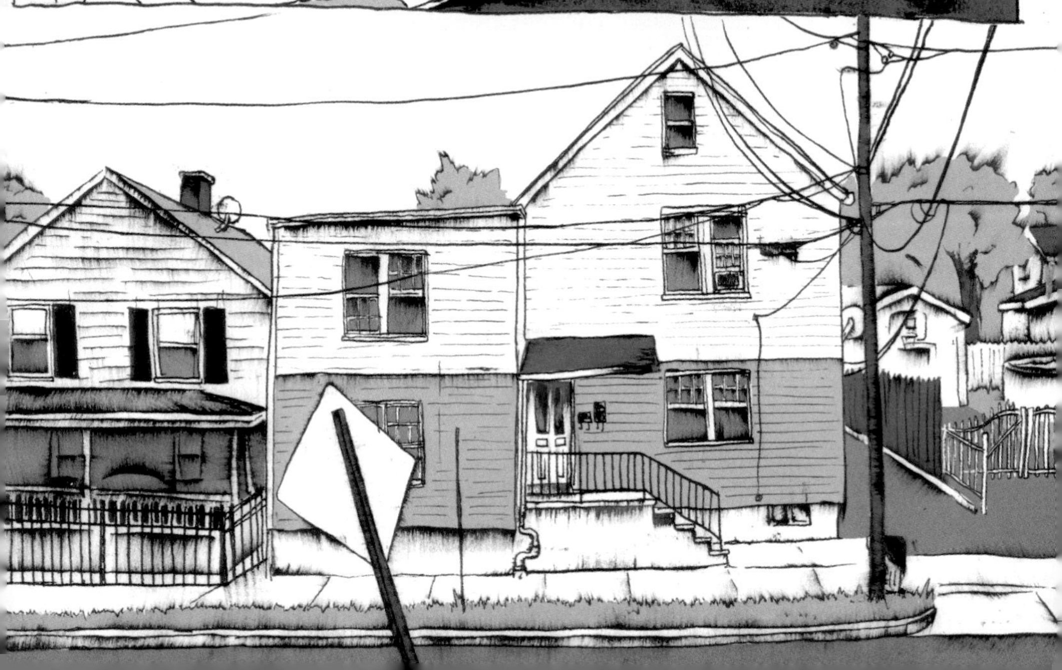

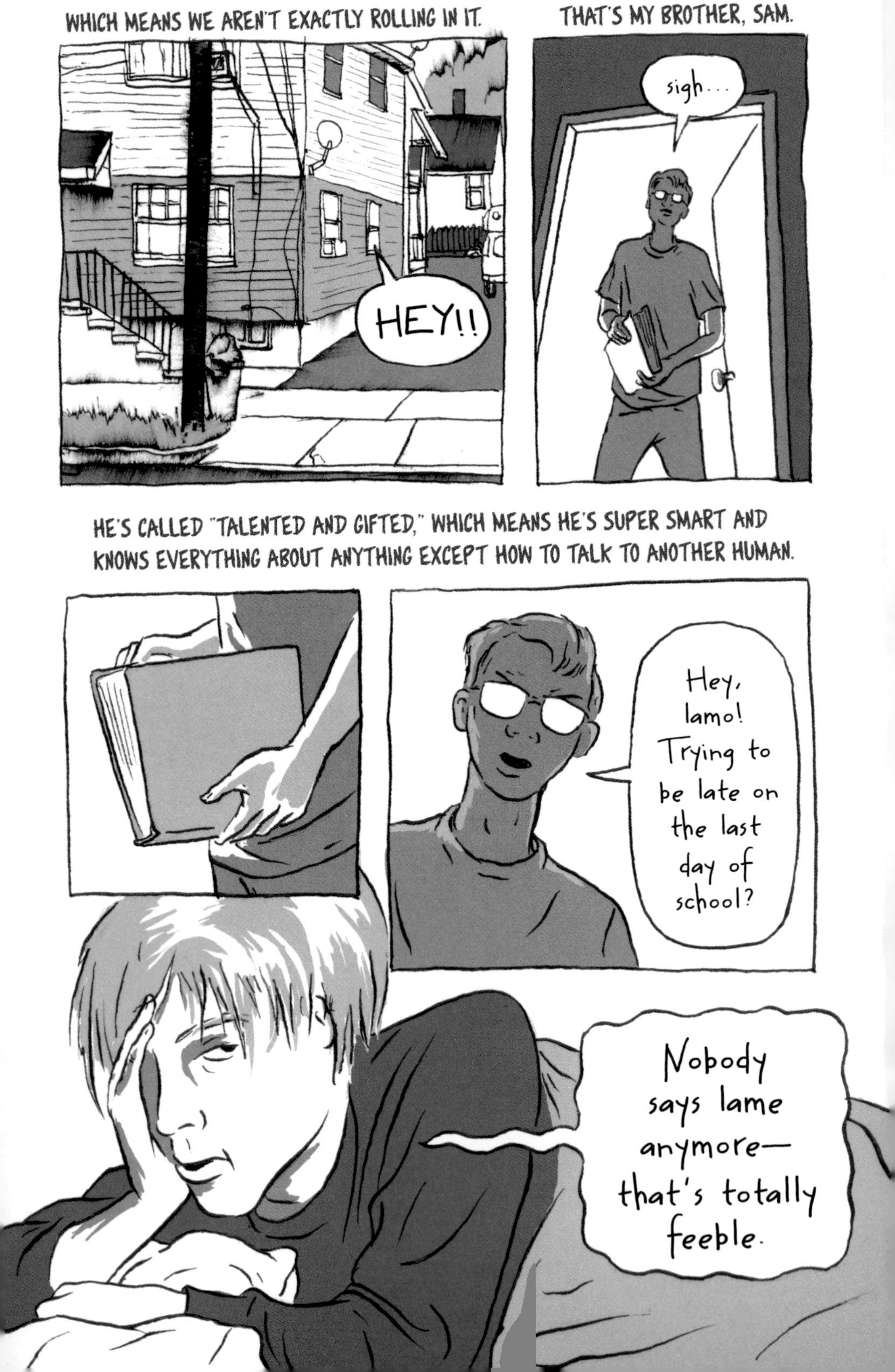
WHICH MEANS WE AREN'T EXACTLY ROLLING IN IT.
HEY!!
THAT'S MY BROTHER, SAM.
sigh...
HE'S CALLED "TALENTED AND GIFTED," WHICH MEANS HE'S SUPER SMART AND KNOWS EVERYTHING ABOUT ANYTHING EXCEPT HOW TO TALK TO ANOTHER HUMAN.
Hey, lamo! Trying to be late on the last day of school?
Nobody says lame anymore— that's totally feeble.

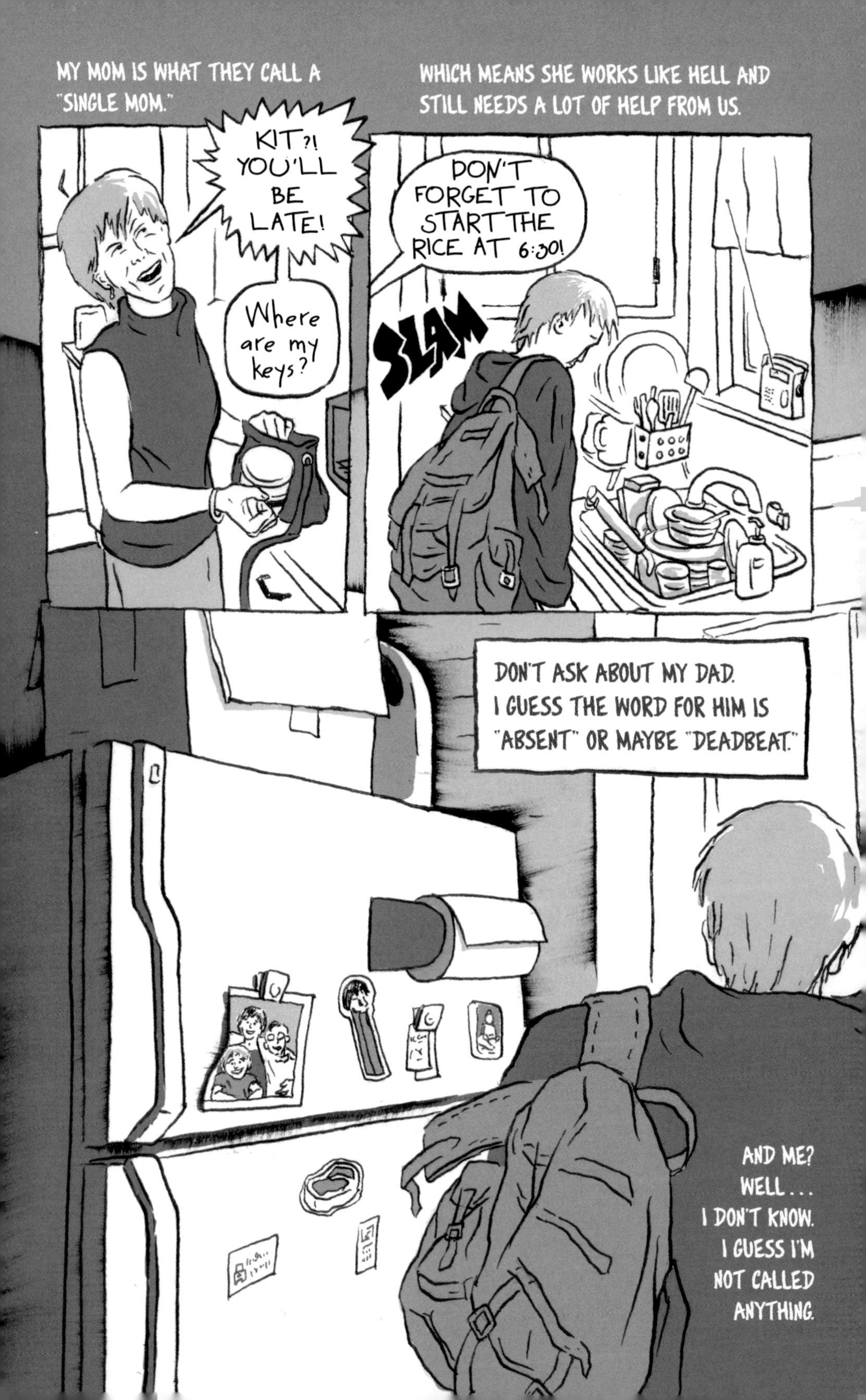
MY MOM IS WHAT THEY CALL A "SINGLE MOM."
WHICH MEANS SHE WORKS LIKE HELL AND STILL NEEDS A LOT OF HELP FROM US.
KIT?! YOU'LL BE LATE!
Where are my keys?
DON'T FORGET TO START THE RICE AT 6:30!
SLAM
DON'T ASK ABOUT MY DAD. I GUESS THE WORD FOR HIM IS "ABSENT" OR MAYBE "DEADBEAT."
AND ME? WELL . . . I DON'T KNOW. I GUESS I'M NOT CALLED ANYTHING.

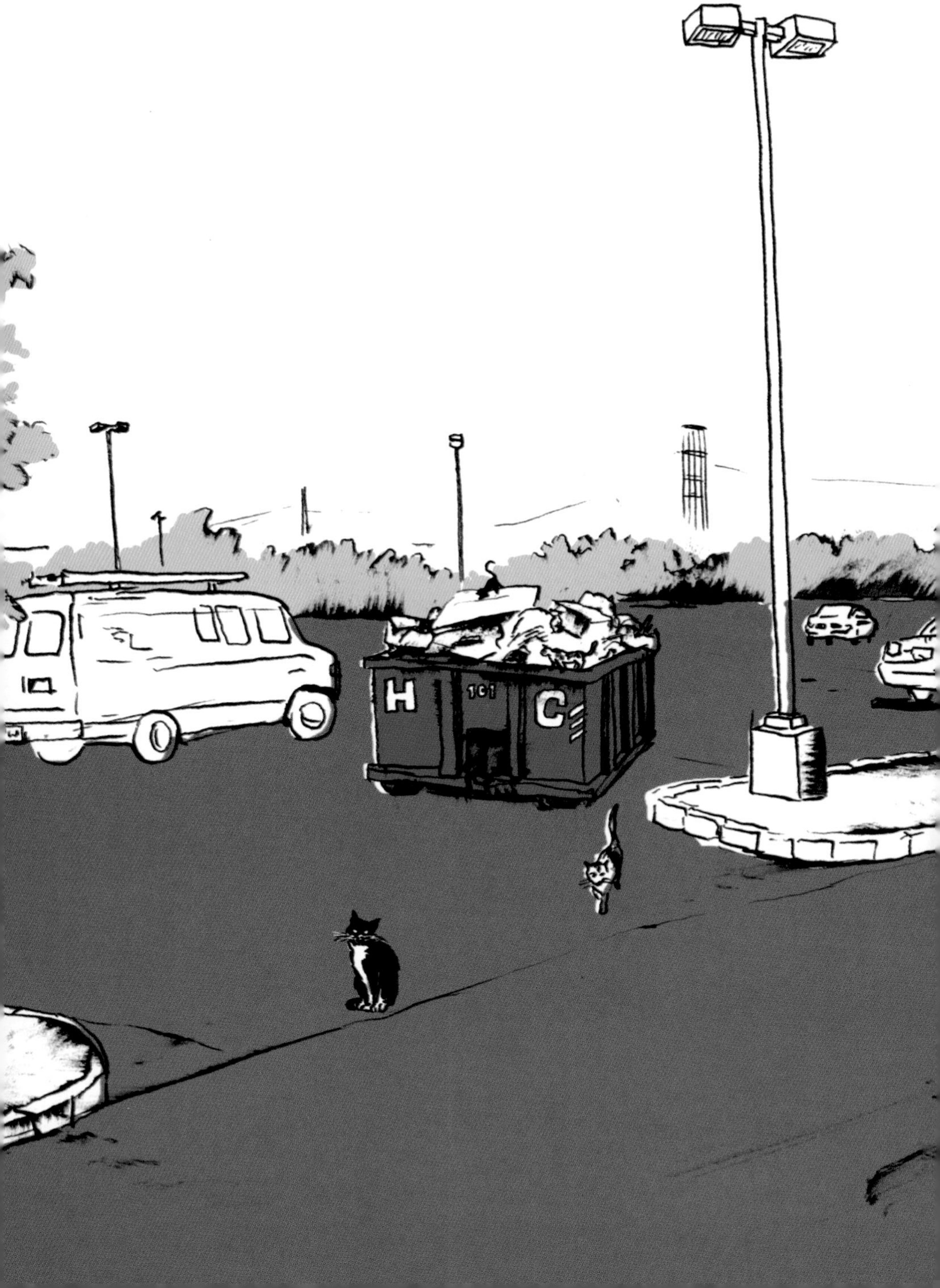
H
101
C

KATMAN

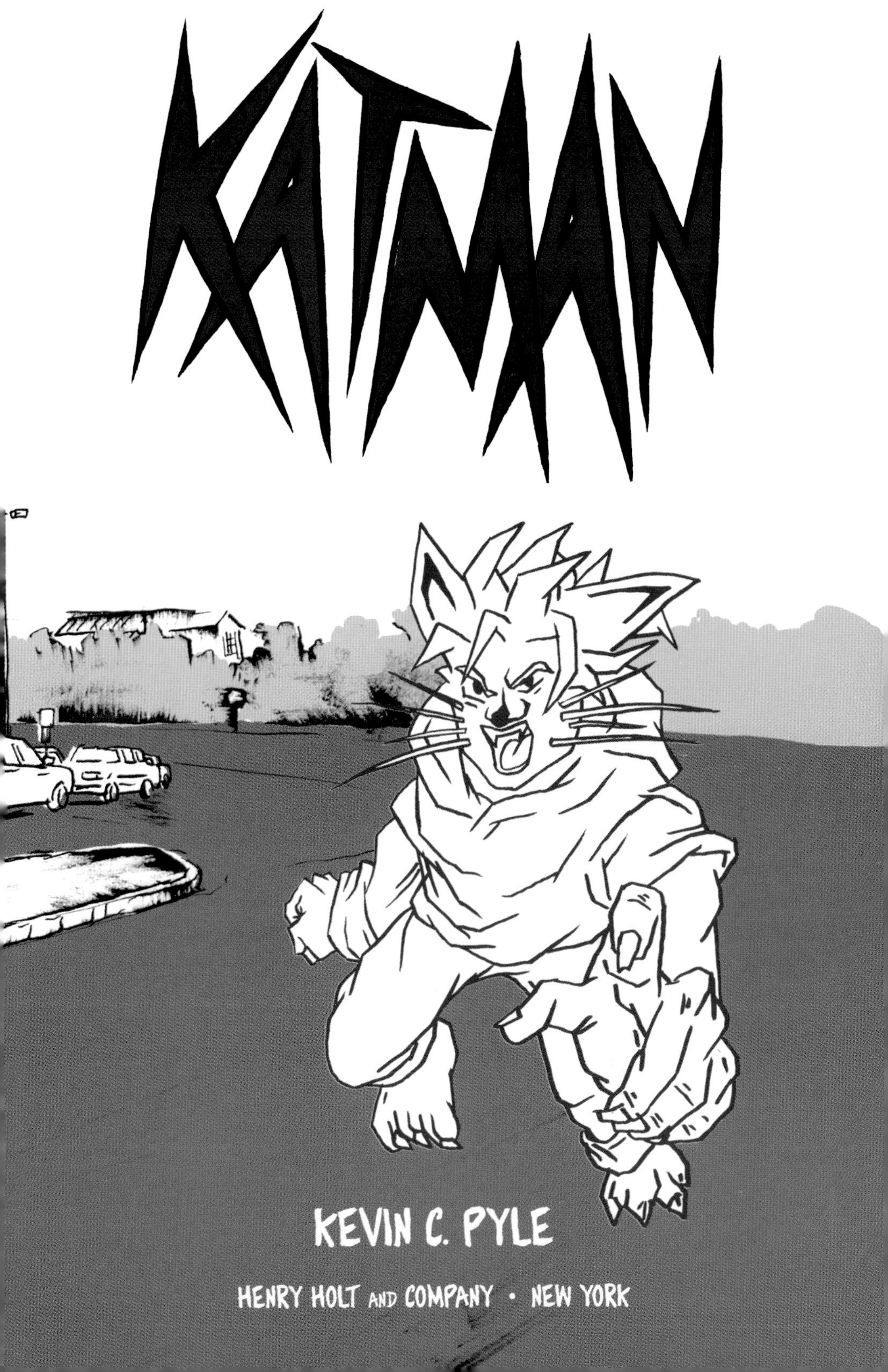

KEVIN C. PYLE

HENRY HOLT AND COMPANY • NEW YORK

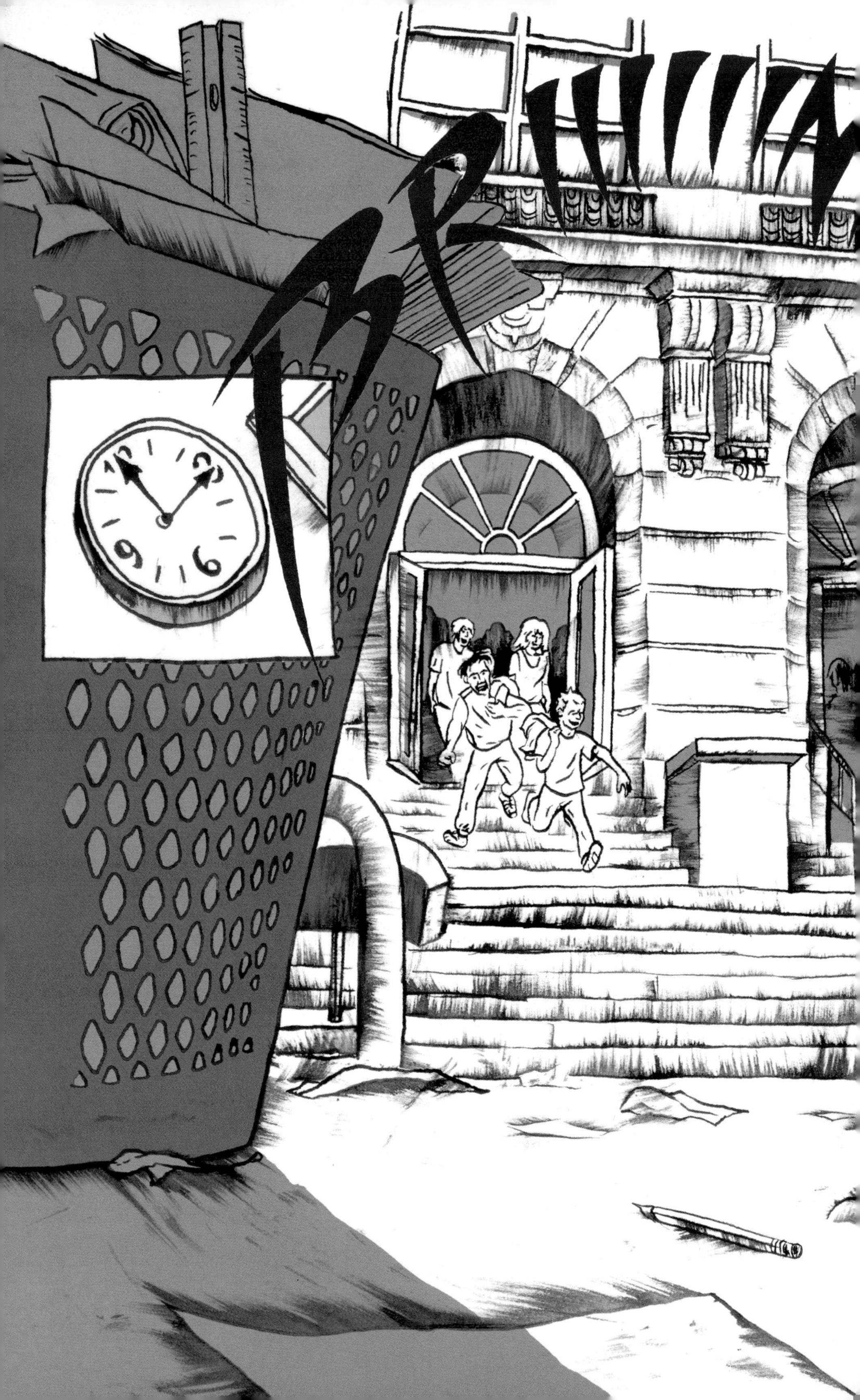

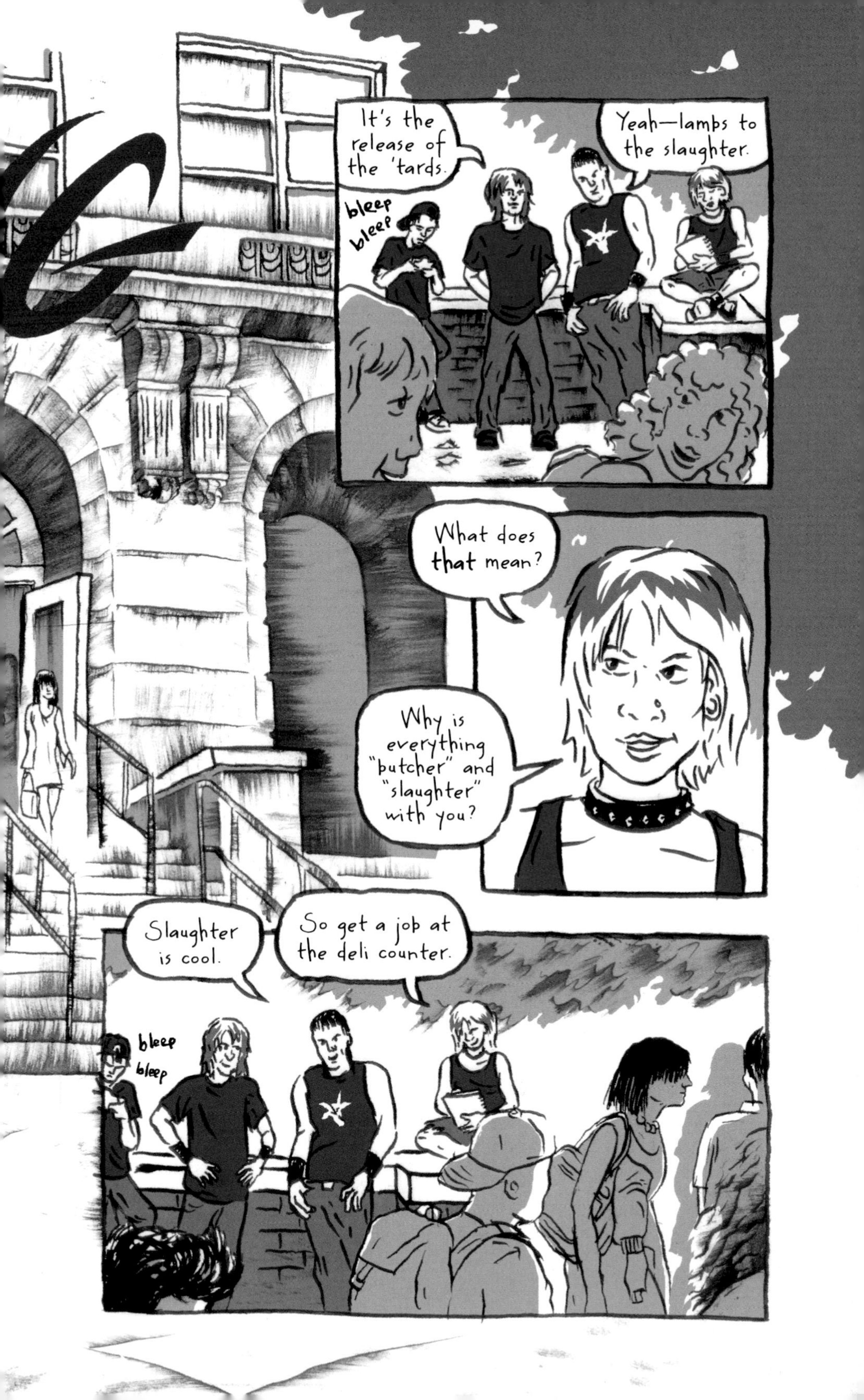
It's the release of the 'tards.
Yeah—lamps to the slaughter.
bleep bleep
What does **that** mean?
Why is everything "butcher" and "slaughter" with you?
Slaughter is cool.
So get a job at the deli counter.
bleep bleep

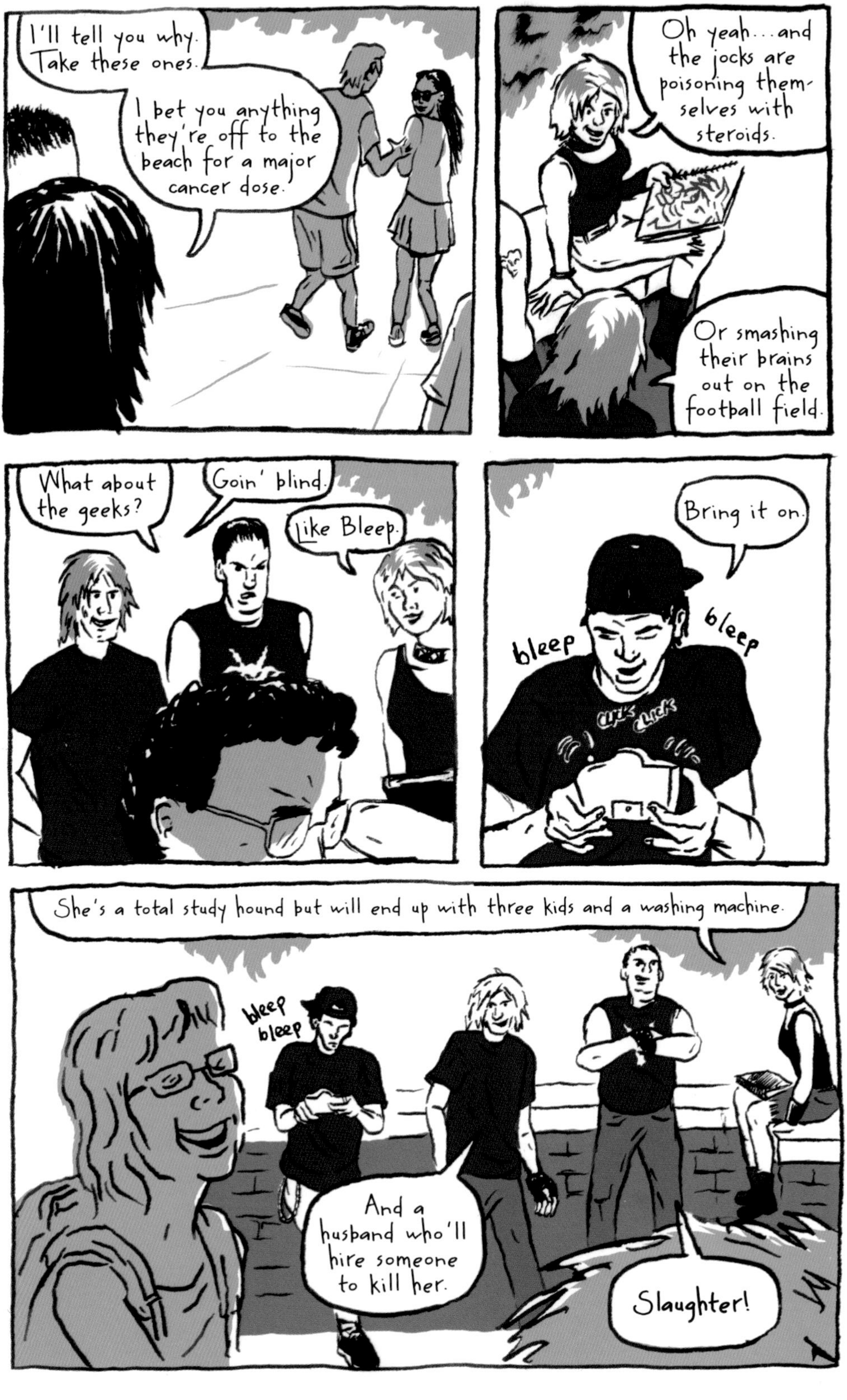
I'll tell you why. Take these ones.
I bet you anything they're off to the beach for a major cancer dose.
Oh yeah... and the jocks are poisoning themselves with steroids.
Or smashing their brains out on the football field.
What about the geeks?
Goin' blind.
Like Bleep.
Bring it on.
bleep
bleep
She's a total study hound but will end up with three kids and a washing machine.
bleep bleep
And a husband who'll hire someone to kill her.
Slaughter!

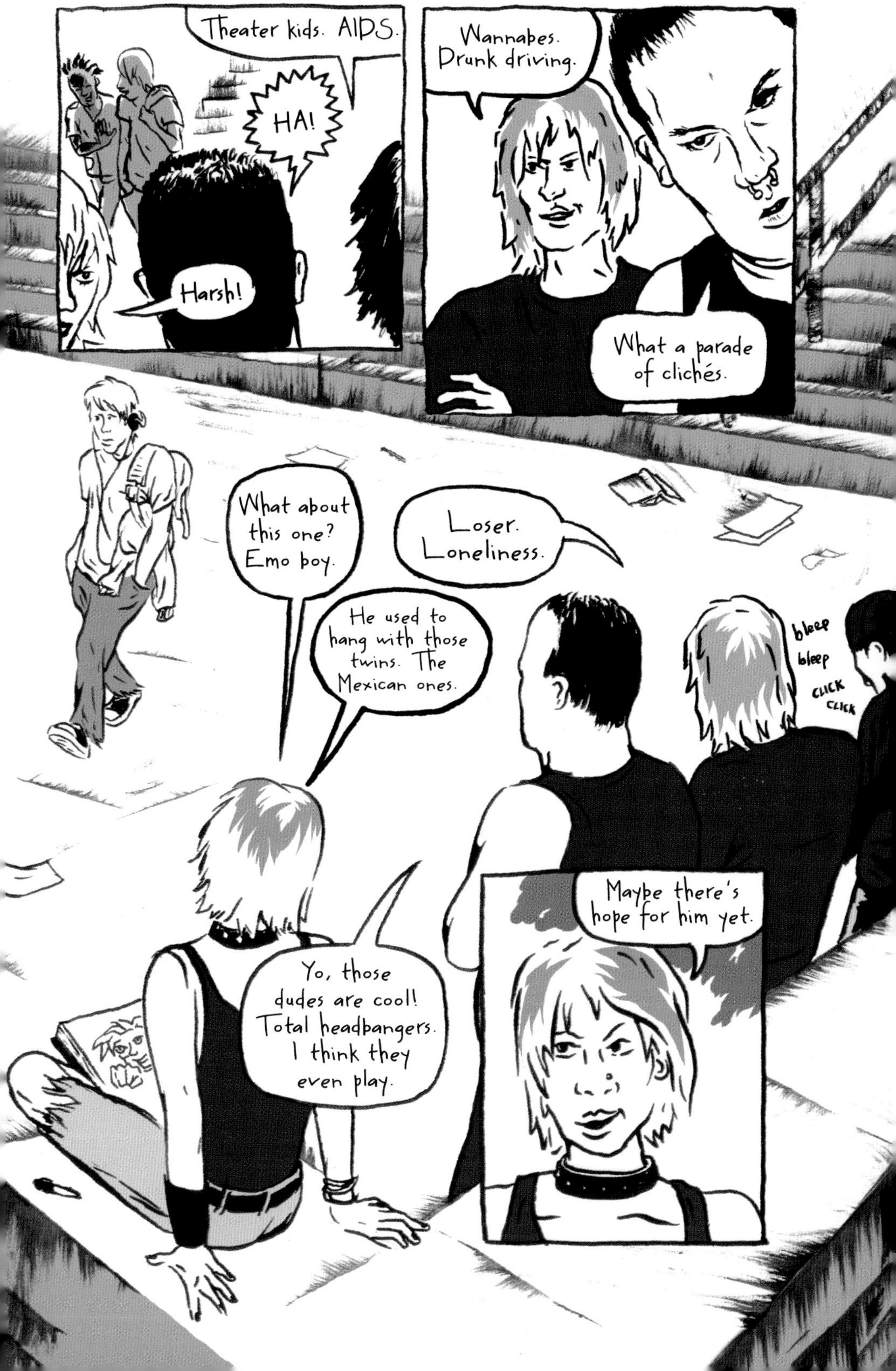
Theater kids. AIDS.
HA!
Harsh!
Wannabes. Drunk driving.
What a parade of clichés.
What about this one? Emo boy.
Loser. Loneliness.
He used to hang with those twins. The Mexican ones.
bleep
bleep
CLICK
CLICK
Yo, those dudes are cool! Total headbangers. I think they even play.
Maybe there's hope for him yet.

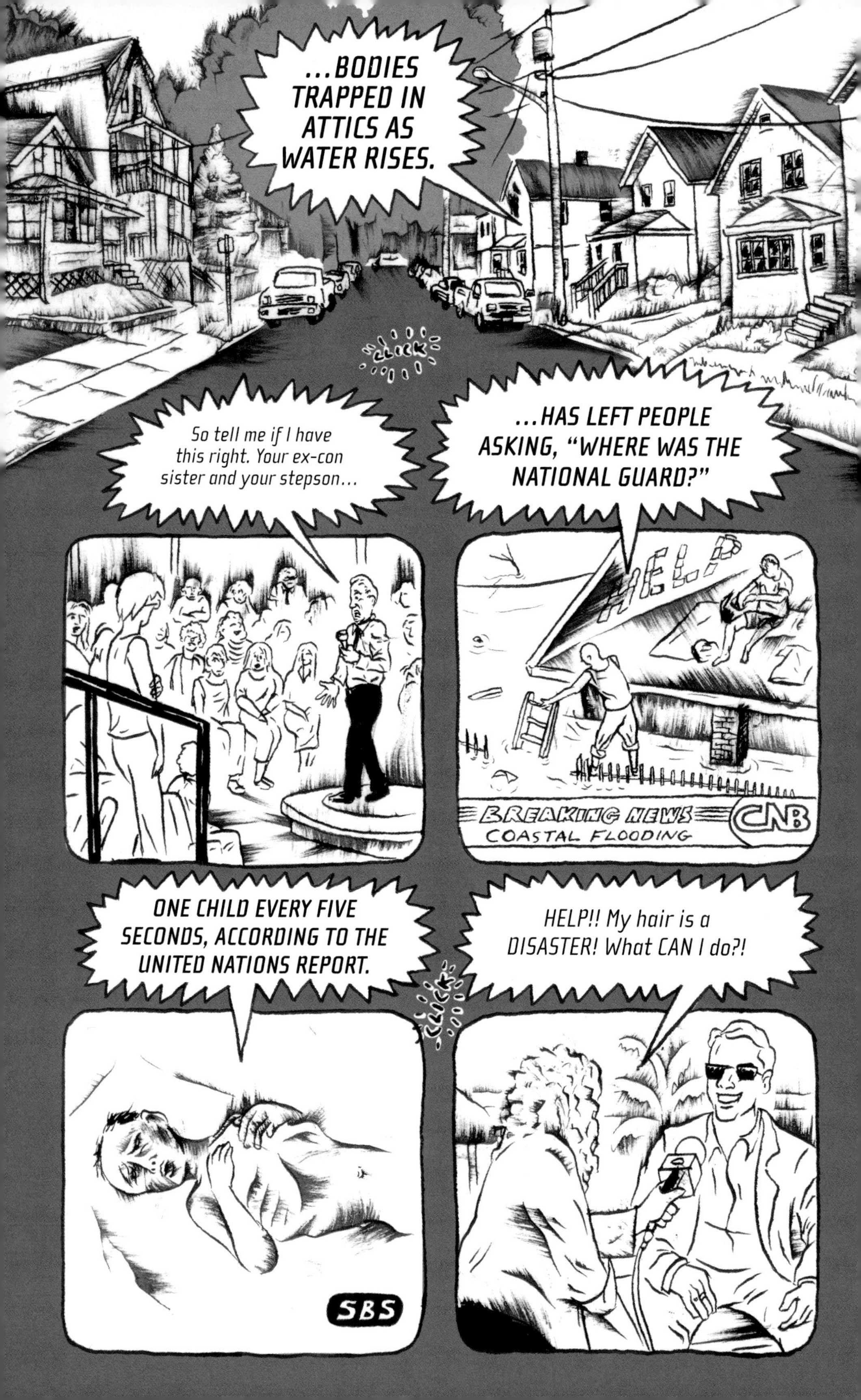

...BODIES TRAPPED IN ATTICS AS WATER RISES.
CLICK
So tell me if I have this right. Your ex-con sister and your stepson...
...HAS LEFT PEOPLE ASKING, "WHERE WAS THE NATIONAL GUARD?"
HELP
BREAKING NEWS
COASTAL FLOODING
CNB
ONE CHILD EVERY FIVE SECONDS, ACCORDING TO THE UNITED NATIONS REPORT.
CLICK
HELP!! My hair is a DISASTER! What CAN I do?!
SBS

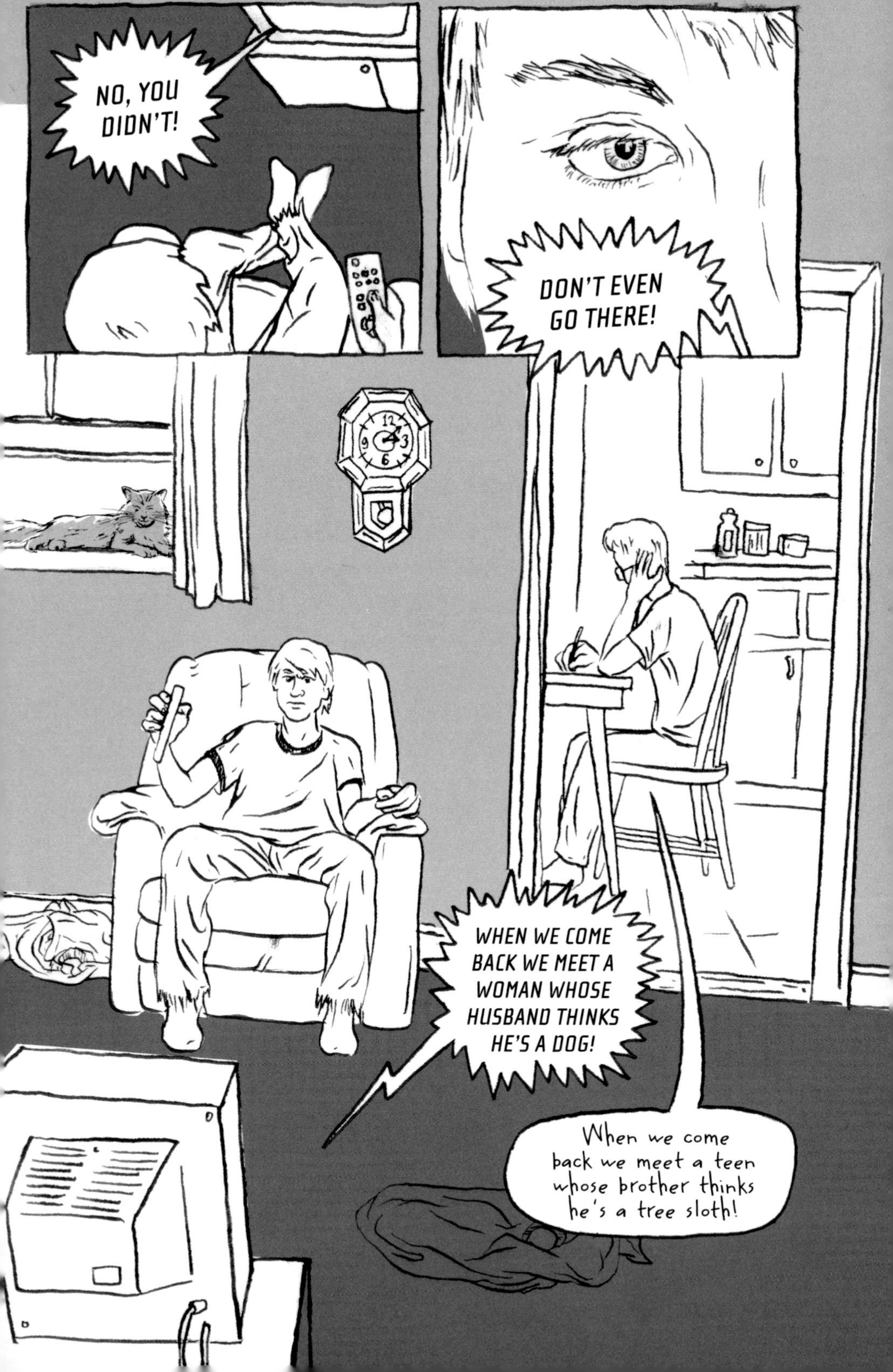
NO, YOU DIDN'T!
DON'T EVEN GO THERE!
WHEN WE COME BACK WE MEET A WOMAN WHOSE HUSBAND THINKS HE'S A DOG!
When we come back we meet a teen whose brother thinks he's a tree sloth!

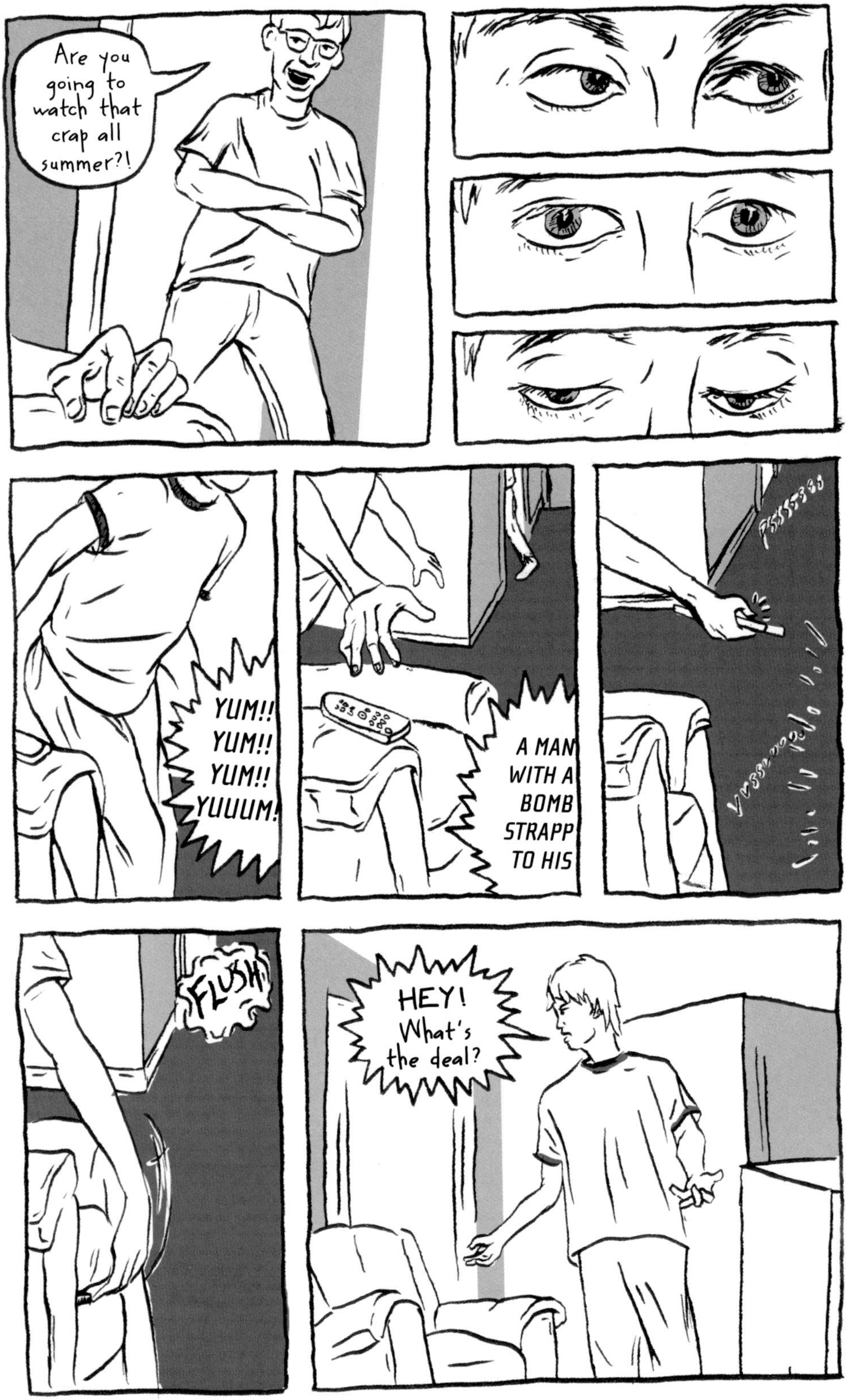
Are you going to watch that crap all summer?!
YUM!! YUM!! YUM!! YUUUM!
A MAN WITH A BOMB STRAPP TO HIS
PSSSSSSS
FLUSH!
HEY! What's the deal?

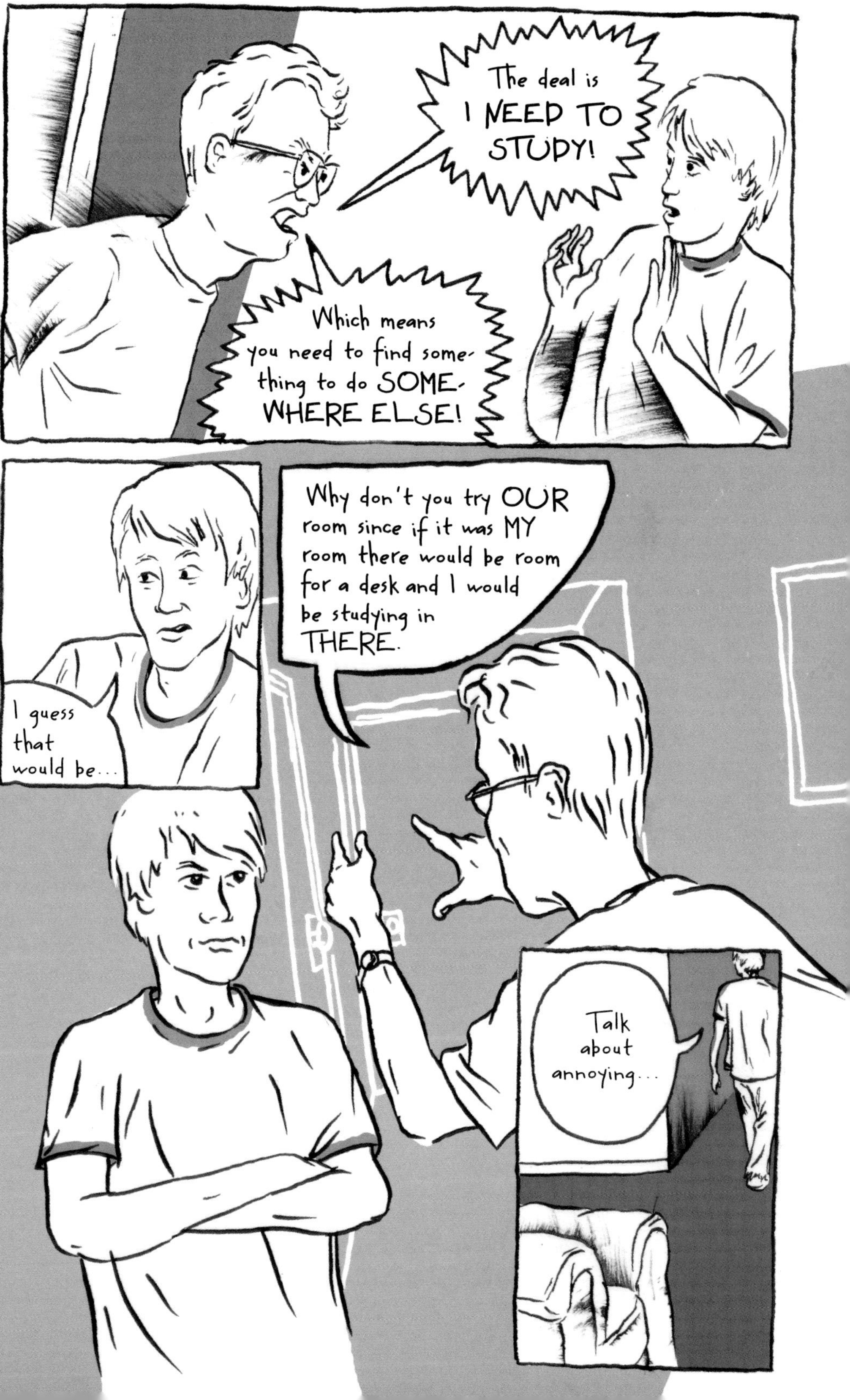
The deal is I NEED TO STUDY!
Which means you need to find some-thing to do SOME-WHERE ELSE!
I guess that would be...
Why don't you try OUR room since if it was MY room there would be room for a desk and I would be studying in THERE.
Talk about annoying...

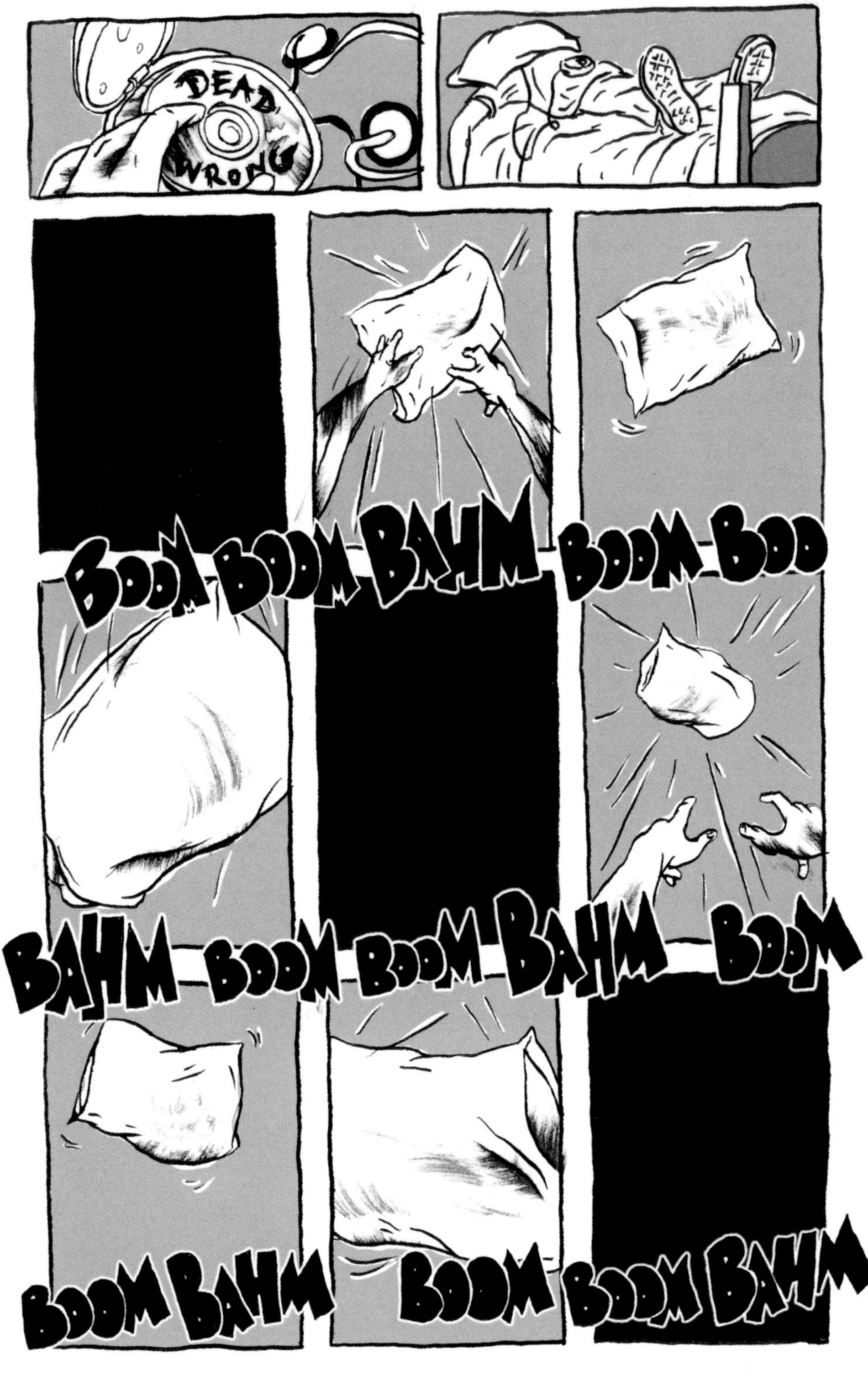
DEAD WRONG
BOOM BOOM BAHM BOOM BOO
BAHM BOOM BOOM BAHM BOOM
BOOM BAHM BOOM BOOM BAHM

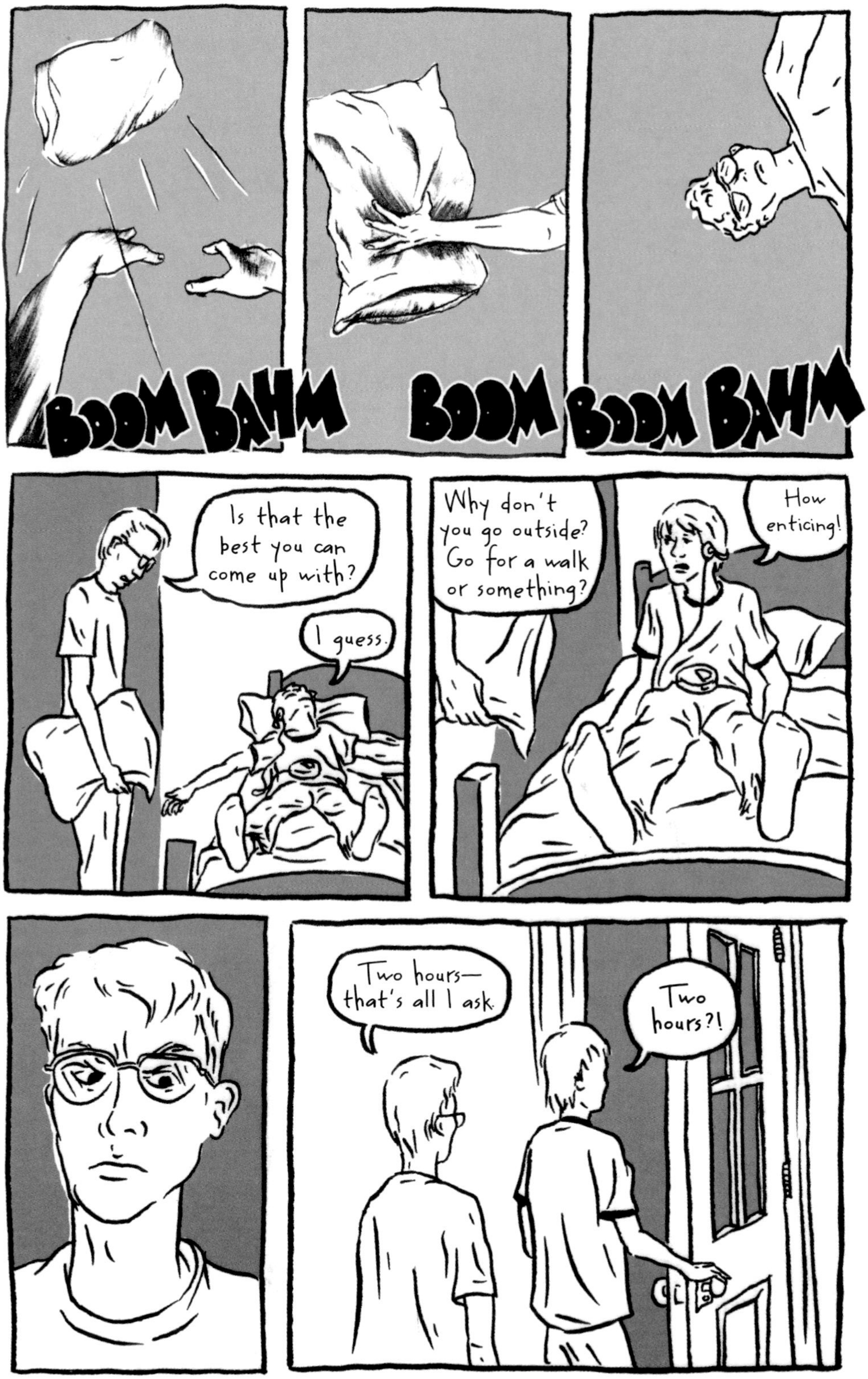
BOOM BAHM
BOOM BOOM BAHM
Is that the best you can come up with?
I guess.
Why don't you go outside? Go for a walk or something?
How enticing!
Two hours— that's all I ask.
Two hours?!

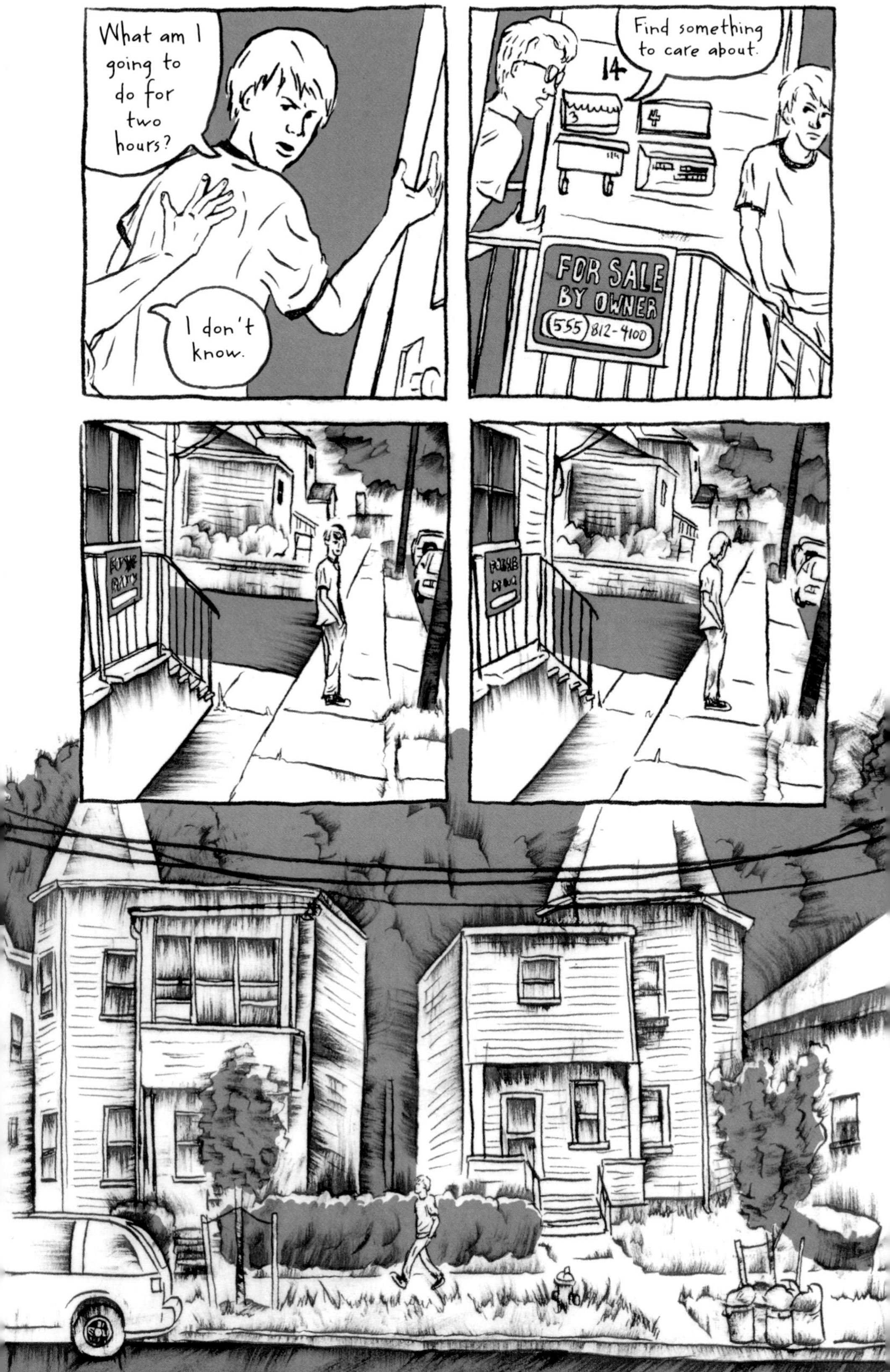
What am I going to do for two hours?
I don't know.
Find something to care about.
14
FOR SALE BY OWNER (555) 812-4100

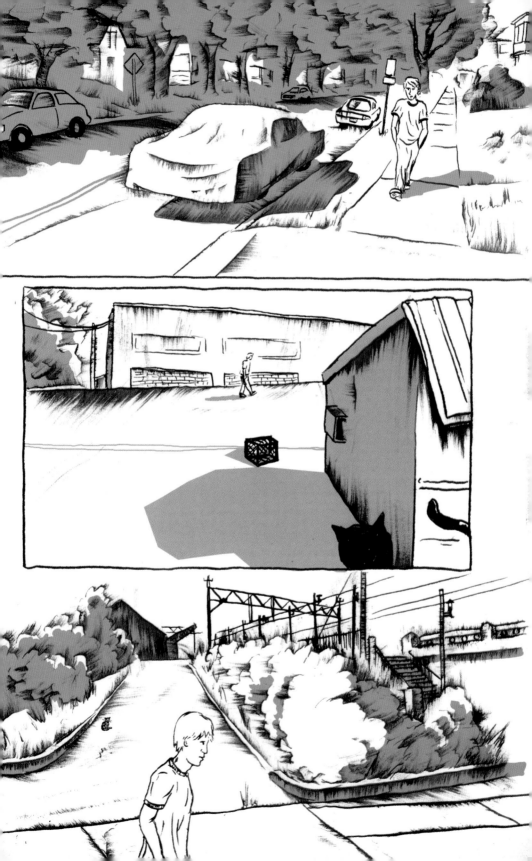

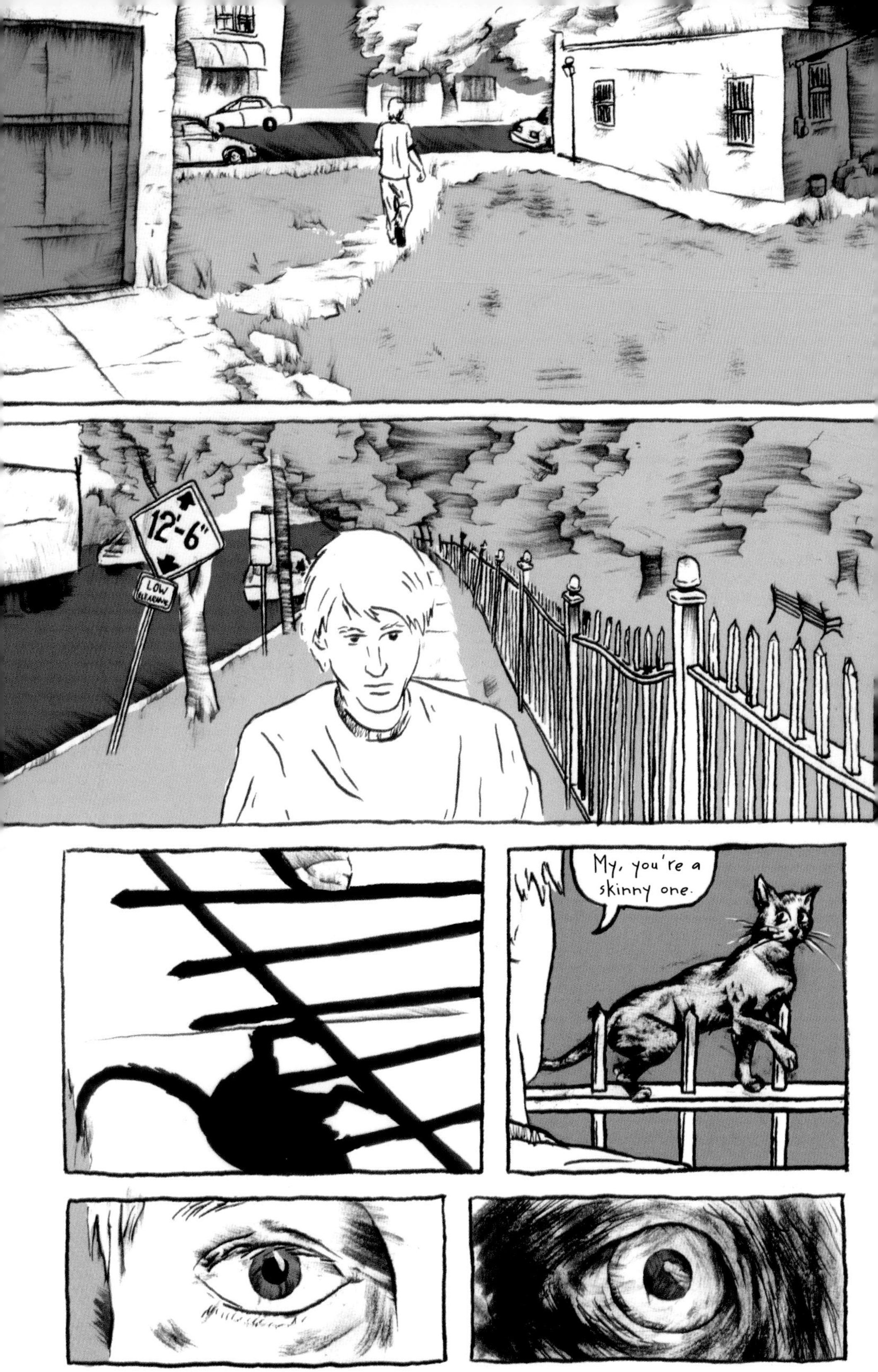
12'-6"
LOW CLEARANCE
My, you're a skinny one.

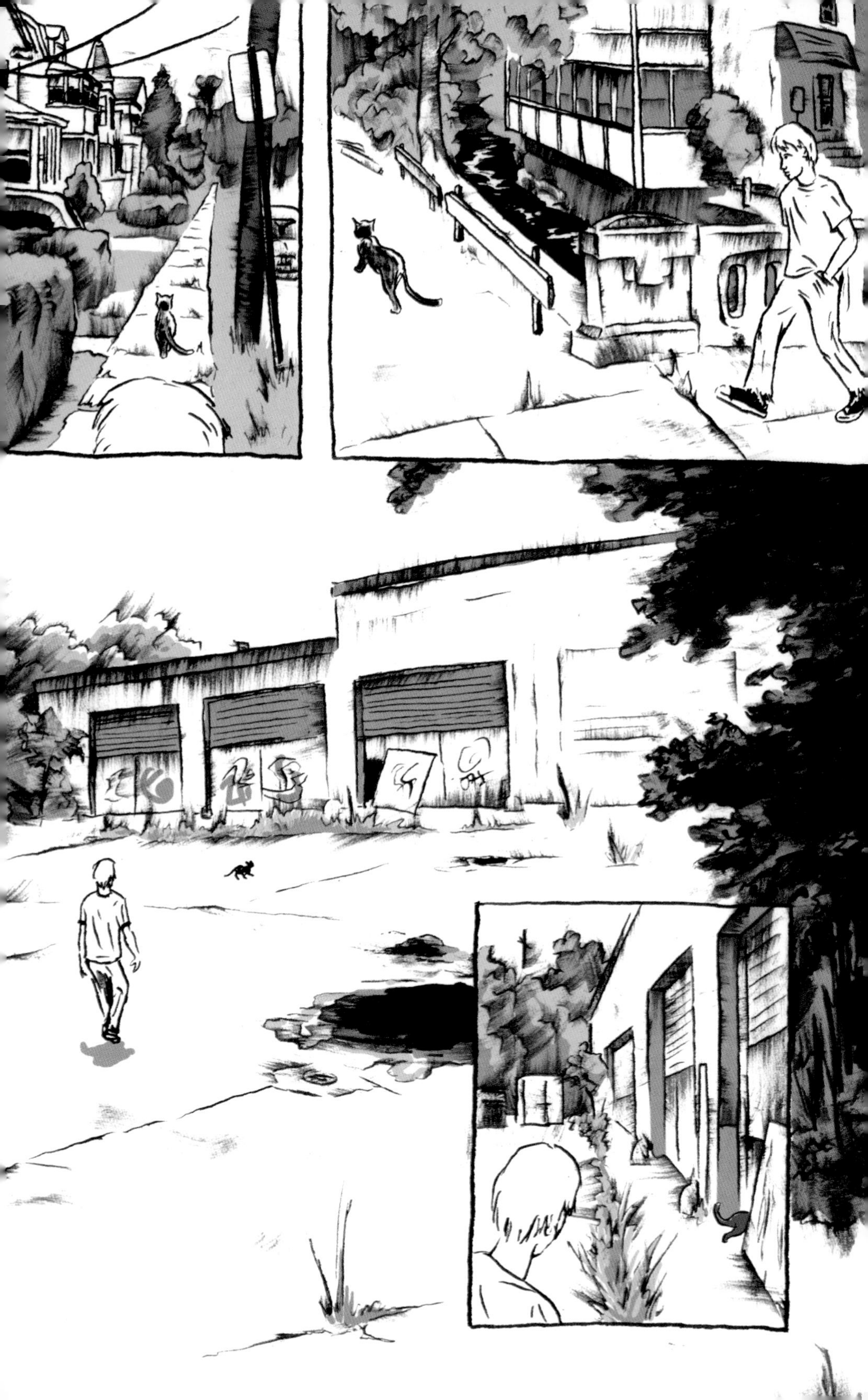

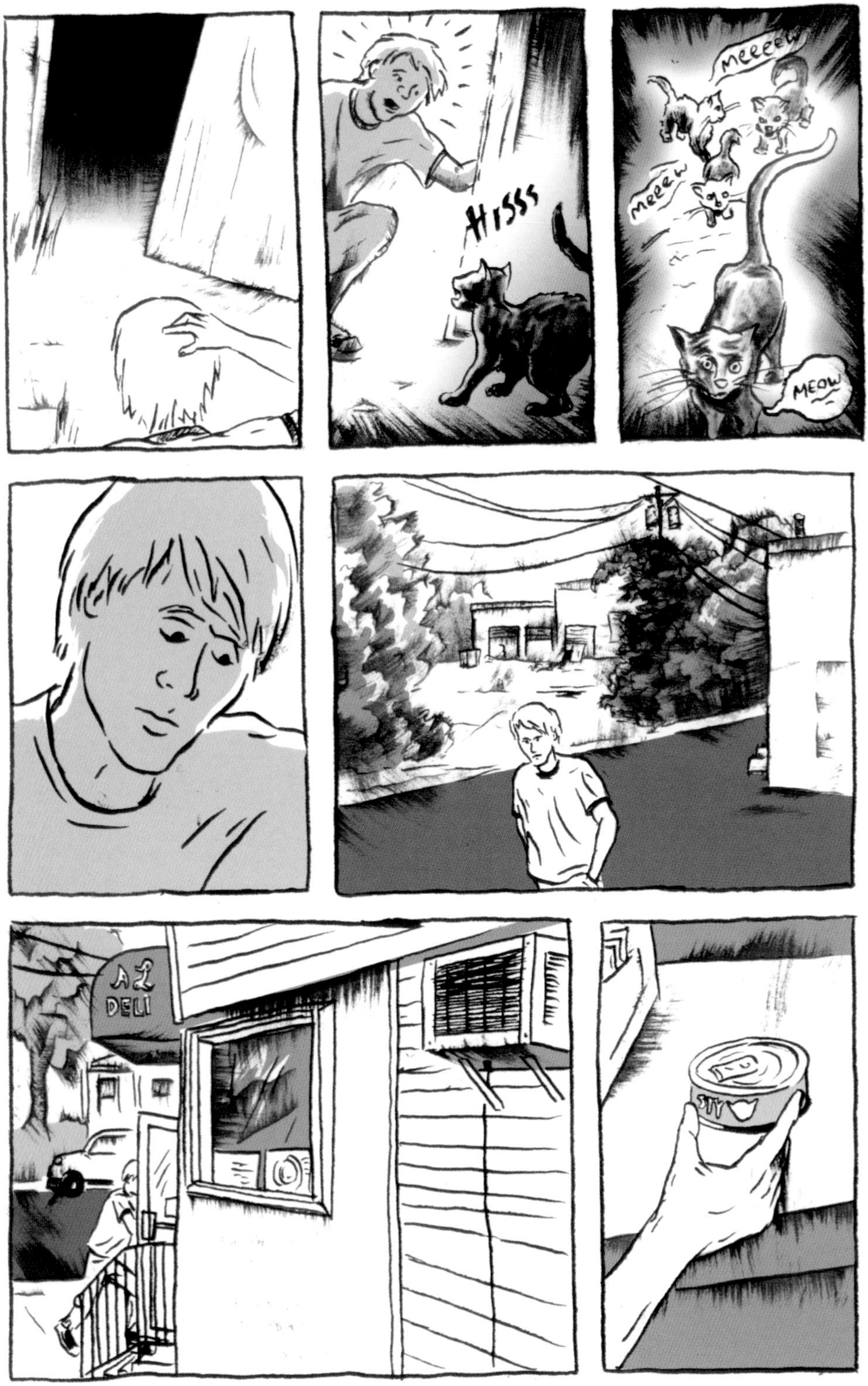
HISSS
Meeeew
meeew
MEOW
A1
DELI

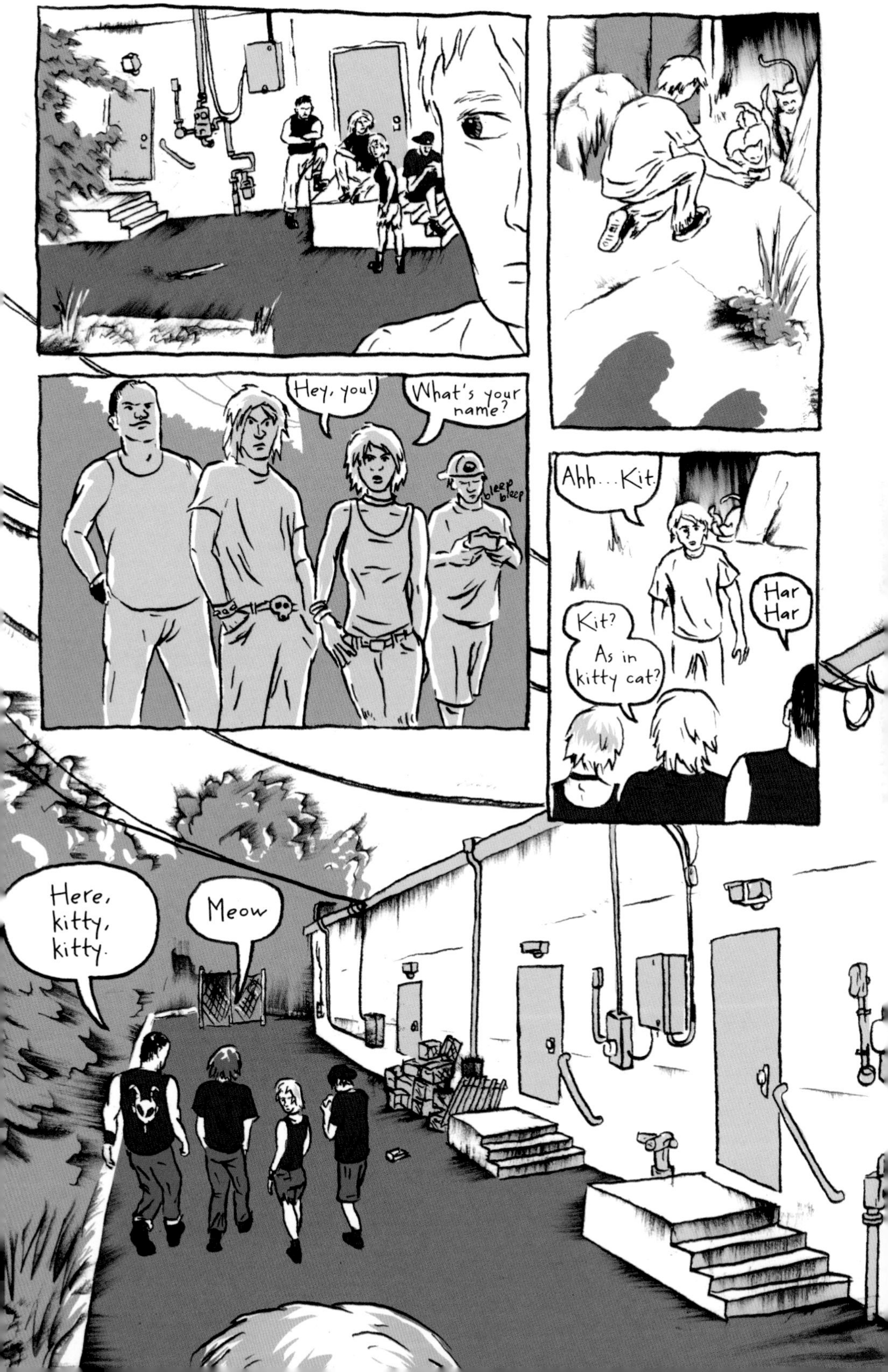
Hey, you!
What's your name?
bleep bleep
Ahh...Kit.
Kit?
As in kitty cat?
Har Har
Here, kitty, kitty.
Meow

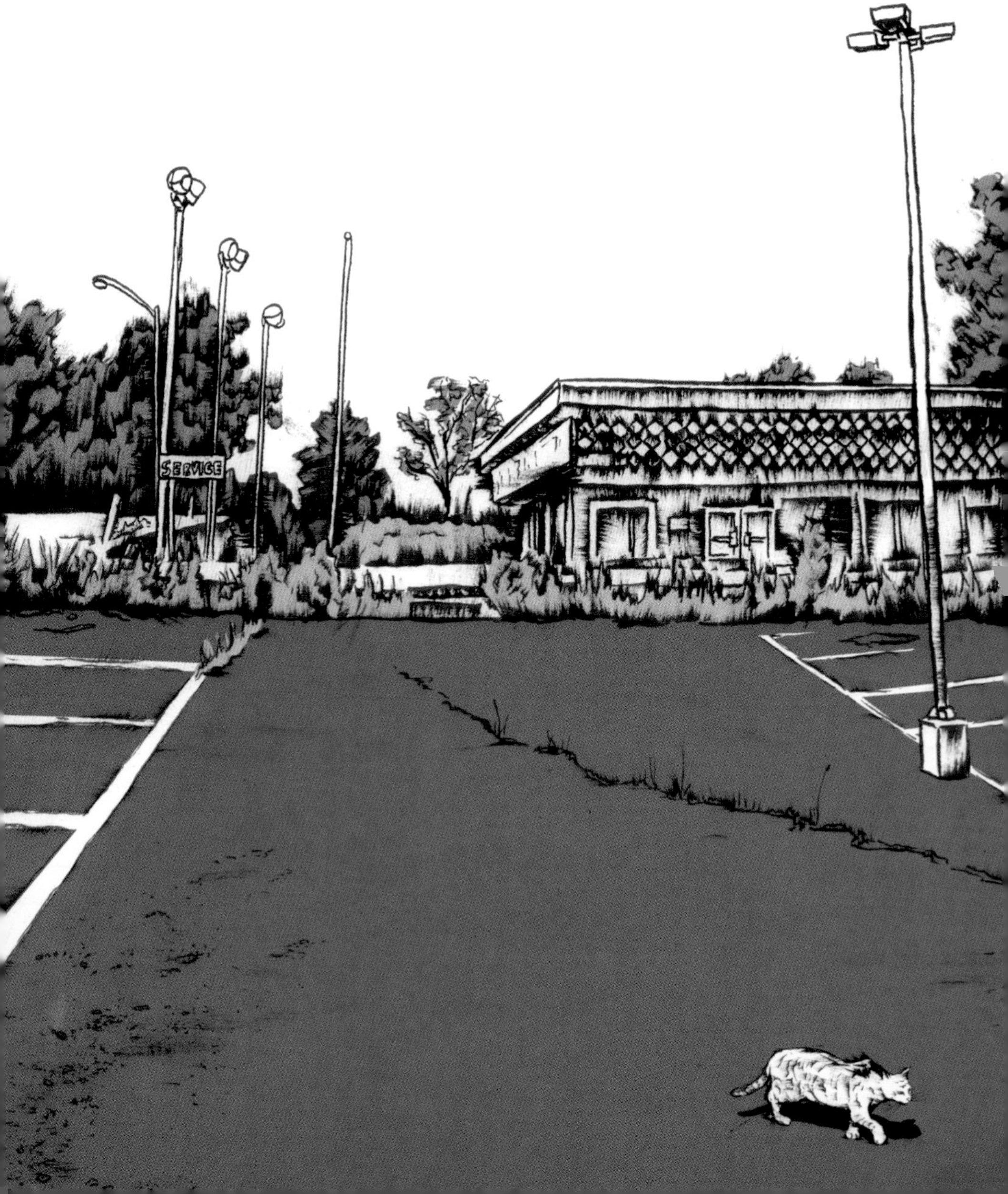
SERVICE

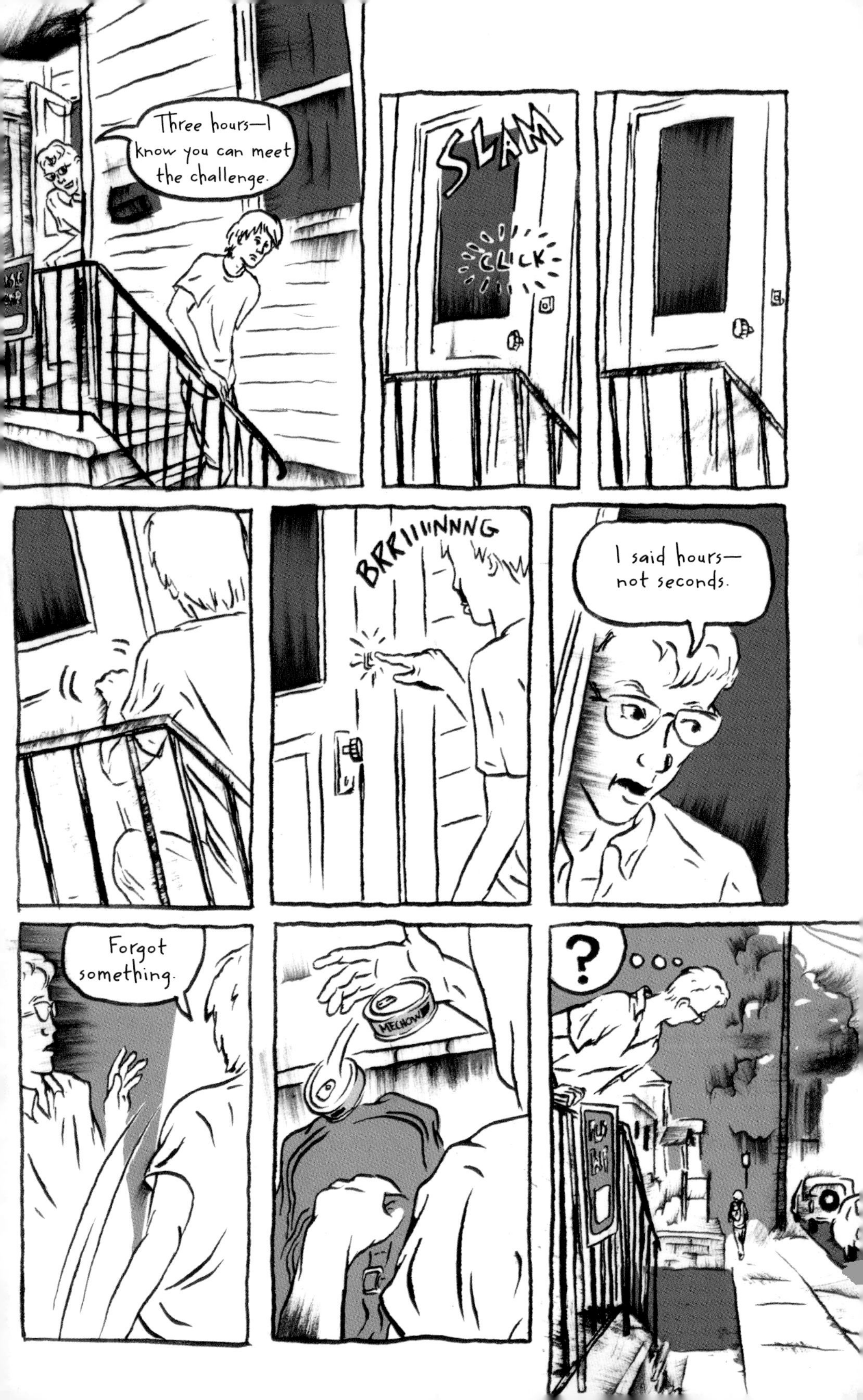
Three hours—I know you can meet the challenge.
SLAM
CLICK
BRRIIINNNG
I said hours—not seconds.
Forgot something.
MEOW
?

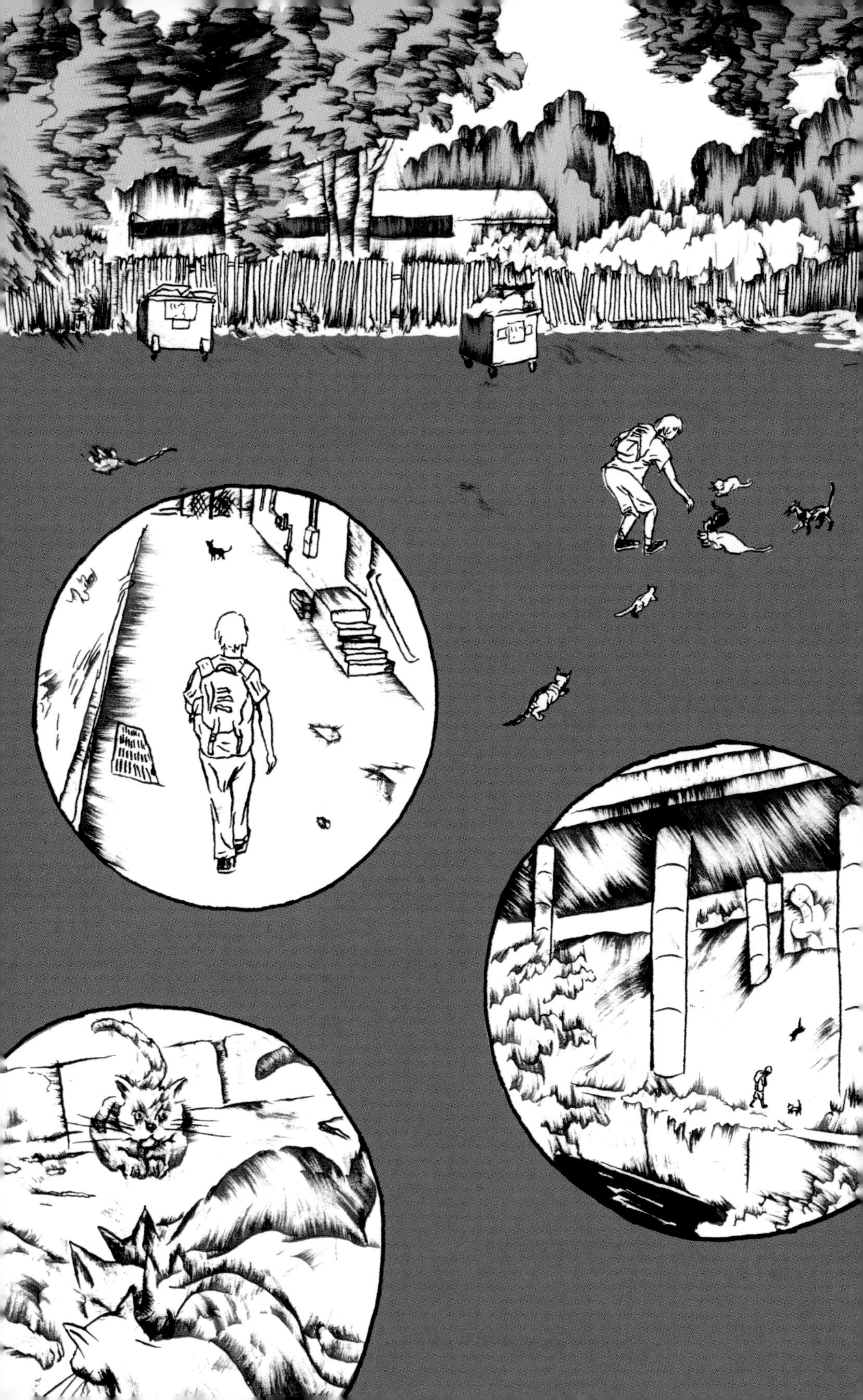

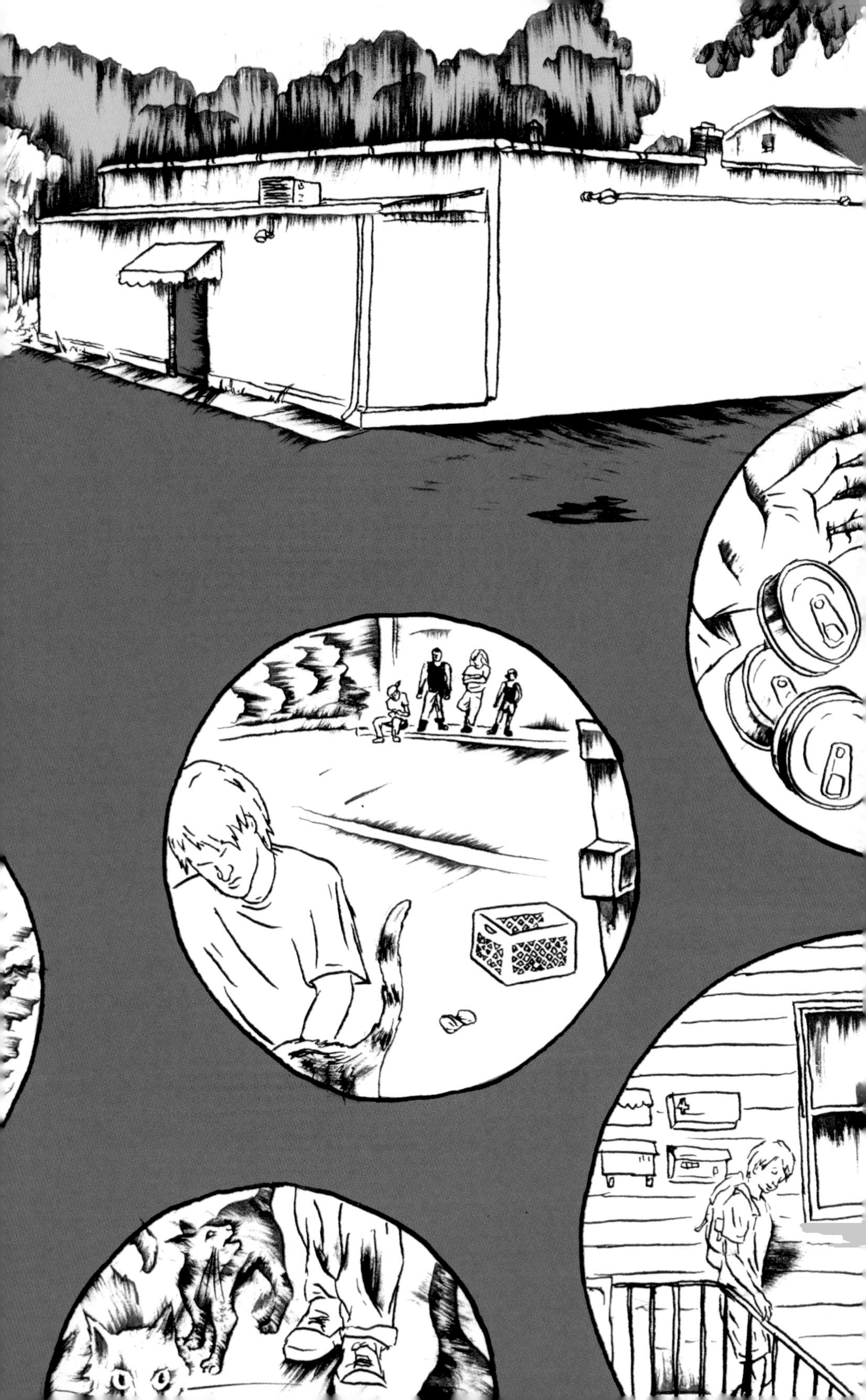

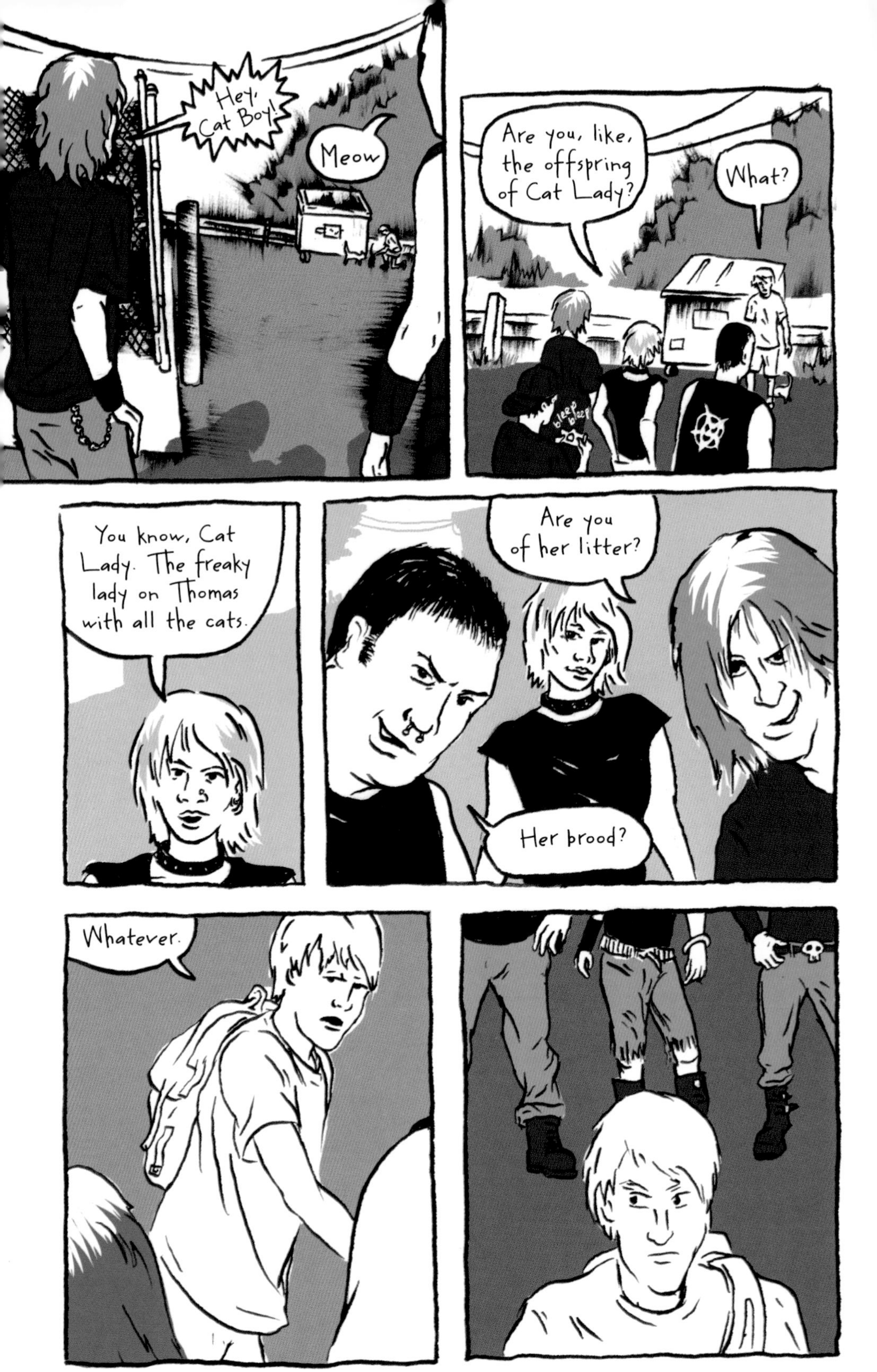
Hey, Cat Boy!
Meow
Are you, like, the offspring of Cat Lady?
What?
bleep bleep
You know, Cat Lady. The freaky lady on Thomas with all the cats.
Are you of her litter?
Her brood?
Whatever.

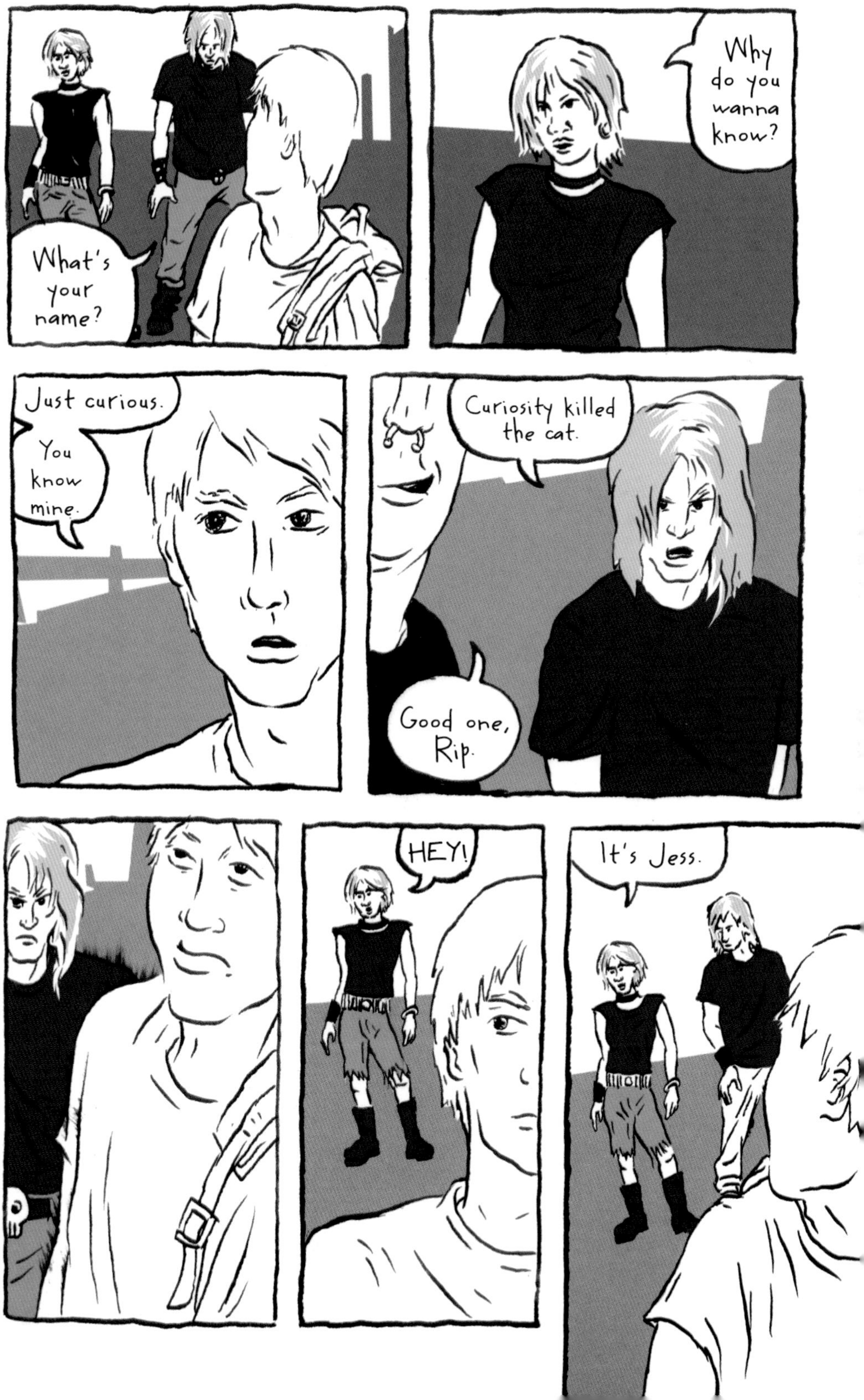
What's your name?
Why do you wanna know?
Just curious.
You know mine.
Curiosity killed the cat.
Good one, Rip.
HEY!
It's Jess.

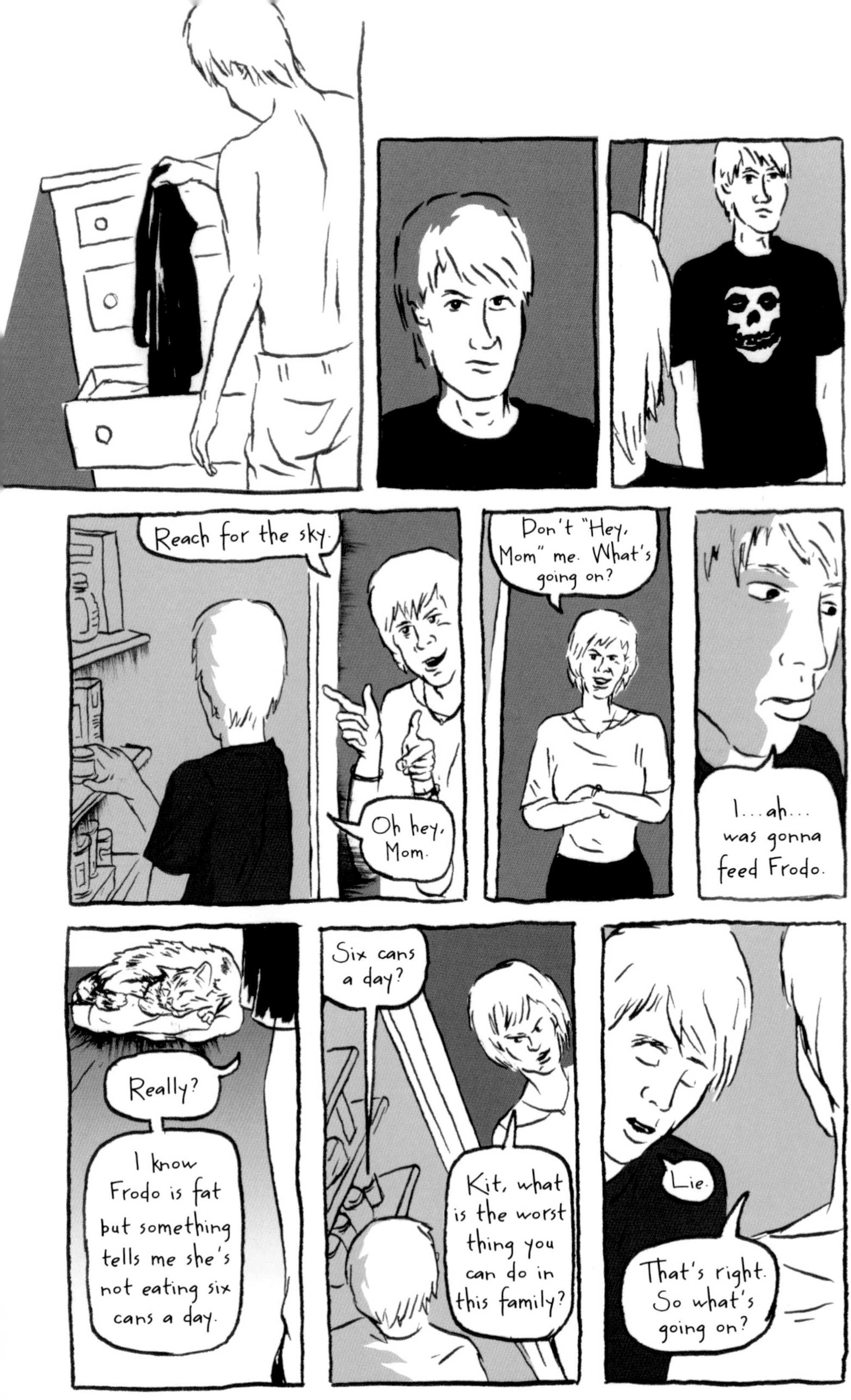
Reach for the sky.
Oh hey, Mom.
Don't "Hey, Mom" me. What's going on?
I...ah... was gonna feed Frodo.
Really?
I know Frodo is fat but something tells me she's not eating six cans a day.
Six cans a day?
Kit, what is the worst thing you can do in this family?
Lie.
That's right. So what's going on?

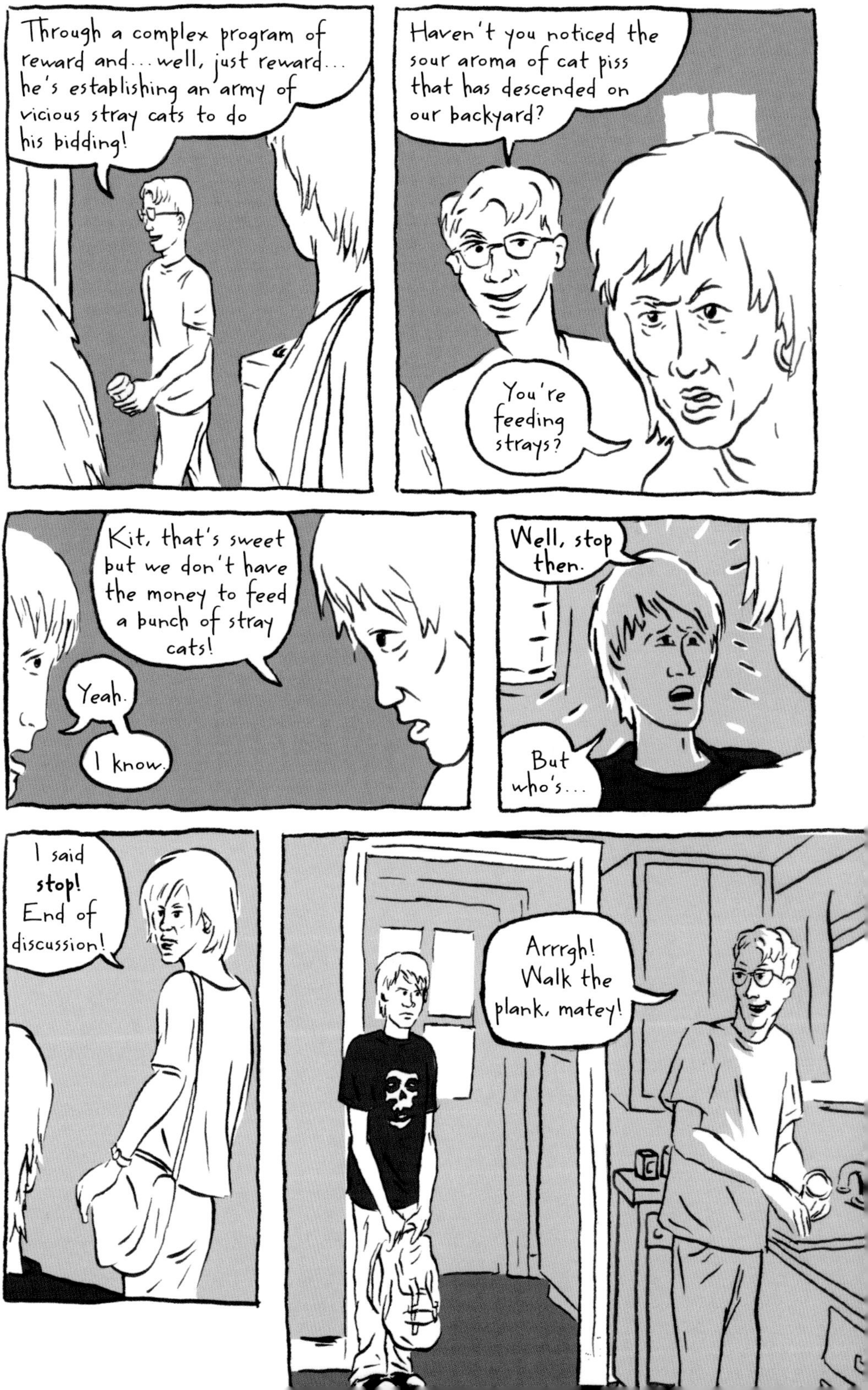

Through a complex program of reward and...well, just reward... he's establishing an army of vicious stray cats to do his bidding!
Haven't you noticed the sour aroma of cat piss that has descended on our backyard?
You're feeding strays?
Kit, that's sweet but we don't have the money to feed a bunch of stray cats!
Yeah.
I know.
Well, stop then.
But who's...
I said **stop!** End of discussion!
Arrrgh! Walk the plank, matey!

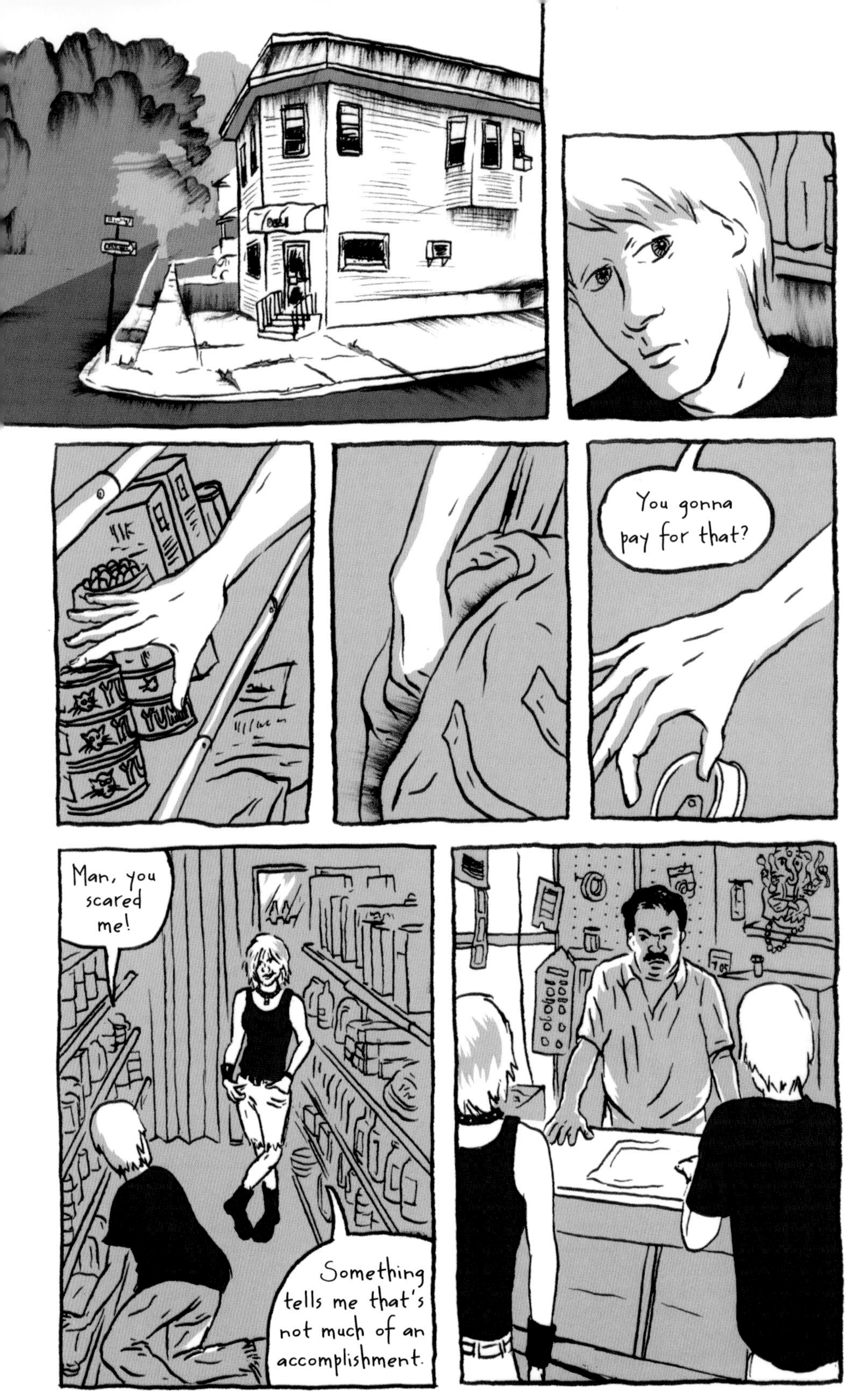
DELI
You gonna pay for that?
Man, you scared me!
Something tells me that's not much of an accomplishment.

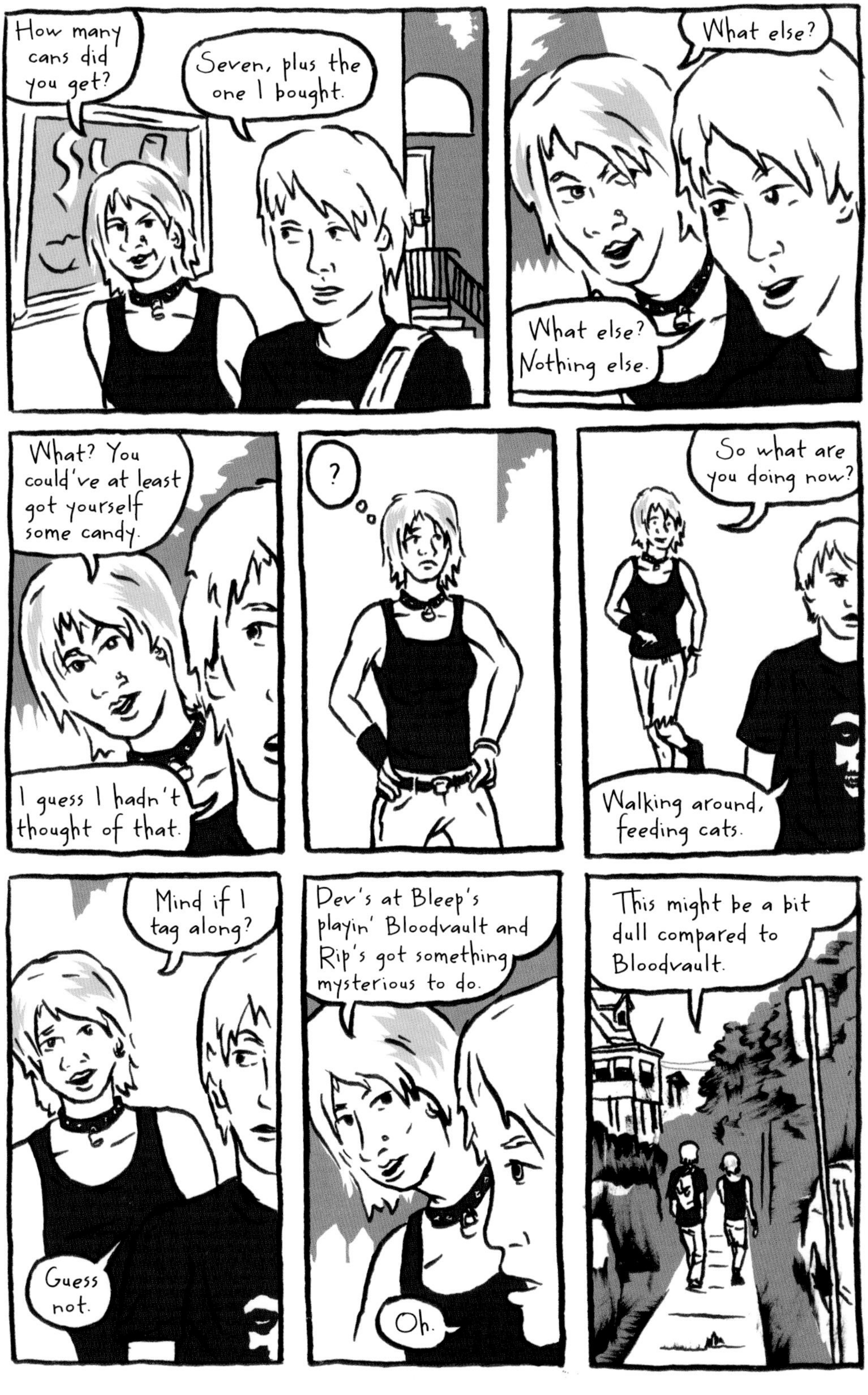
How many cans did you get?
Seven, plus the one I bought.
What else?
What else? Nothing else.
What? You could've at least got yourself some candy.
I guess I hadn't thought of that.
?
So what are you doing now?
Walking around, feeding cats.
Mind if I tag along?
Guess not.
Dev's at Bleep's playin' Bloodvault and Rip's got something mysterious to do.
Oh.
This might be a bit dull compared to Bloodvault.

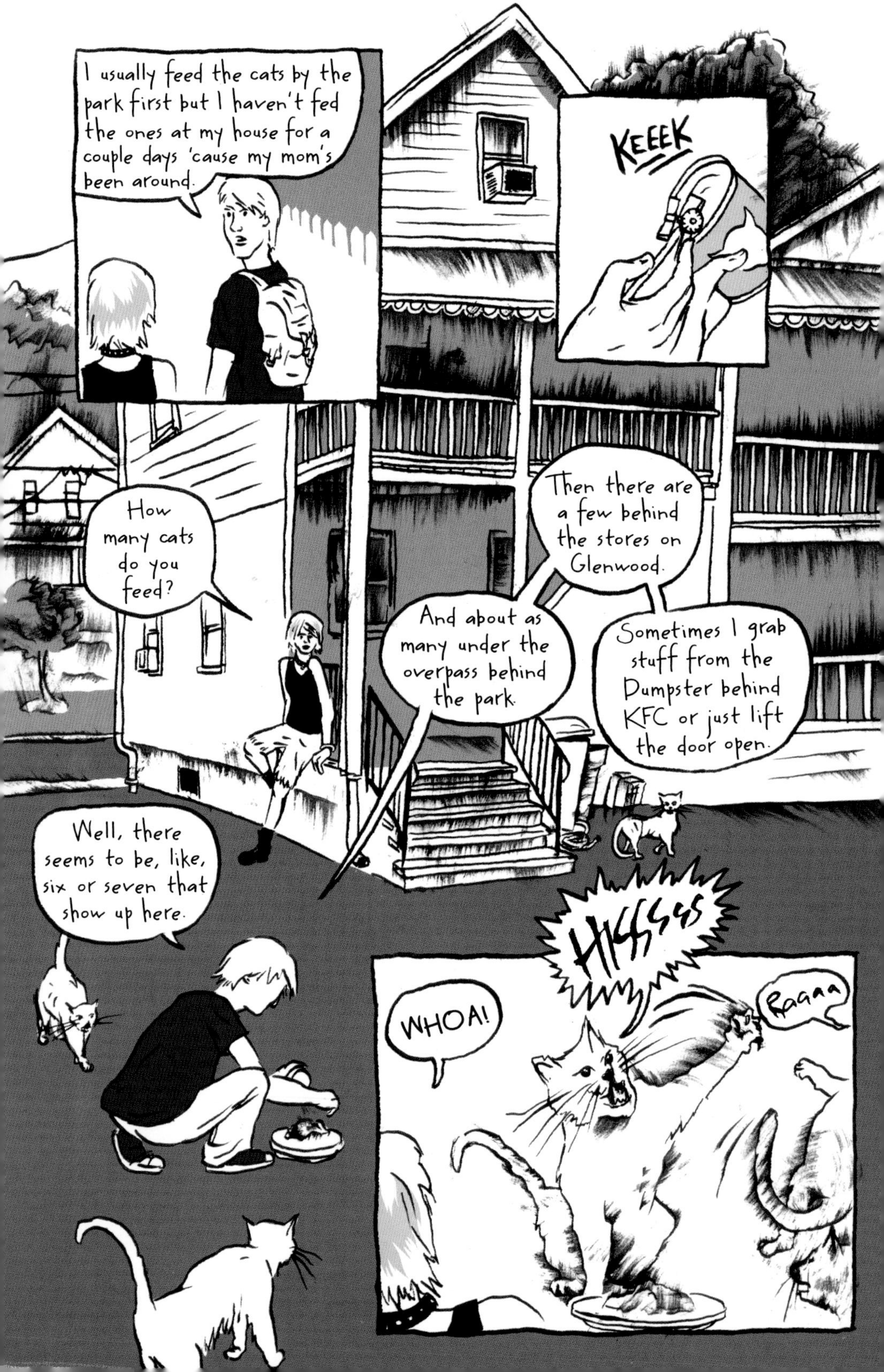
I usually feed the cats by the park first but I haven't fed the ones at my house for a couple days 'cause my mom's been around.
KEEEK
How many cats do you feed?
Well, there seems to be, like, six or seven that show up here.
Then there are a few behind the stores on Glenwood.
And about as many under the overpass behind the park.
Sometimes I grab stuff from the Dumpster behind KFC or just lift the door open.
HISSSS
WHOA!
Raaaa

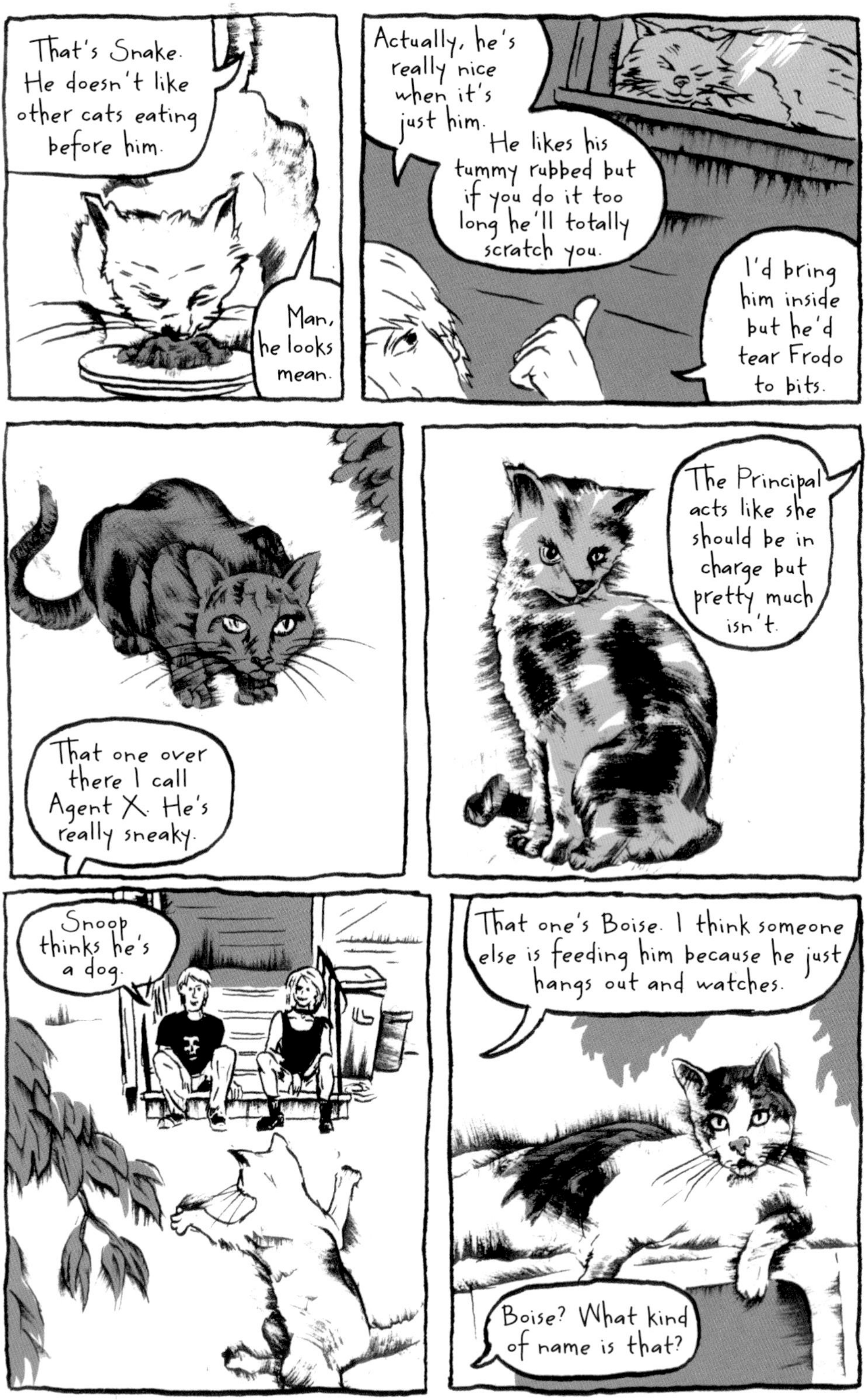
That's Snake. He doesn't like other cats eating before him.
Man, he looks mean.
Actually, he's really nice when it's just him.
He likes his tummy rubbed but if you do it too long he'll totally scratch you.
I'd bring him inside but he'd tear Frodo to bits.
That one over there I call Agent X. He's really sneaky.
The Principal acts like she should be in charge but pretty much isn't.
Snoop thinks he's a dog.
That one's Boise. I think someone else is feeding him because he just hangs out and watches.
Boise? What kind of name is that?

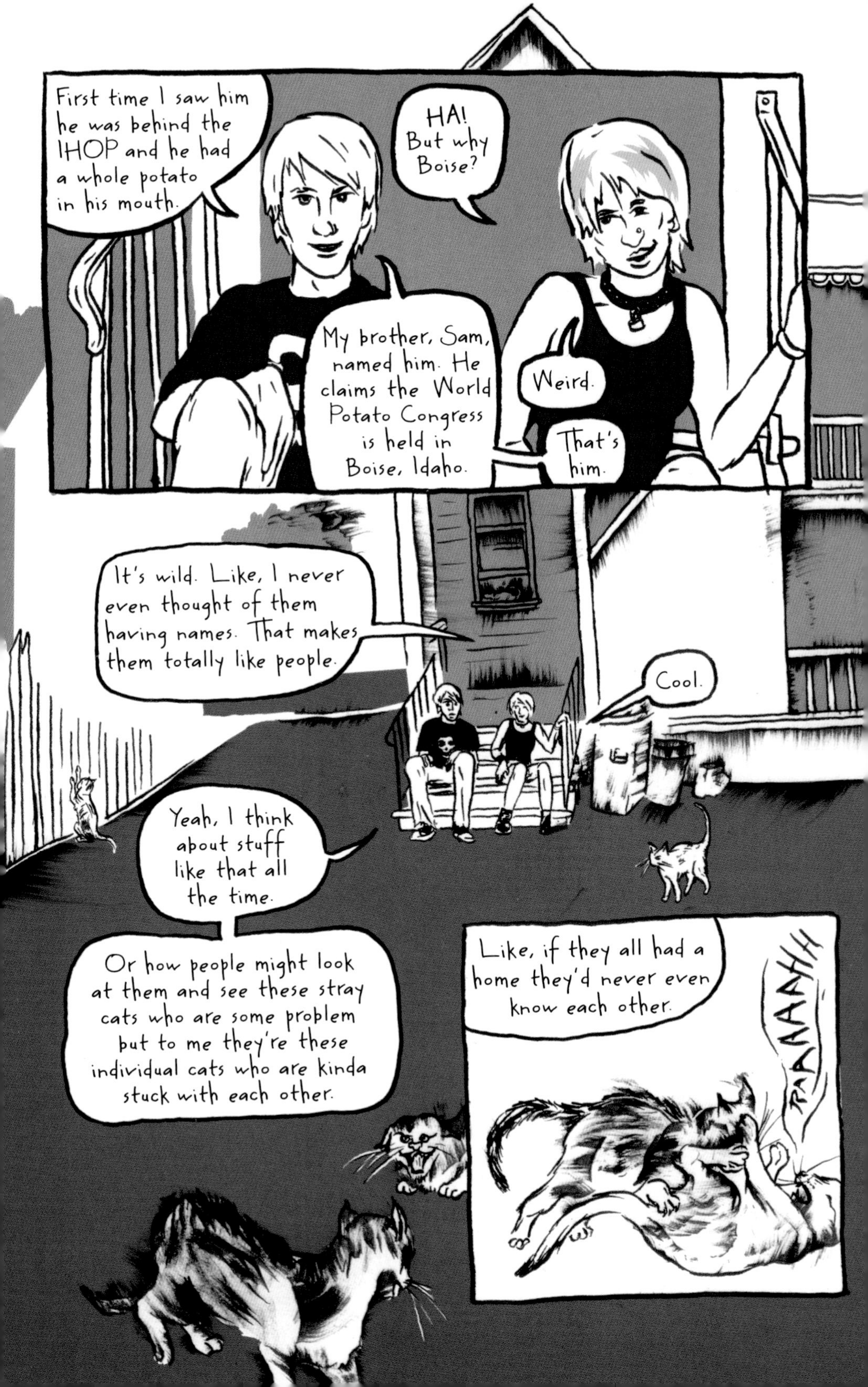
First time I saw him he was behind the IHOP and he had a whole potato in his mouth.
HA! But why Boise?
My brother, Sam, named him. He claims the World Potato Congress is held in Boise, Idaho.
Weird.
That's him.
It's wild. Like, I never even thought of them having names. That makes them totally like people.
Cool.
Yeah, I think about stuff like that all the time.
Or how people might look at them and see these stray cats who are some problem but to me they're these individual cats who are kinda stuck with each other.
Like, if they all had a home they'd never even know each other.
RAAAAAHH

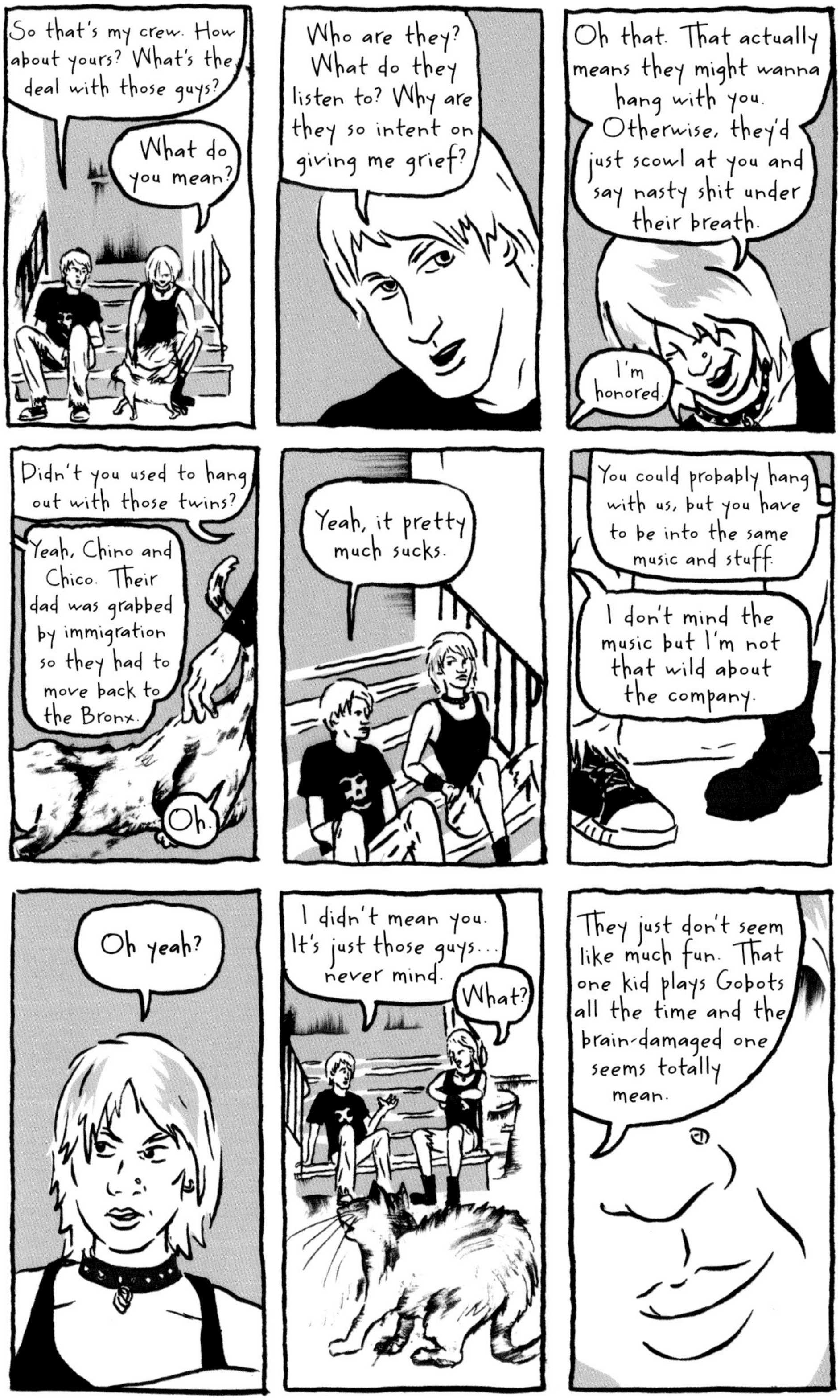
So that's my crew. How about yours? What's the deal with those guys?
What do you mean?
Who are they? What do they listen to? Why are they so intent on giving me grief?
Oh that. That actually means they might wanna hang with you. Otherwise, they'd just scowl at you and say nasty shit under their breath.
I'm honored.
Didn't you used to hang out with those twins?
Yeah, Chino and Chico. Their dad was grabbed by immigration so they had to move back to the Bronx.
Oh.
Yeah, it pretty much sucks.
You could probably hang with us, but you have to be into the same music and stuff.
I don't mind the music but I'm not that wild about the company.
Oh yeah?
I didn't mean you. It's just those guys... never mind.
What?
They just don't seem like much fun. That one kid plays Gobots all the time and the brain-damaged one seems totally mean.

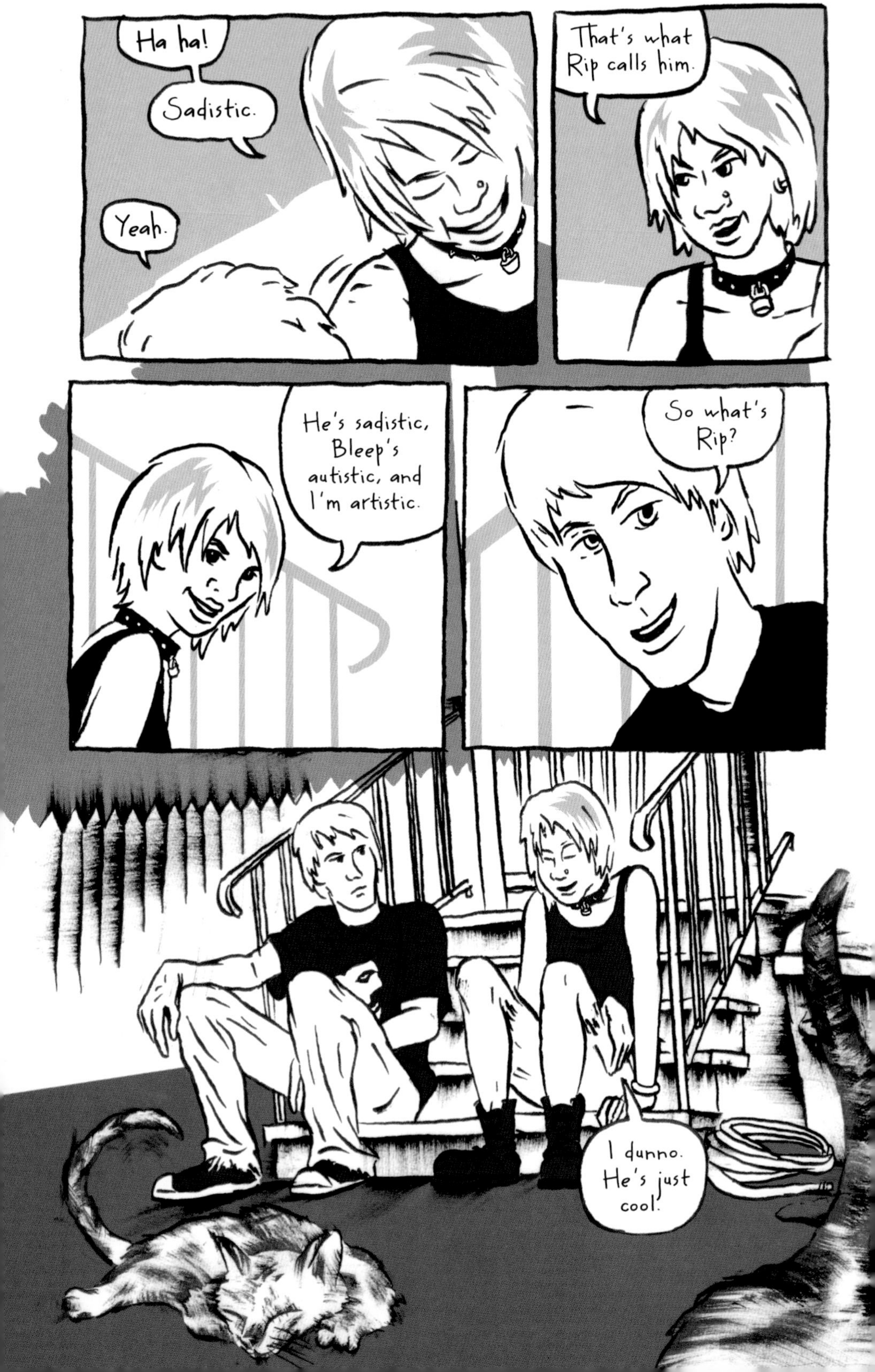
Ha ha!
Sadistic.
Yeah.
That's what Rip calls him.
He's sadistic, Bleep's autistic, and I'm artistic.
So what's Rip?
I dunno. He's just cool.

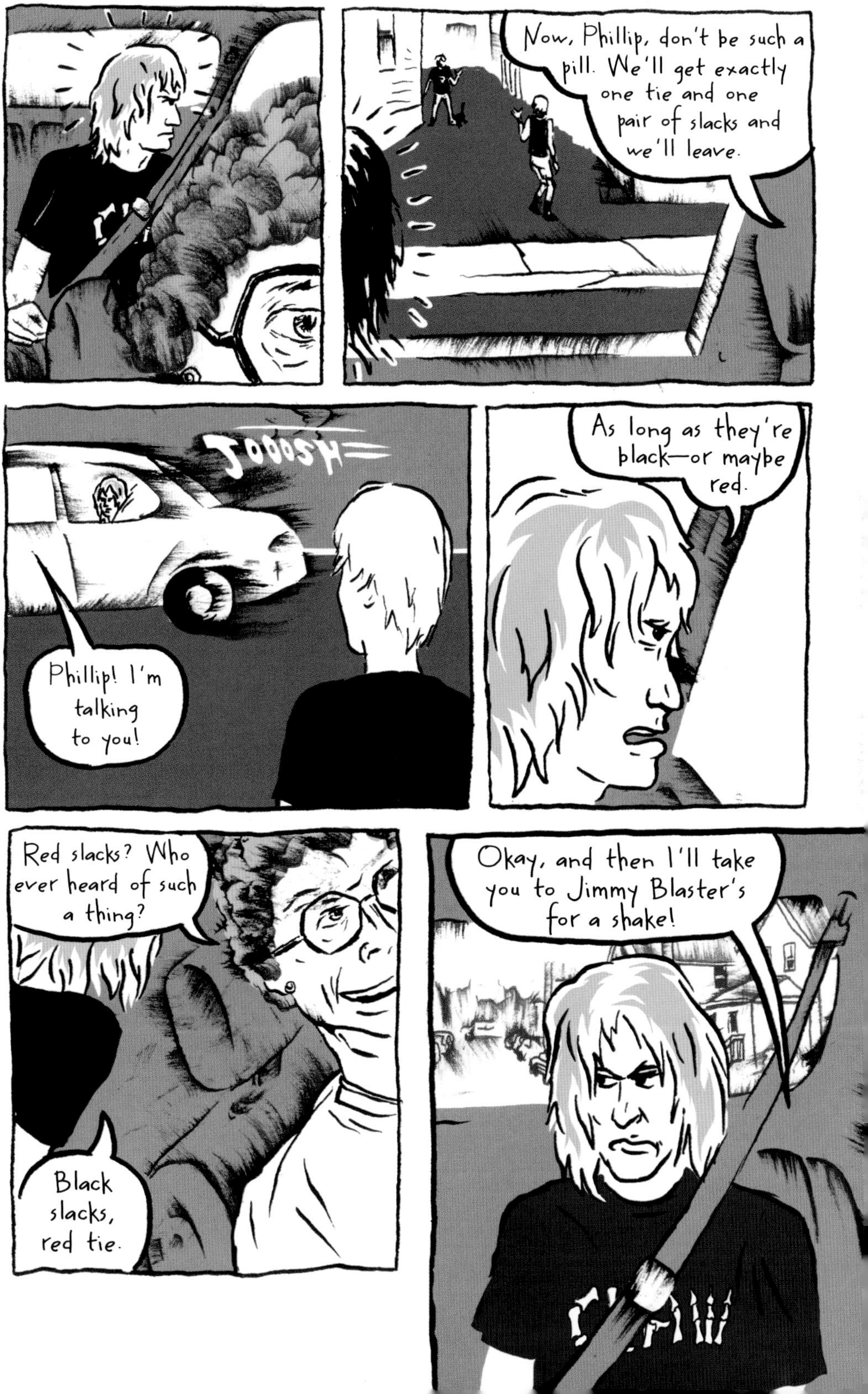
Now, Phillip, don't be such a pill. We'll get exactly one tie and one pair of slacks and we'll leave.
JOOOSH
Phillip! I'm talking to you!
As long as they're black—or maybe red.
Red slacks? Who ever heard of such a thing?
Black slacks, red tie.
Okay, and then I'll take you to Jimmy Blaster's for a shake!

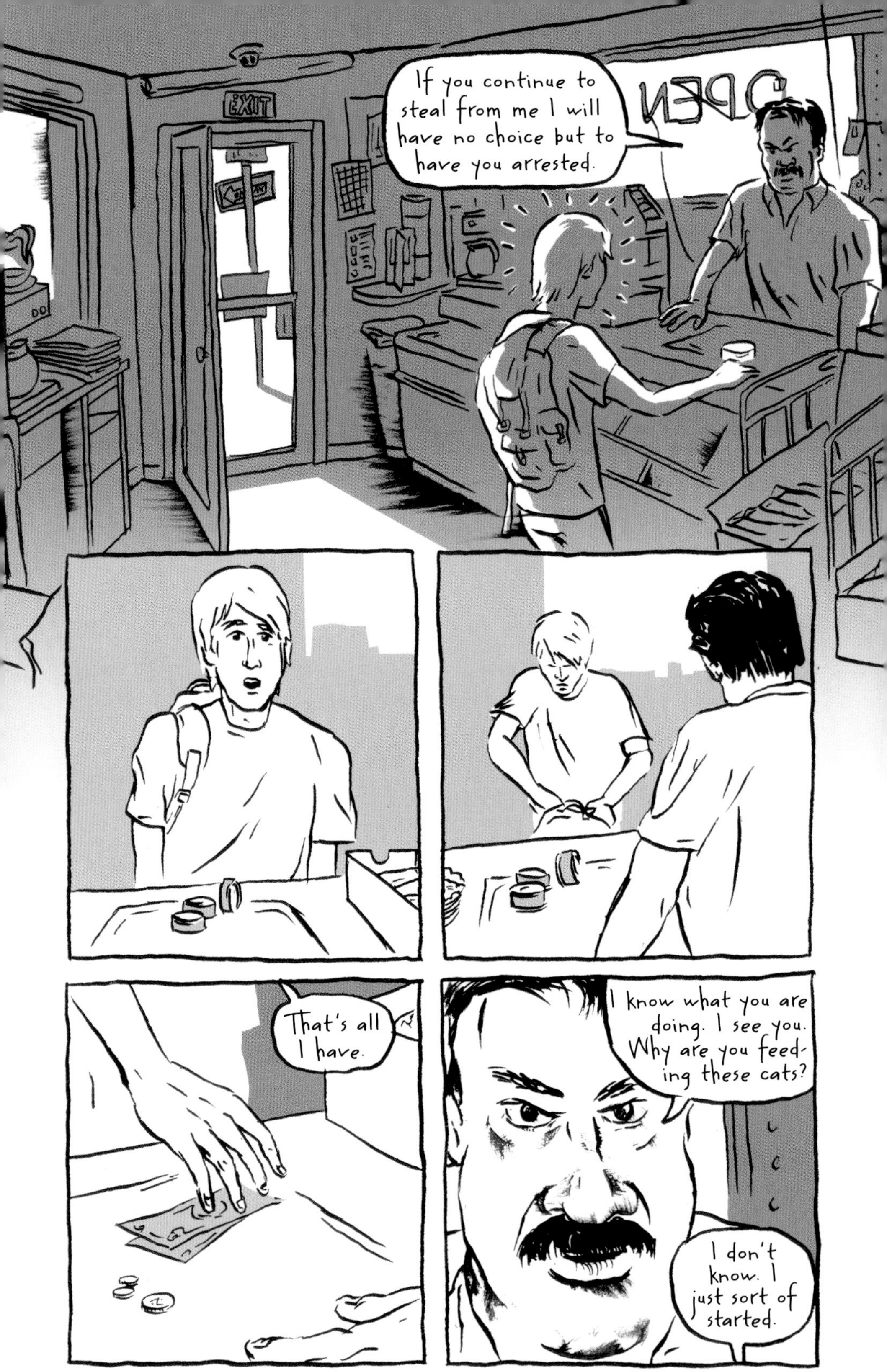
EXIT
OPEN
If you continue to steal from me I will have no choice but to have you arrested.
That's all I have.
I know what you are doing. I see you. Why are you feeding these cats?
I don't know. I just sort of started.

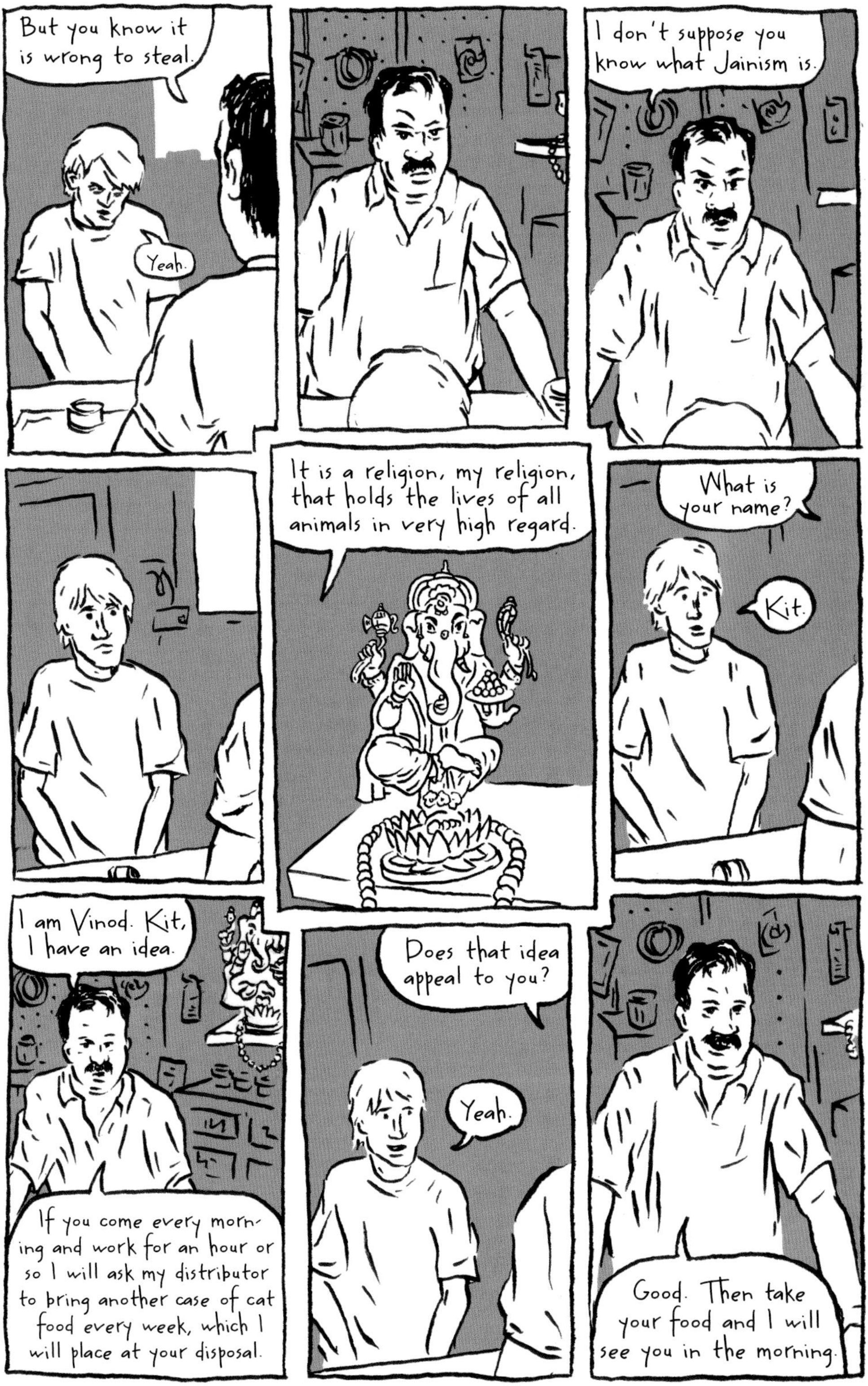
But you know it is wrong to steal.
Yeah.
I don't suppose you know what Jainism is.
It is a religion, my religion, that holds the lives of all animals in very high regard.
What is your name?
Kit.
I am Vinod. Kit, I have an idea.
If you come every morning and work for an hour or so I will ask my distributor to bring another case of cat food every week, which I will place at your disposal.
Does that idea appeal to you?
Yeah.
Good. Then take your food and I will see you in the morning.

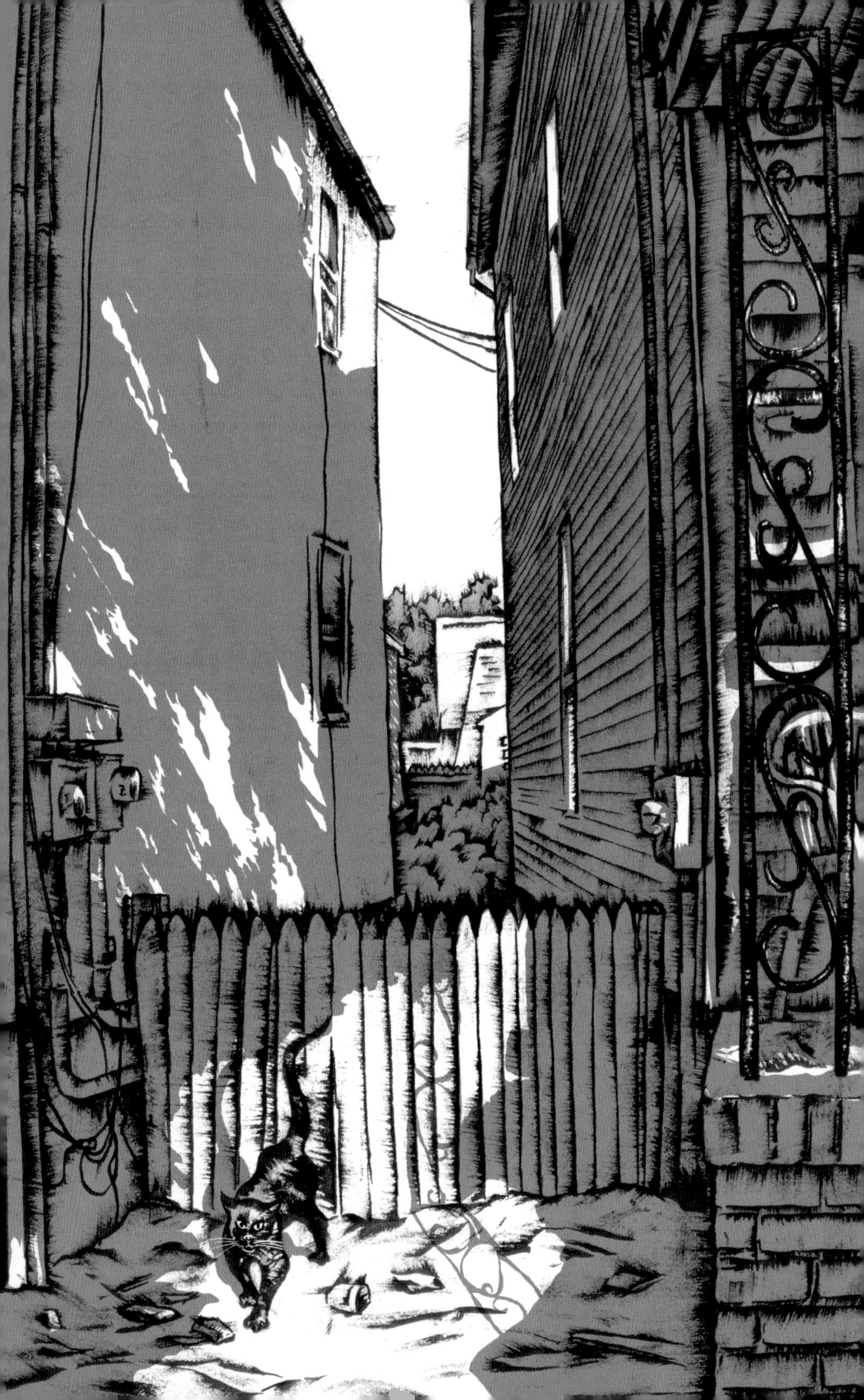

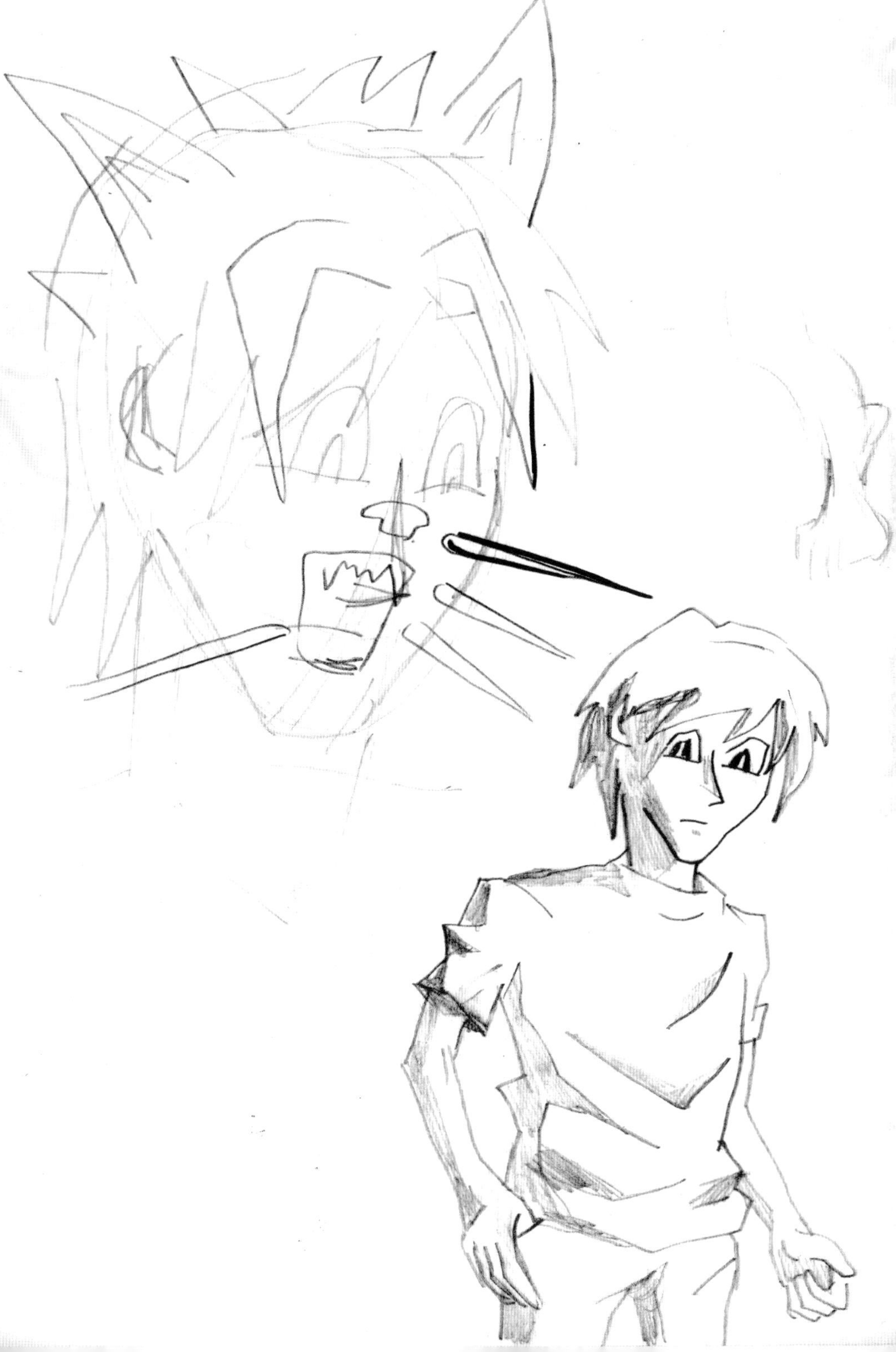

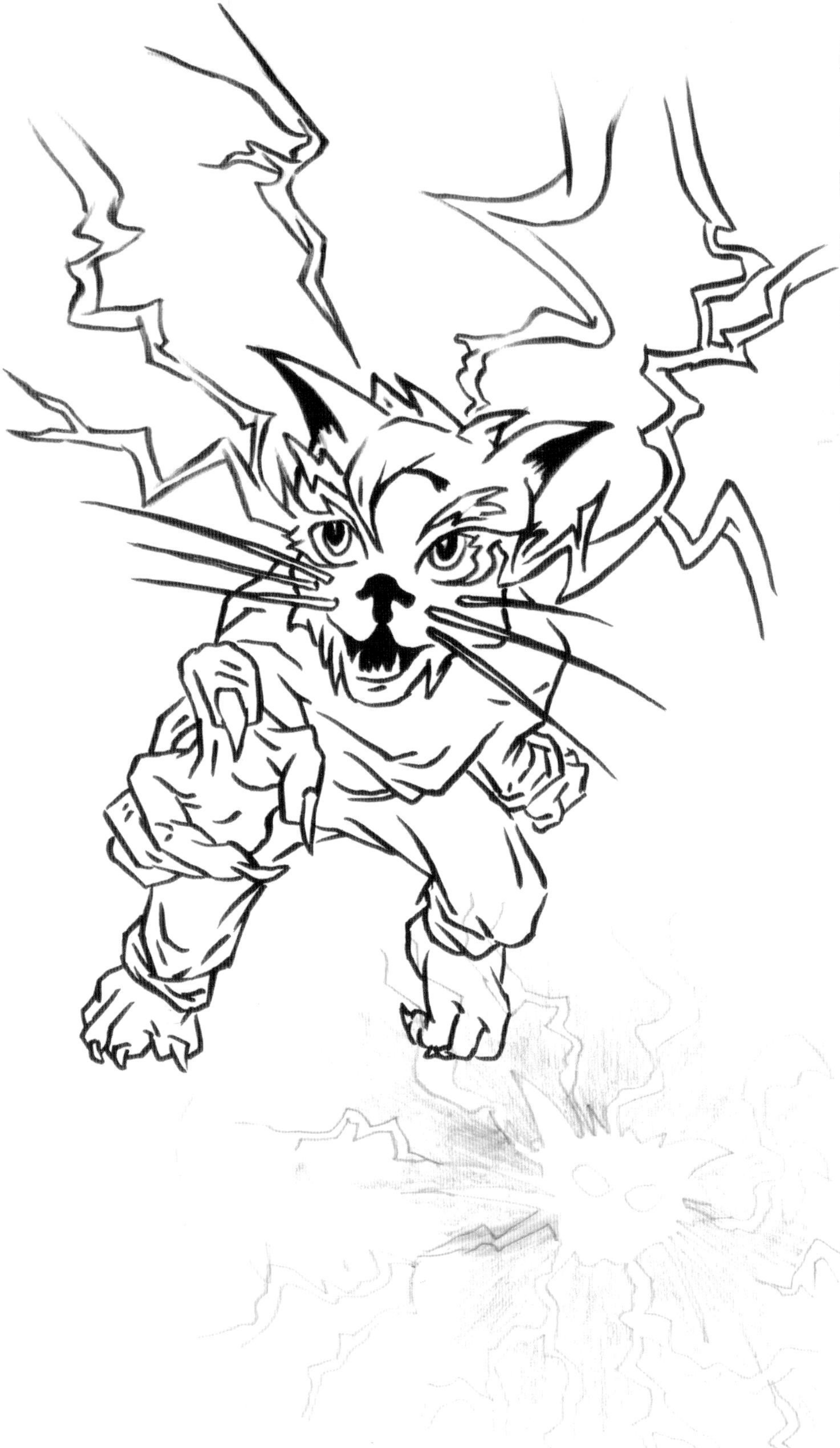

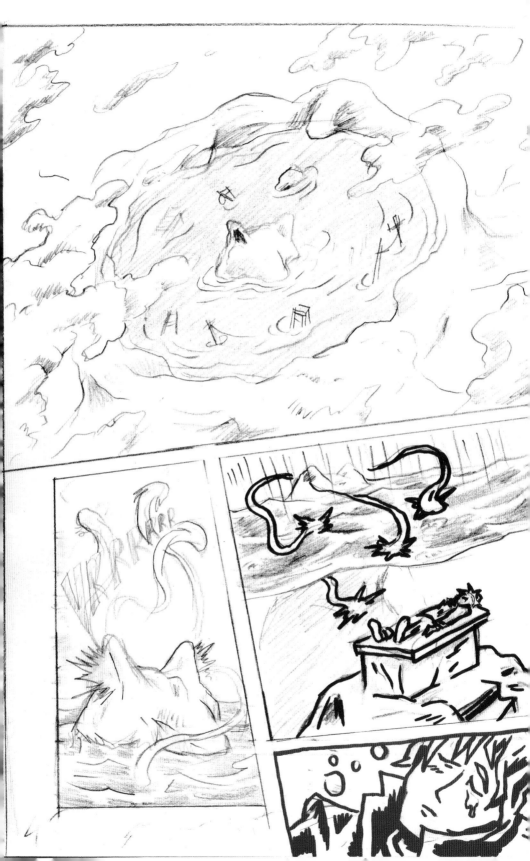

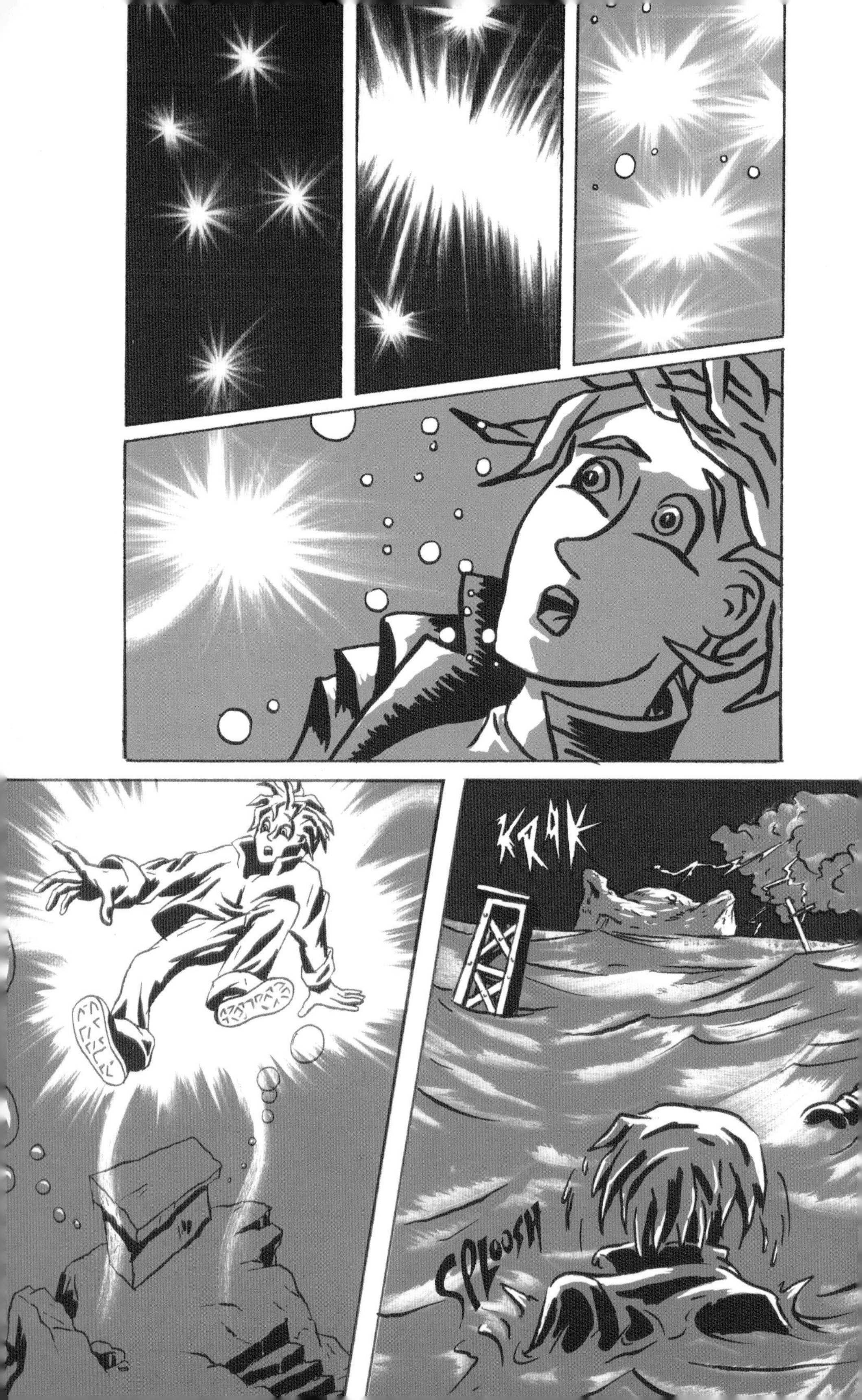
KRAK
SPLOOSH

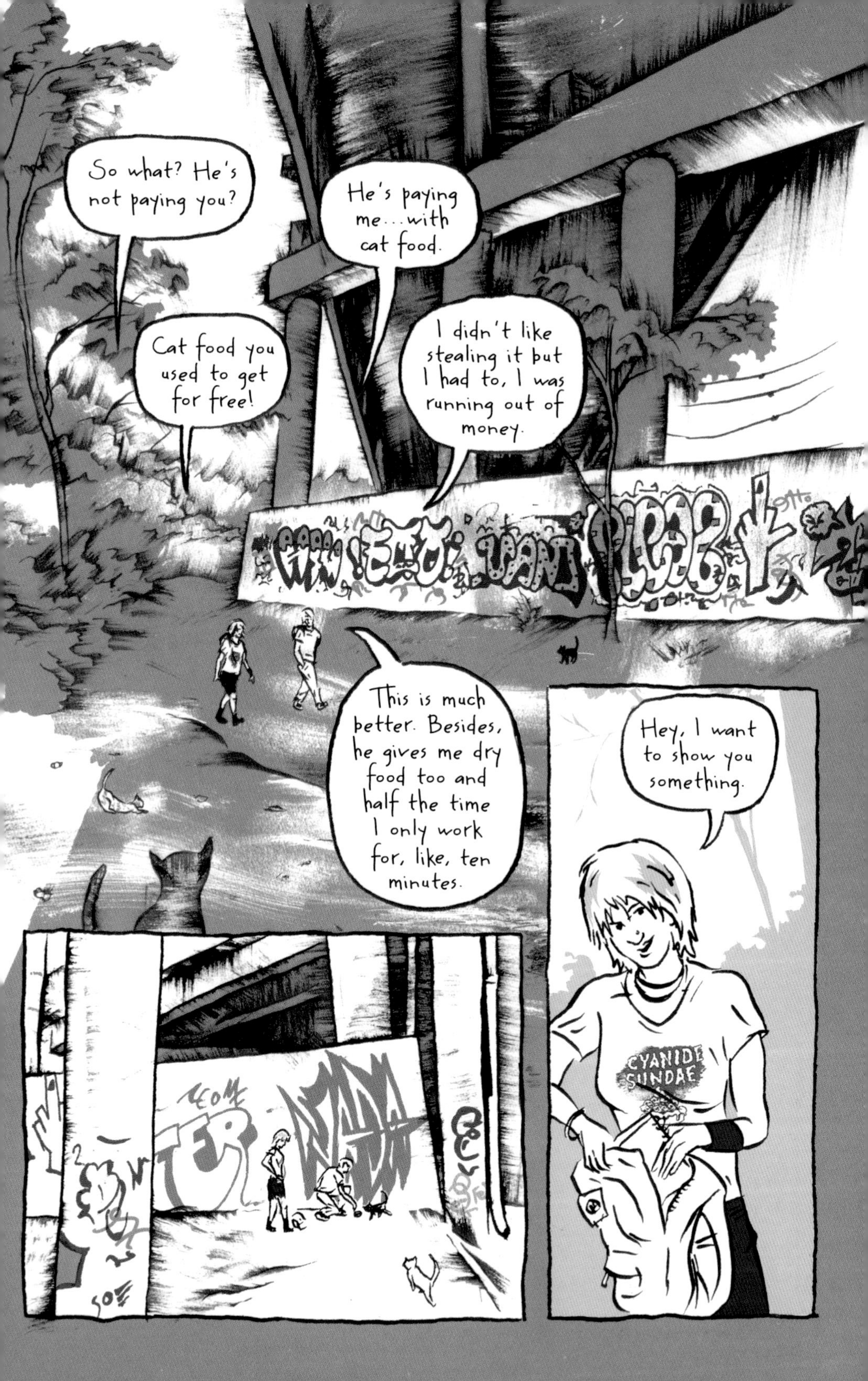
So what? He's not paying you?
He's paying me...with cat food.
Cat food you used to get for free!
I didn't like stealing it but I had to, I was running out of money.
This is much better. Besides, he gives me dry food too and half the time I only work for, like, ten minutes.
Hey, I want to show you something.
CYANIDE SUNDAE

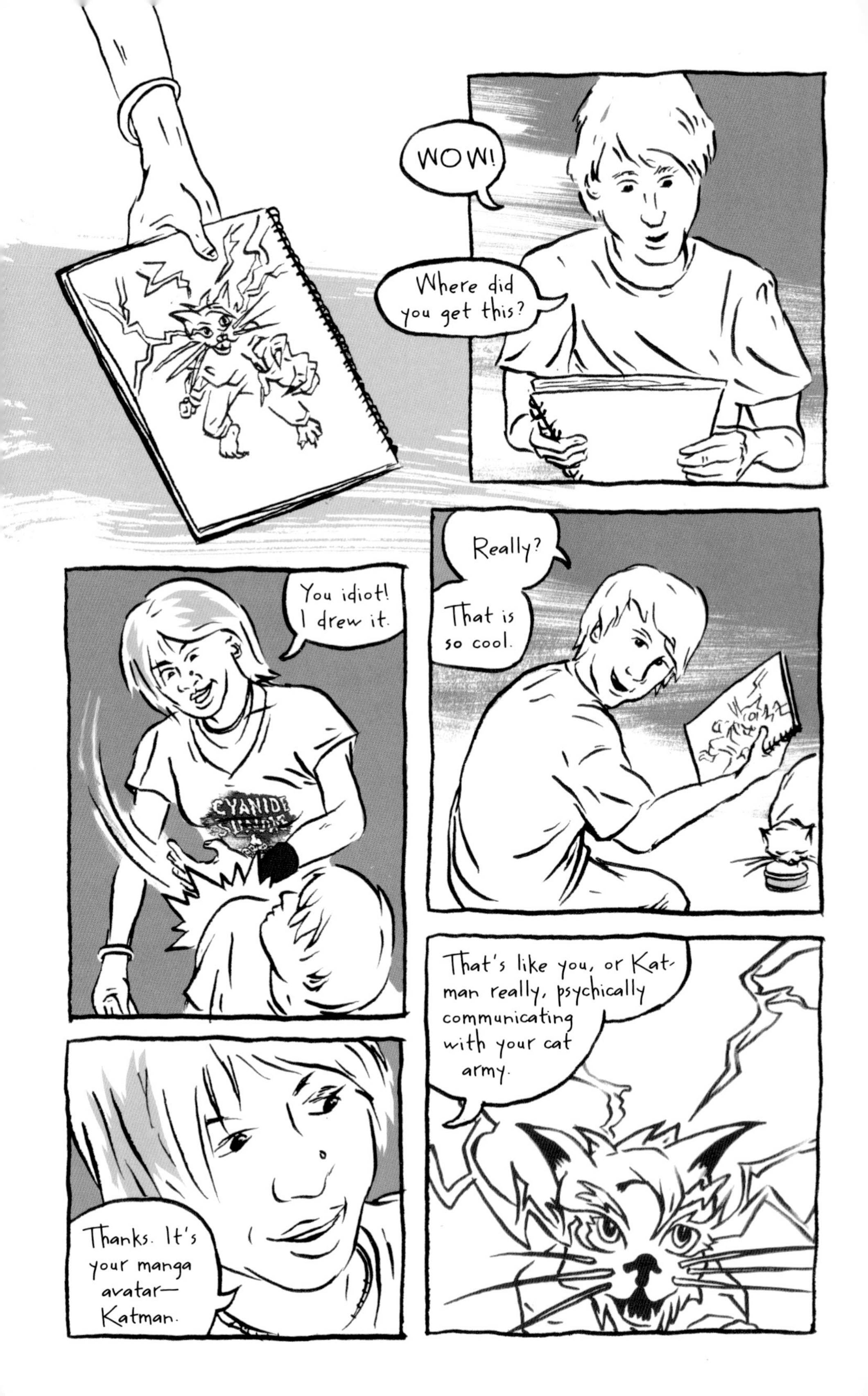
WOW!
Where did you get this?
You idiot! I drew it.
CYANIDE
Really?
That is so cool.
Thanks. It's your manga avatar—Katman.
That's like you, or Kat-man really, psychically communicating with your cat army.

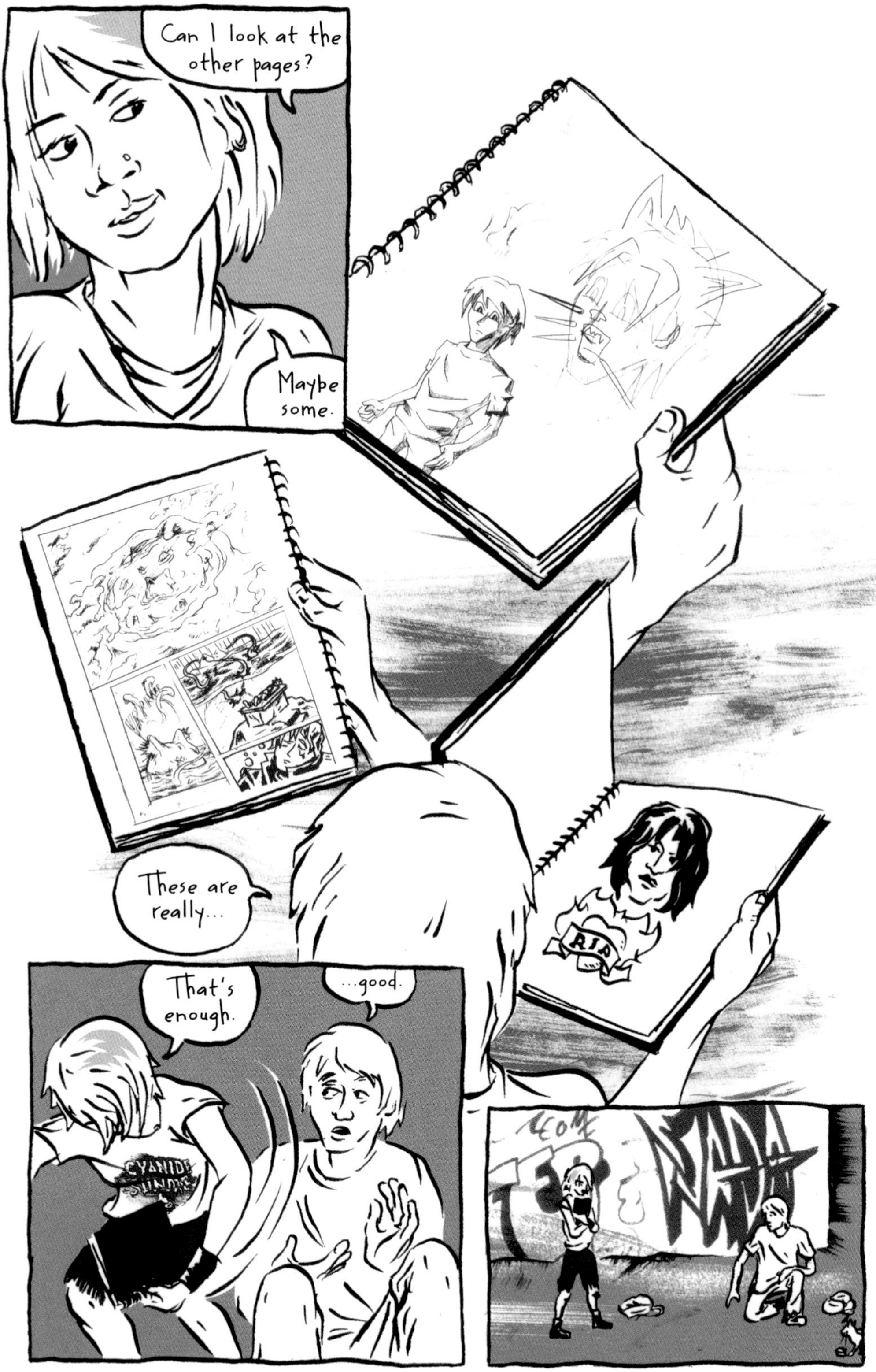
Can I look at the other pages?
Maybe some.
These are really...
That's enough.
...good.
CYANIDE SUNDAE

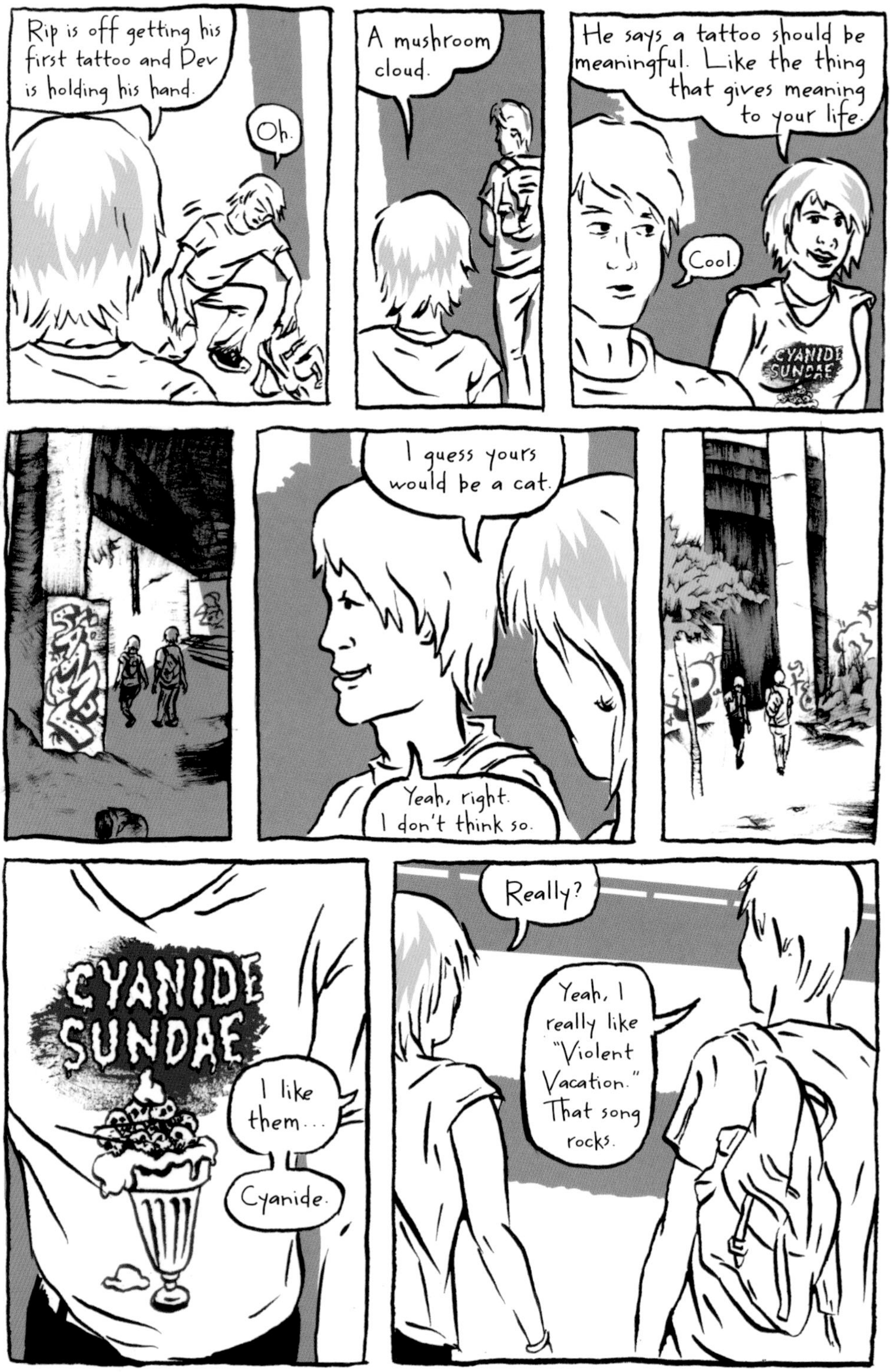

Rip is off getting his first tattoo and Dev is holding his hand.
Oh.
A mushroom cloud.
He says a tattoo should be meaningful. Like the thing that gives meaning to your life.
Cool.
CYANIDE SUNDAE
I guess yours would be a cat.
Yeah, right. I don't think so.
CYANIDE SUNDAE
I like them...
Cyanide.
Really?
Yeah, I really like "Violent Vacation." That song rocks.

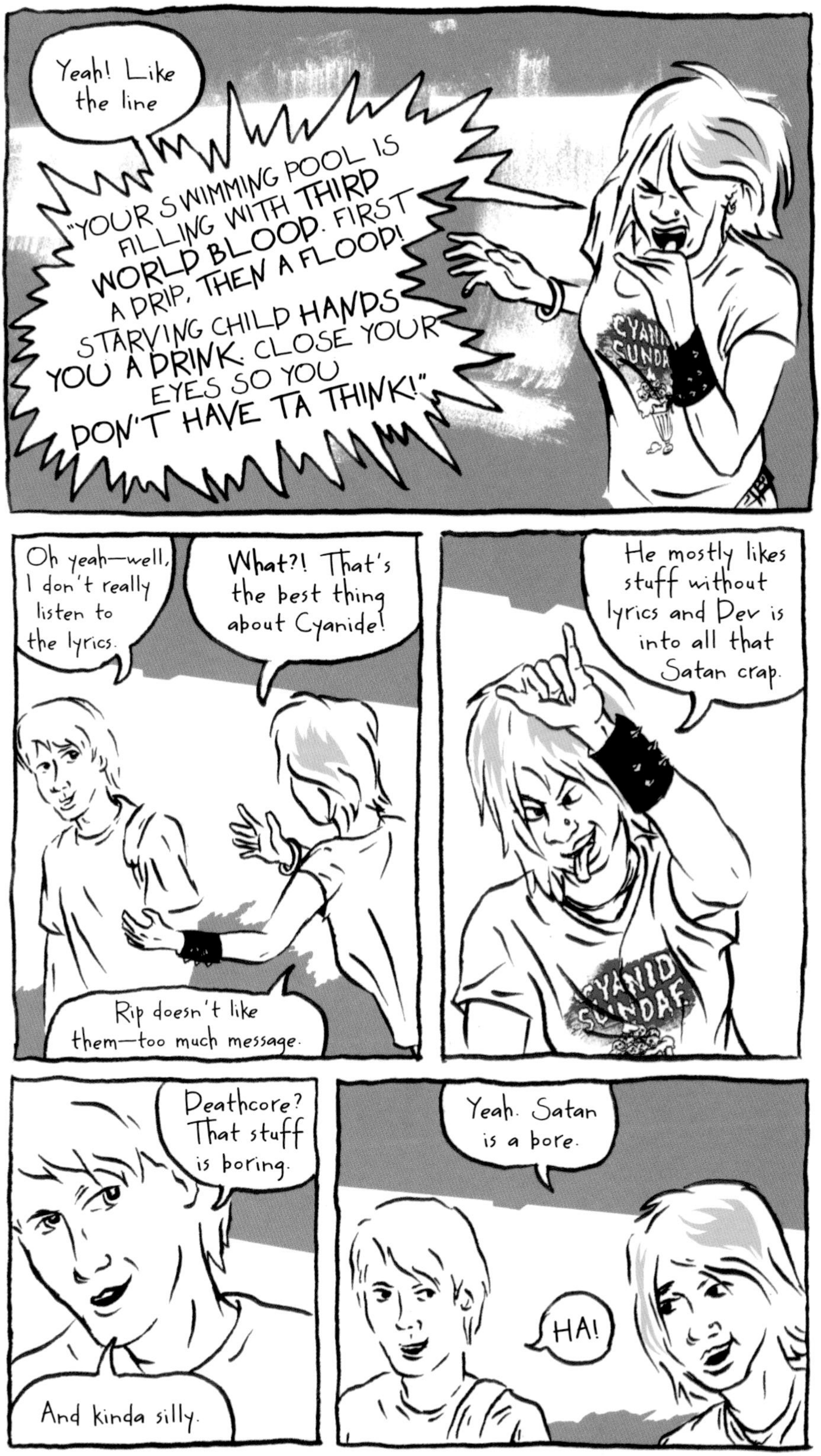

Yeah! Like the line
"YOUR SWIMMING POOL IS FILLING WITH THIRD WORLD BLOOD. FIRST A DRIP, THEN A FLOOD! STARVING CHILD HANDS YOU A DRINK. CLOSE YOUR EYES SO YOU DON'T HAVE TA THINK!"
Oh yeah—well, I don't really listen to the lyrics.
What?! That's the best thing about Cyanide!
Rip doesn't like them—too much message.
He mostly likes stuff without lyrics and Dev is into all that Satan crap.
Deathcore? That stuff is boring.
And kinda silly.
Yeah. Satan is a bore.
HA!

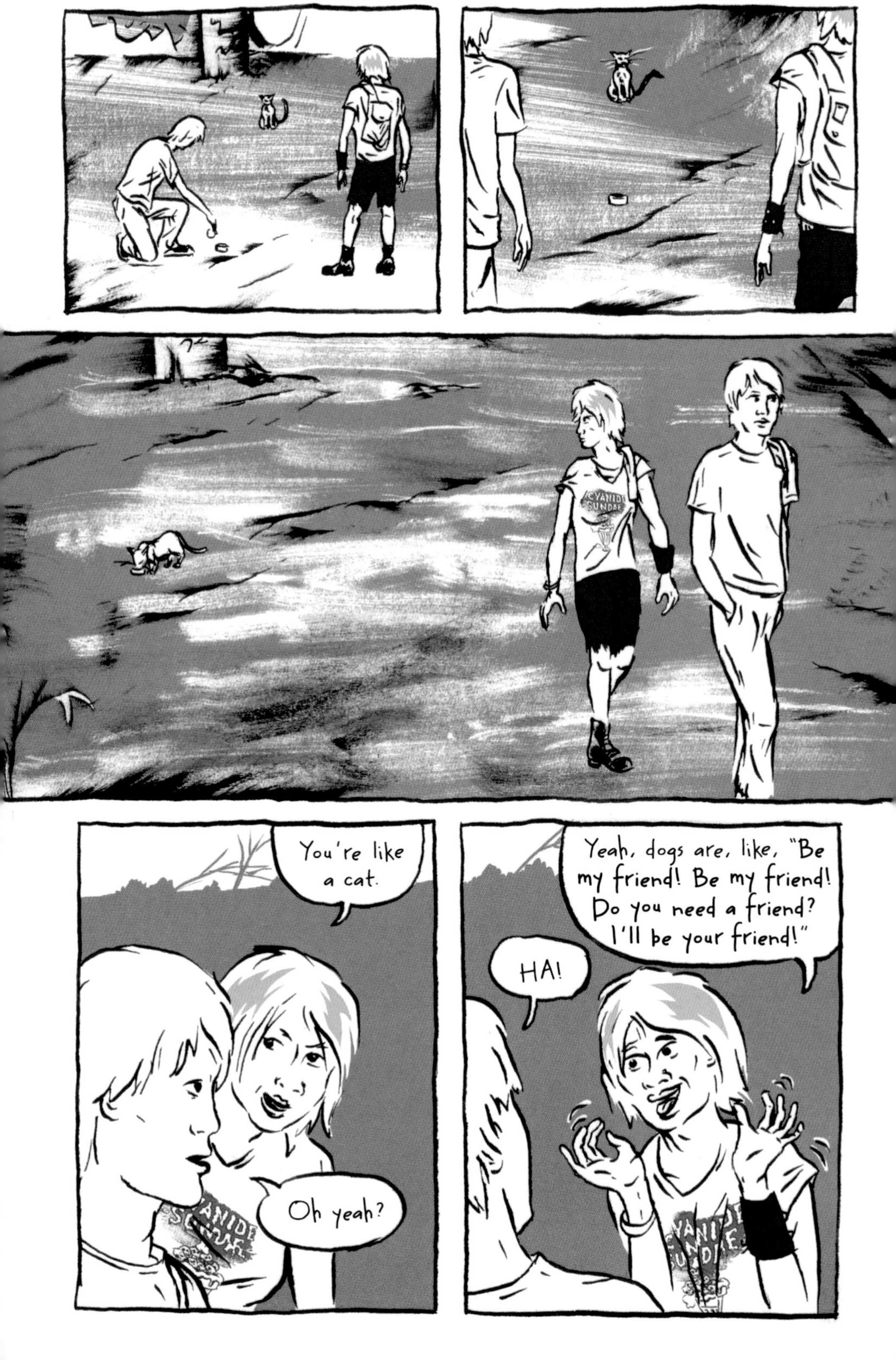
You're like a cat.
Oh yeah?
Yeah, dogs are, like, "Be my friend! Be my friend! Do you need a friend? I'll be your friend!"
HA!

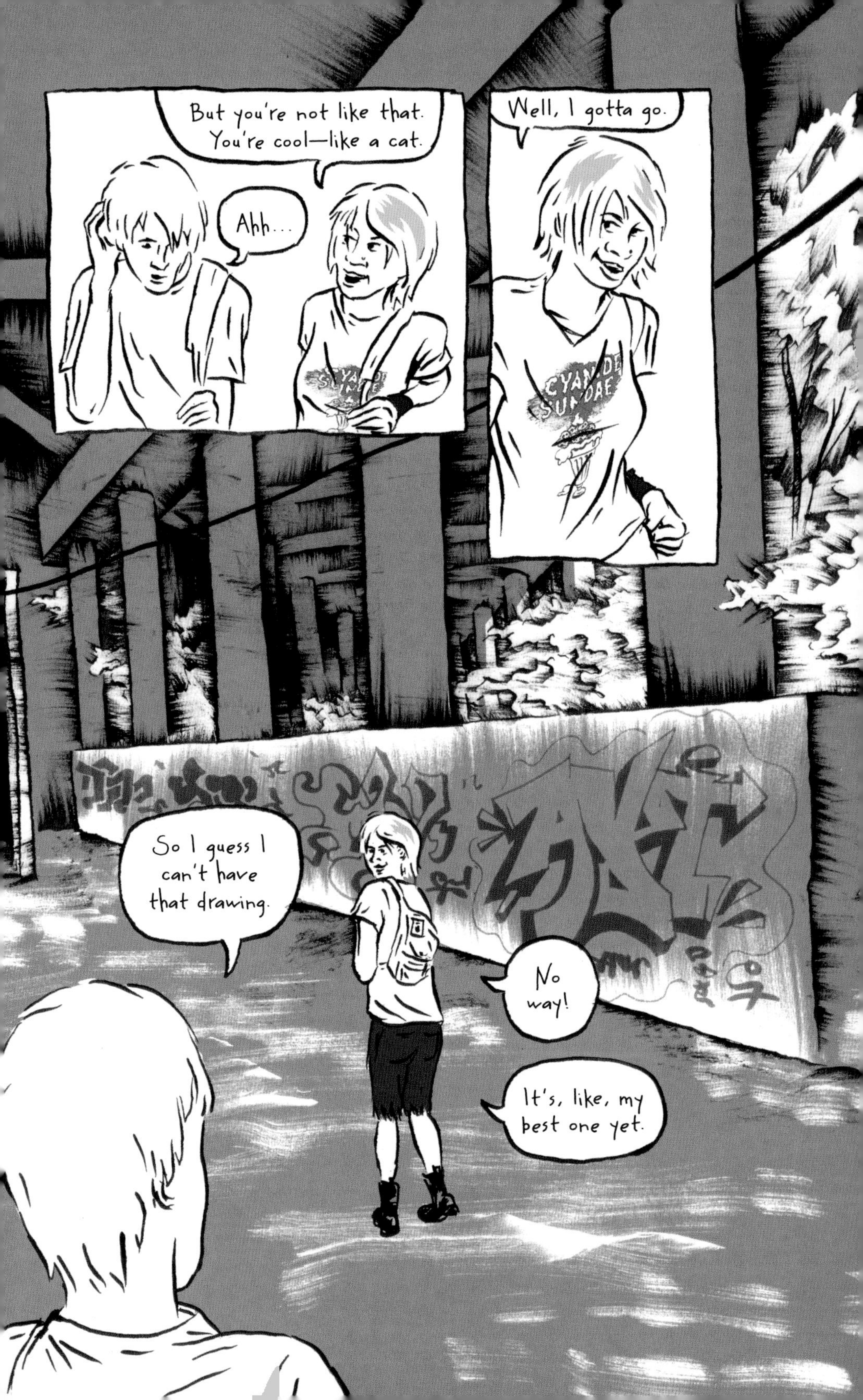
But you're not like that. You're cool—like a cat.
Ahh...
Well, I gotta go.
CYANIDE SUNDAE
So I guess I can't have that drawing.
No way!
It's, like, my best one yet.

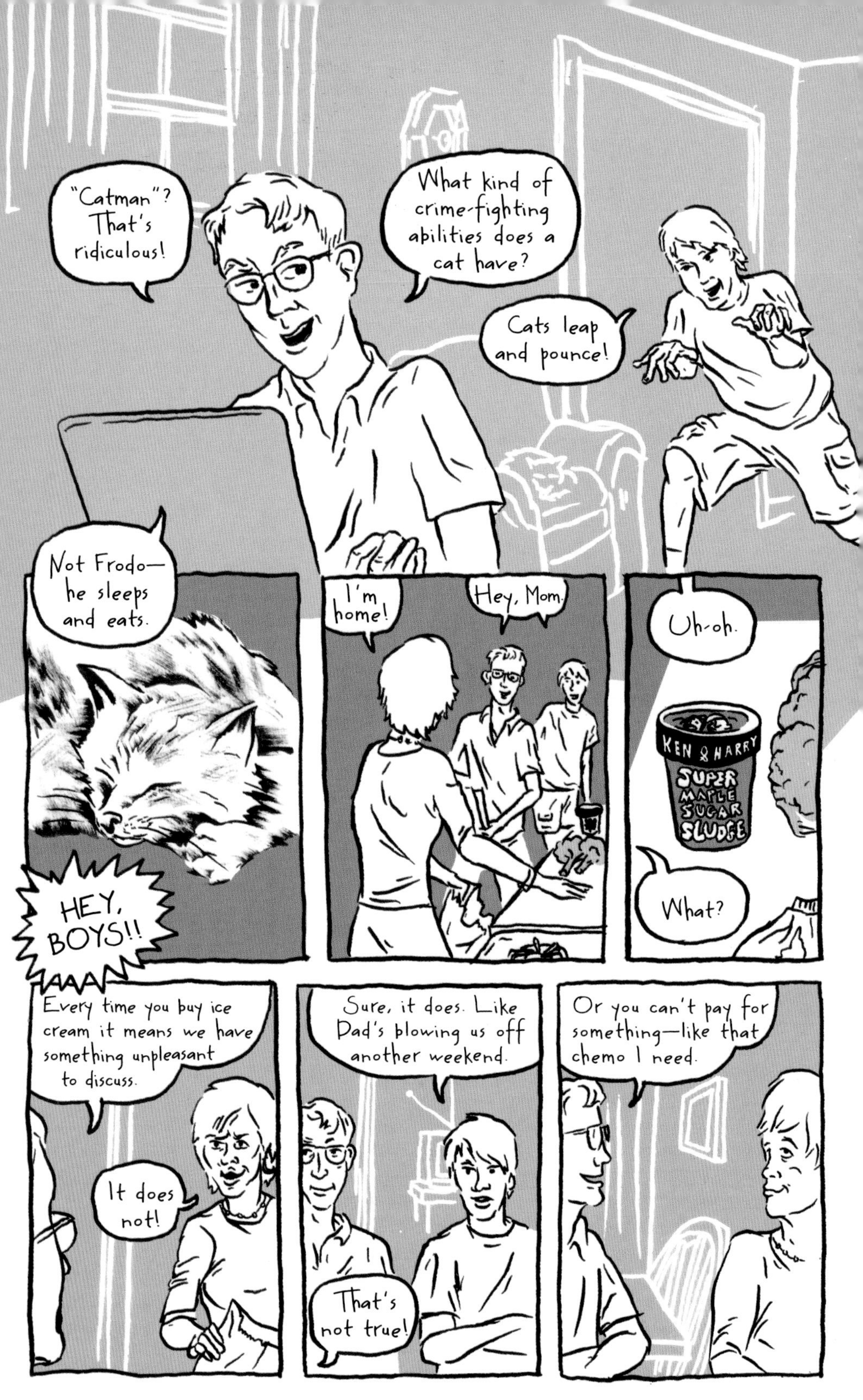
"Catman"? That's ridiculous!
What kind of crime-fighting abilities does a cat have?
Cats leap and pounce!
Not Frodo— he sleeps and eats.
HEY, BOYS!!
I'm home!
Hey, Mom.
Uh-oh.
KEN & HARRY
SUPER MAPLE SUGAR SLUDGE
What?
Every time you buy ice cream it means we have something unpleasant to discuss.
It does not!
Sure, it does. Like Dad's blowing us off another weekend.
That's not true!
Or you can't pay for something—like that chemo I need.

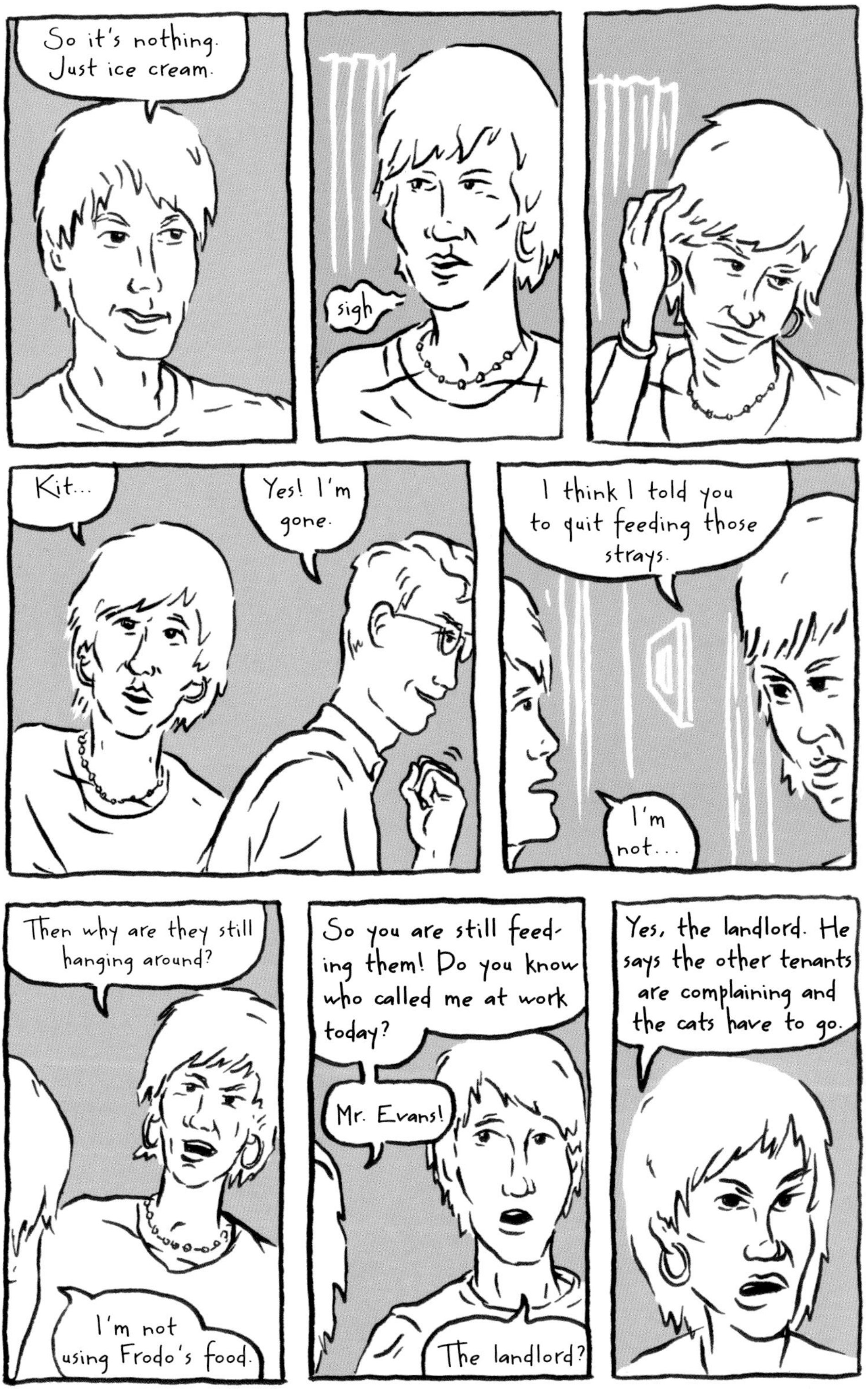

So it's nothing. Just ice cream.
sigh
Kit...
Yes! I'm gone.
I think I told you to quit feeding those strays.
I'm not...
Then why are they still hanging around?
I'm not using Frodo's food.
So you are still feeding them! Do you know who called me at work today?
Mr. Evans!
The landlord?
Yes, the landlord. He says the other tenants are complaining and the cats have to go.

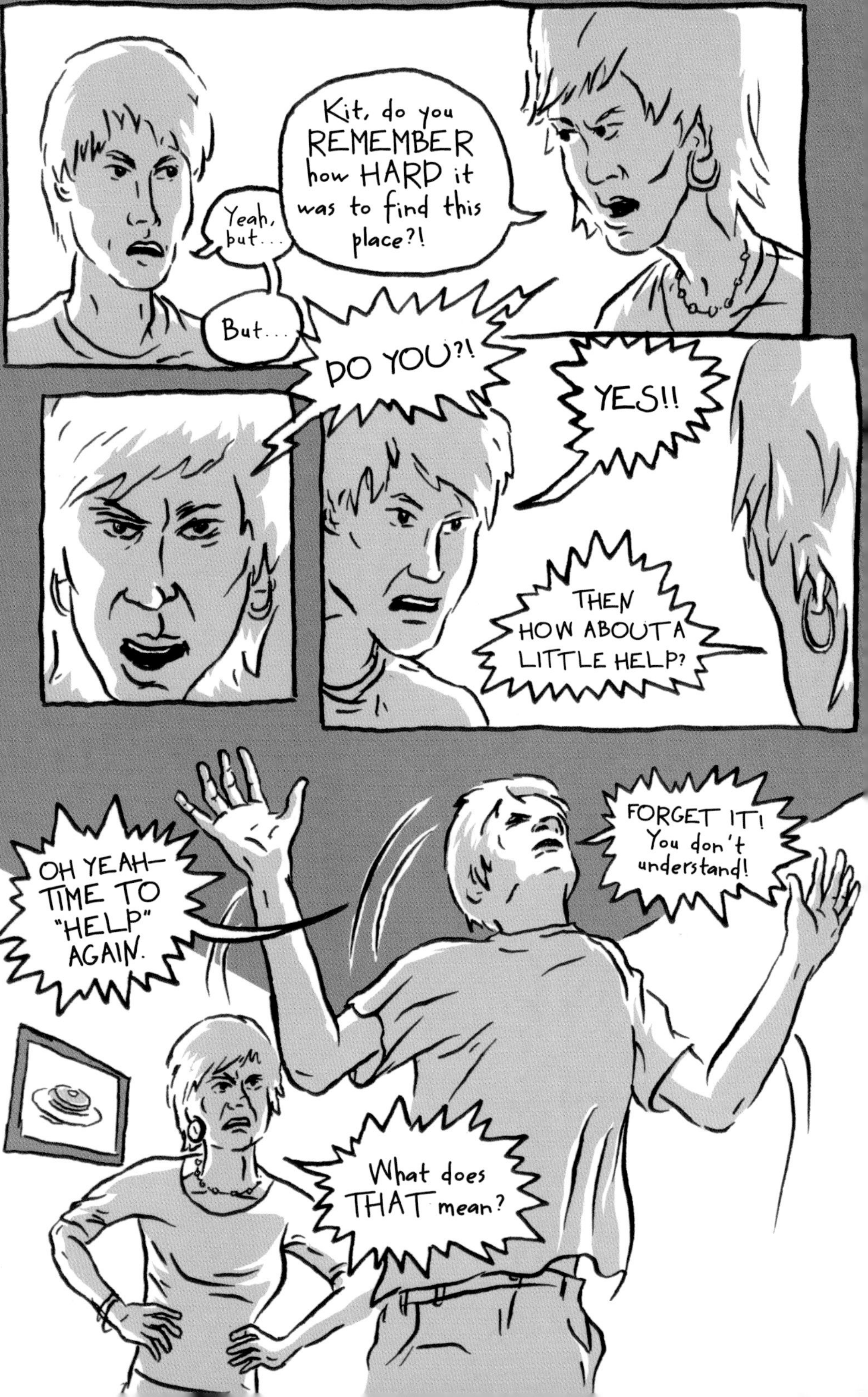
Kit, do you REMEMBER how HARD it was to find this place?!
Yeah, but...
But...
DO YOU?!
YES!!
THEN HOW ABOUT A LITTLE HELP?
OH YEAH— TIME TO "HELP" AGAIN.
FORGET IT! You don't understand!
What does THAT mean?

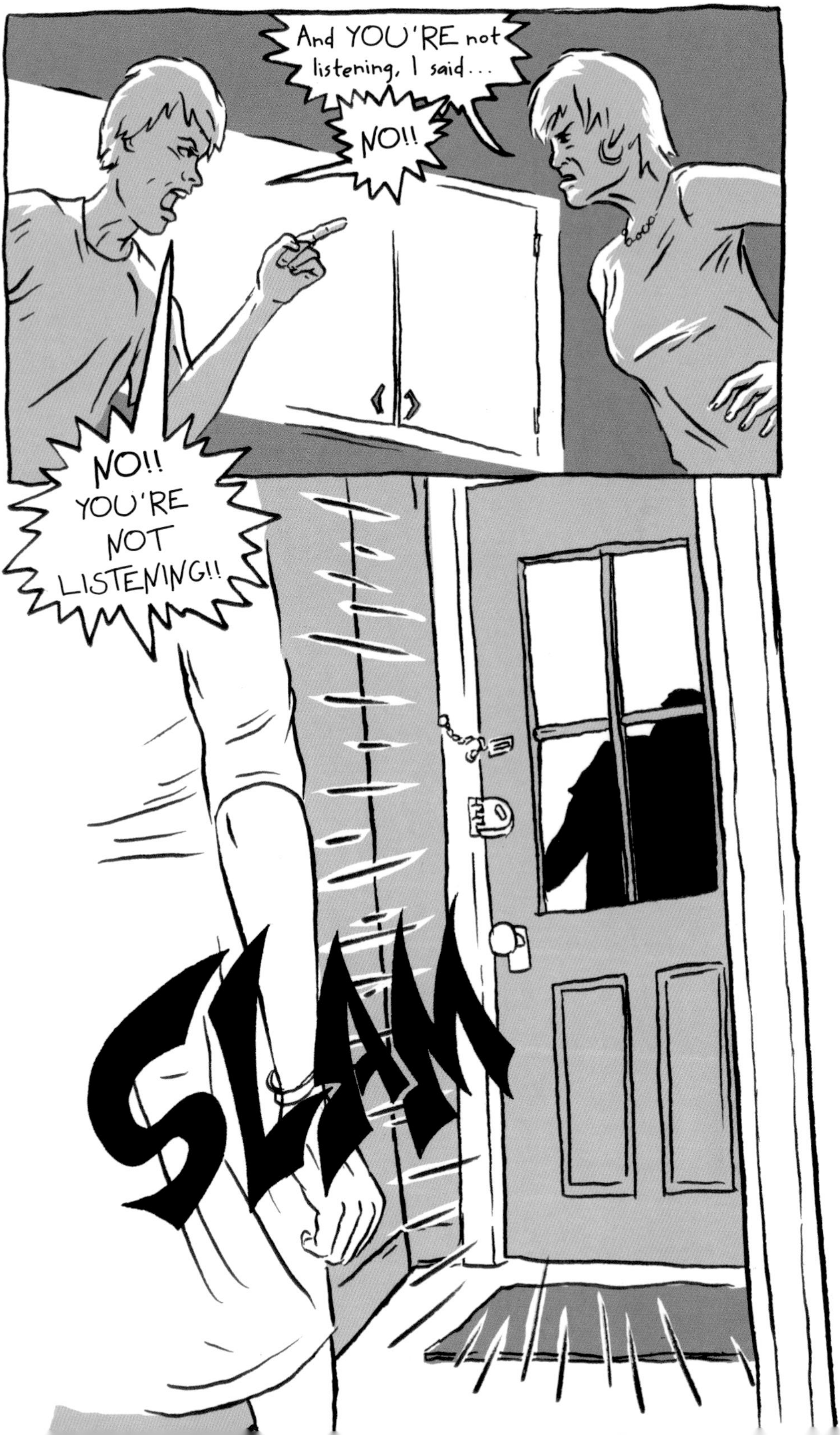
And YOU'RE not listening, I said...
NO!!
NO!! YOU'RE NOT LISTENING!!
SLAM

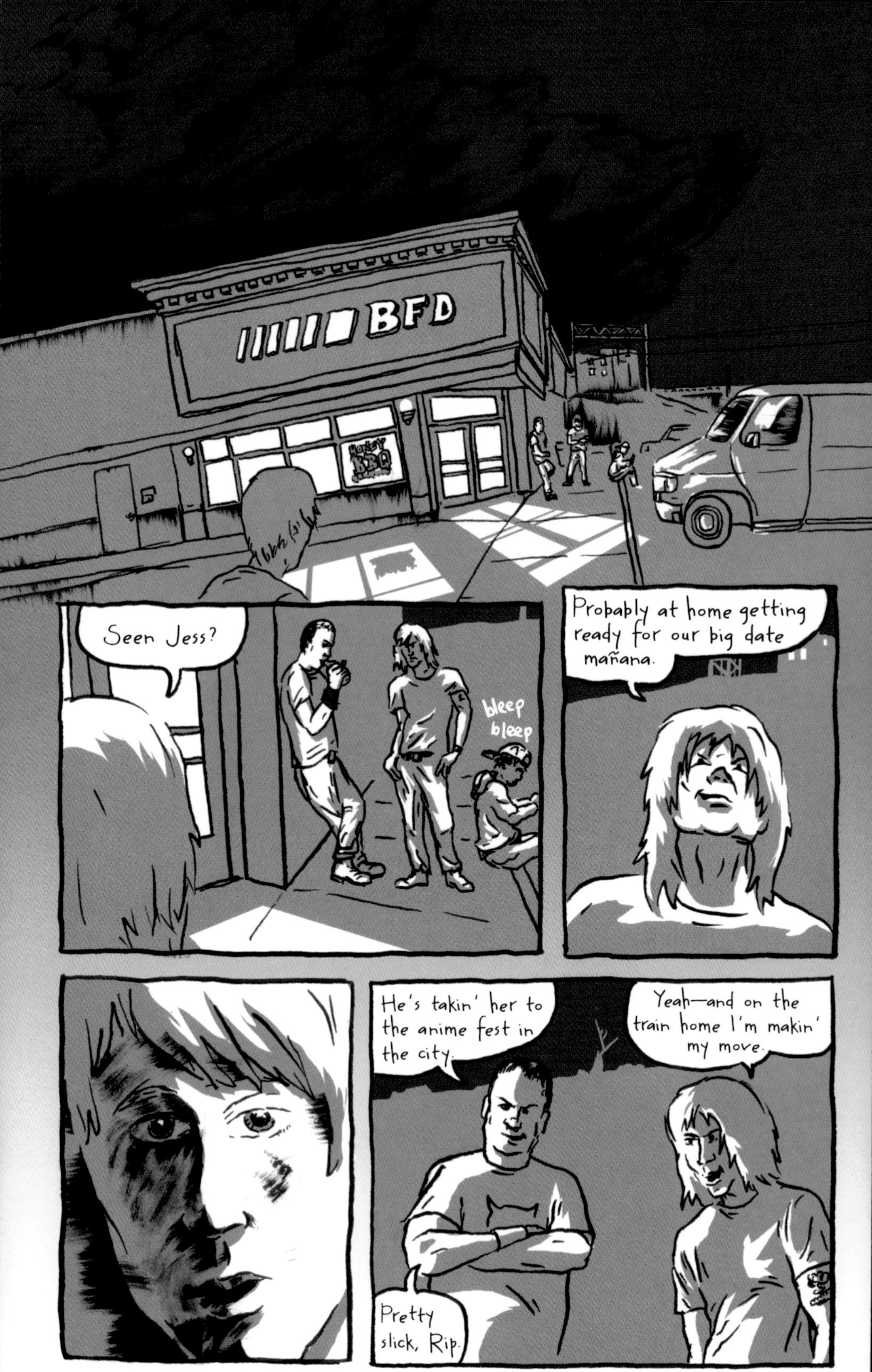
BFD
Seen Jess?
bleep bleep
Probably at home getting ready for our big date mañana.
He's takin' her to the anime fest in the city.
Yeah—and on the train home I'm makin' my move.
Pretty slick, Rip.

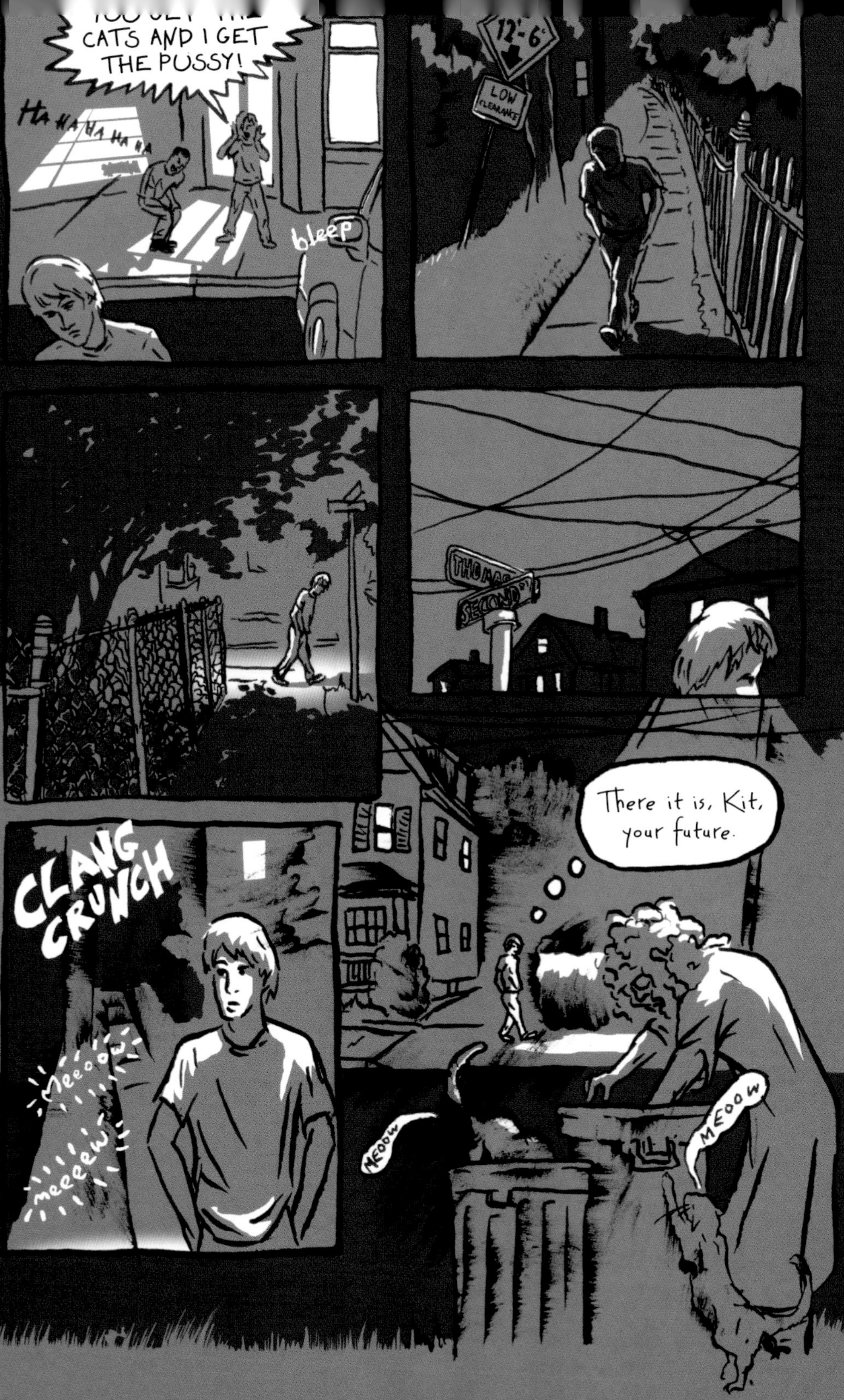
CATS AND I GET
THE PUSSY!
HA HA HA HA HA HA
bleep
12'-6"
LOW CLEARANCE
THOMAS
SECOND ST
There it is, Kit, your future.
CLANG
CRUNCH
Meeooow
meeeew
MEOOW
MEOOW

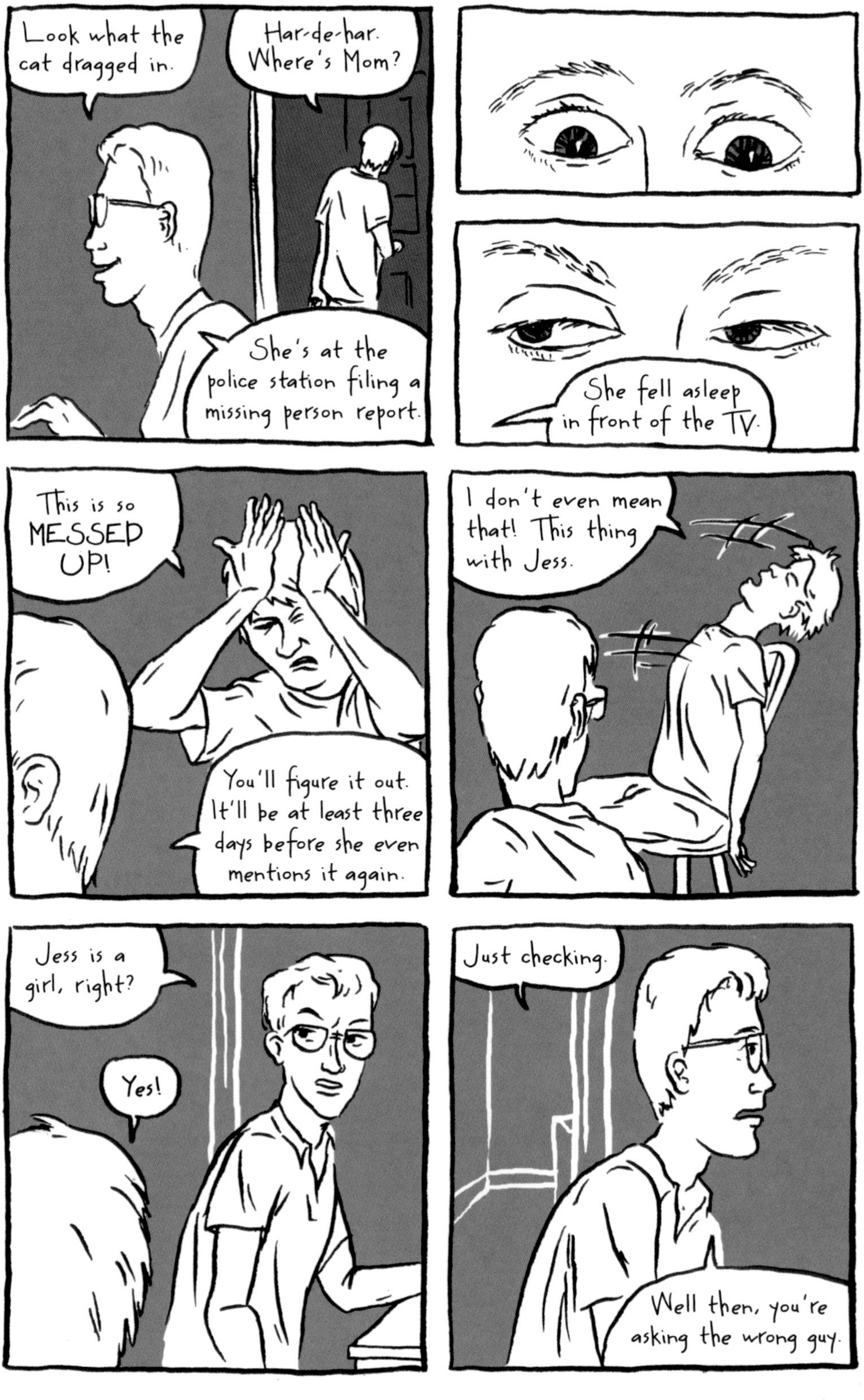
Look what the cat dragged in.
Har-de-har. Where's Mom?
She's at the police station filing a missing person report.
She fell asleep in front of the TV.
This is so MESSED UP!
You'll figure it out. It'll be at least three days before she even mentions it again.
I don't even mean that! This thing with Jess.
Jess is a girl, right?
Yes!
Just checking.
Well then, you're asking the wrong guy.

What? You don't think about them?

Are you crazy? Yeah, I think about them. That doesn't mean I understand them.

Except enough to know they aren't interested in someone like me.

I'm not exactly "cool."

They're not all like that.

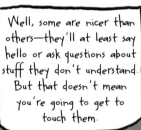

Well, some are nicer than others—they'll at least say hello or ask questions about stuff they don't understand. But that doesn't mean you're going to get to touch them.

You're like a cat.

You have to be "cool" to do that.

I just try not to think about it. It just gets me all sweaty.

Well, I guess I got plenty to figure out with these stupid cats.

That I can help you with.

Try "A" for animal shelter.

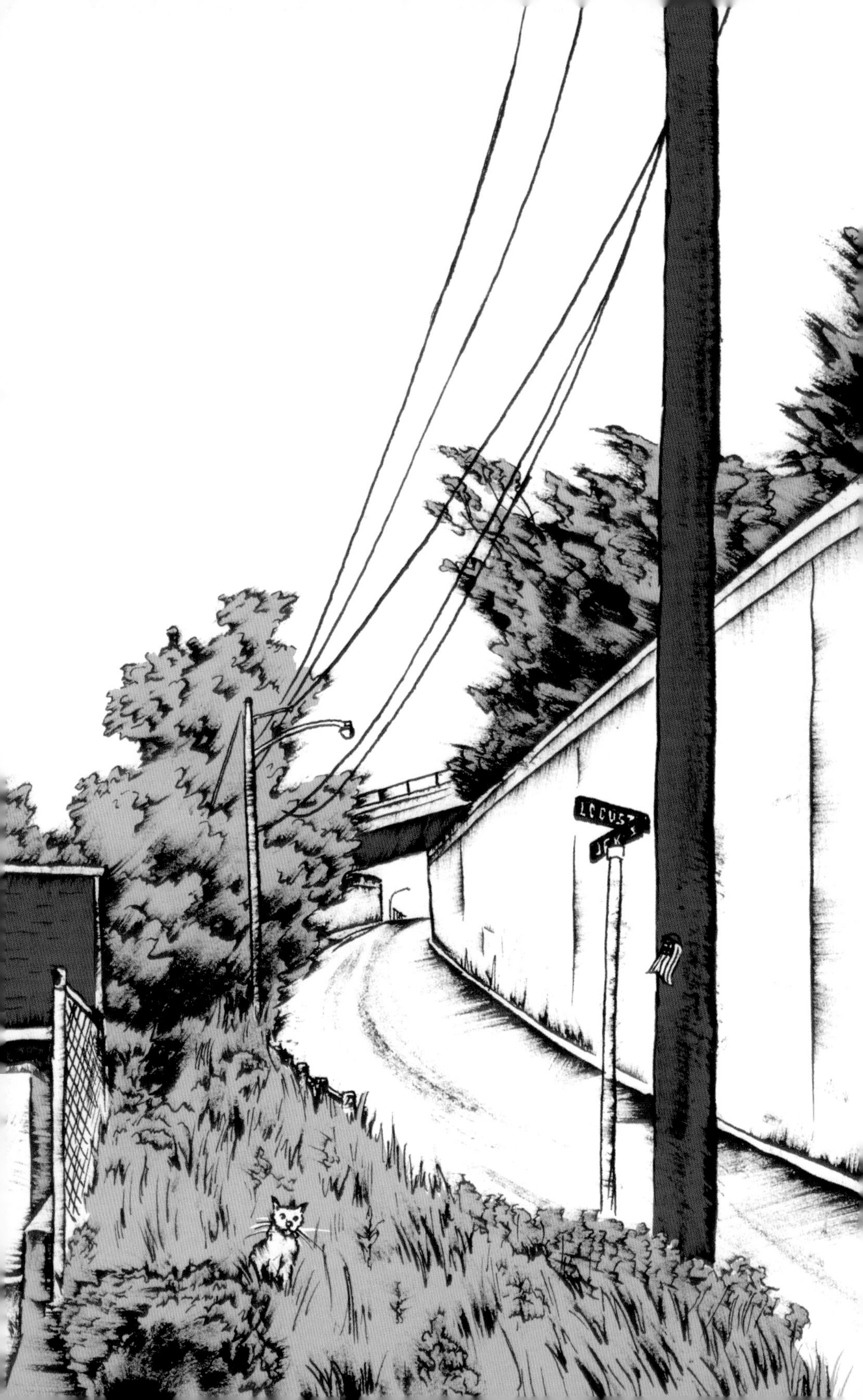
LOCUST

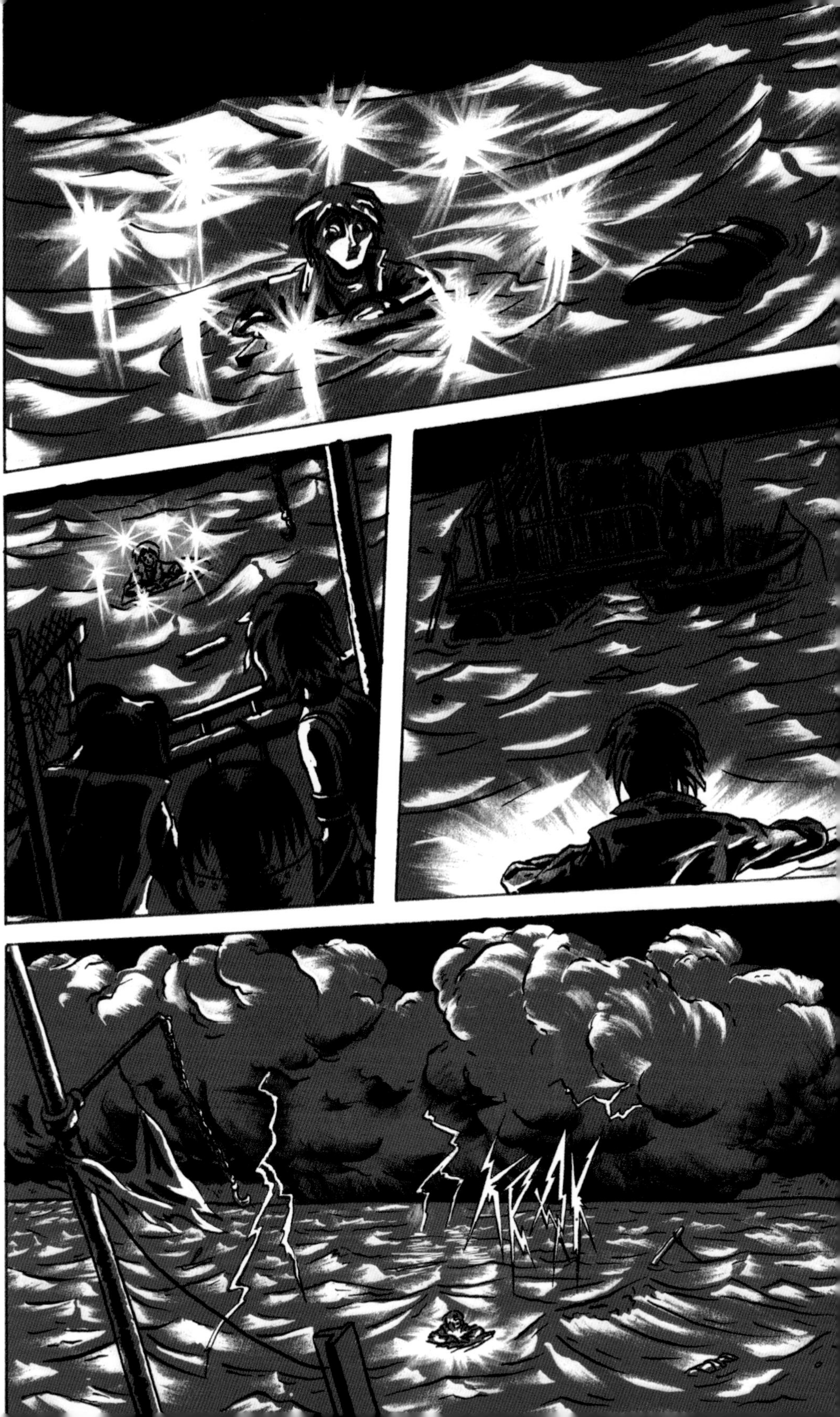
KRAK

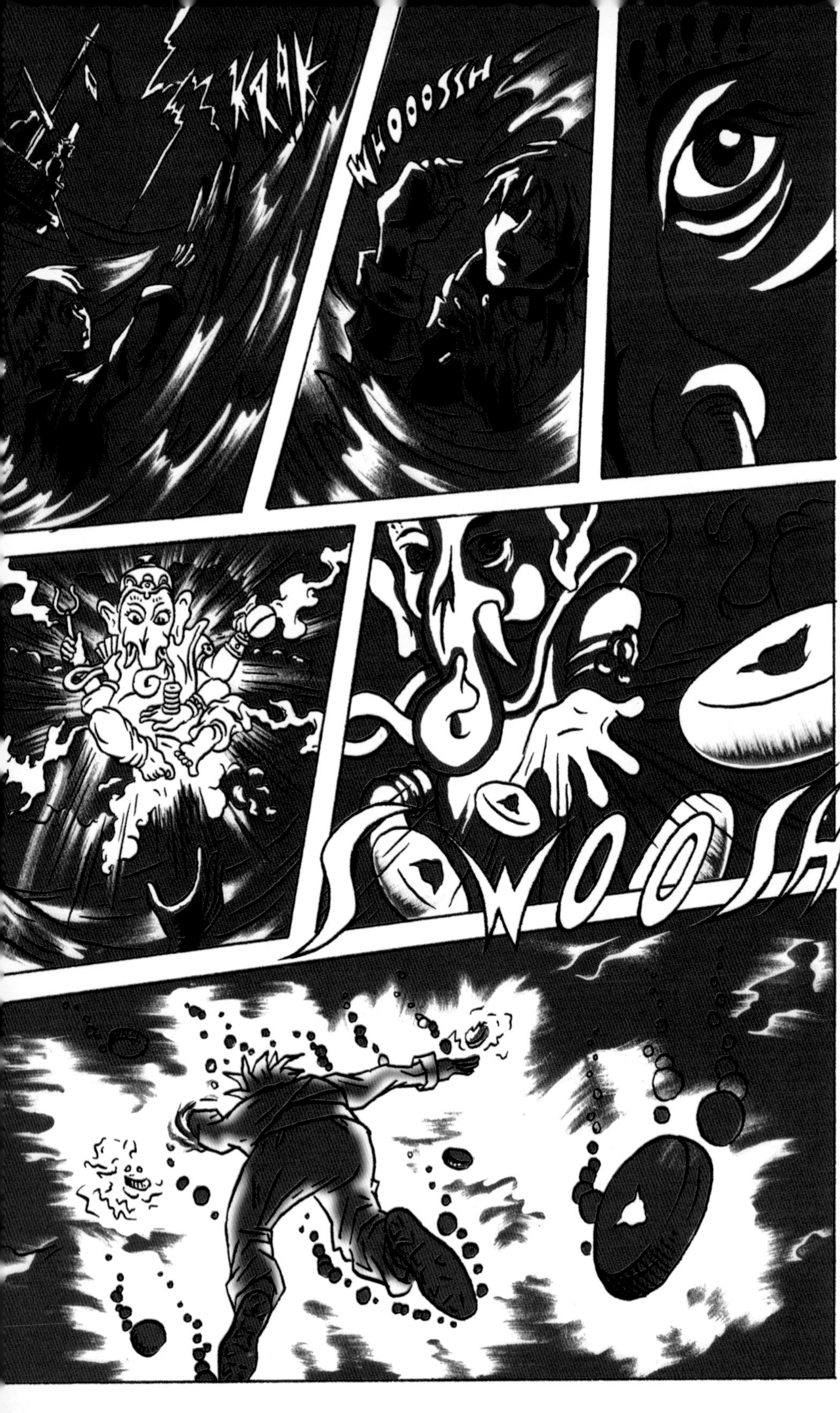
KRAK
WHOOOSSH
SWOOSH

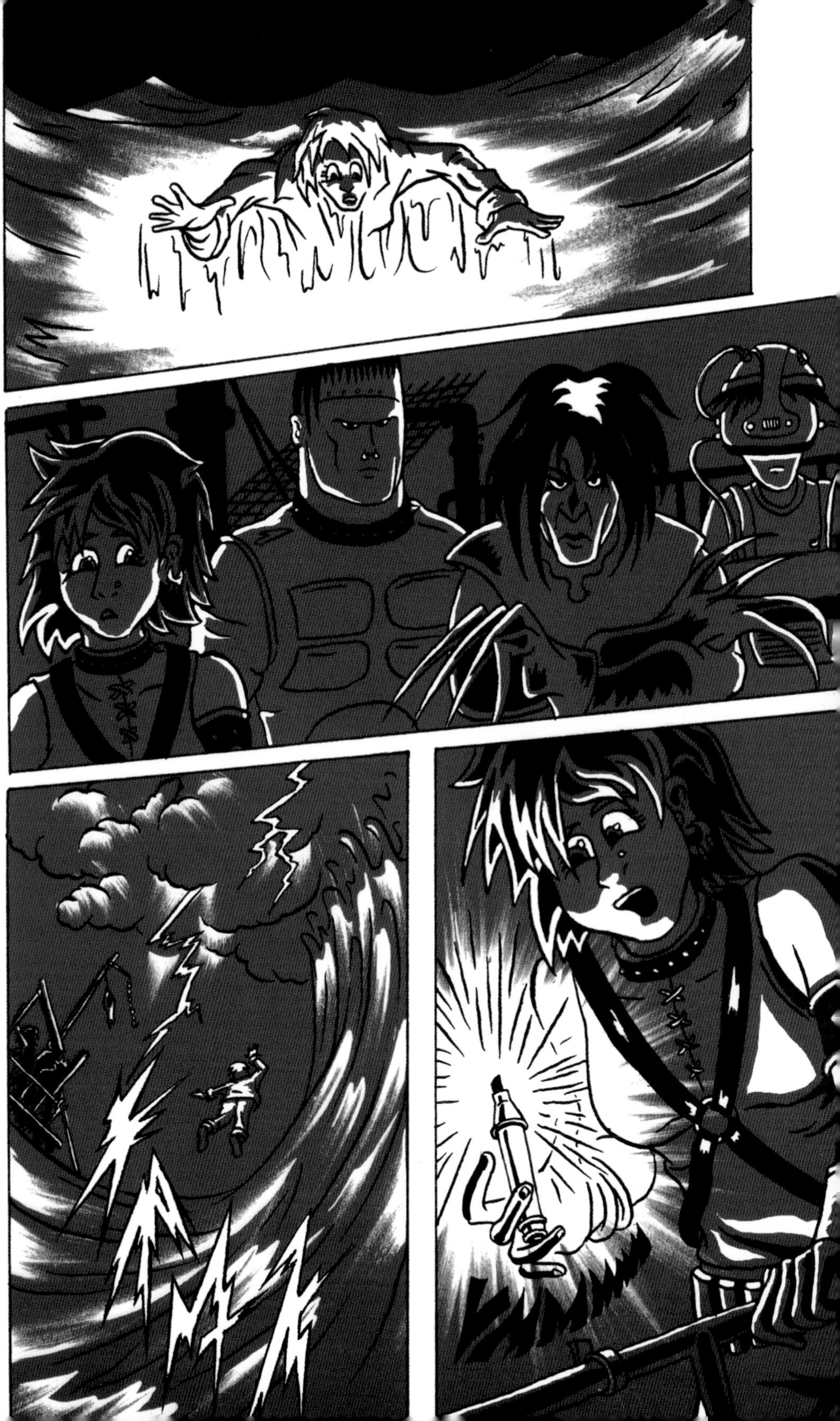

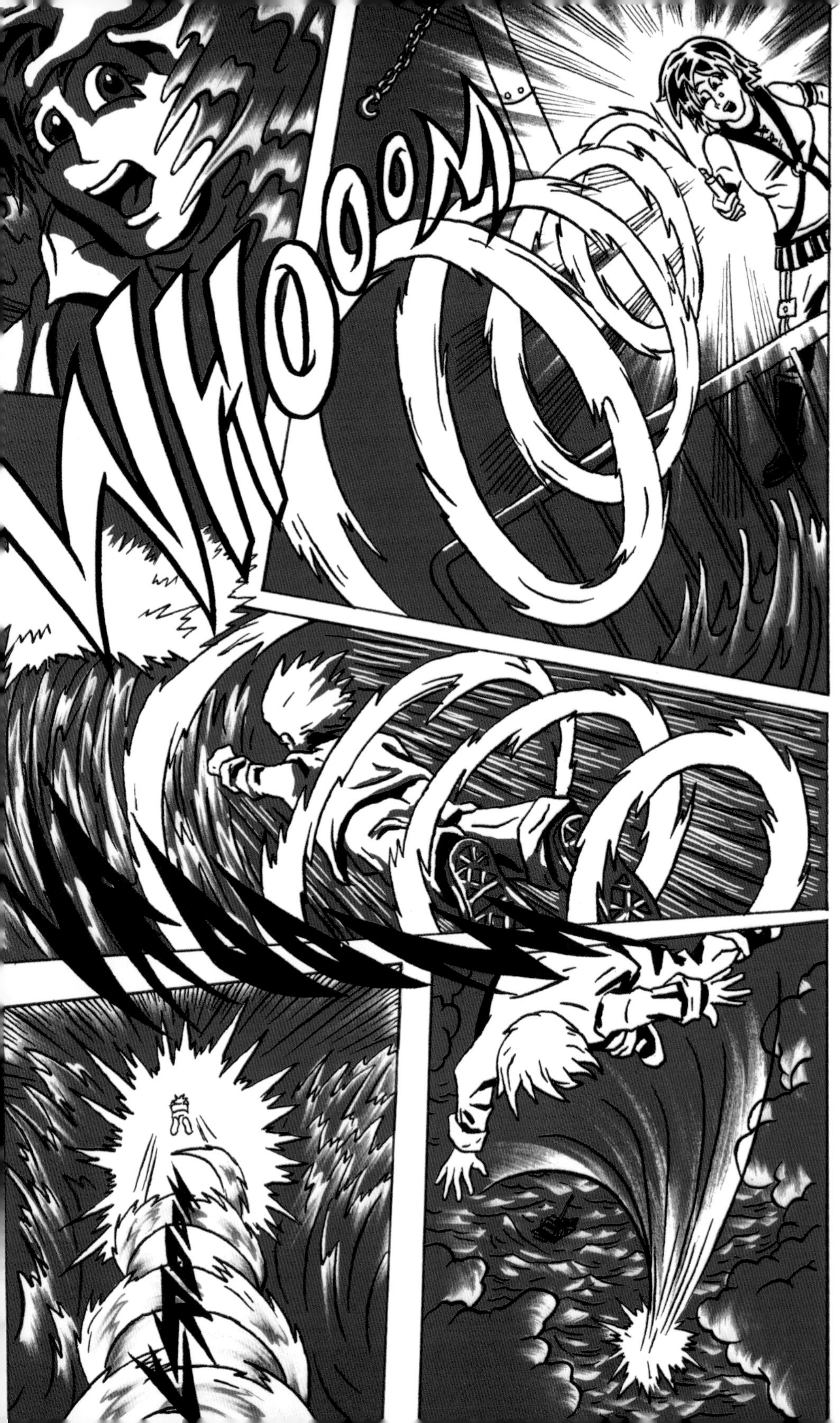
WHOOOOM

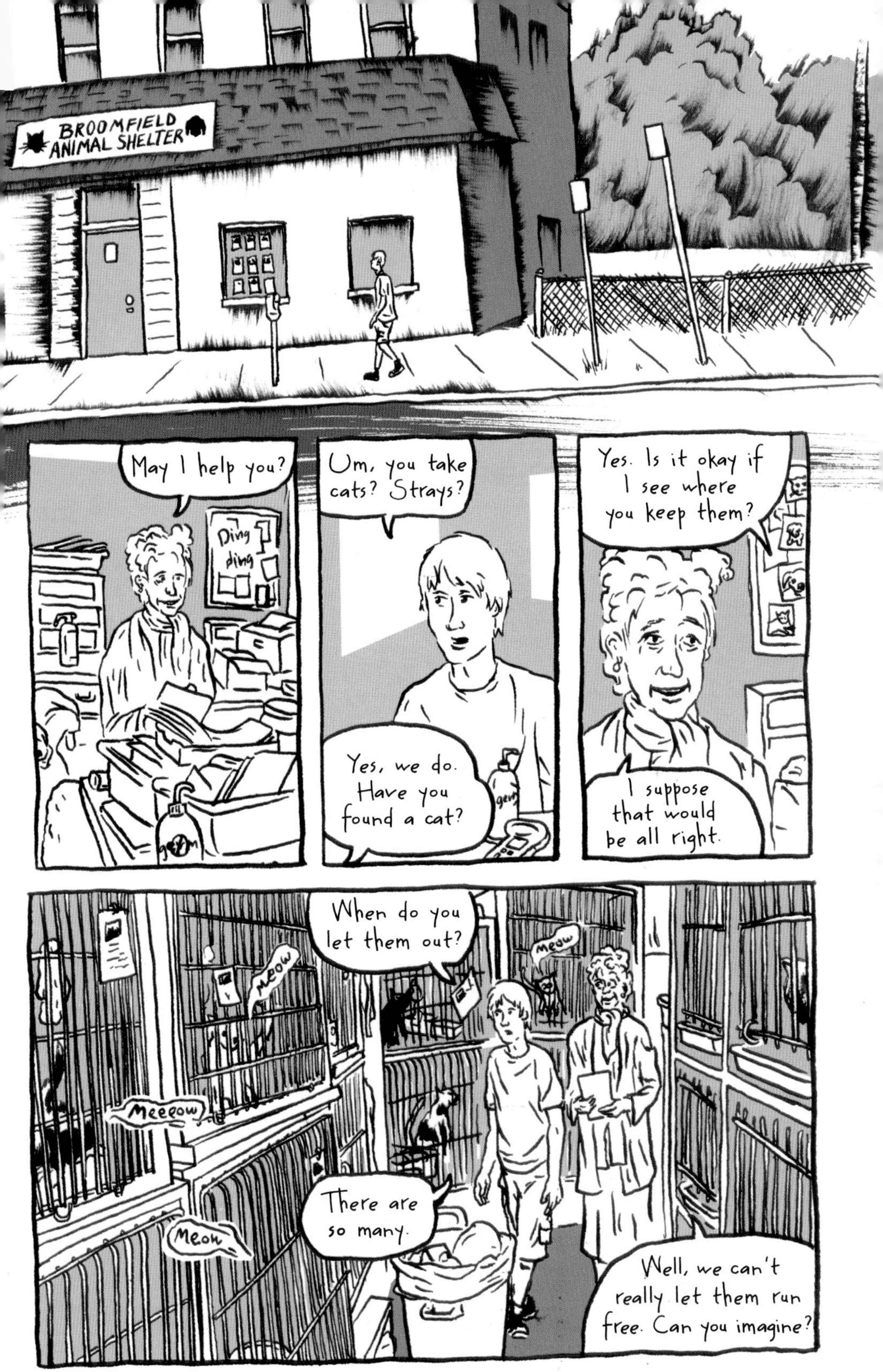
BROOMFIELD ANIMAL SHELTER
May I help you?
Ding ding
Um, you take cats? Strays?
Yes, we do. Have you found a cat?
Yes. Is it okay if I see where you keep them?
I suppose that would be all right.
When do you let them out?
meow
meow
Meeeow
There are so many.
Meow
Well, we can't really let them run free. Can you imagine?

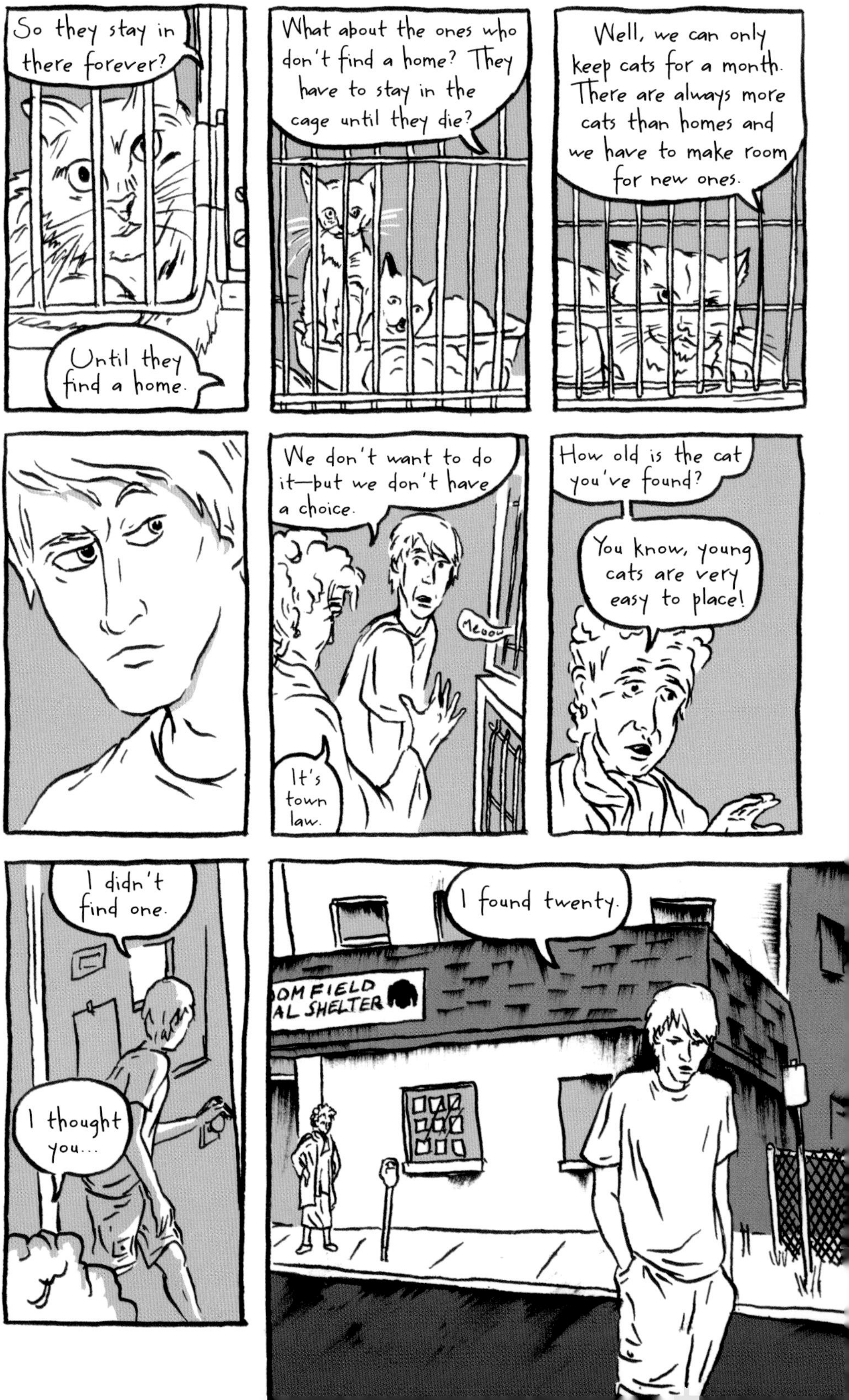
So they stay in there forever?
Until they find a home.
What about the ones who don't find a home? They have to stay in the cage until they die?
Well, we can only keep cats for a month. There are always more cats than homes and we have to make room for new ones.
We don't want to do it—but we don't have a choice.
It's town law.
Meoow
How old is the cat you've found?
You know, young cats are very easy to place!
I didn't find one.
I thought you...
I found twenty.
OMFIELD
AL SHELTER

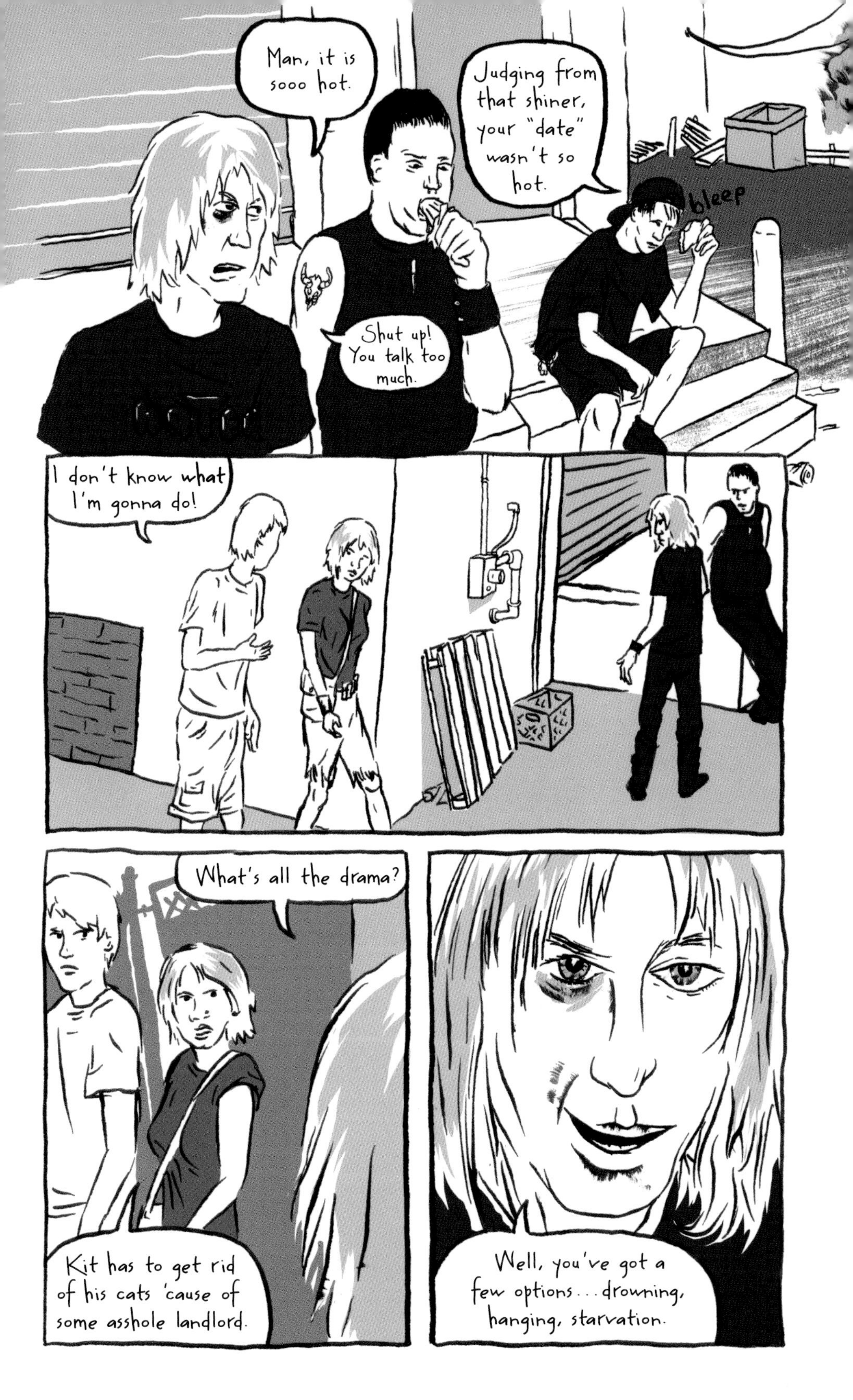

Man, it is sooo hot.
Judging from that shiner, your "date" wasn't so hot.
bleep
Shut up! You talk too much.
I don't know what I'm gonna do!
What's all the drama?
Kit has to get rid of his cats 'cause of some asshole landlord.
Well, you've got a few options... drowning, hanging, starvation.

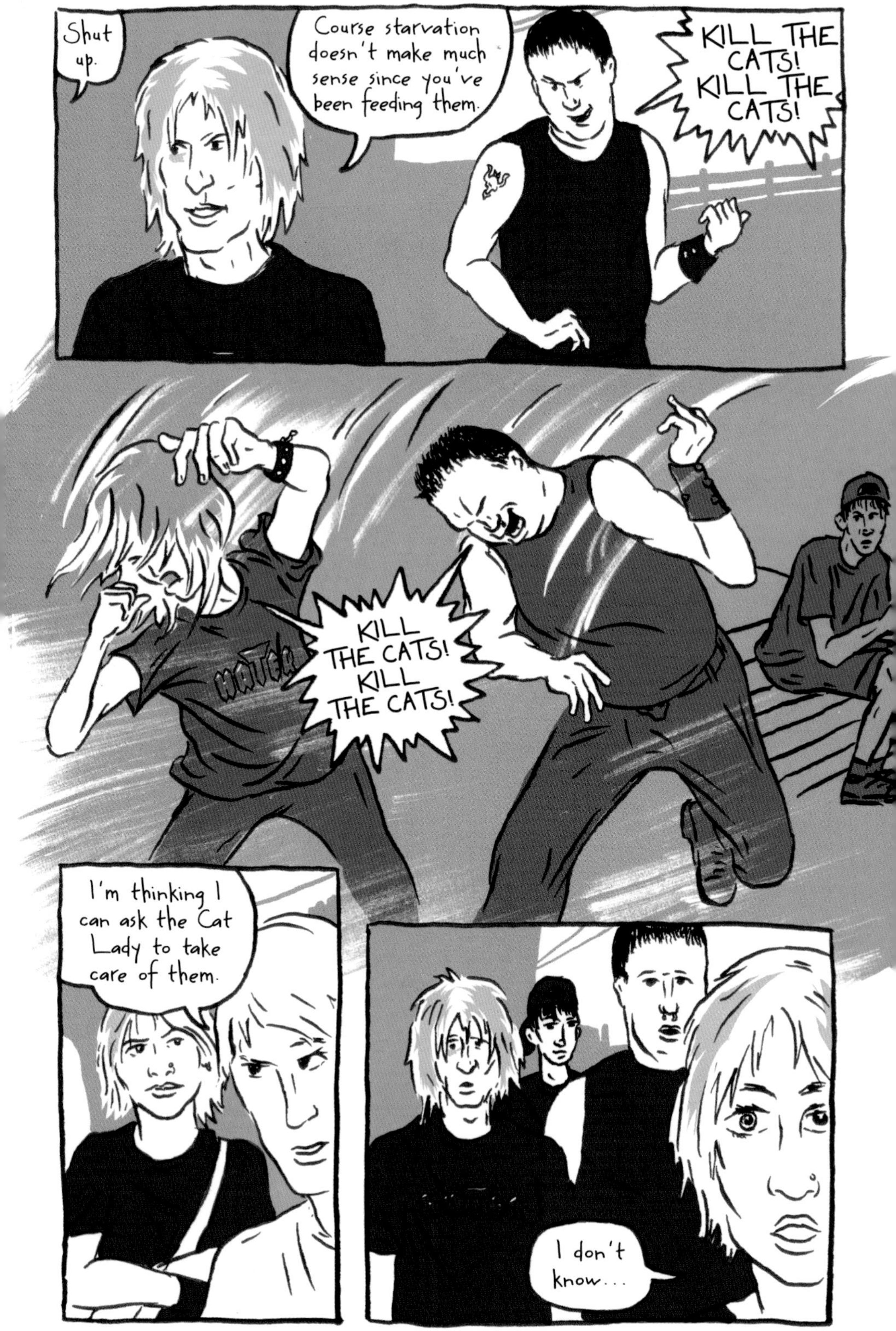
Shut up.
Course starvation doesn't make much sense since you've been feeding them.
KILL THE CATS! KILL THE CATS!
KILL THE CATS! KILL THE CATS!
I'm thinking I can ask the Cat Lady to take care of them.
I don't know...

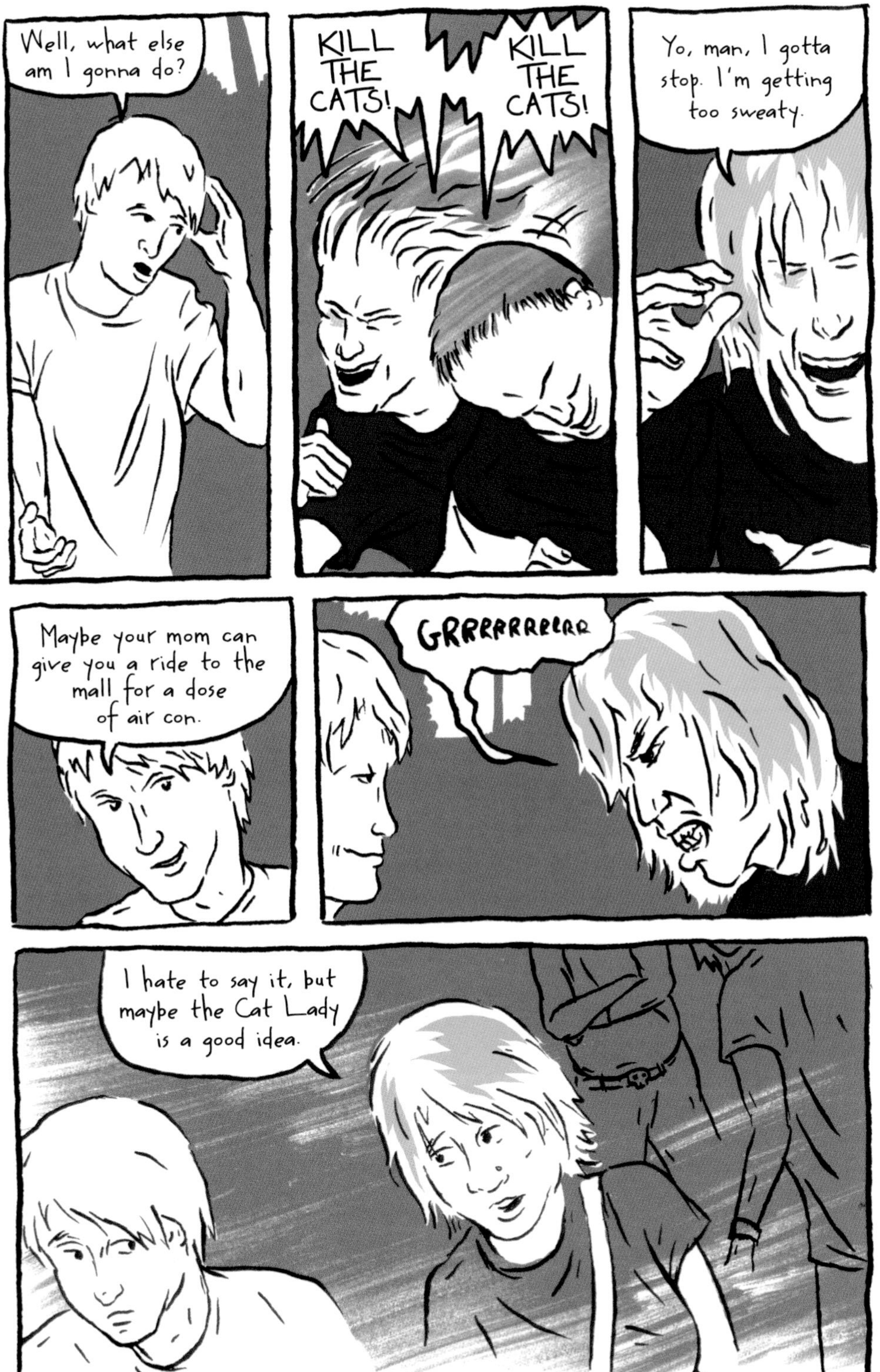
Well, what else am I gonna do?
KILL THE CATS!
KILL THE CATS!
Yo, man, I gotta stop. I'm getting too sweaty.
Maybe your mom can give you a ride to the mall for a dose of air con.
GRRRRRRRRRR
I hate to say it, but maybe the Cat Lady is a good idea.

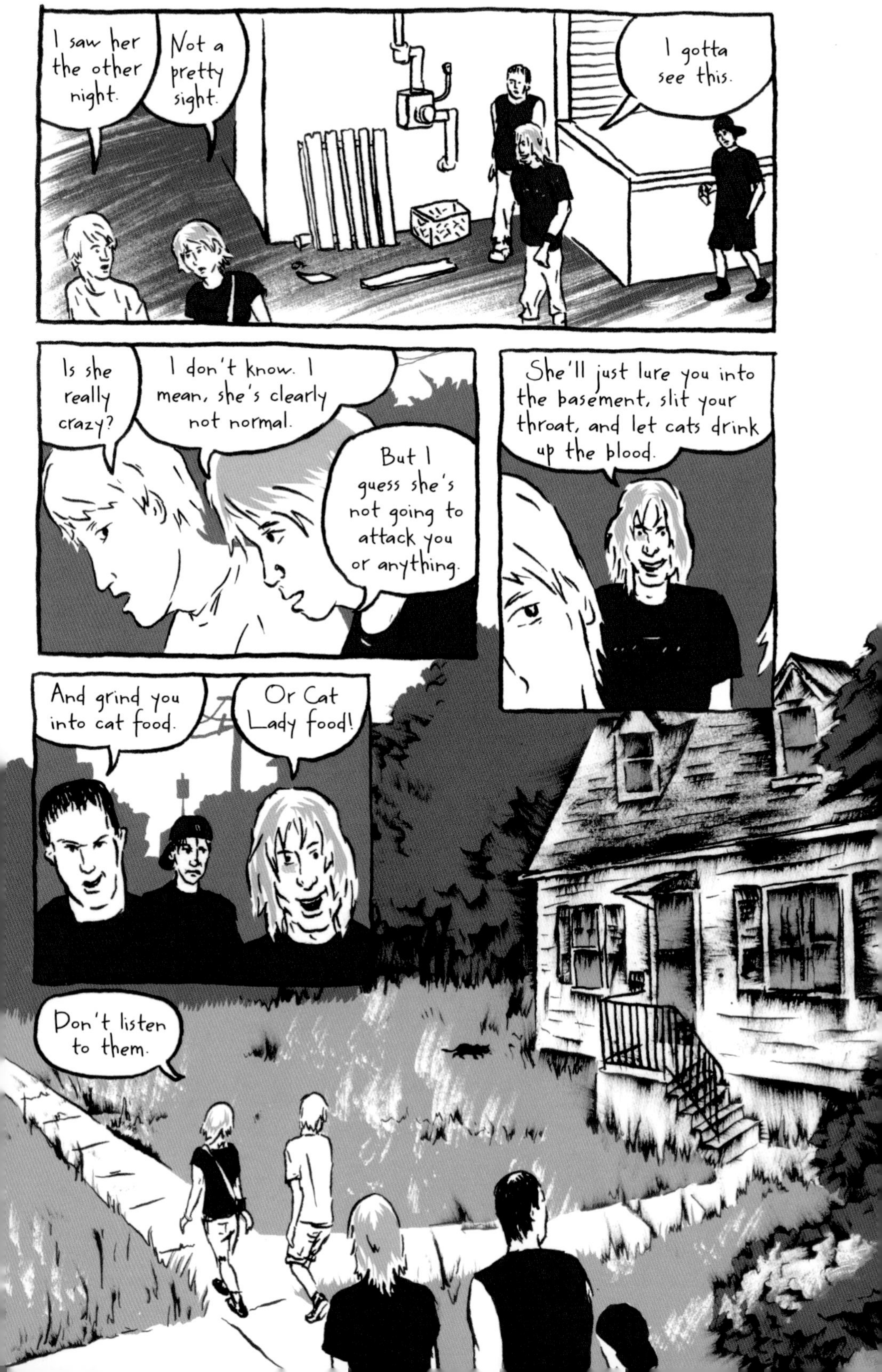
I saw her the other night.
Not a pretty sight.
I gotta see this.
Is she really crazy?
I don't know. I mean, she's clearly not normal.
But I guess she's not going to attack you or anything.
She'll just lure you into the basement, slit your throat, and let cats drink up the blood.
And grind you into cat food.
Or Cat Lady food!
Don't listen to them.

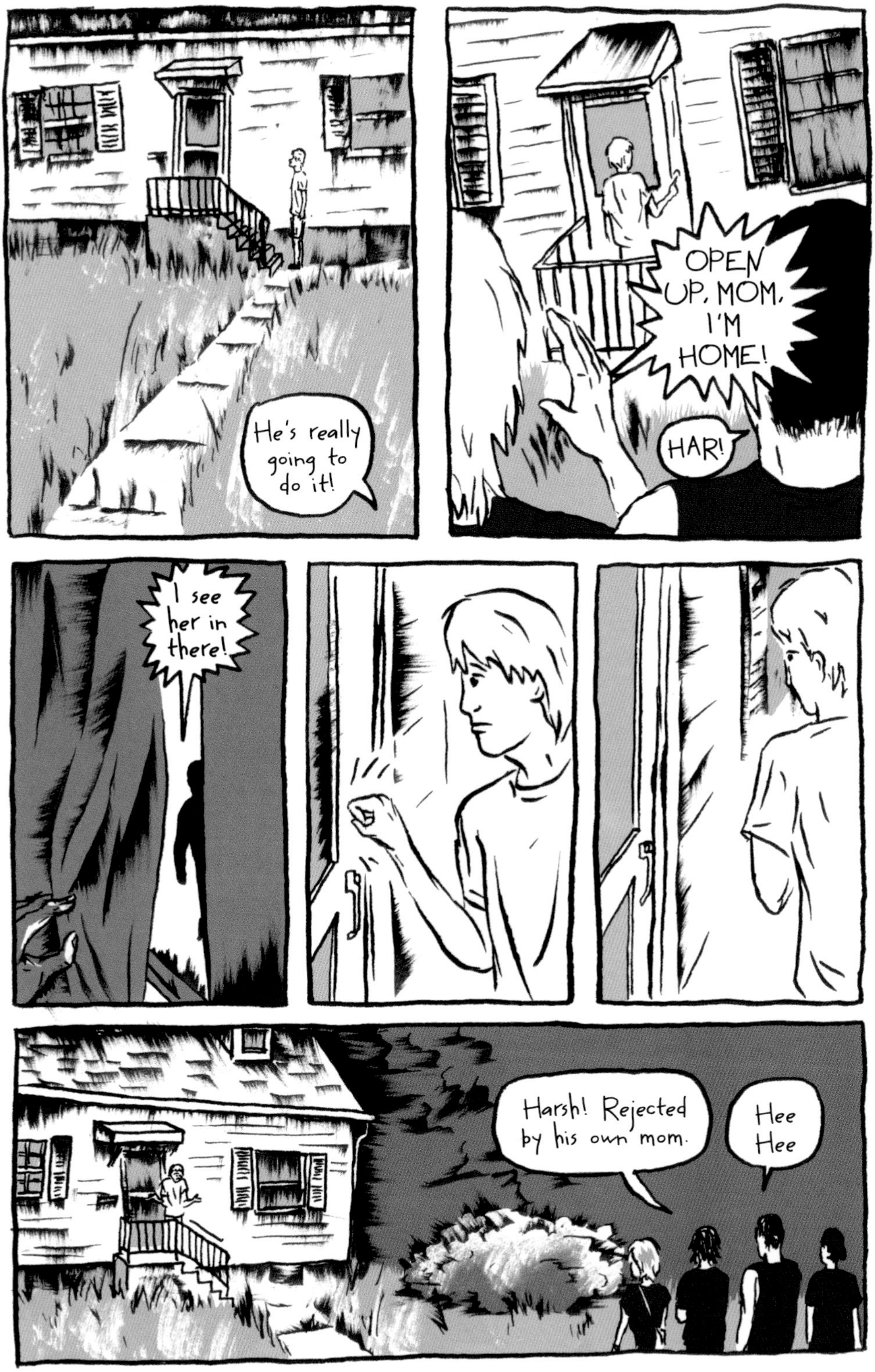
He's really going to do it!
OPEN UP, MOM, I'M HOME!
HAR!
I see her in there!
Harsh! Rejected by his own mom.
Hee Hee

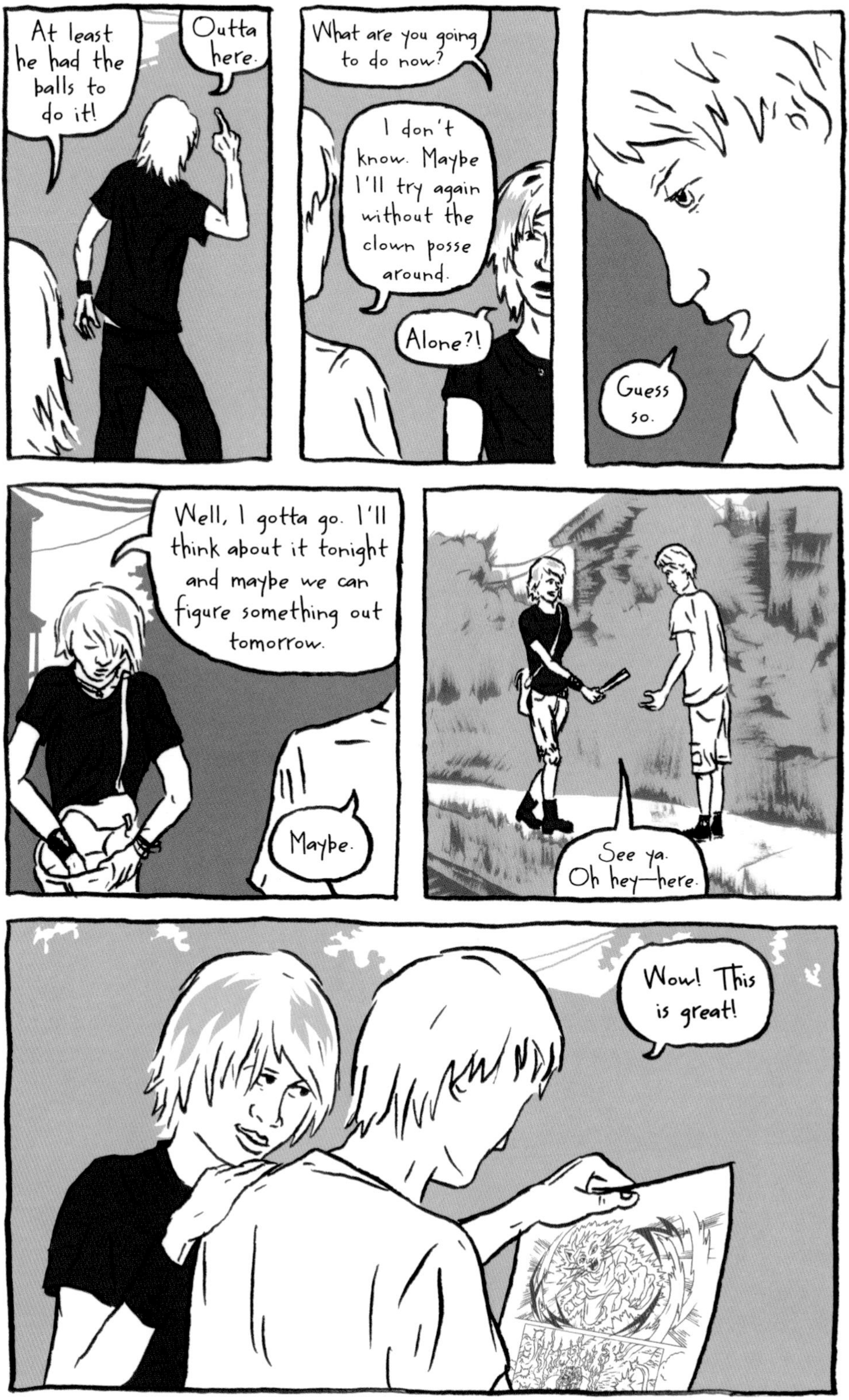
At least he had the balls to do it!
Outta here.
What are you going to do now?
I don't know. Maybe I'll try again without the clown posse around.
Alone?!
Guess so.
Well, I gotta go. I'll think about it tonight and maybe we can figure something out tomorrow.
Maybe.
See ya. Oh hey—here.
Wow! This is great!

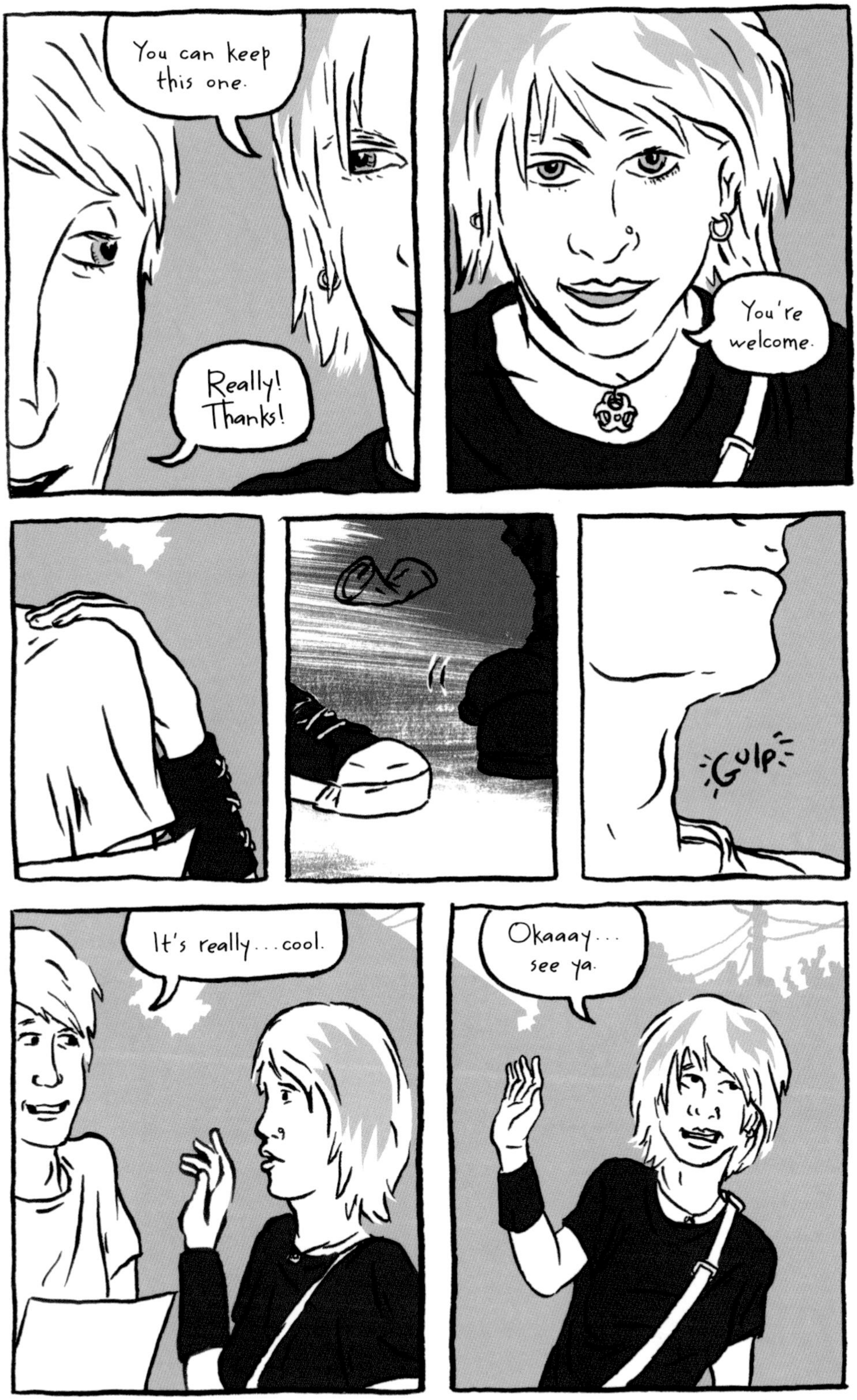
You can keep this one.
Really! Thanks!
You're welcome.
GULP
It's really . . . cool.
Okaaay . . . see ya.

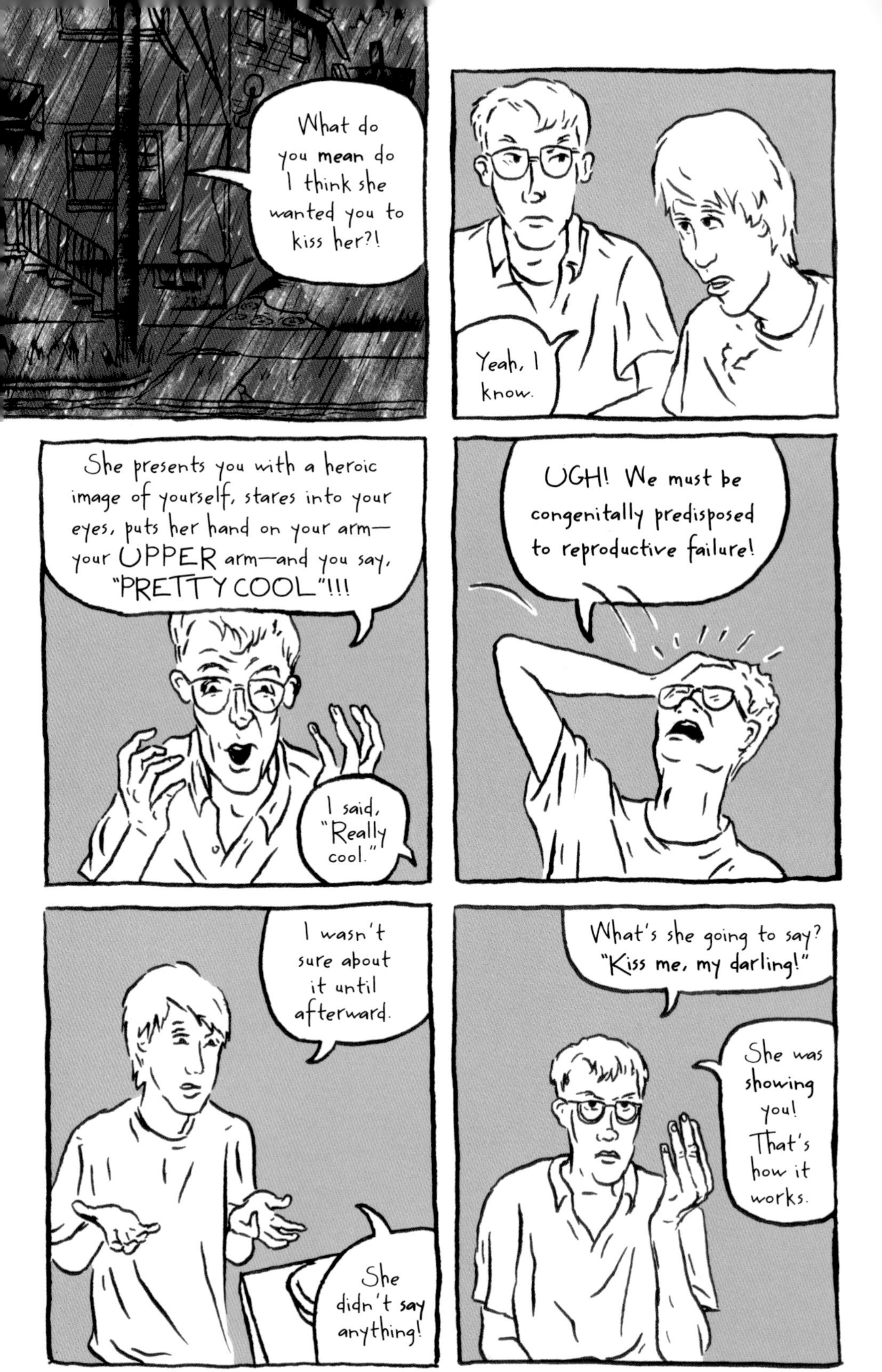
What do you mean do I think she wanted you to kiss her?!
Yeah, I know.
She presents you with a heroic image of yourself, stares into your eyes, puts her hand on your arm— your UPPER arm—and you say, "PRETTY COOL"!!!
I said, "Really cool."
UGH! We must be congenitally predisposed to reproductive failure!
I wasn't sure about it until afterward.
She didn't say anything!
What's she going to say? "Kiss me, my darling!"
She was showing you! That's how it works.

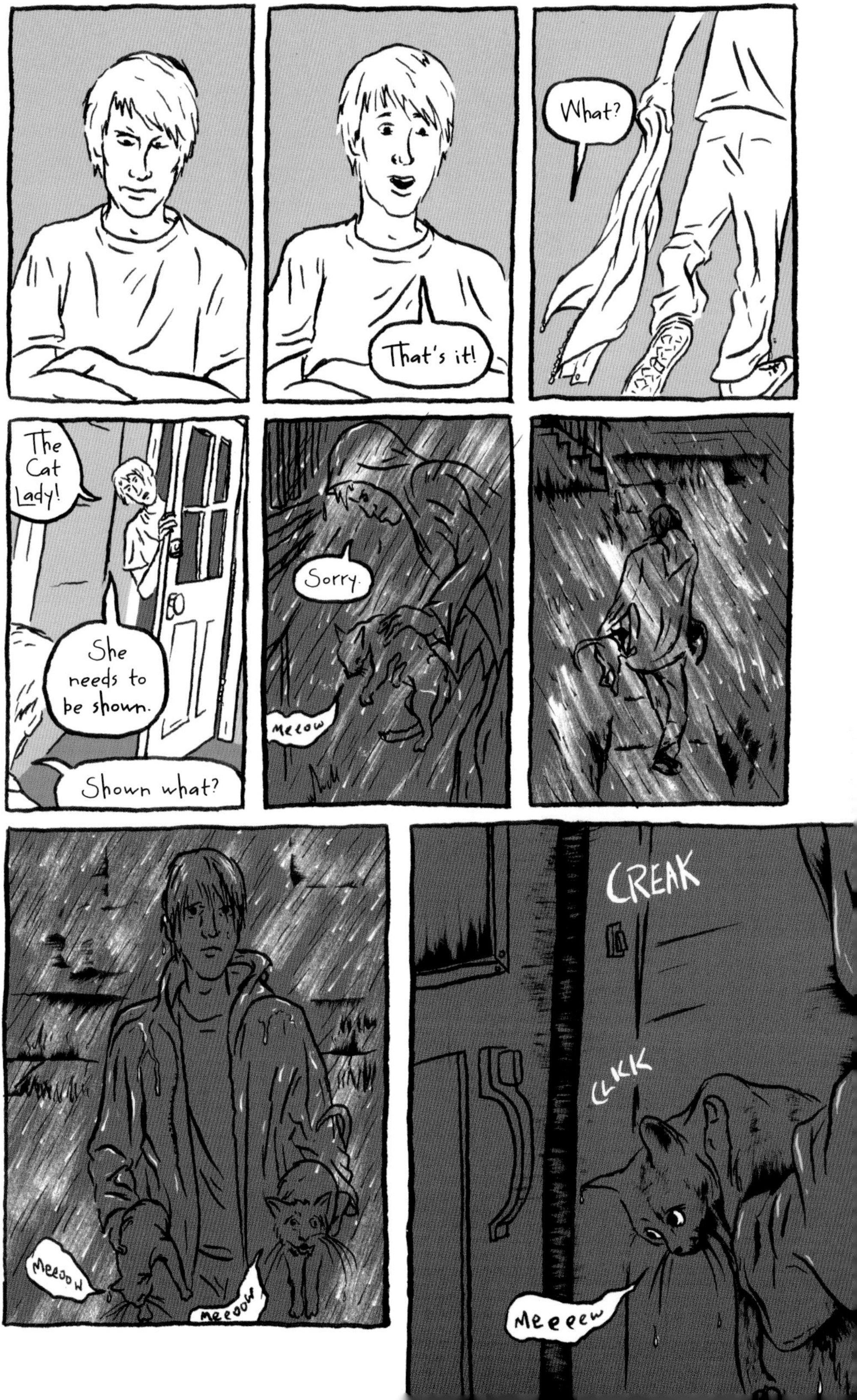

That's it!
What?
The Cat Lady!
She needs to be shown.
Shown what?
Sorry.
Meeow
Meeoow
Meeoow
CREAK
CLKK
Meeeew

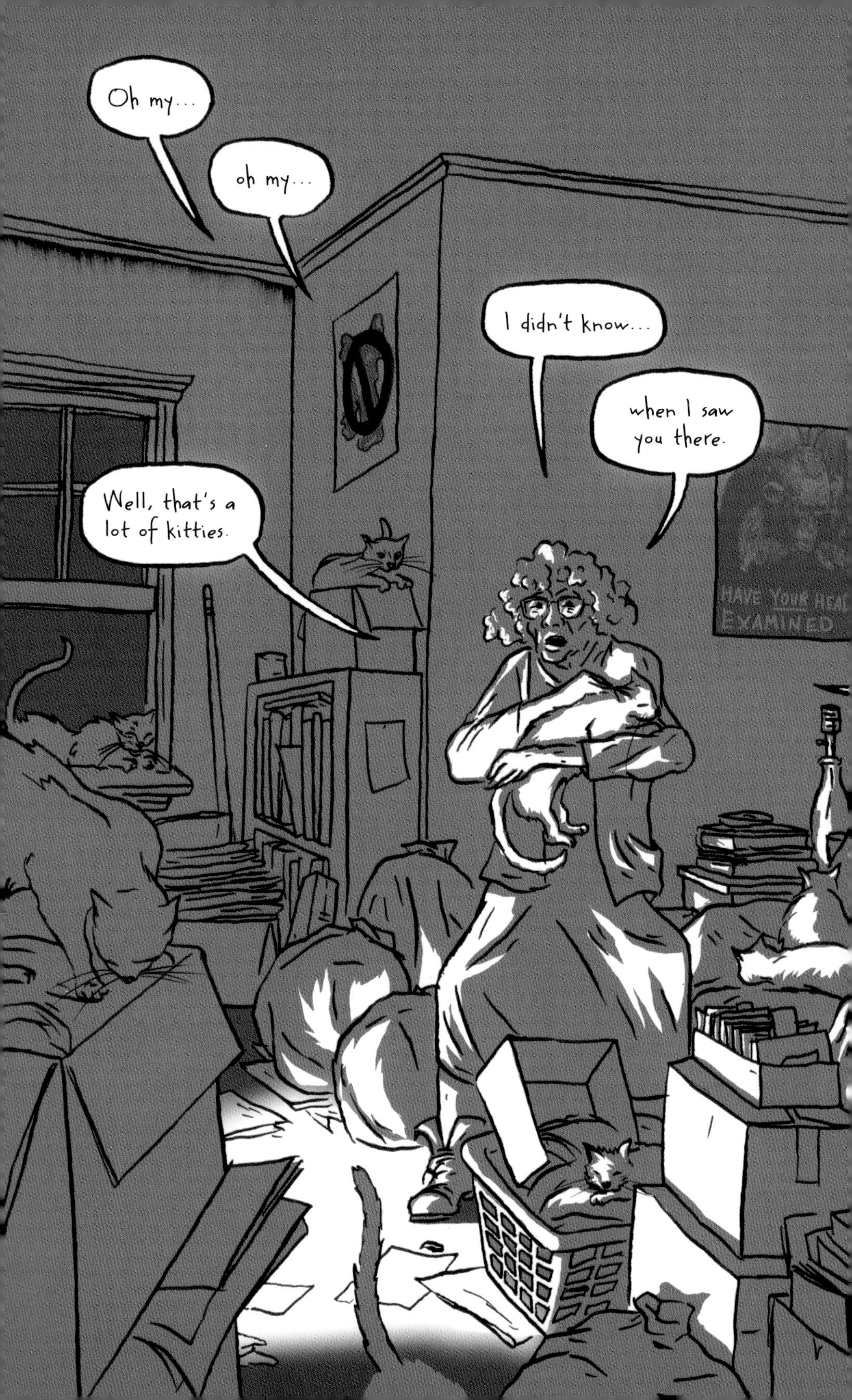
Oh my...
oh my...
Well, that's a lot of kitties.
I didn't know...
when I saw you there.
HAVE YOUR HEA
EXAMINED

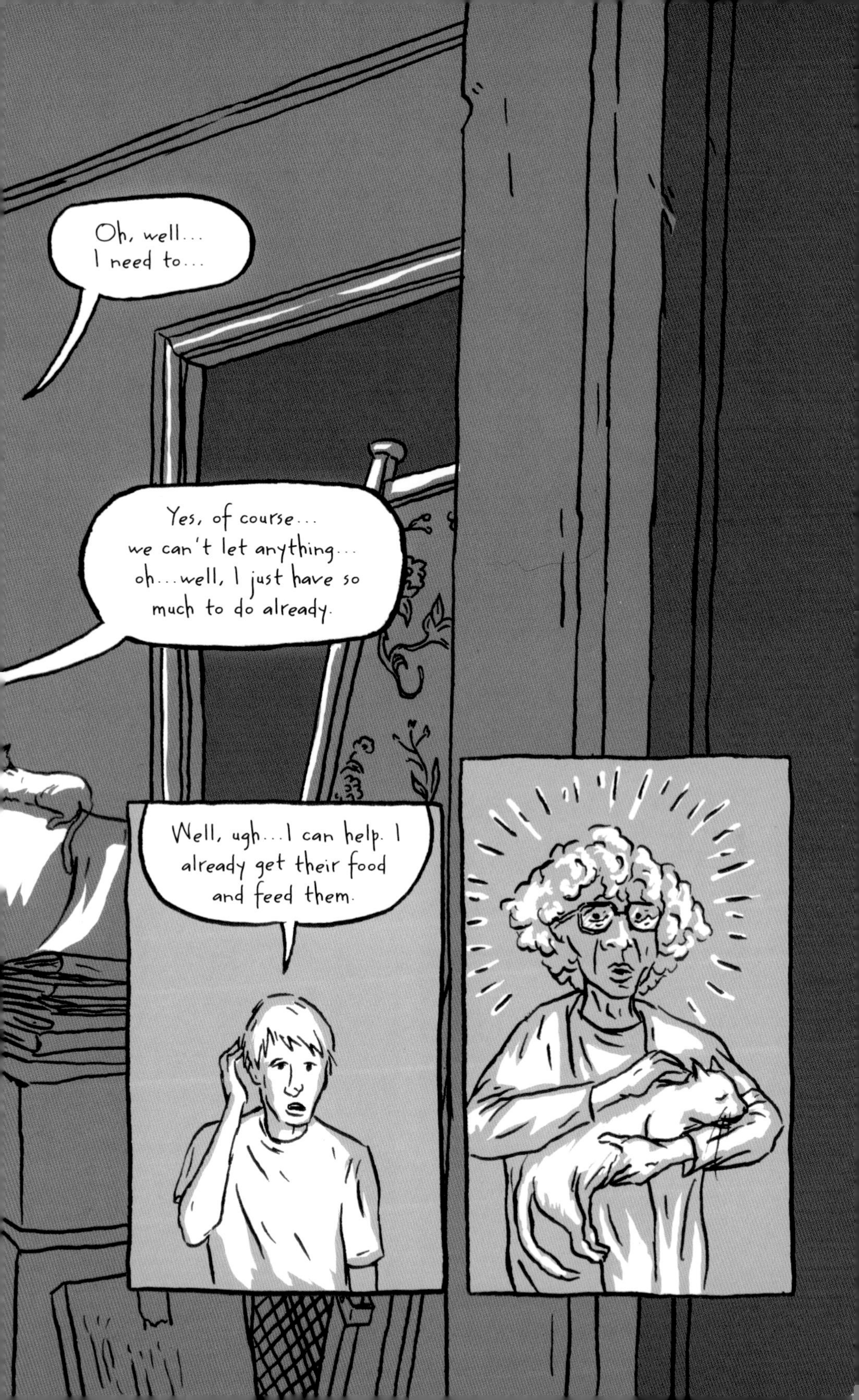
Oh, well... I need to...
Yes, of course... we can't let anything... oh...well, I just have so much to do already.
Well, ugh...I can help. I already get their food and feed them.

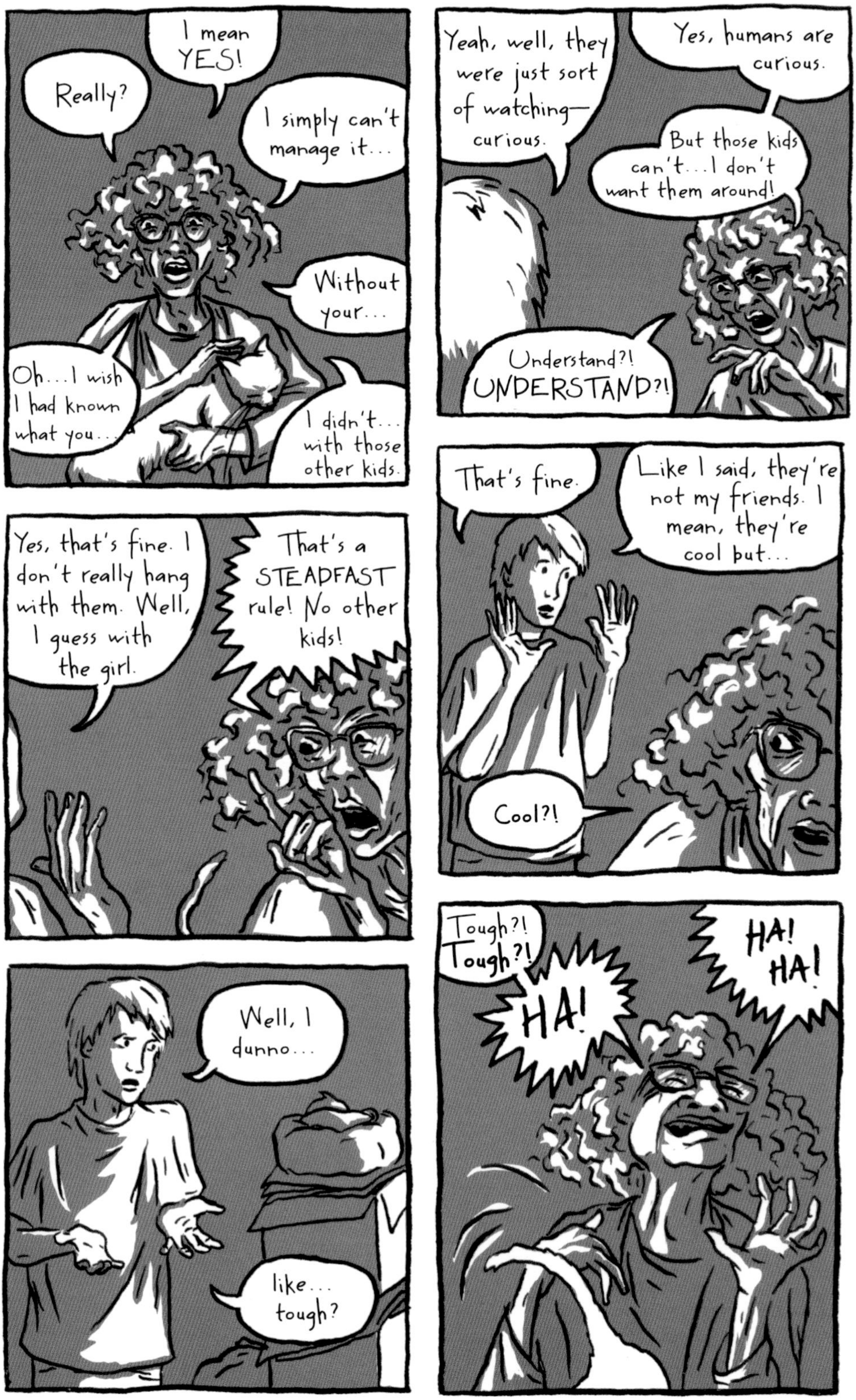
Really?
I mean YES!
I simply can't manage it...
Without your...
Oh...I wish I had known what you...
I didn't... with those other kids.
Yeah, well, they were just sort of watching—curious.
Yes, humans are curious.
But those kids can't...I don't want them around!
Understand?! UNDERSTAND?!
Yes, that's fine. I don't really hang with them. Well, I guess with the girl.
That's a STEADFAST rule! No other kids!
That's fine.
Like I said, they're not my friends. I mean, they're cool but...
Cool?!
Well, I dunno...
like... tough?
Tough?! Tough?!
HA!
HA! HA!

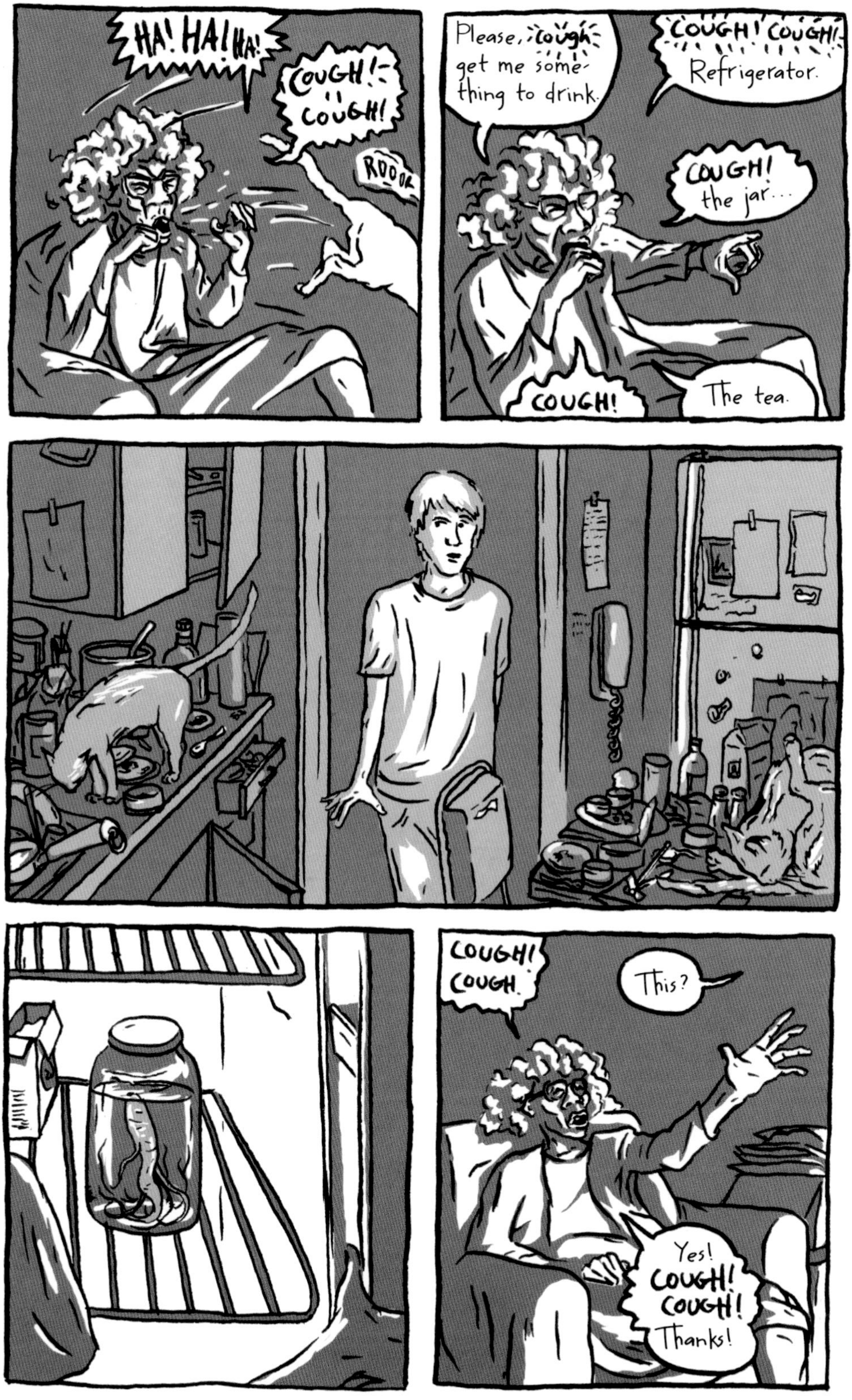
HA! HA! HA!
COUGH! COUGH!
ROOOR
Please, cough get me something to drink.
COUGH! COUGH! Refrigerator.
COUGH! the jar...
COUGH!
The tea.
COUGH! COUGH.
This?
Yes! COUGH! COUGH! Thanks!

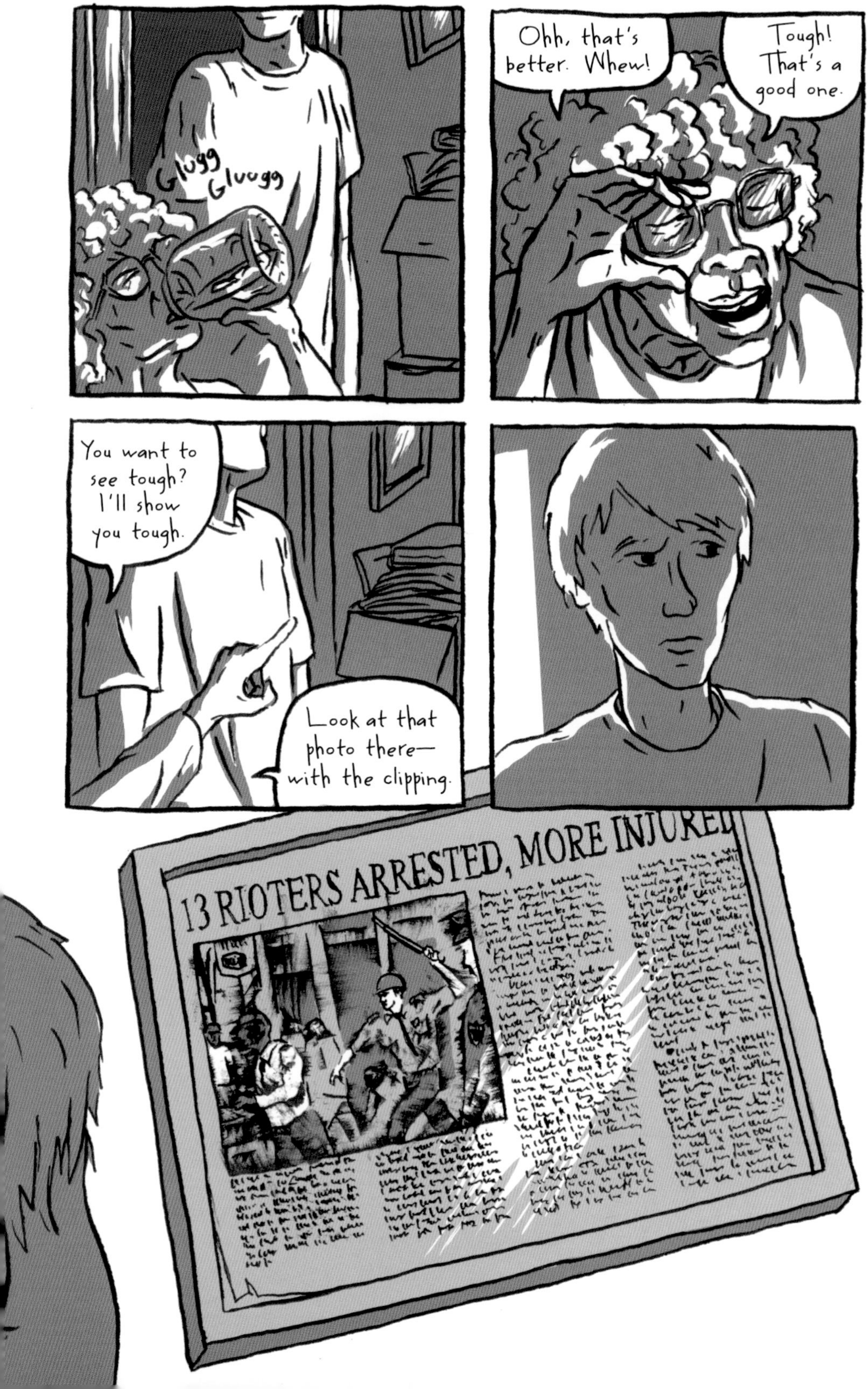
Glugg
Gluugg
Ohh, that's better. Whew!
Tough! That's a good one.
You want to see tough? I'll show you tough.
Look at that photo there—with the clipping.
13 RIOTERS ARRESTED, MORE INJURED

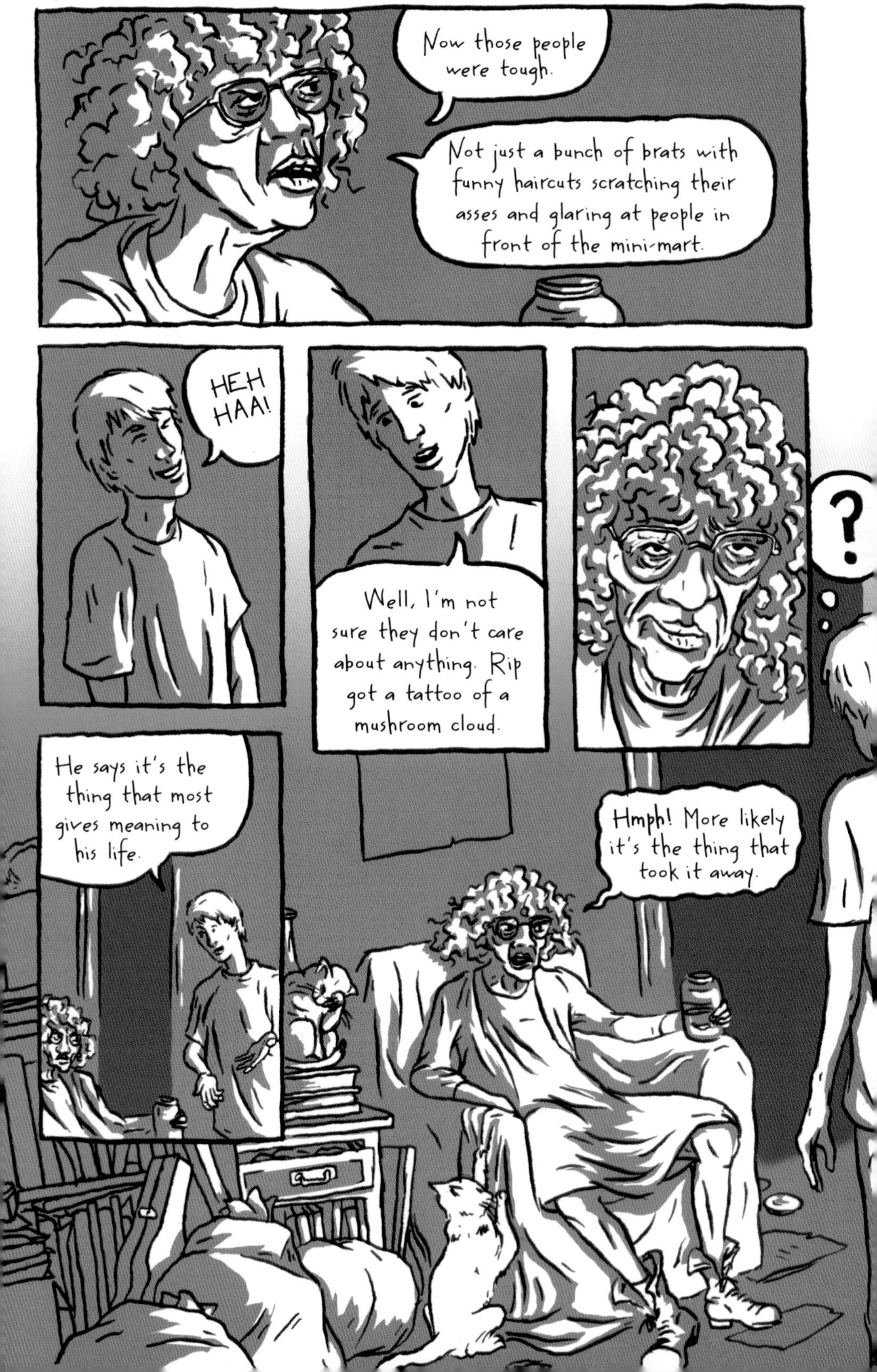
Now those people were tough.
Not just a bunch of brats with funny haircuts scratching their asses and glaring at people in front of the mini-mart.
HEH HAA!
Well, I'm not sure they don't care about anything. Rip got a tattoo of a mushroom cloud.
?
He says it's the thing that most gives meaning to his life.
Hmph! More likely it's the thing that took it away.

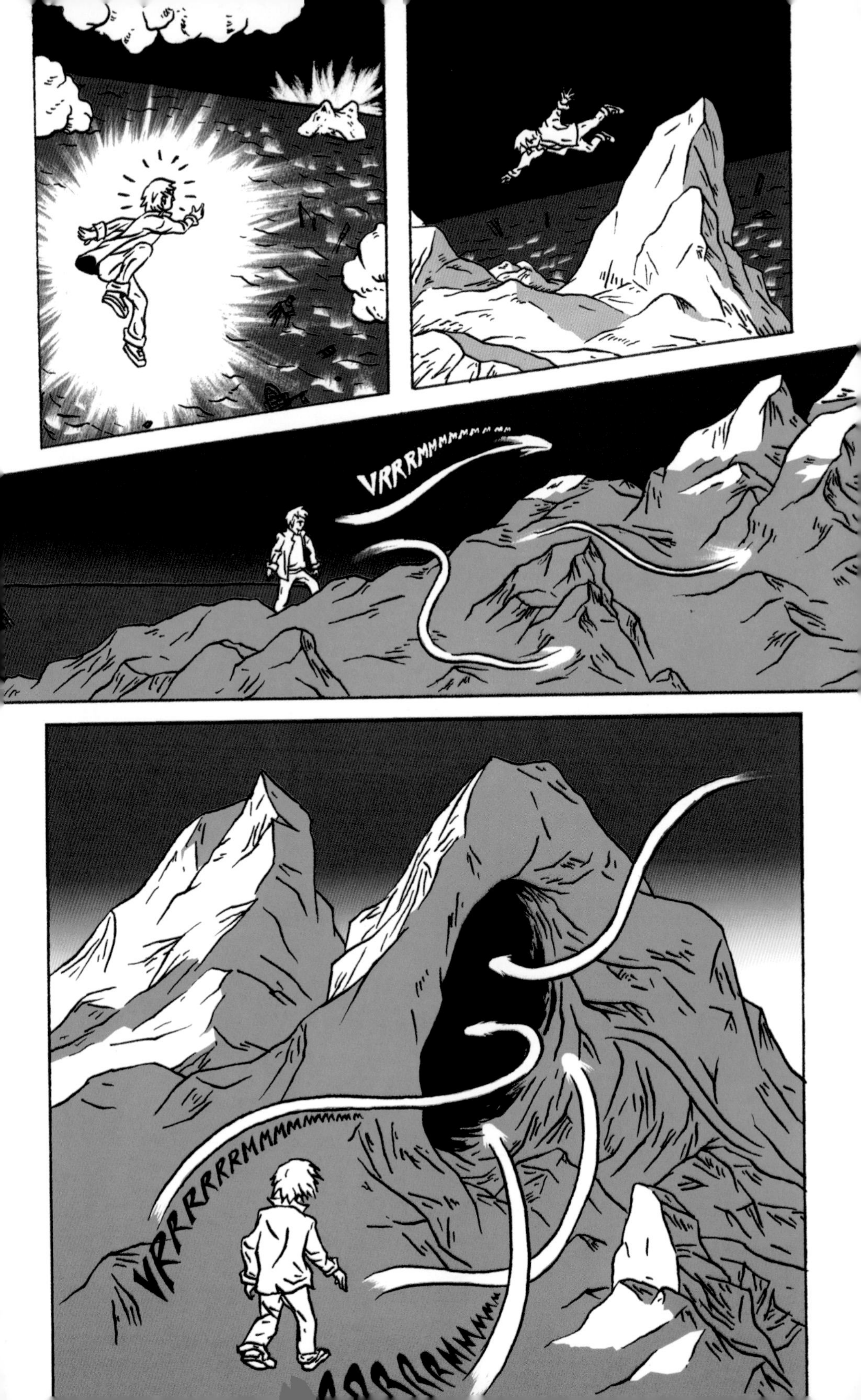
VRRRMMMMMMMMMmm
VRRRRRRRMMMMMMMMmmmm

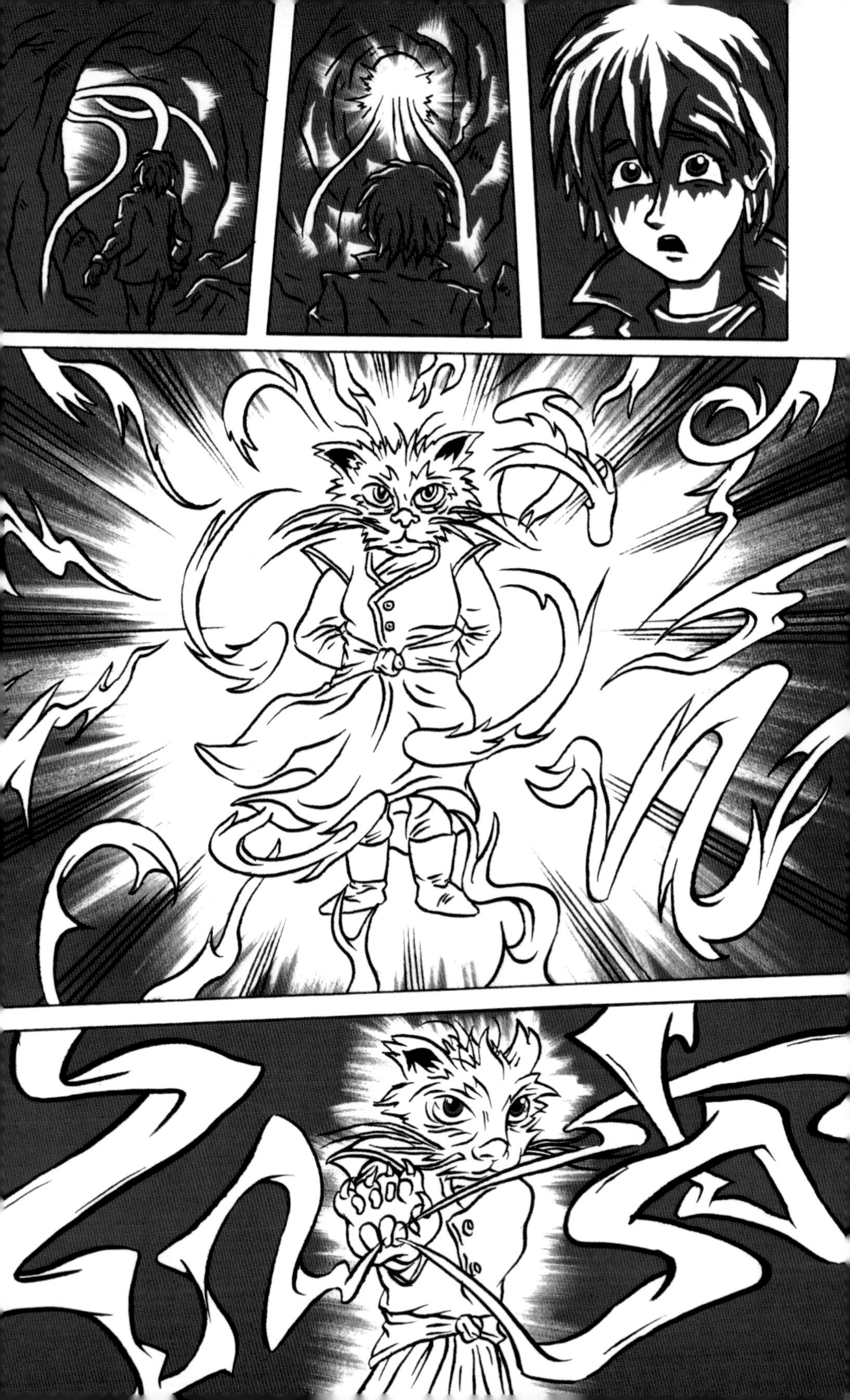

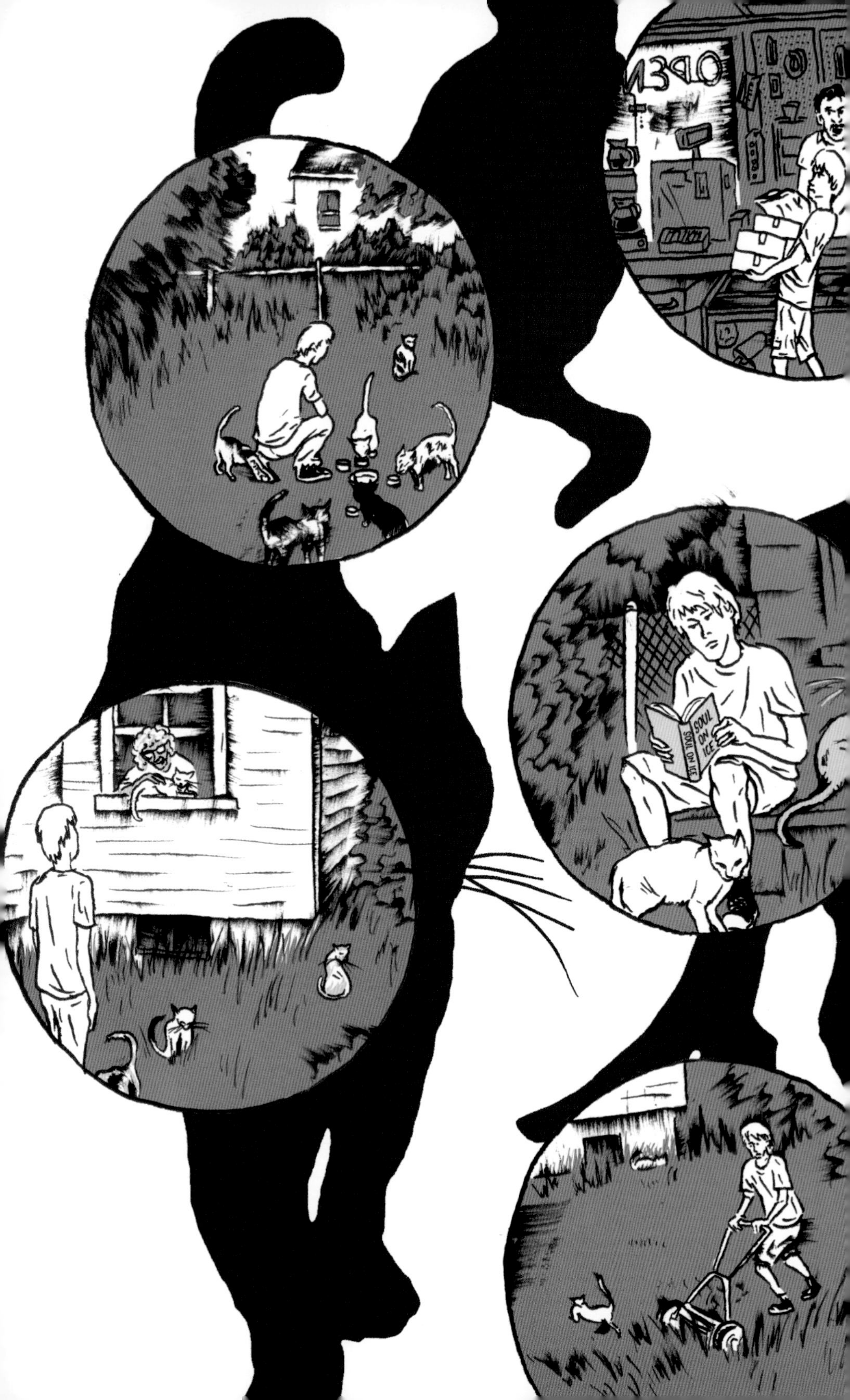
OPEN
SOUL ON ICE
SOUL ON ICE

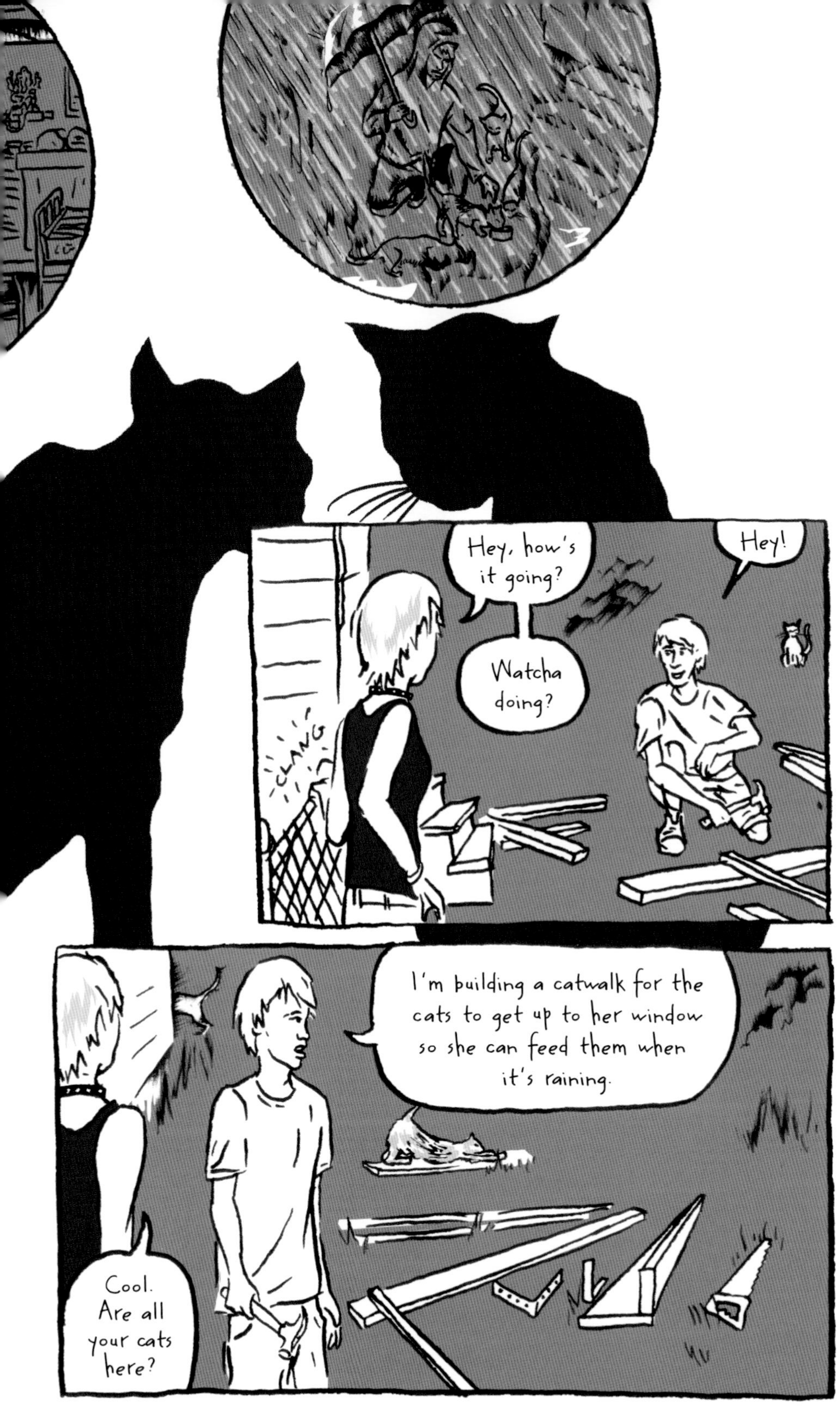
Hey, how's it going?
Watcha doing?
Hey!
CLANG
I'm building a catwalk for the cats to get up to her window so she can feed them when it's raining.
Cool. Are all your cats here?

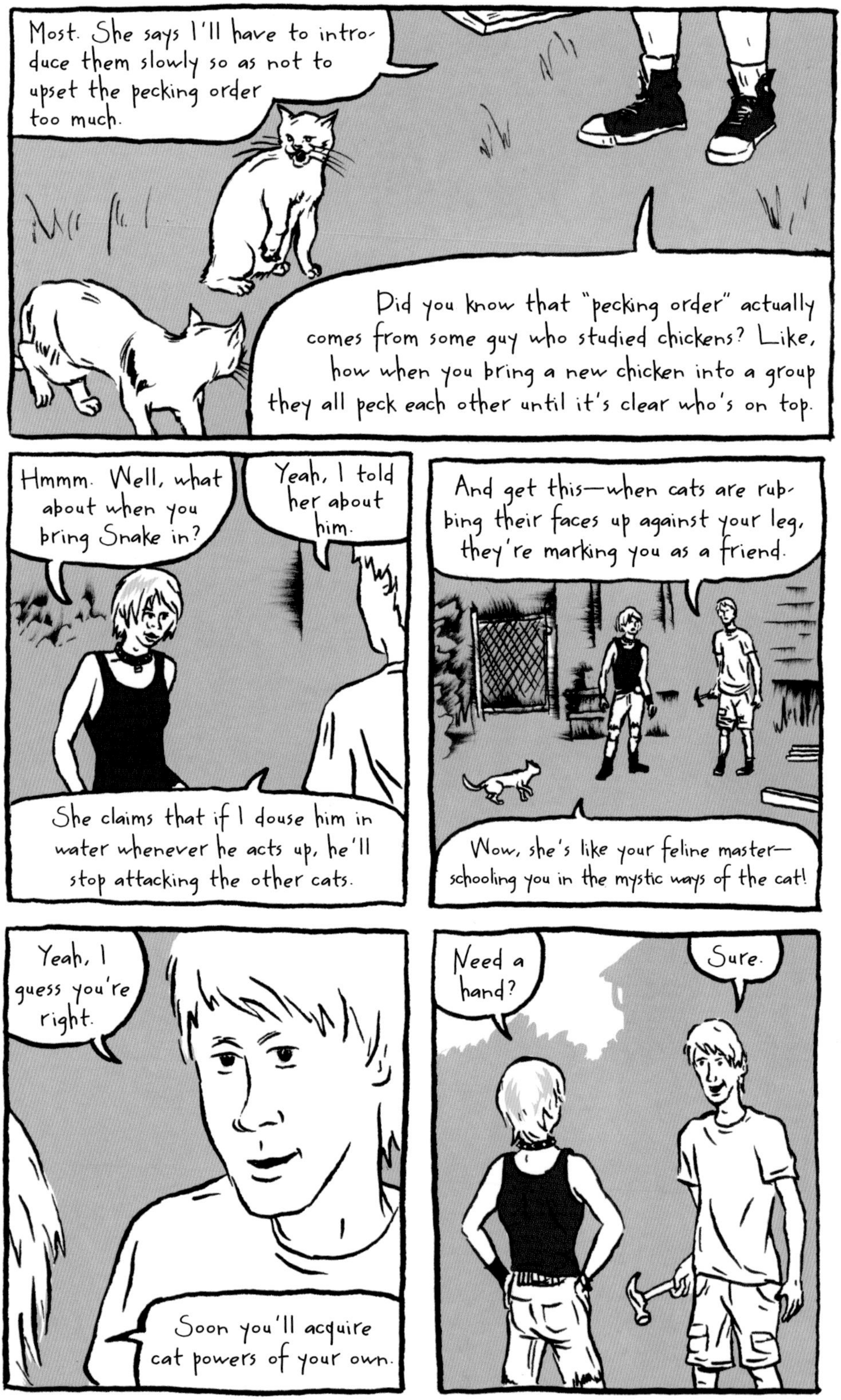
Most. She says I'll have to introduce them slowly so as not to upset the pecking order too much.
Did you know that "pecking order" actually comes from some guy who studied chickens? Like, how when you bring a new chicken into a group they all peck each other until it's clear who's on top.
Hmmm. Well, what about when you bring Snake in?
Yeah, I told her about him.
She claims that if I douse him in water whenever he acts up, he'll stop attacking the other cats.
And get this—when cats are rubbing their faces up against your leg, they're marking you as a friend.
Wow, she's like your feline master—schooling you in the mystic ways of the cat!
Yeah, I guess you're right.
Soon you'll acquire cat powers of your own.
Need a hand?
Sure.

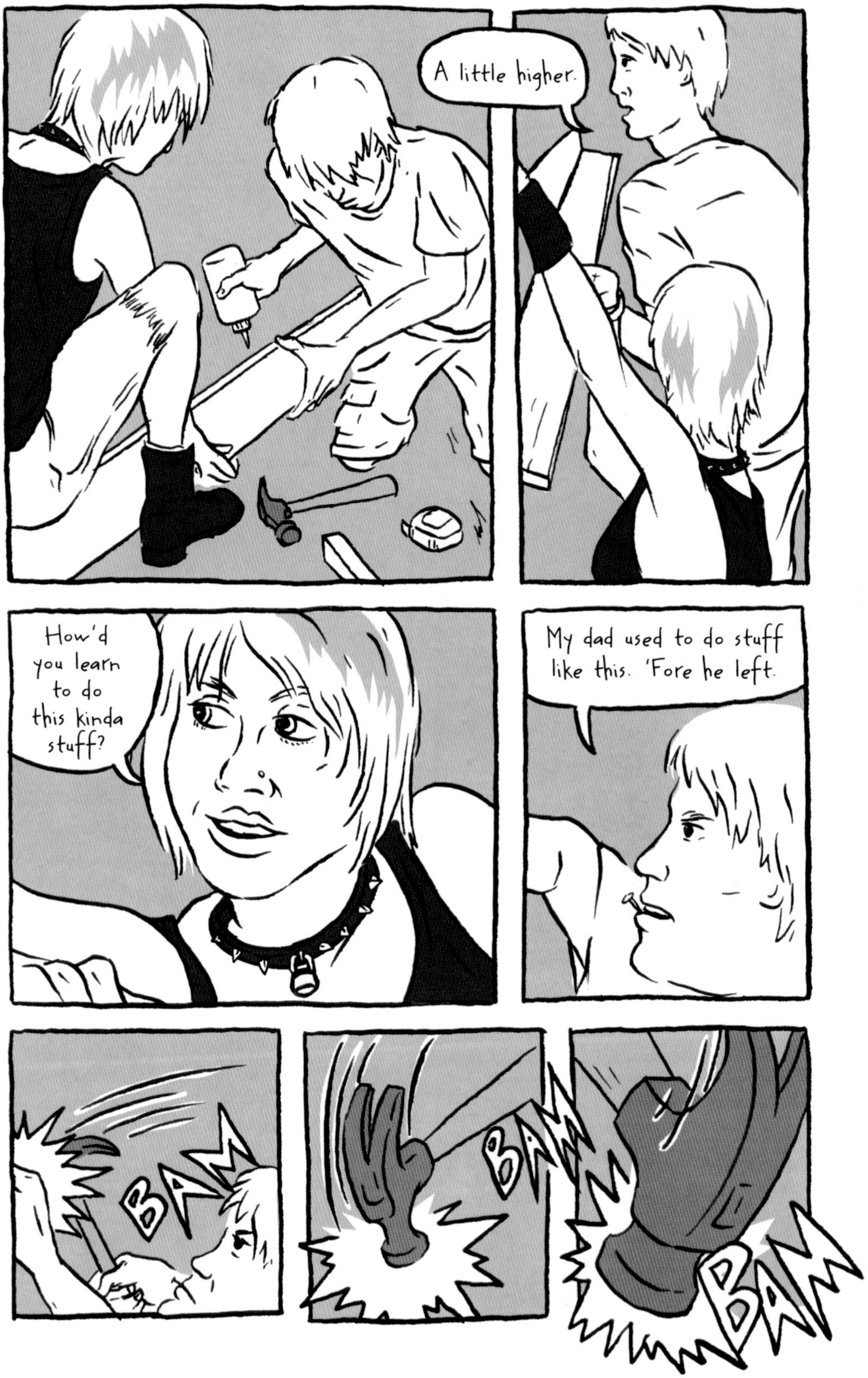
A little higher.
How'd you learn to do this kinda stuff?
My dad used to do stuff like this. 'Fore he left.
BAM
BAM
BAM

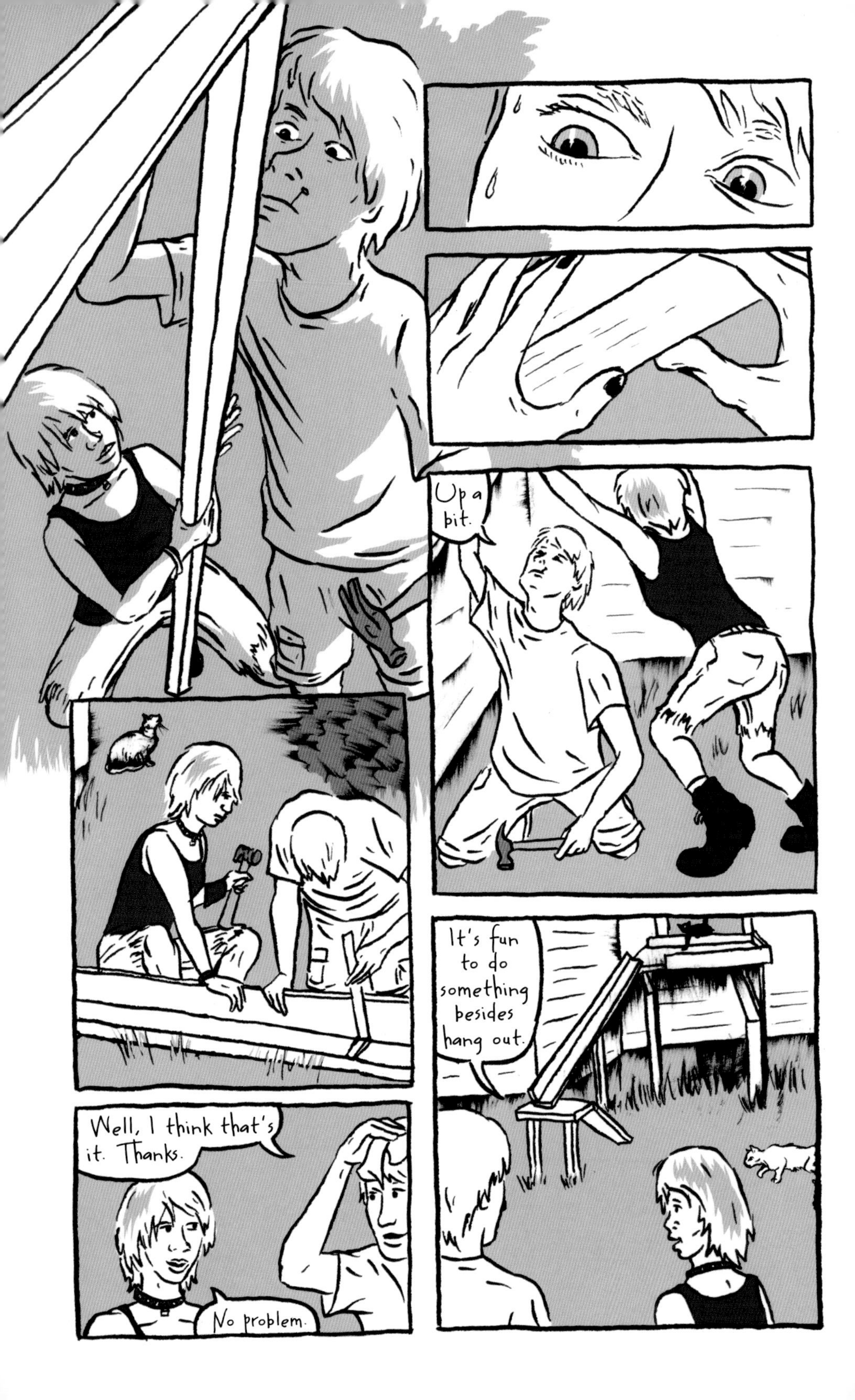
Up a bit.
It's fun to do something besides hang out.
Well, I think that's it. Thanks.
No problem.

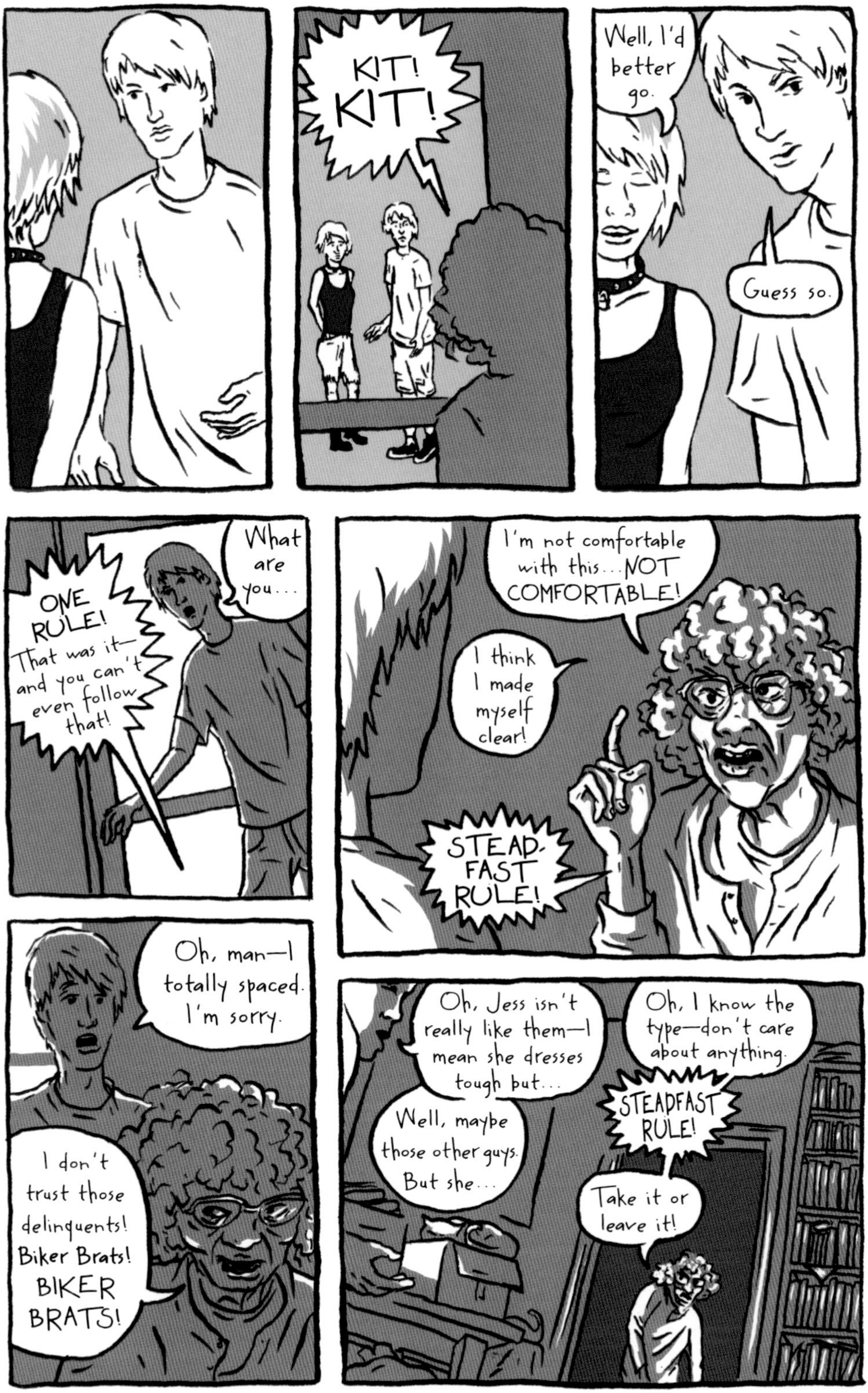
KIT! KIT!
Well, I'd better go.
Guess so.
ONE RULE! That was it—and you can't even follow that!
What are you...
I'm not comfortable with this...NOT COMFORTABLE!
I think I made myself clear!
STEAD-FAST RULE!
Oh, man—I totally spaced. I'm sorry.
I don't trust those delinquents! Biker Brats! BIKER BRATS!
Oh, Jess isn't really like them—I mean she dresses tough but...
Oh, I know the type—don't care about anything.
Well, maybe those other guys. But she...
STEADFAST RULE!
Take it or leave it!

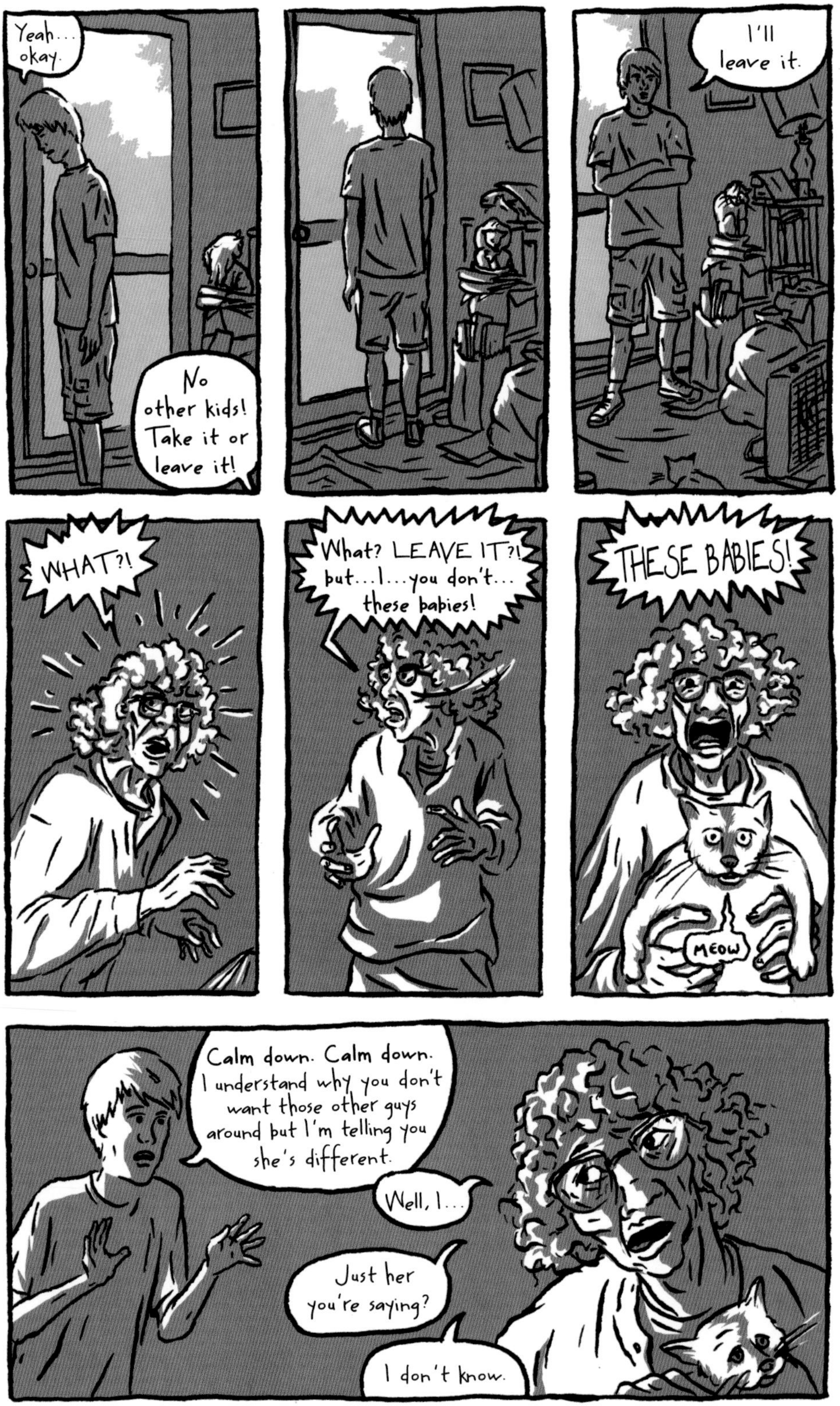
Yeah... okay.
No other kids! Take it or leave it!
I'll leave it.
WHAT?!
What? LEAVE IT?! but...I...you don't... these babies!
THESE BABIES!
MEOW
Calm down. Calm down. I understand why you don't want those other guys around but I'm telling you she's different.
Well, I...
Just her you're saying?
I don't know.

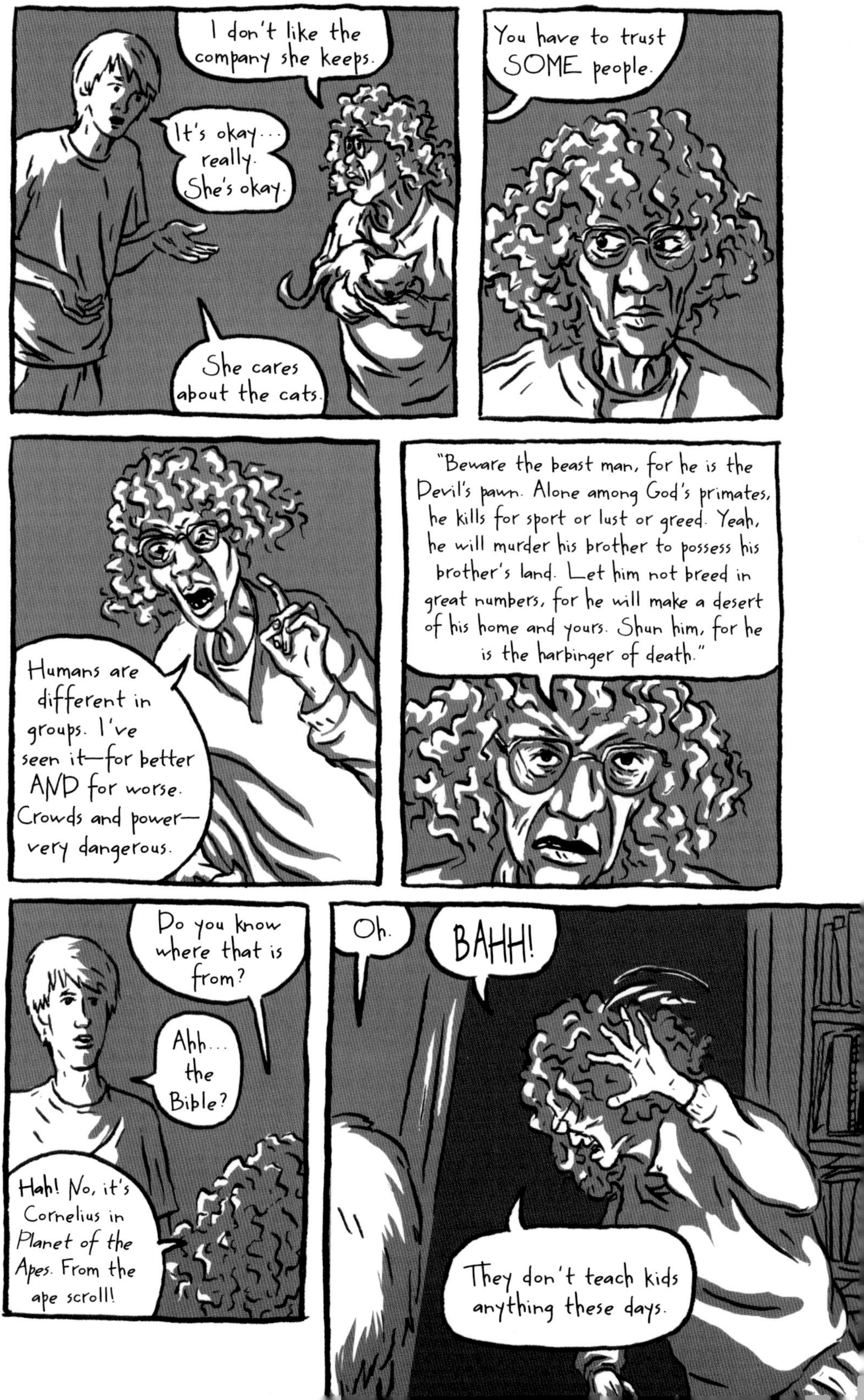
I don't like the company she keeps.
It's okay... really. She's okay.
She cares about the cats.
You have to trust SOME people.
Humans are different in groups. I've seen it—for better AND for worse. Crowds and power—very dangerous.
"Beware the beast man, for he is the Devil's pawn. Alone among God's primates, he kills for sport or lust or greed. Yeah, he will murder his brother to possess his brother's land. Let him not breed in great numbers, for he will make a desert of his home and yours. Shun him, for he is the harbinger of death."
Do you know where that is from?
Ahh... the Bible?
Hah! No, it's Cornelius in *Planet of the Apes*. From the ape scroll!
Oh.
BAHH!
They don't teach kids anything these days.

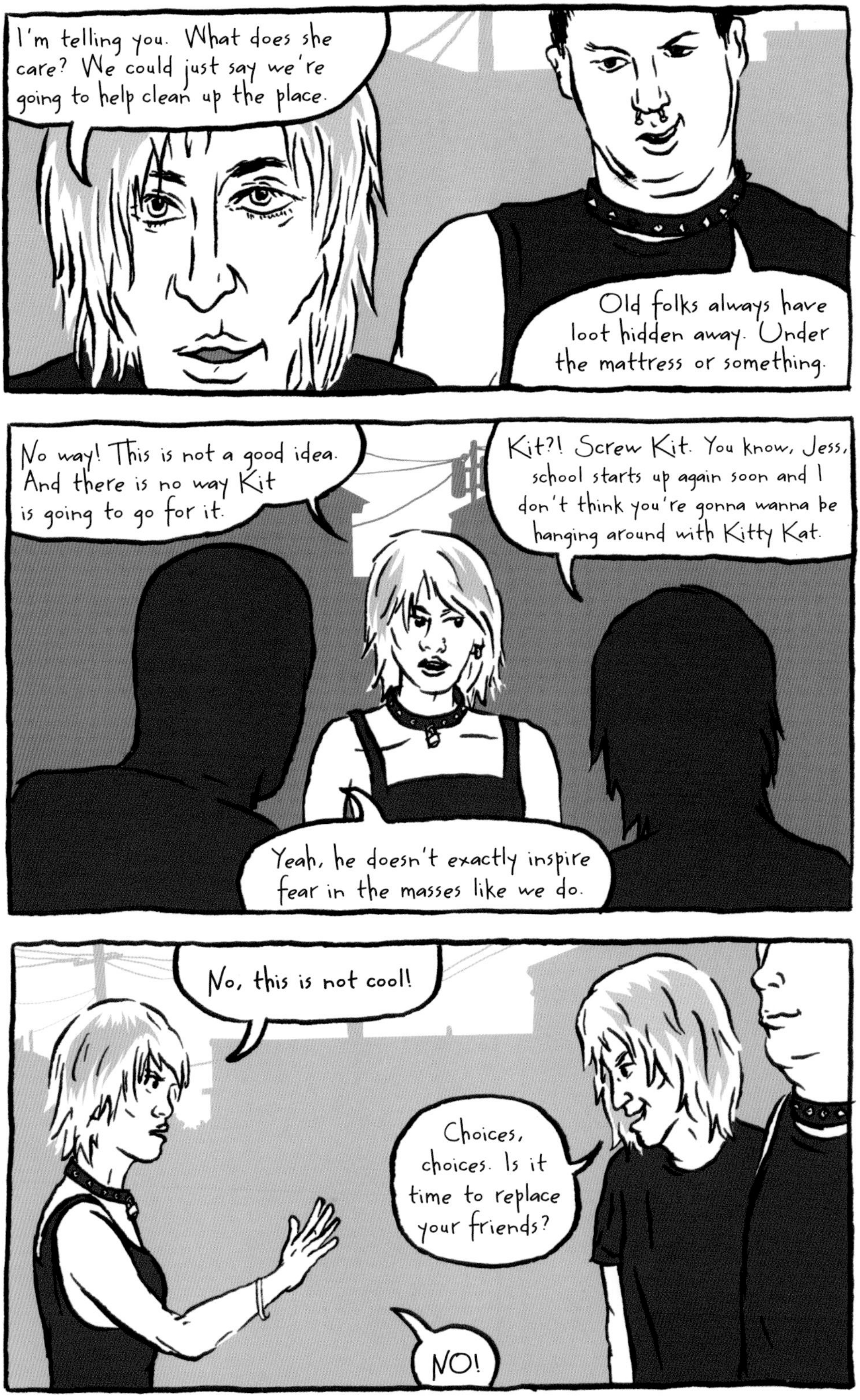
I'm telling you. What does she care? We could just say we're going to help clean up the place.
Old folks always have loot hidden away. Under the mattress or something.
No way! This is not a good idea. And there is no way Kit is going to go for it.
Kit?! Screw Kit. You know, Jess, school starts up again soon and I don't think you're gonna wanna be hanging around with Kitty Kat.
Yeah, he doesn't exactly inspire fear in the masses like we do.
No, this is not cool!
Choices, choices. Is it time to replace your friends?
NO!

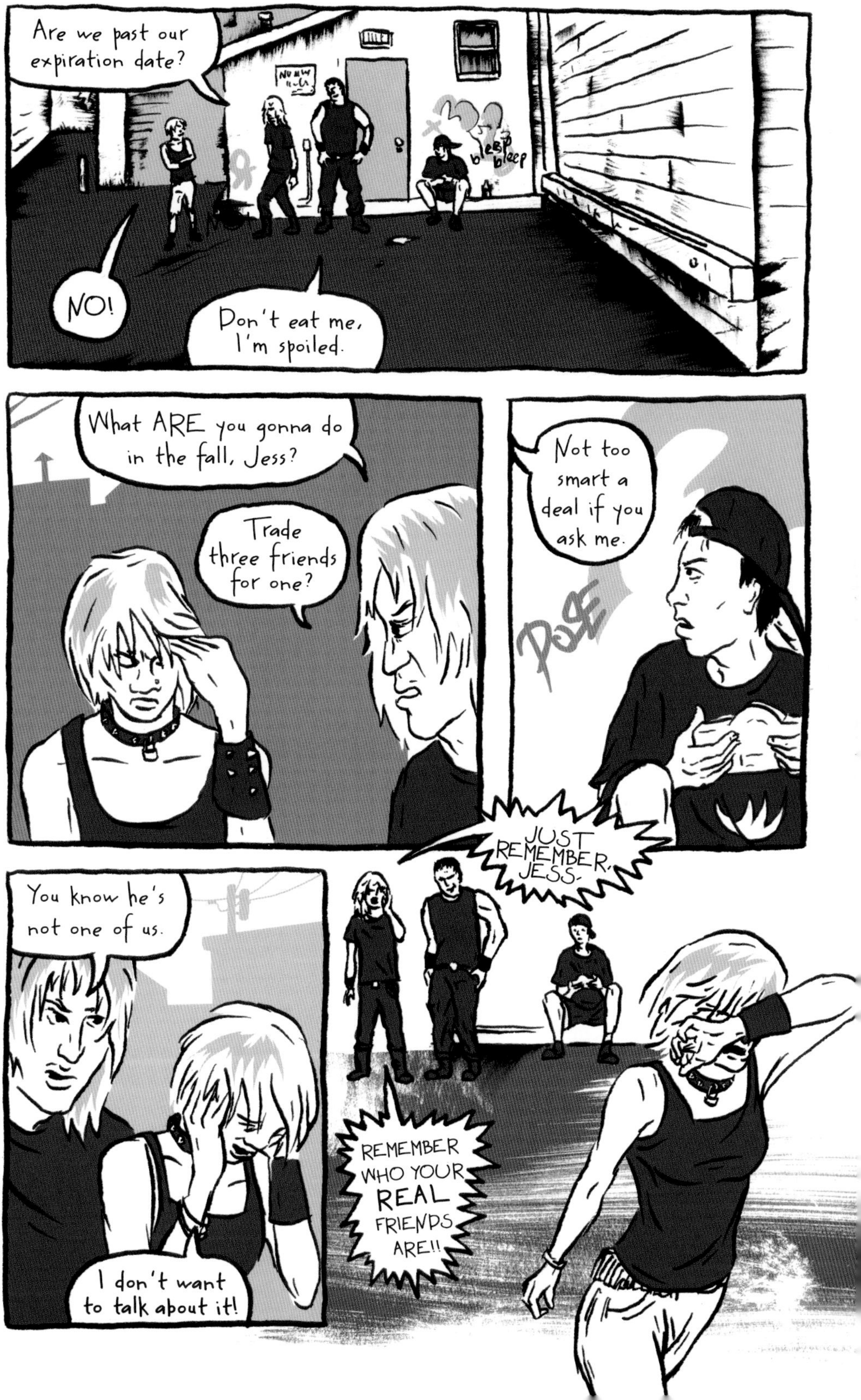
Are we past our expiration date?
NO!
Don't eat me, I'm spoiled.
What ARE you gonna do in the fall, Jess?
Trade three friends for one?
Not too smart a deal if you ask me.
JUST REMEMBER, JESS-
You know he's not one of us.
I don't want to talk about it!
REMEMBER WHO YOUR REAL FRIENDS ARE!!

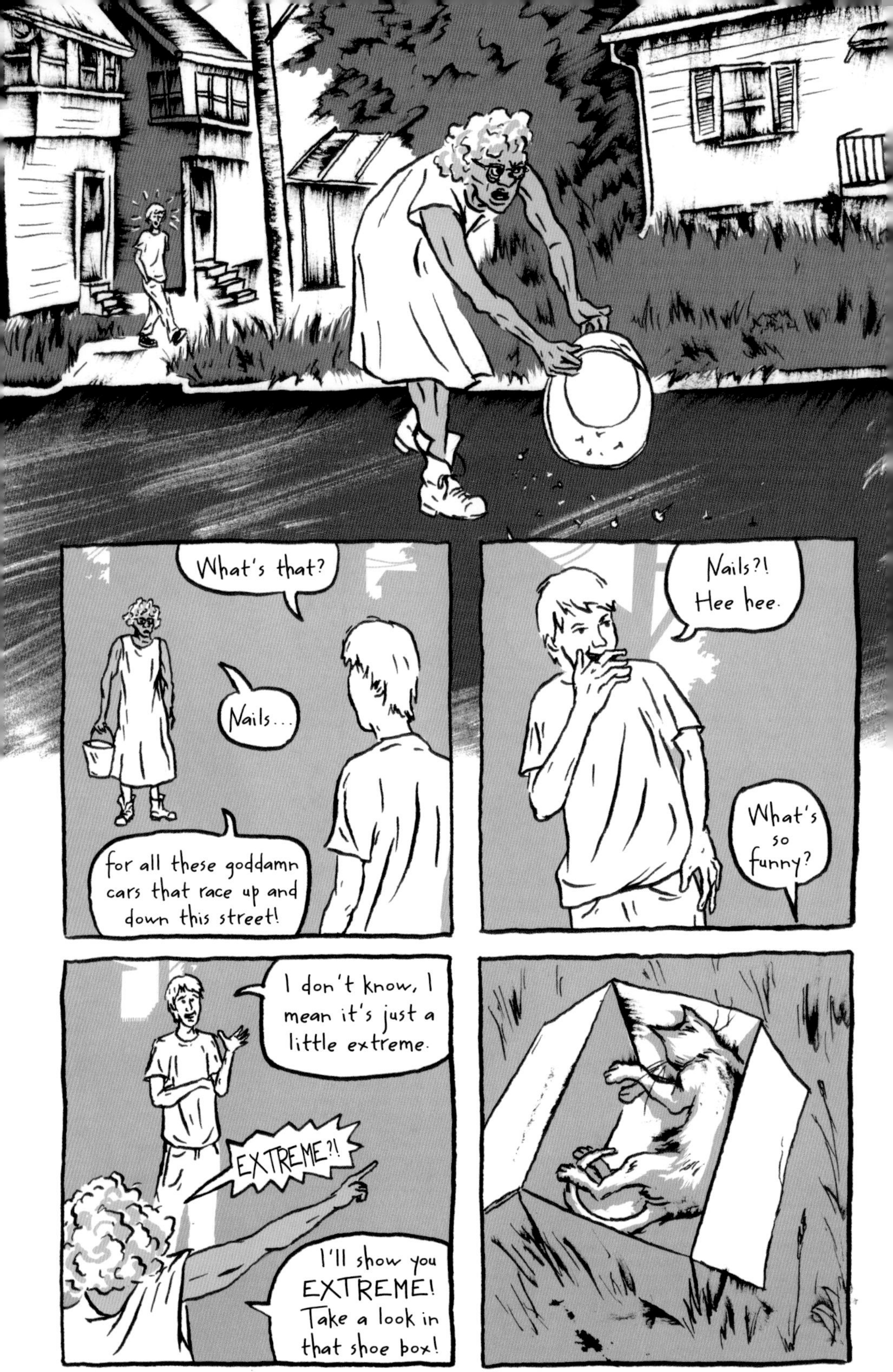
What's that?
Nails...
for all these goddamn cars that race up and down this street!
Nails?! Hee hee.
What's so funny?
I don't know, I mean it's just a little extreme.
EXTREME?!
I'll show you EXTREME! Take a look in that shoe box!

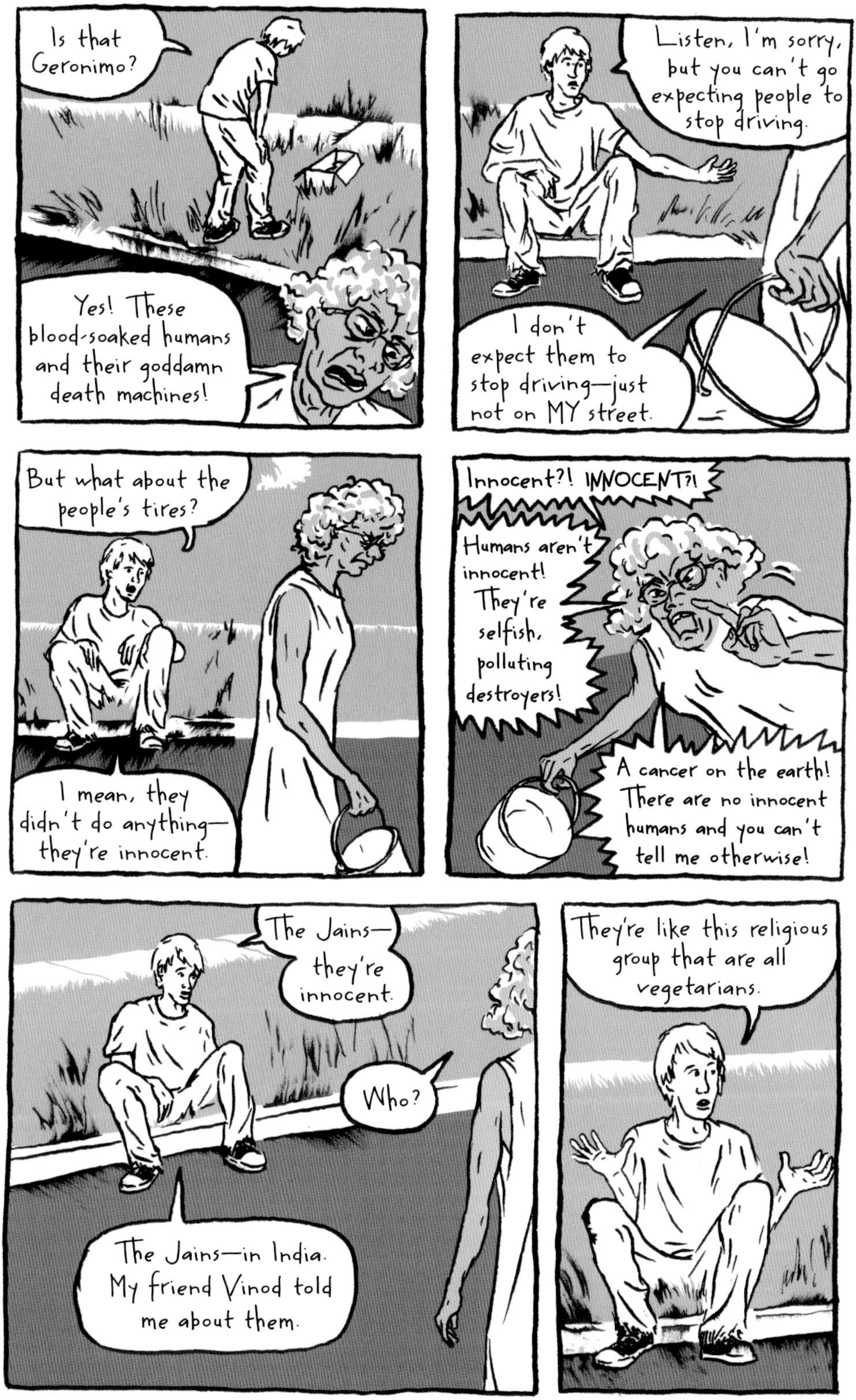
Is that Geronimo?
Yes! These blood-soaked humans and their goddamn death machines!
Listen, I'm sorry, but you can't go expecting people to stop driving.
I don't expect them to stop driving—just not on MY street.
But what about the people's tires?
I mean, they didn't do anything—they're innocent.
Innocent?! INNOCENT?!
Humans aren't innocent! They're selfish, polluting destroyers!
A cancer on the earth! There are no innocent humans and you can't tell me otherwise!
The Jains—they're innocent.
Who?
The Jains—in India. My friend Vinod told me about them.
They're like this religious group that are all vegetarians.

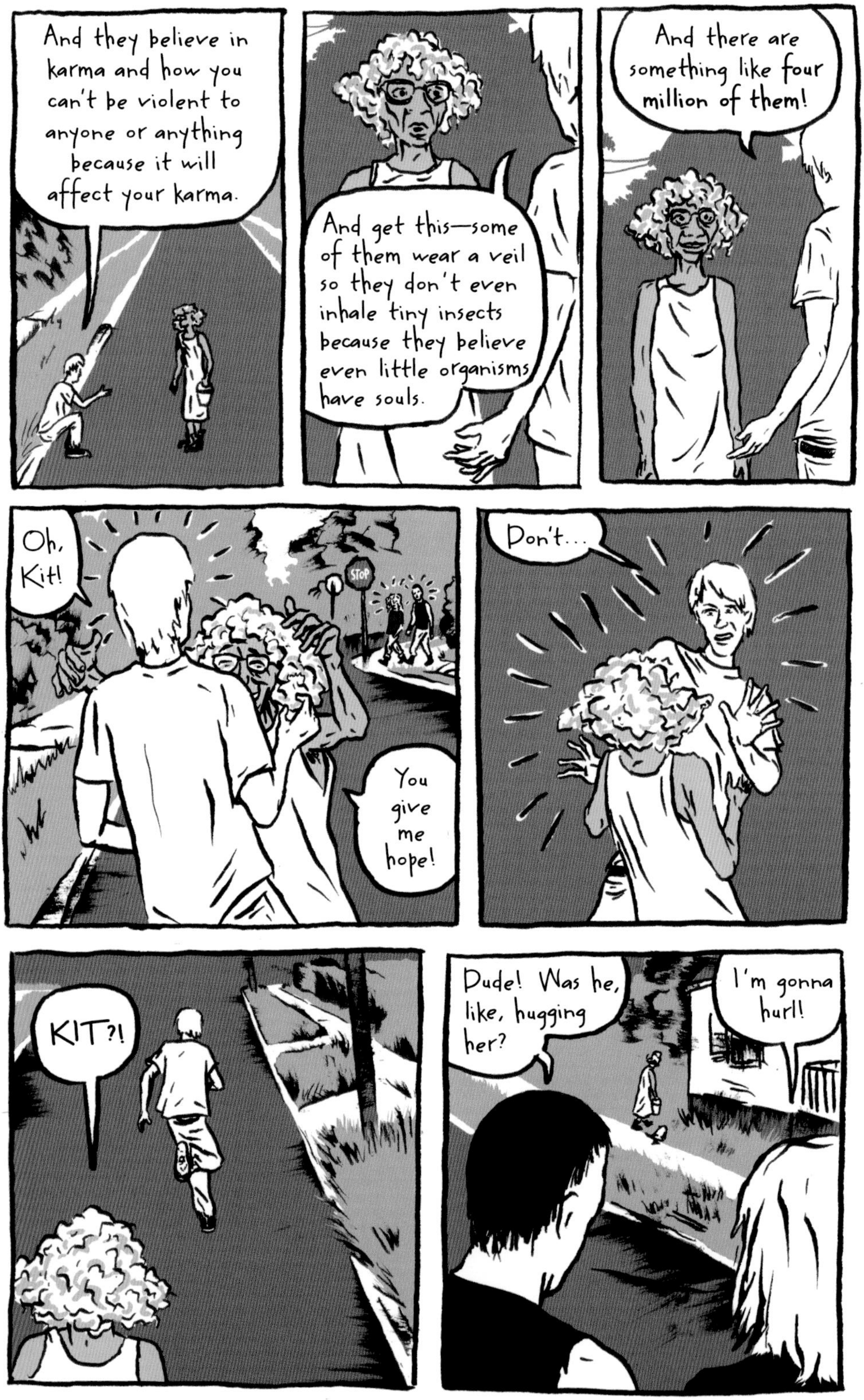
And they believe in karma and how you can't be violent to anyone or anything because it will affect your karma.
And get this—some of them wear a veil so they don't even inhale tiny insects because they believe even little organisms have souls.
And there are something like four million of them!
Oh, Kit!
STOP
You give me hope!
Don't...
KIT?!
Dude! Was he, like, hugging her?
I'm gonna hurl!

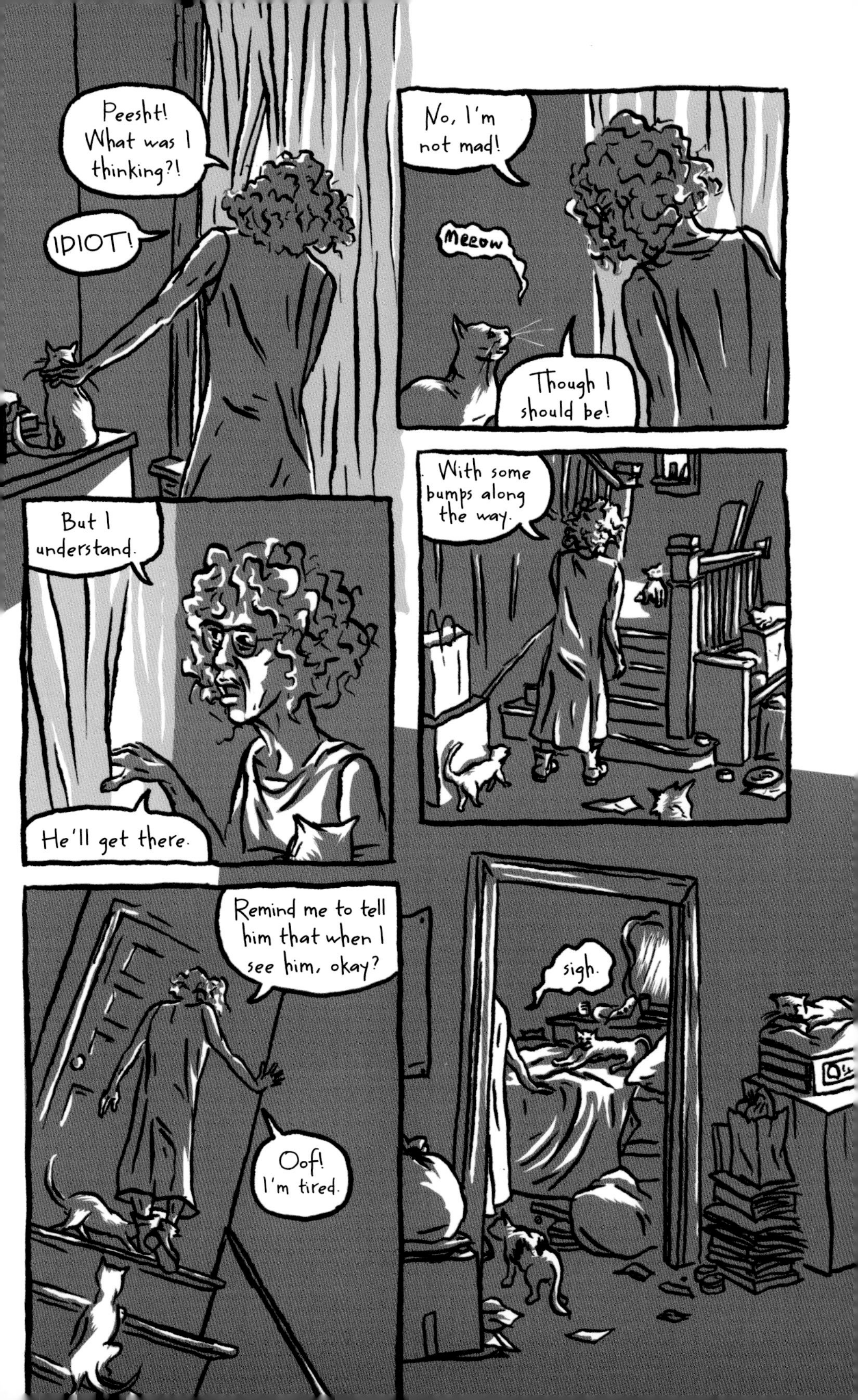
Peesht! What was I thinking?!
IDIOT!
No, I'm not mad!
Meeow
Though I should be!
But I understand.
He'll get there.
With some bumps along the way.
Remind me to tell him that when I see him, okay?
Oof! I'm tired.
sigh.

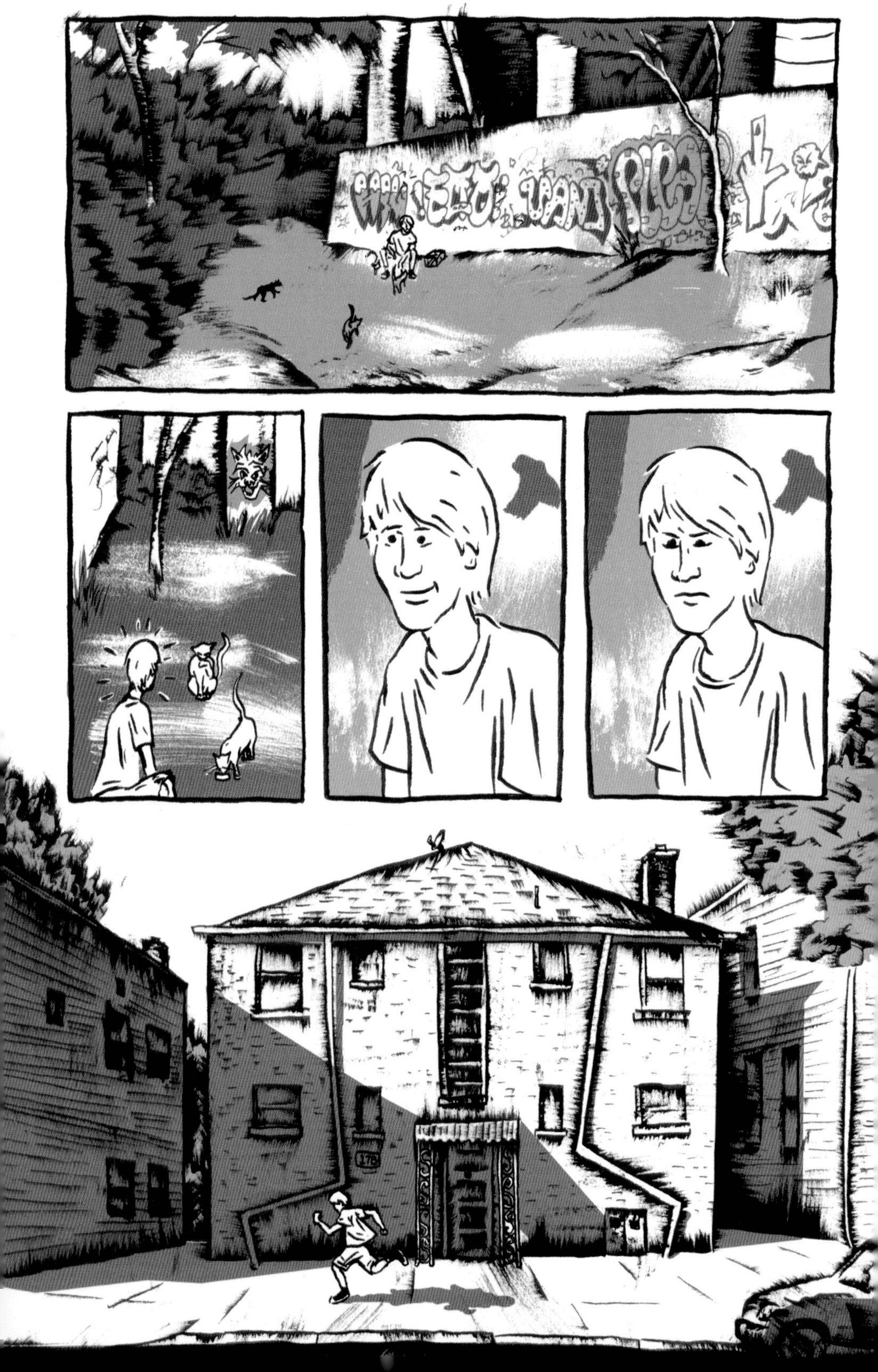

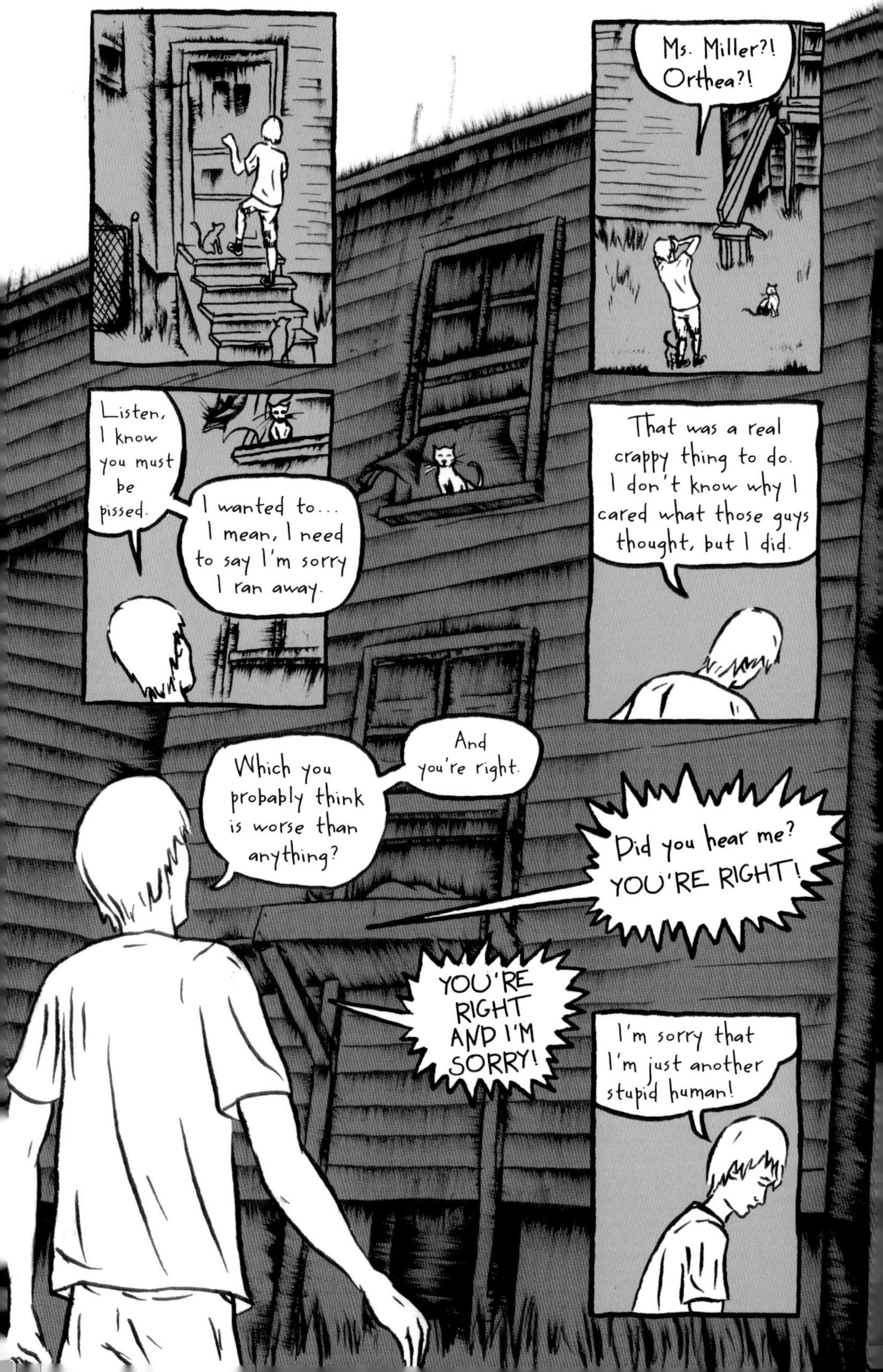
Ms. Miller?! Orthea?!
Listen, I know you must be pissed.
I wanted to... I mean, I need to say I'm sorry I ran away.
That was a real crappy thing to do. I don't know why I cared what those guys thought, but I did.
Which you probably think is worse than anything?
And you're right.
Did you hear me? YOU'RE RIGHT!
YOU'RE RIGHT AND I'M SORRY!
I'm sorry that I'm just another stupid human!

Meeow

Ms. Miller?

Meeow

opened fire on rioters.

wing to
Newark's
e of the
Newark
of sub-
t rates
, pur-
est of
with
city
tion.

Orthea Miller

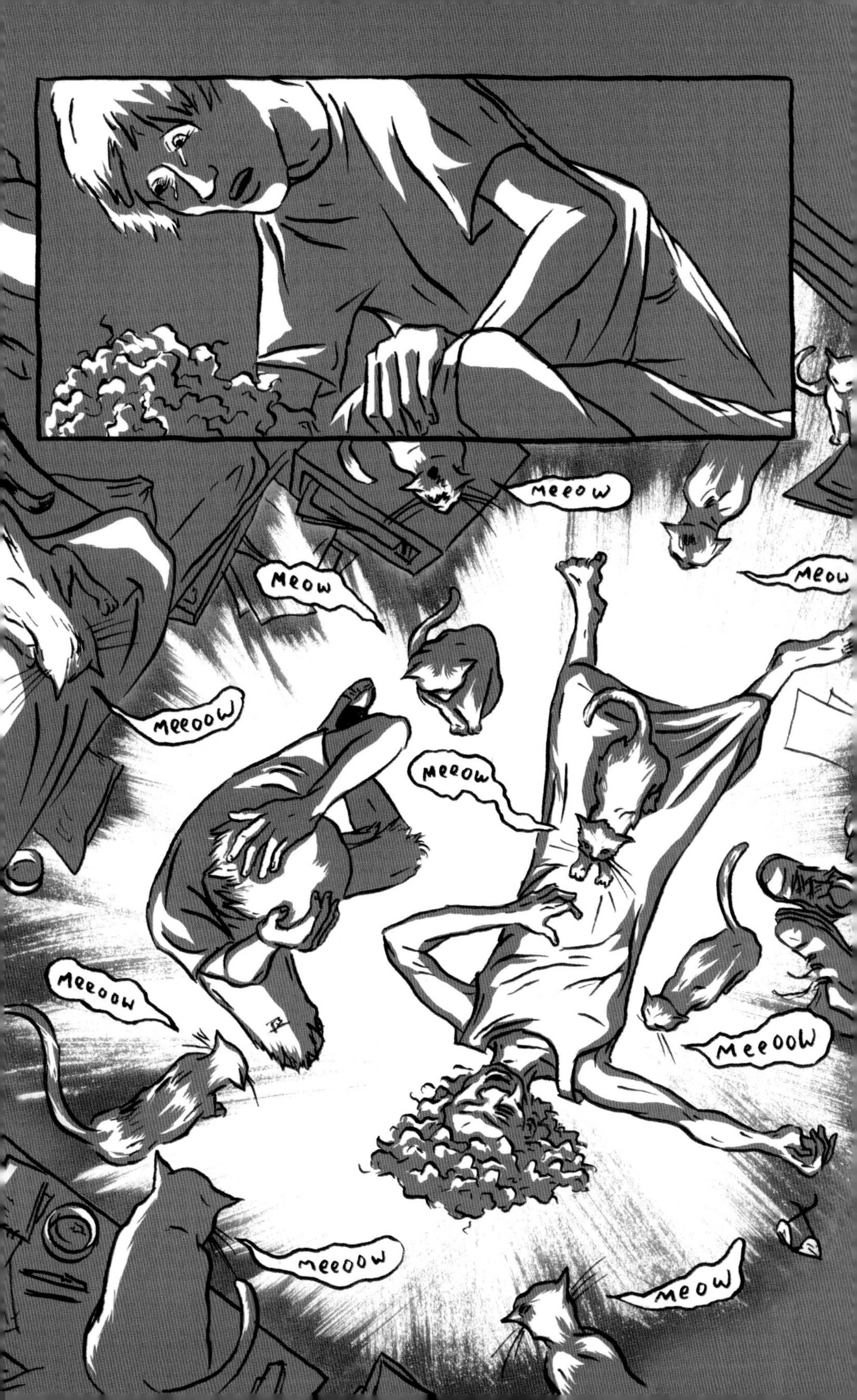
Meeow
Meow
Meow
Meeoow
Meeow
Meeoow
MeeooW
meeoow
Meow

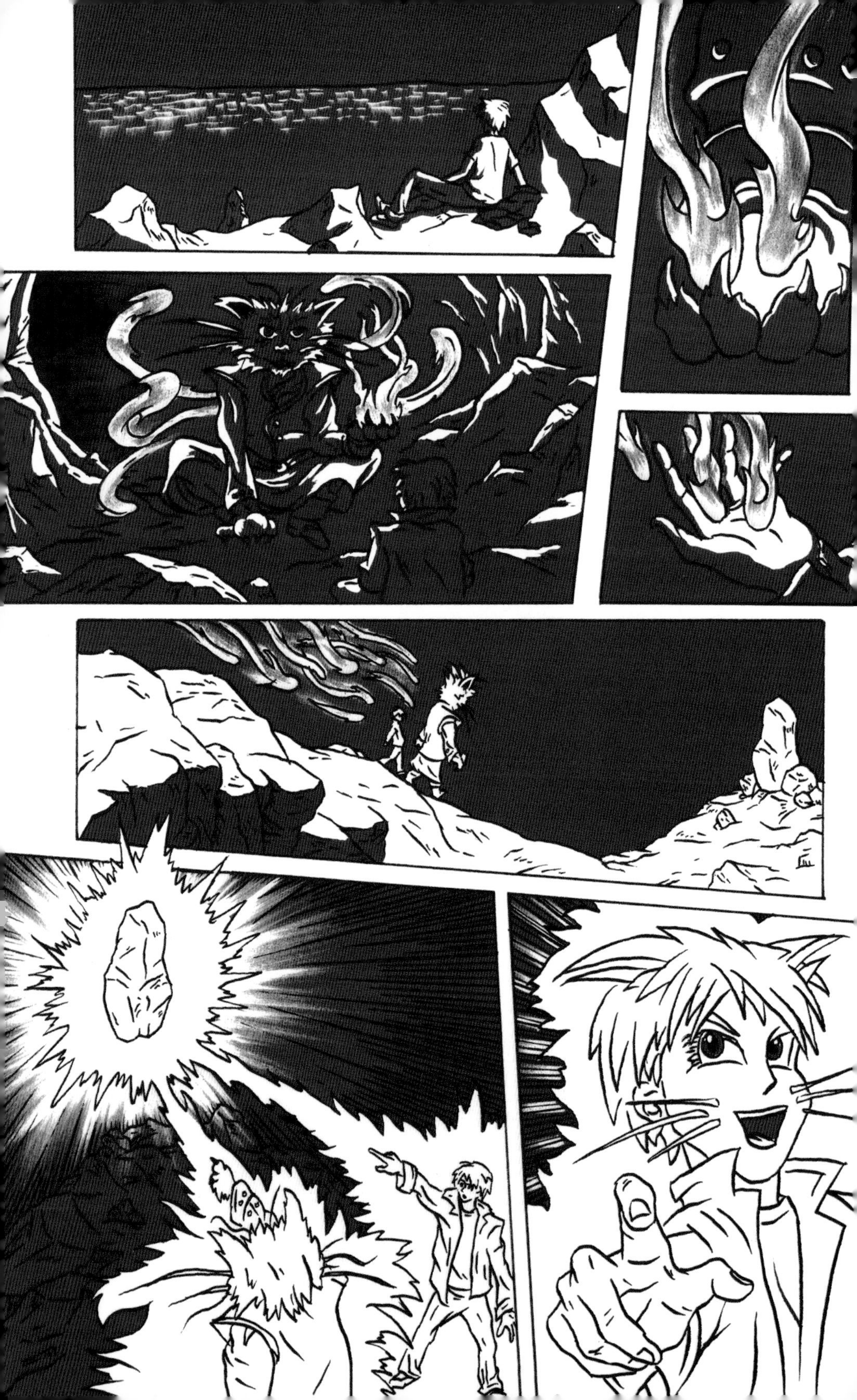

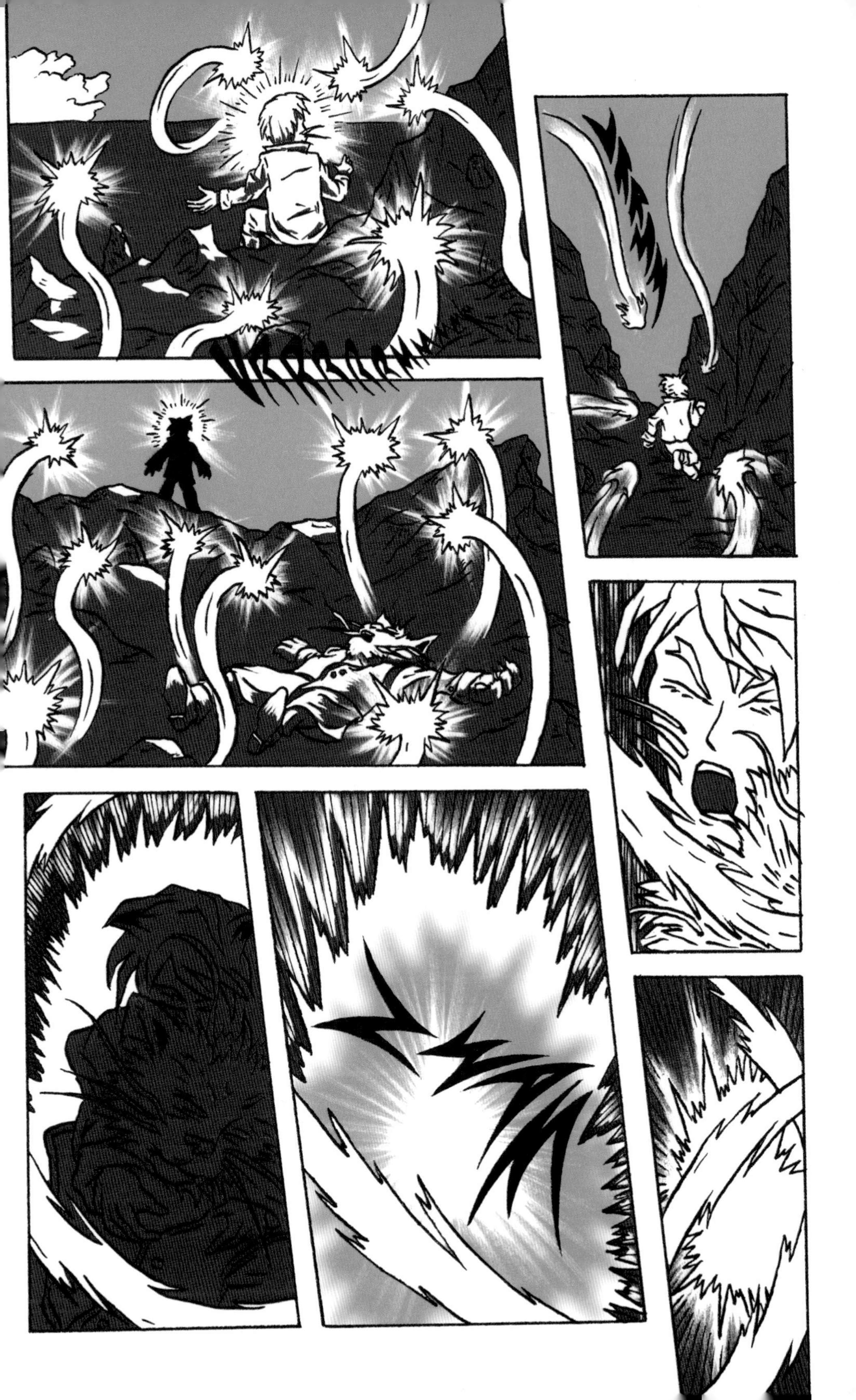

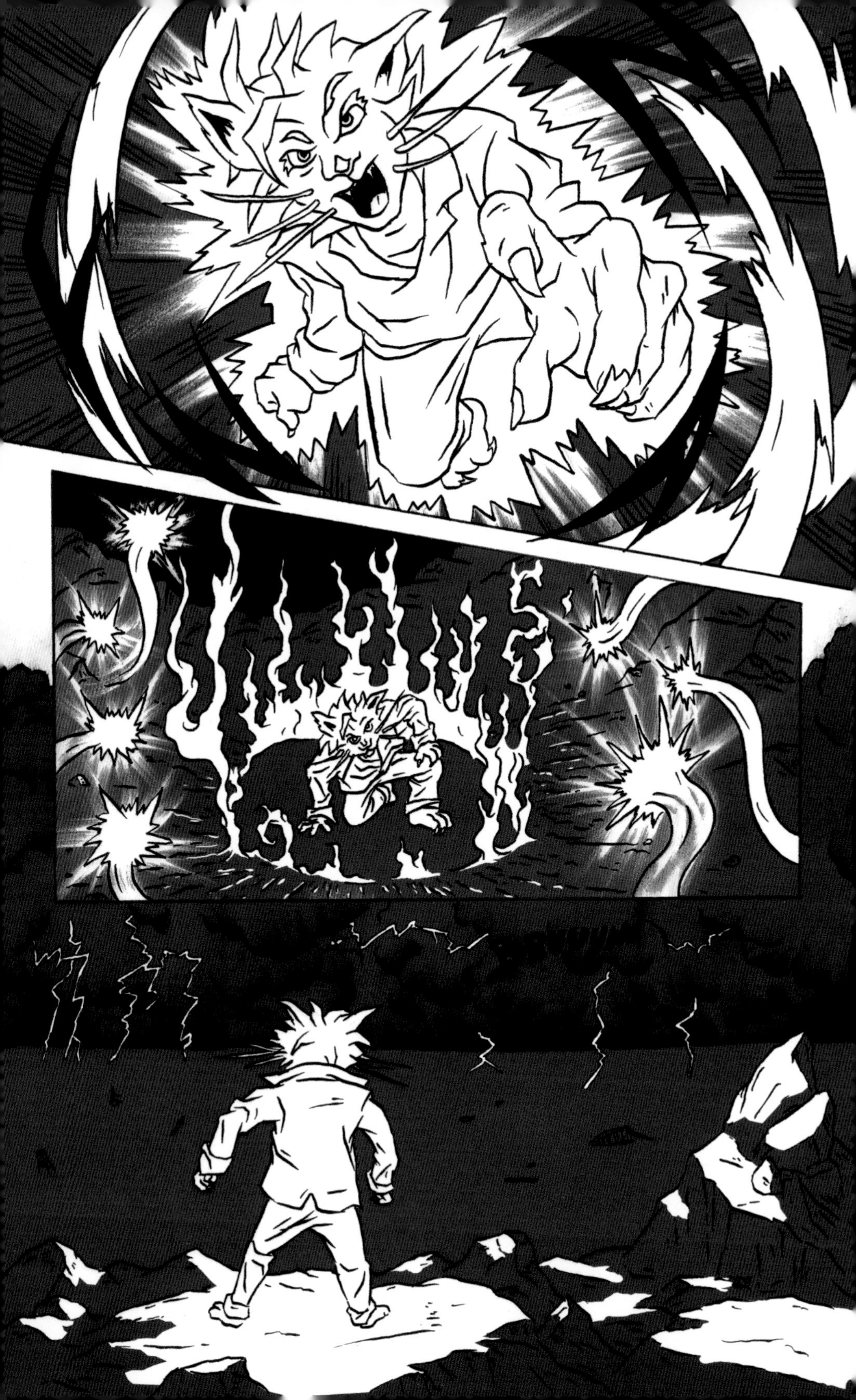

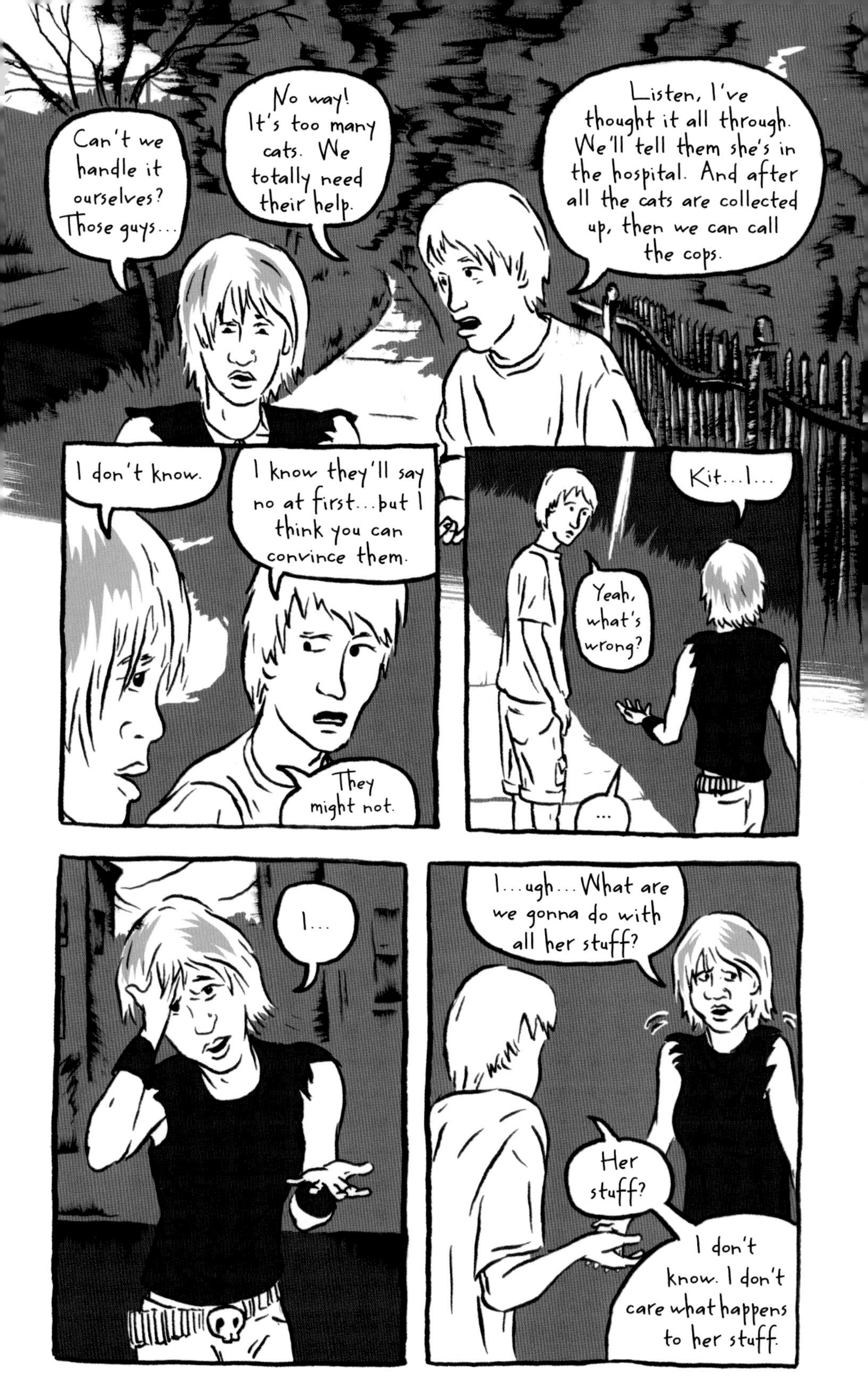
Can't we handle it ourselves? Those guys...
No way! It's too many cats. We totally need their help.
Listen, I've thought it all through. We'll tell them she's in the hospital. And after all the cats are collected up, then we can call the cops.
I don't know.
I know they'll say no at first...but I think you can convince them.
They might not.
Kit...I...
Yeah, what's wrong?
...
I...
I...ugh...What are we gonna do with all her stuff?
Her stuff?
I don't know. I don't care what happens to her stuff.

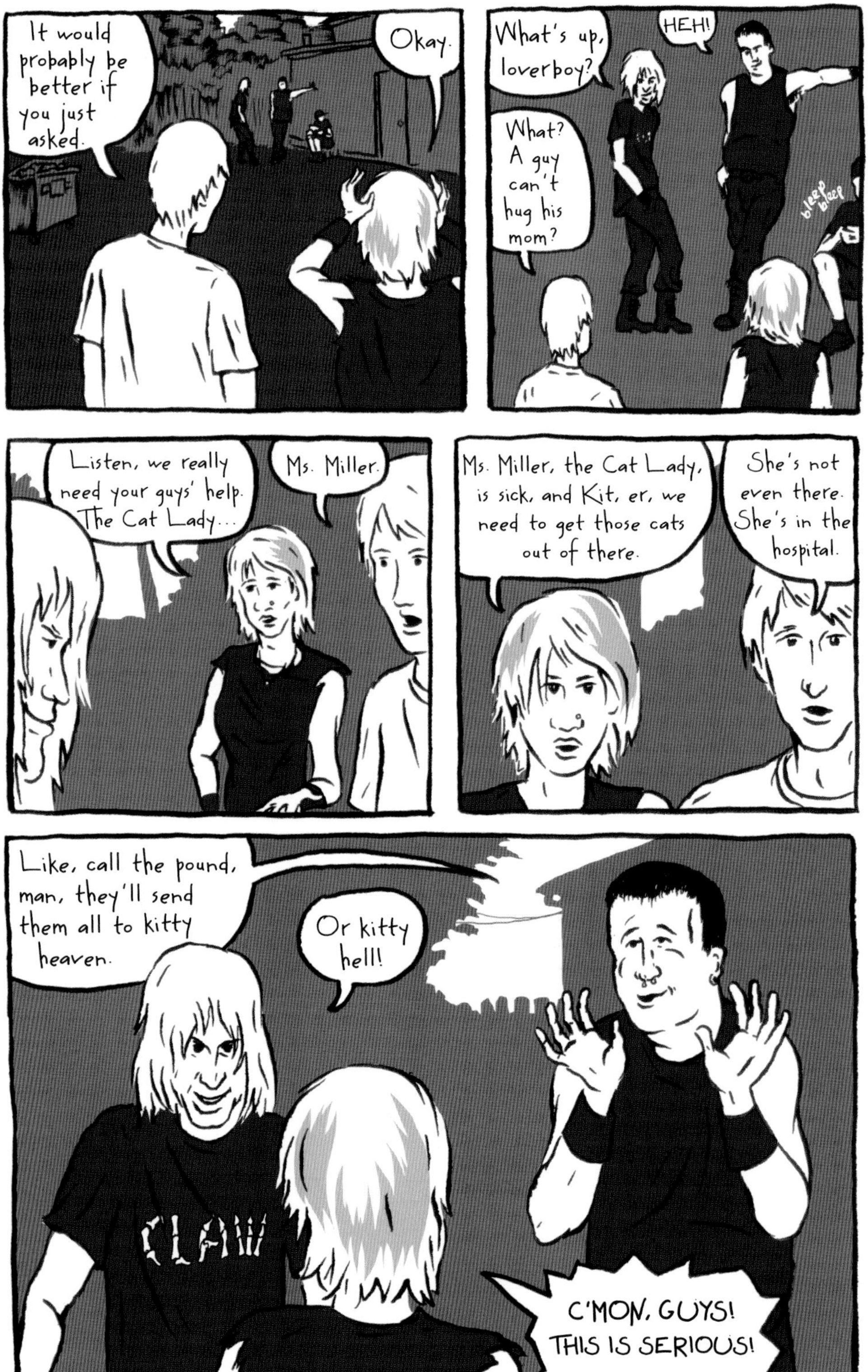
It would probably be better if you just asked.
Okay.
What's up, loverboy?
HEH!
What? A guy can't hug his mom?
bleep bleep
Listen, we really need your guys' help. The Cat Lady...
Ms. Miller.
Ms. Miller, the Cat Lady, is sick, and Kit, er, we need to get those cats out of there.
She's not even there. She's in the hospital.
Like, call the pound, man, they'll send them all to kitty heaven.
Or kitty hell!
CLAW
C'MON, GUYS! THIS IS SERIOUS!

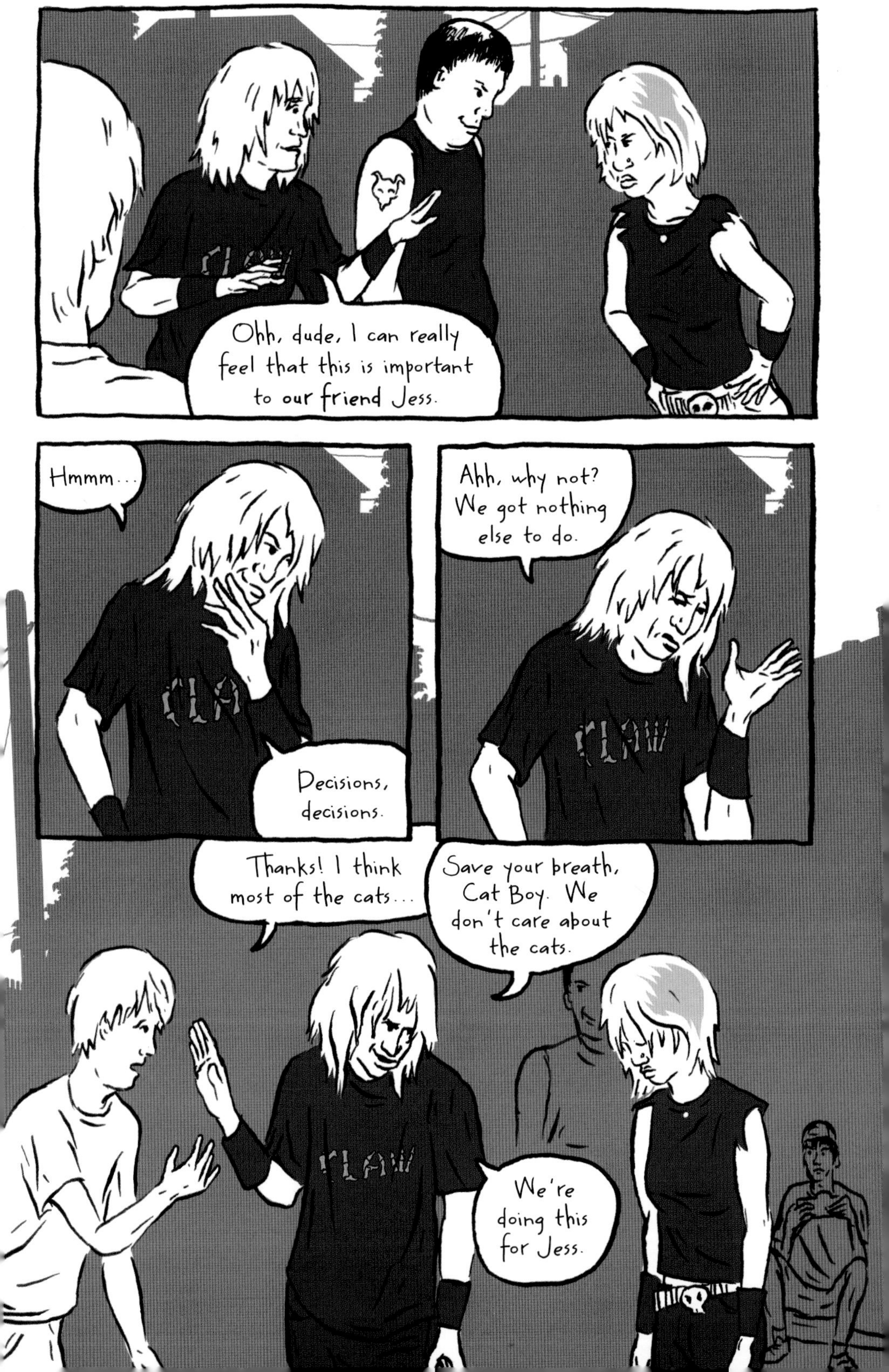
Ohh, dude, I can really feel that this is important to our friend Jess.
Hmmm...
Decisions, decisions.
Ahh, why not? We got nothing else to do.
Thanks! I think most of the cats...
Save your breath, Cat Boy. We don't care about the cats.
We're doing this for Jess.

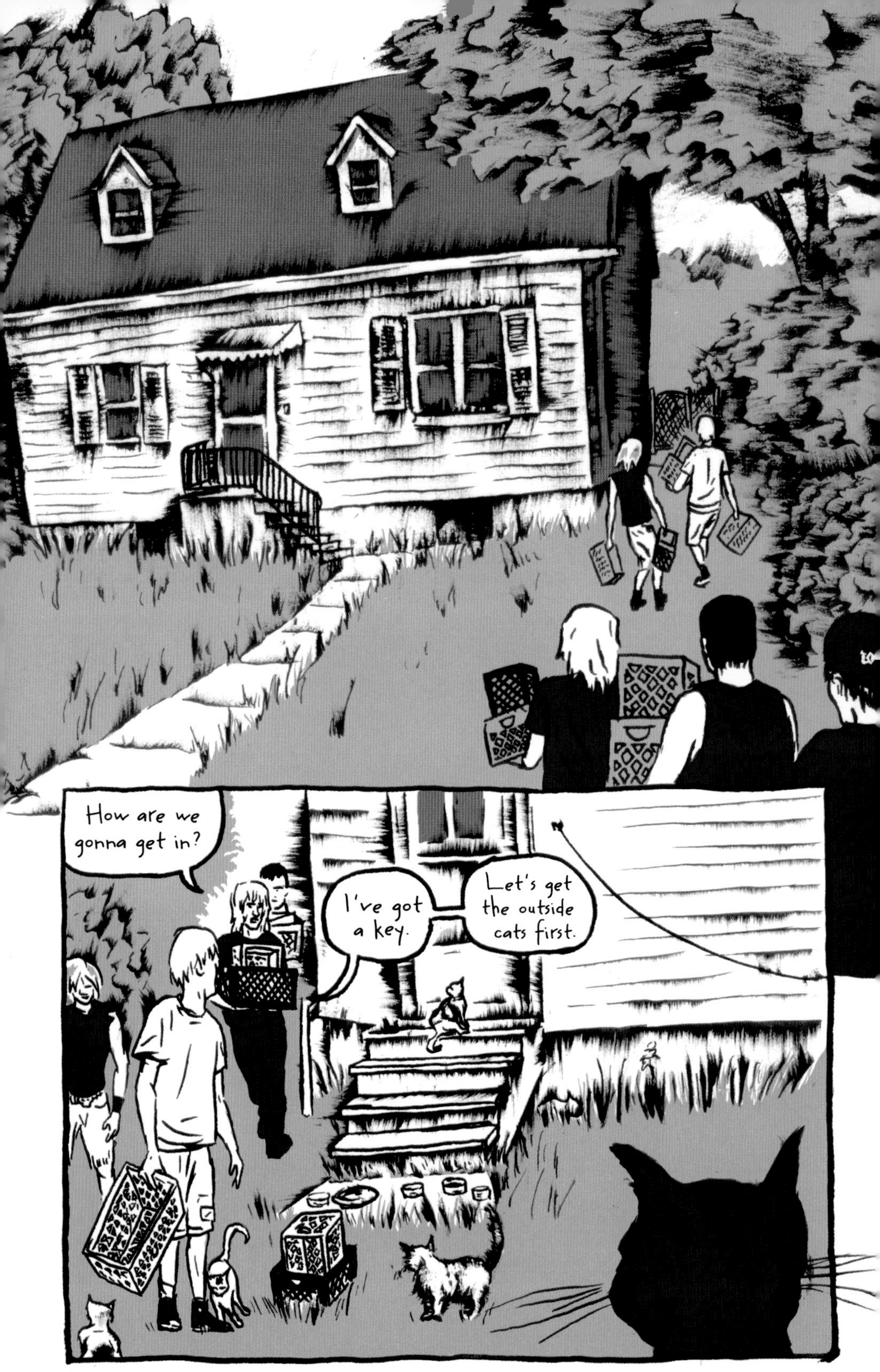
How are we gonna get in?
I've got a key.
Let's get the outside cats first.

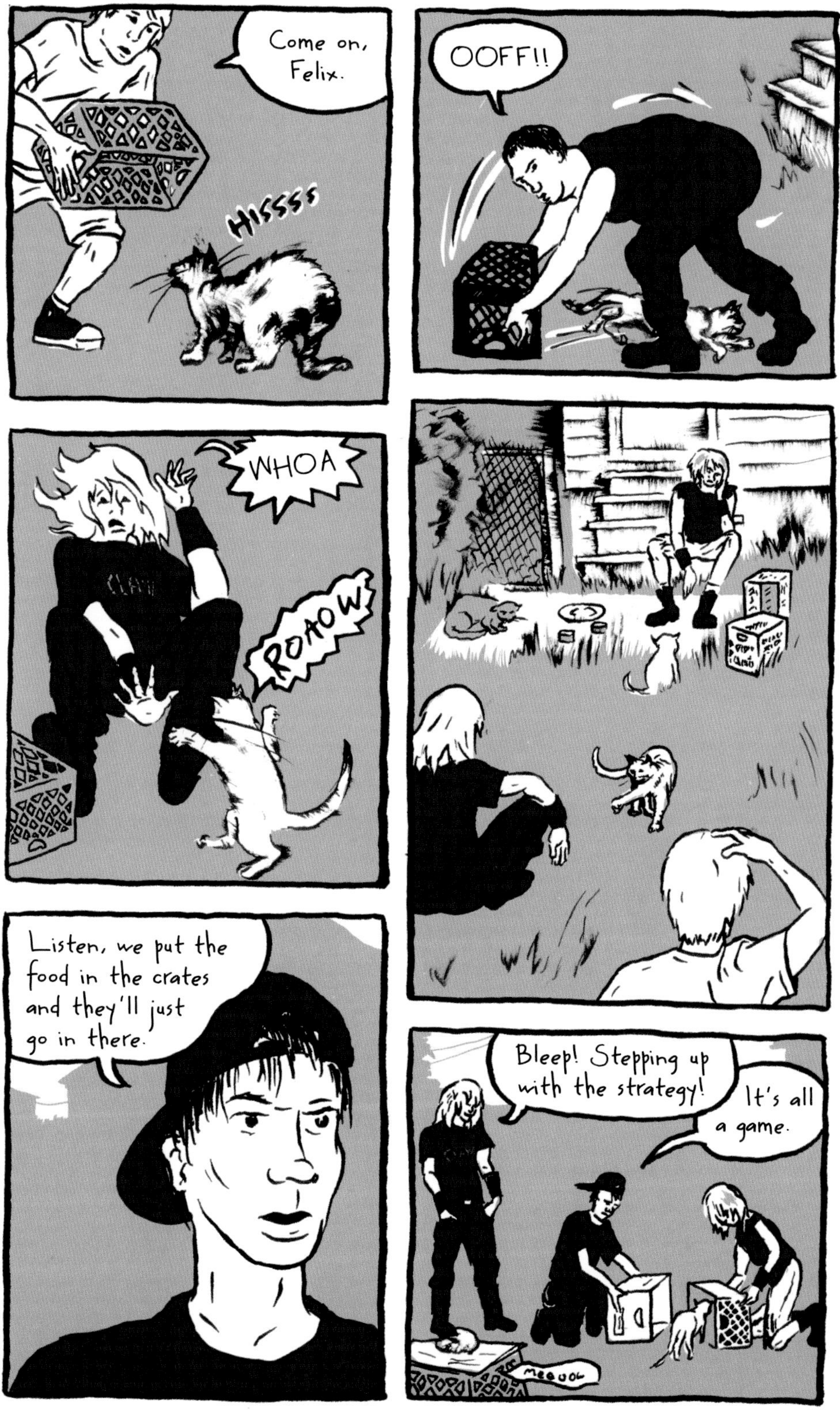
Come on, Felix.
HISSSS
OOFF!!
WHOA
ROAOW
Listen, we put the food in the crates and they'll just go in there.
Bleep! Stepping up with the strategy!
It's all a game.

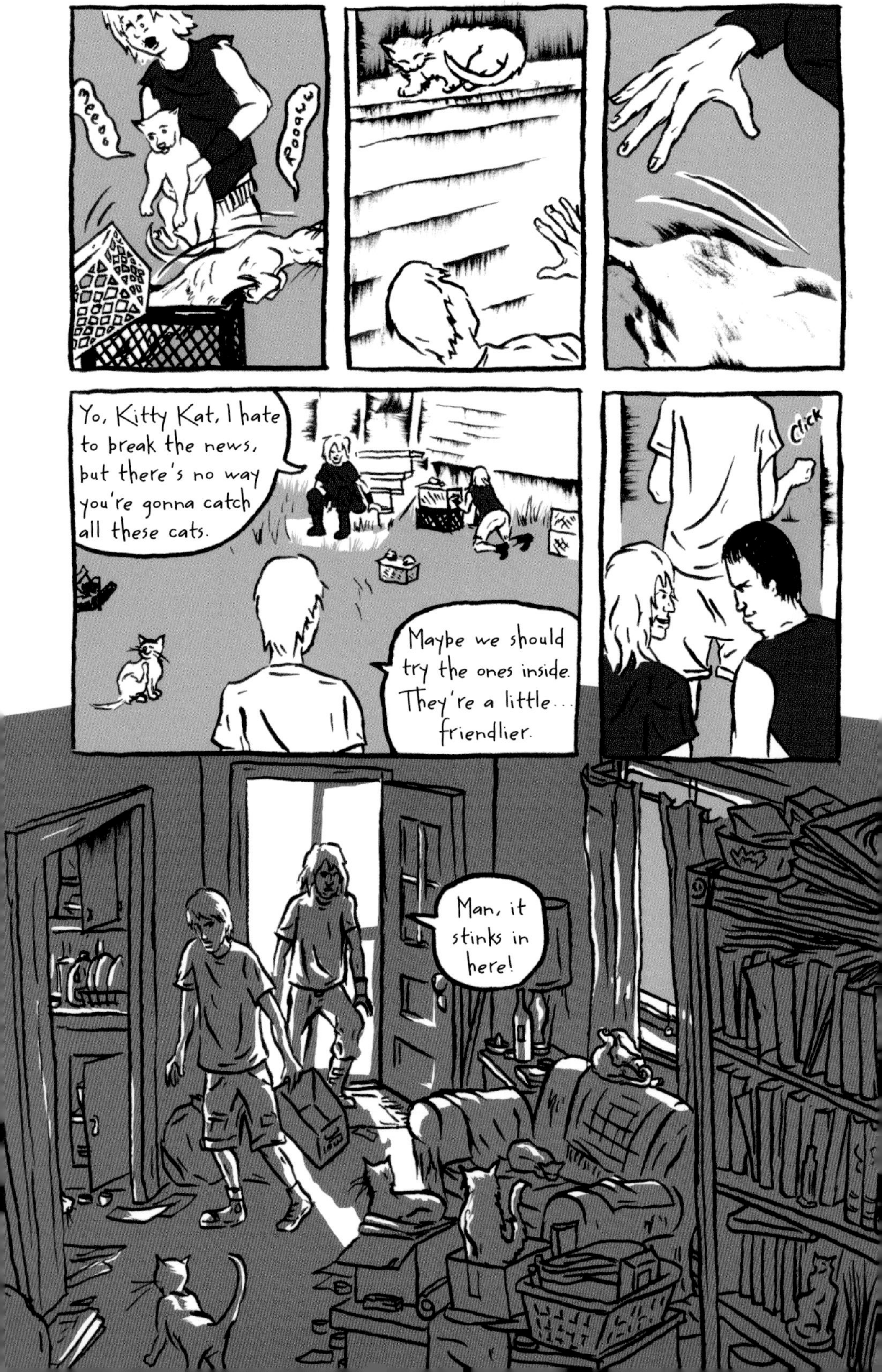

meeoo
Rooaww
Yo, Kitty Kat, I hate to break the news, but there's no way you're gonna catch all these cats.
Maybe we should try the ones inside. They're a little... friendlier.
click
Man, it stinks in here!

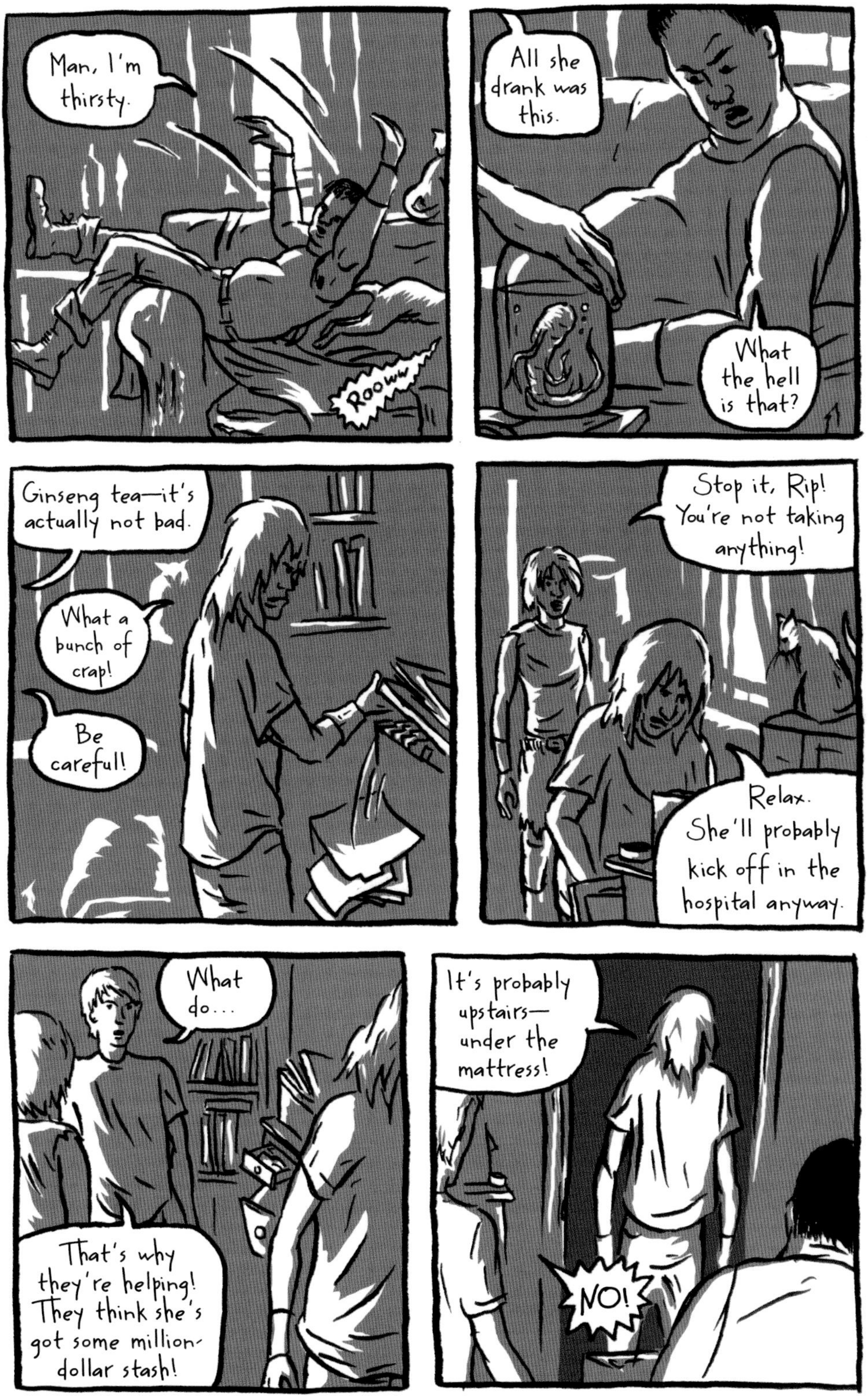
Man, I'm thirsty.
ROOWW
All she drank was this.
What the hell is that?
Ginseng tea—it's actually not bad.
What a bunch of crap!
Be careful!
Stop it, Rip! You're not taking anything!
Relax. She'll probably kick off in the hospital anyway.
What do...
That's why they're helping! They think she's got some million-dollar stash!
It's probably upstairs—under the mattress!
NO!

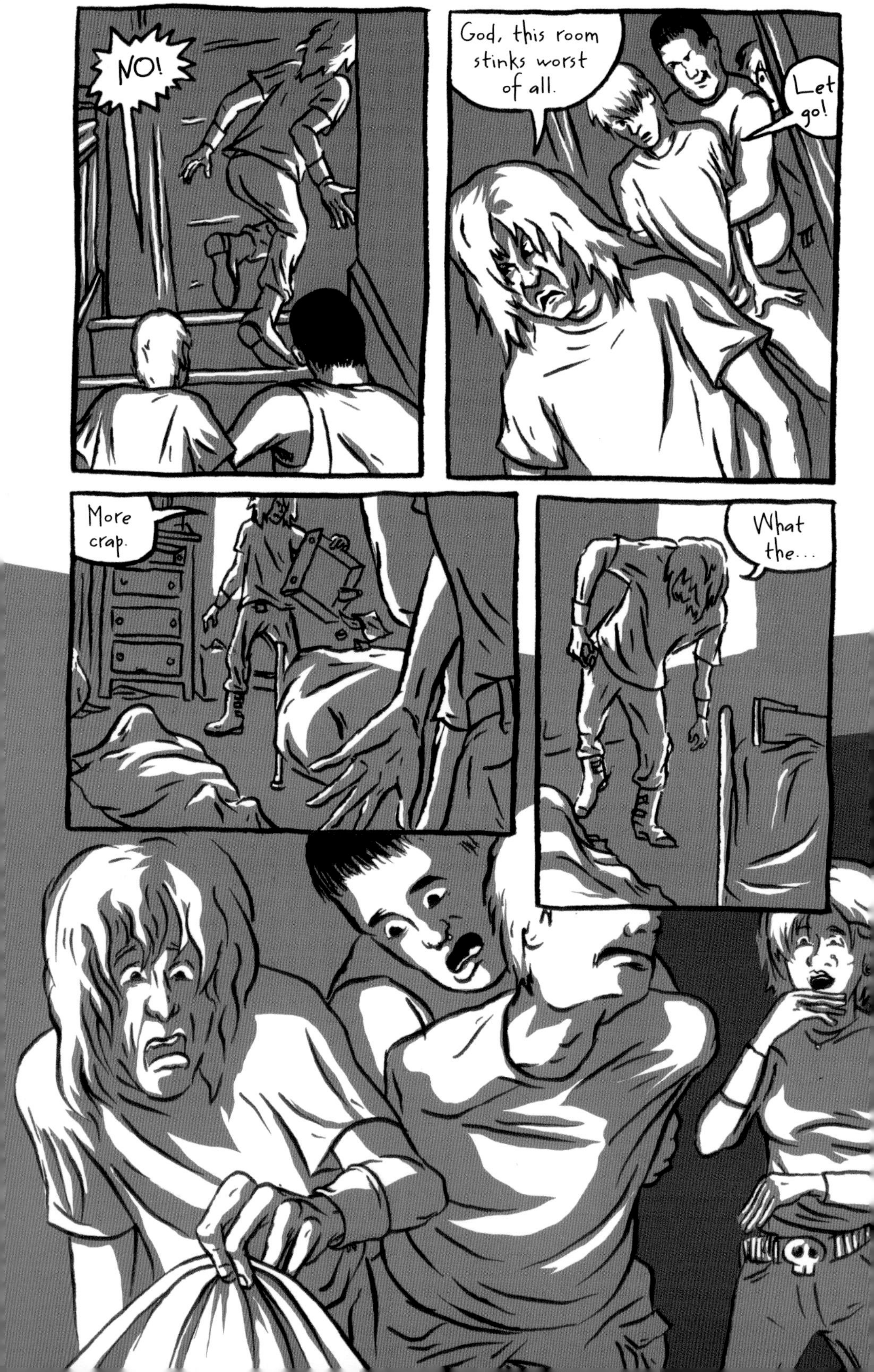
NO!
God, this room stinks worst of all.
Let go!
More crap.
What the...

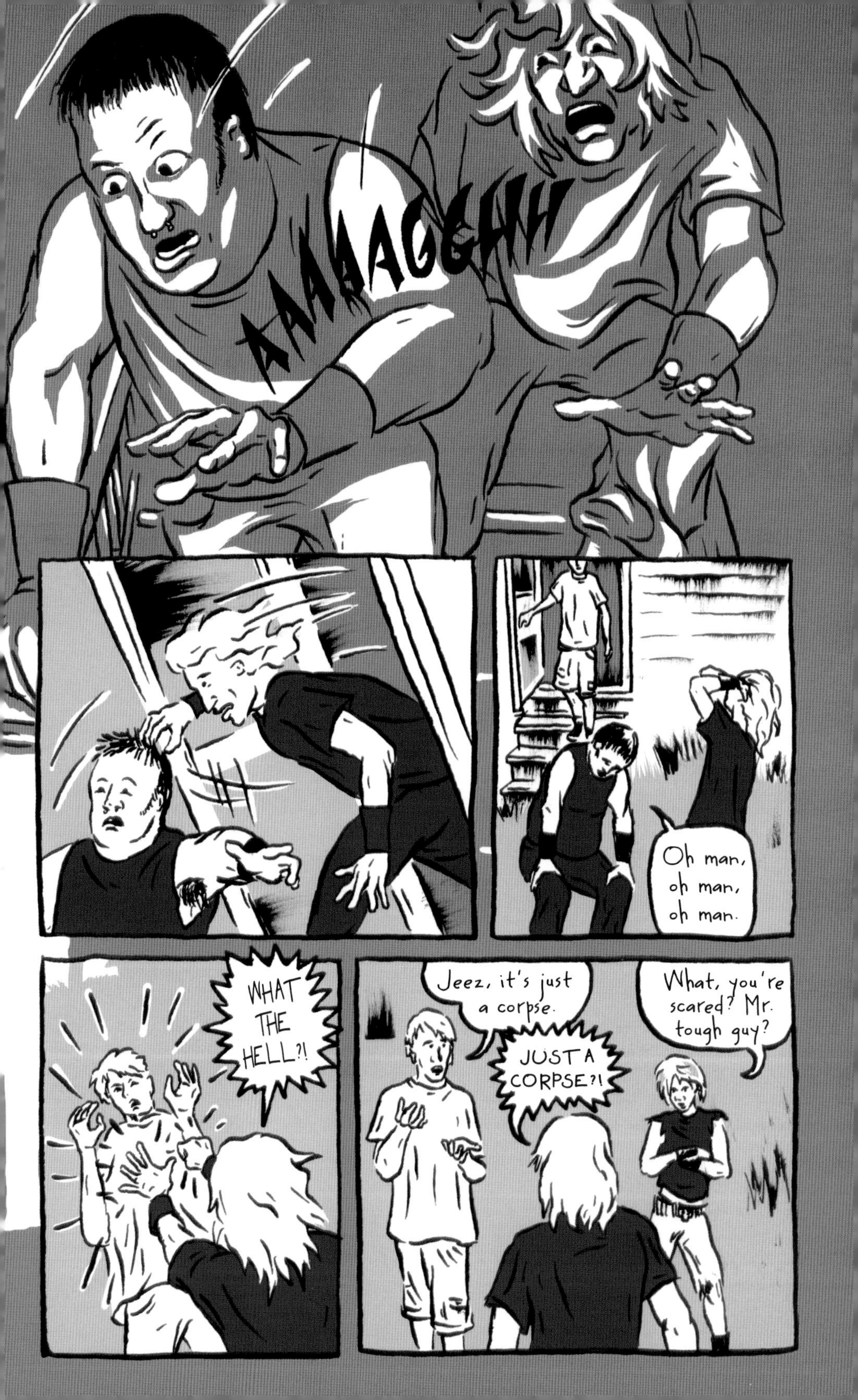
AAAAAGGHHH
Oh man,
oh man,
oh man.
WHAT THE HELL?!
Jeez, it's just a corpse.
JUST A CORPSE?!
What, you're scared? Mr. tough guy?

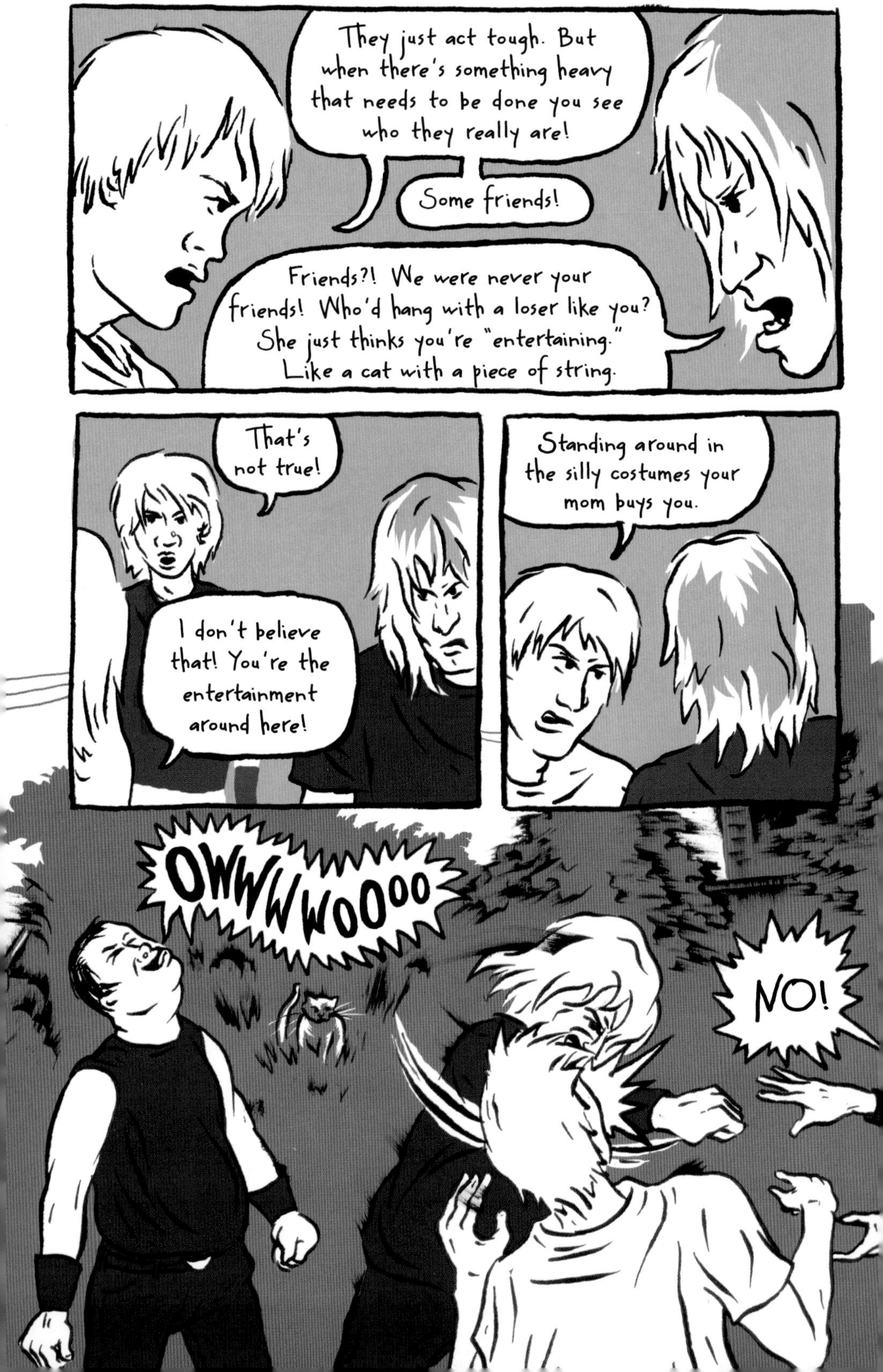
They just act tough. But when there's something heavy that needs to be done you see who they really are!
Some friends!
Friends?! We were never your friends! Who'd hang with a loser like you? She just thinks you're "entertaining." Like a cat with a piece of string.
That's not true!
I don't believe that! You're the entertainment around here!
Standing around in the silly costumes your mom buys you.
OWWWWOOOO
NO!

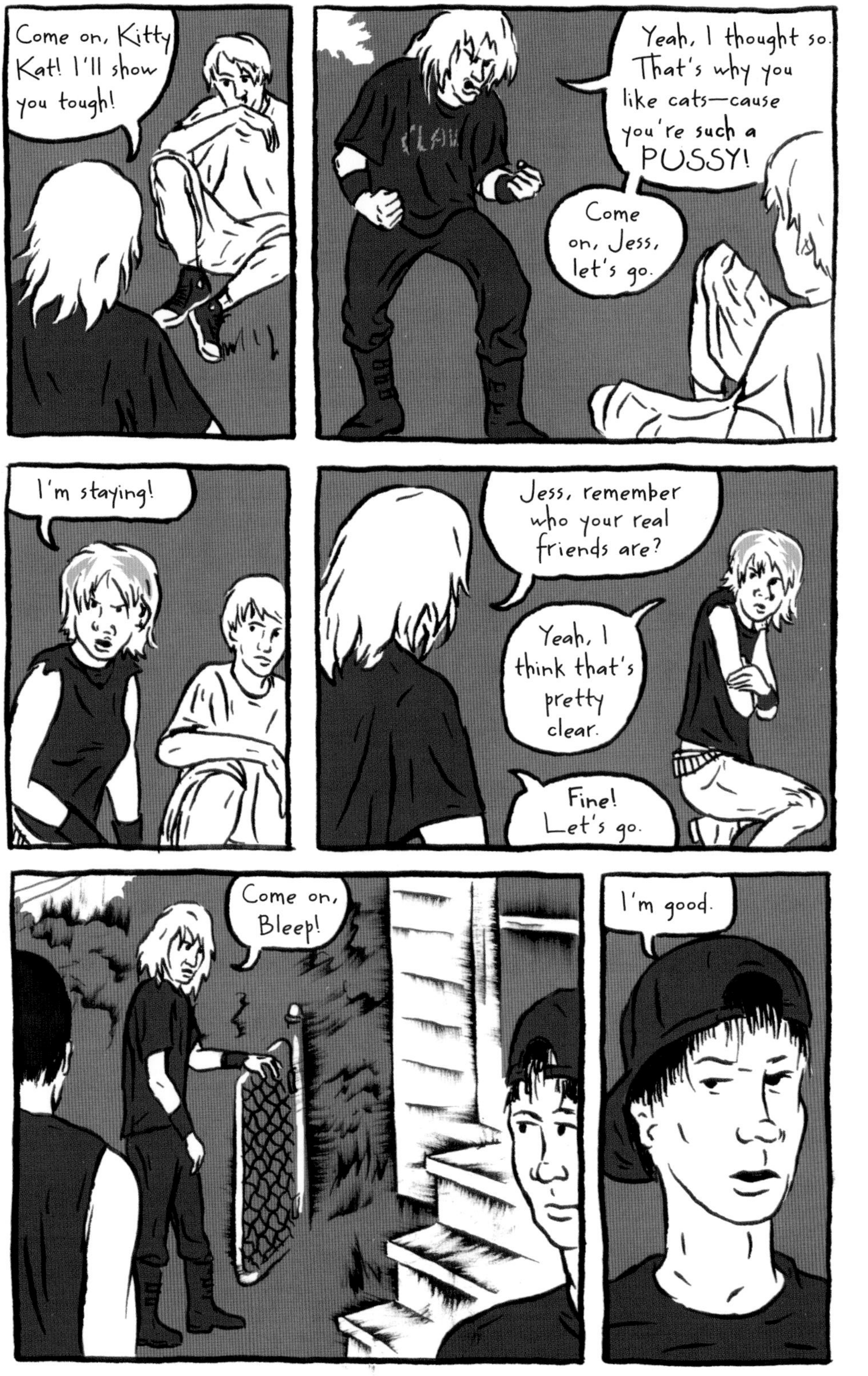
Come on, Kitty Kat! I'll show you tough!
Yeah, I thought so. That's why you like cats—cause you're such a PUSSY!
Come on, Jess, let's go.
I'm staying!
Jess, remember who your real friends are?
Yeah, I think that's pretty clear.
Fine! Let's go.
Come on, Bleep!
I'm good.

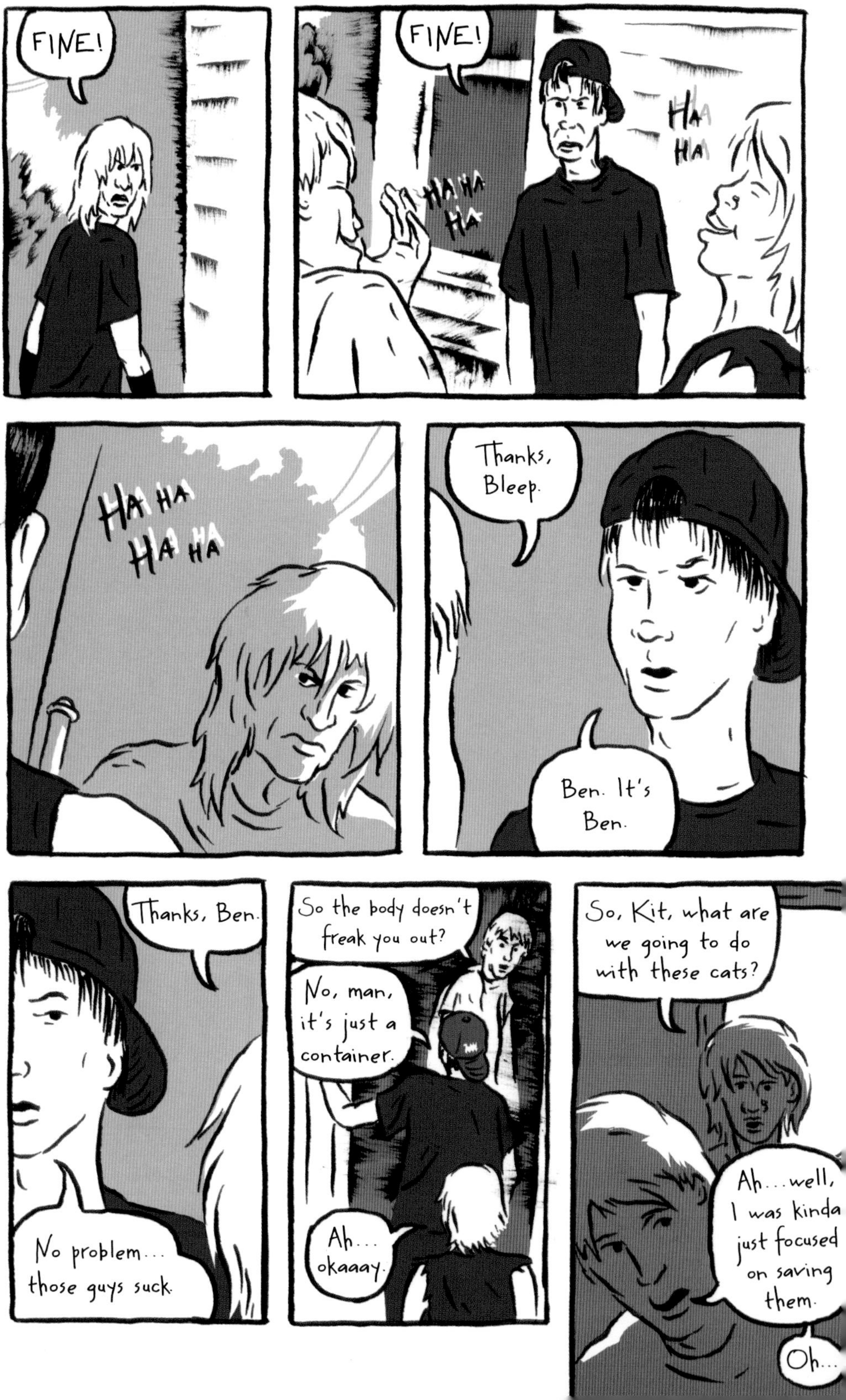
FINE!
FINE!
HA HA
HA HA HA
HA HA
HA HA
Thanks, Bleep.
Ben. It's Ben.
Thanks, Ben.
No problem... those guys suck.
So the body doesn't freak you out?
No, man, it's just a container.
Ah... okaaay.
So, Kit, what are we going to do with these cats?
Ah...well, I was kinda just focused on saving them.
Oh...

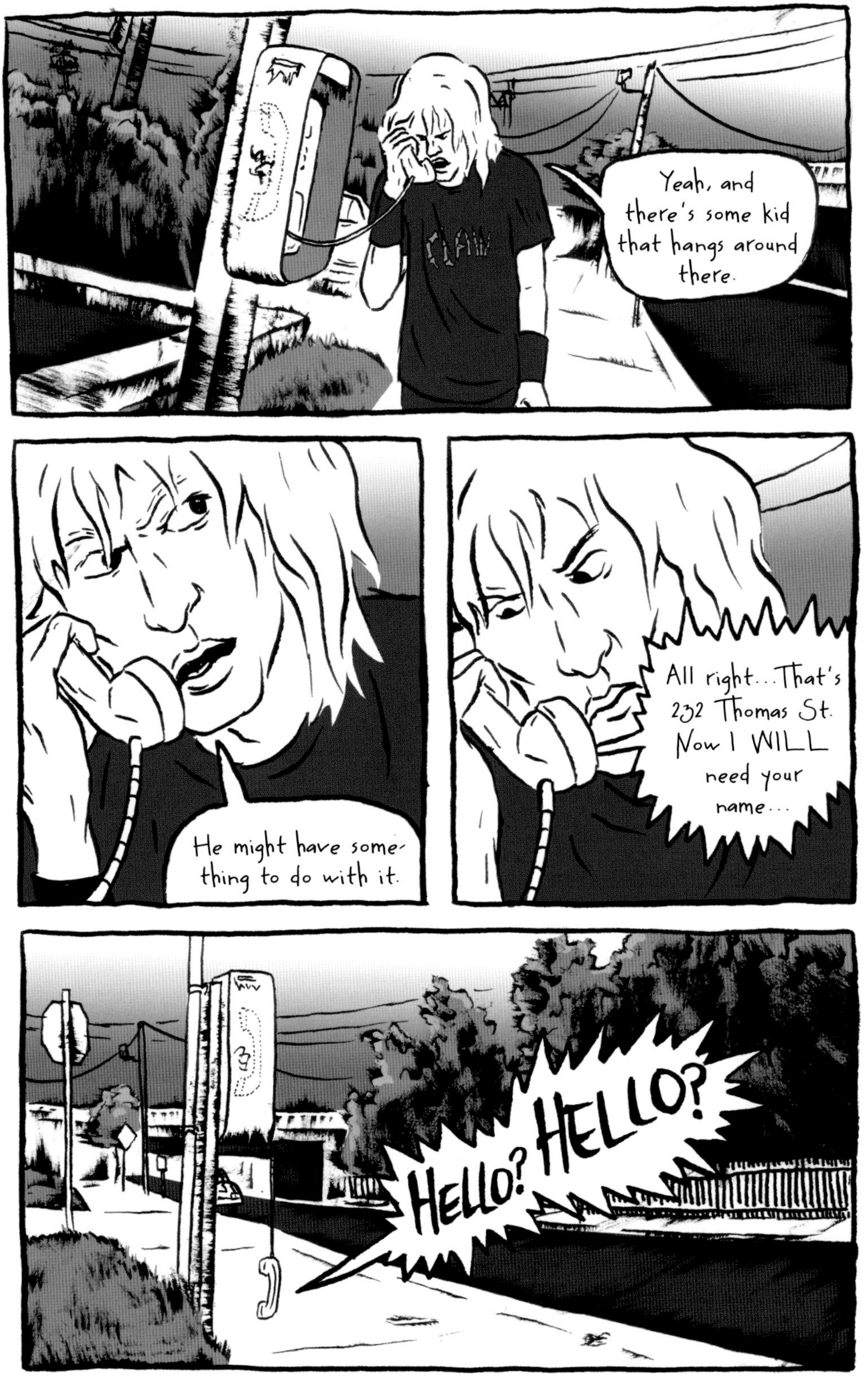
Yeah, and there's some kid that hangs around there.
He might have something to do with it.
All right... That's 232 Thomas St. Now I WILL need your name...
HELLO? HELLO?

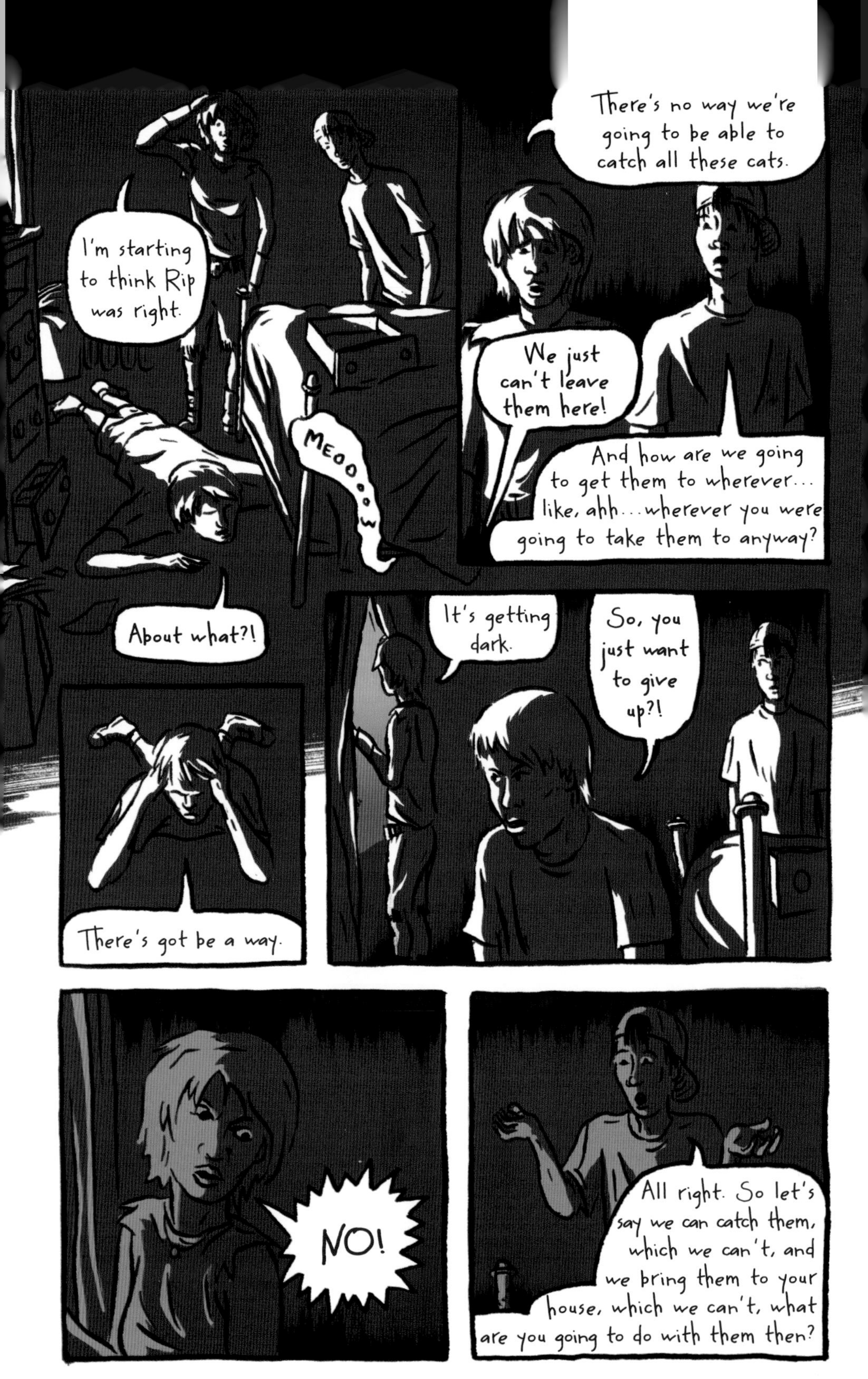
I'm starting to think Rip was right.
MEOO...W
About what?!
There's no way we're going to be able to catch all these cats.
We just can't leave them here!
And how are we going to get them to wherever... like, ahh...wherever you were going to take them to anyway?
There's got be a way.
It's getting dark.
So, you just want to give up?!
NO!
All right. So let's say we can catch them, which we can't, and we bring them to your house, which we can't, what are you going to do with them then?

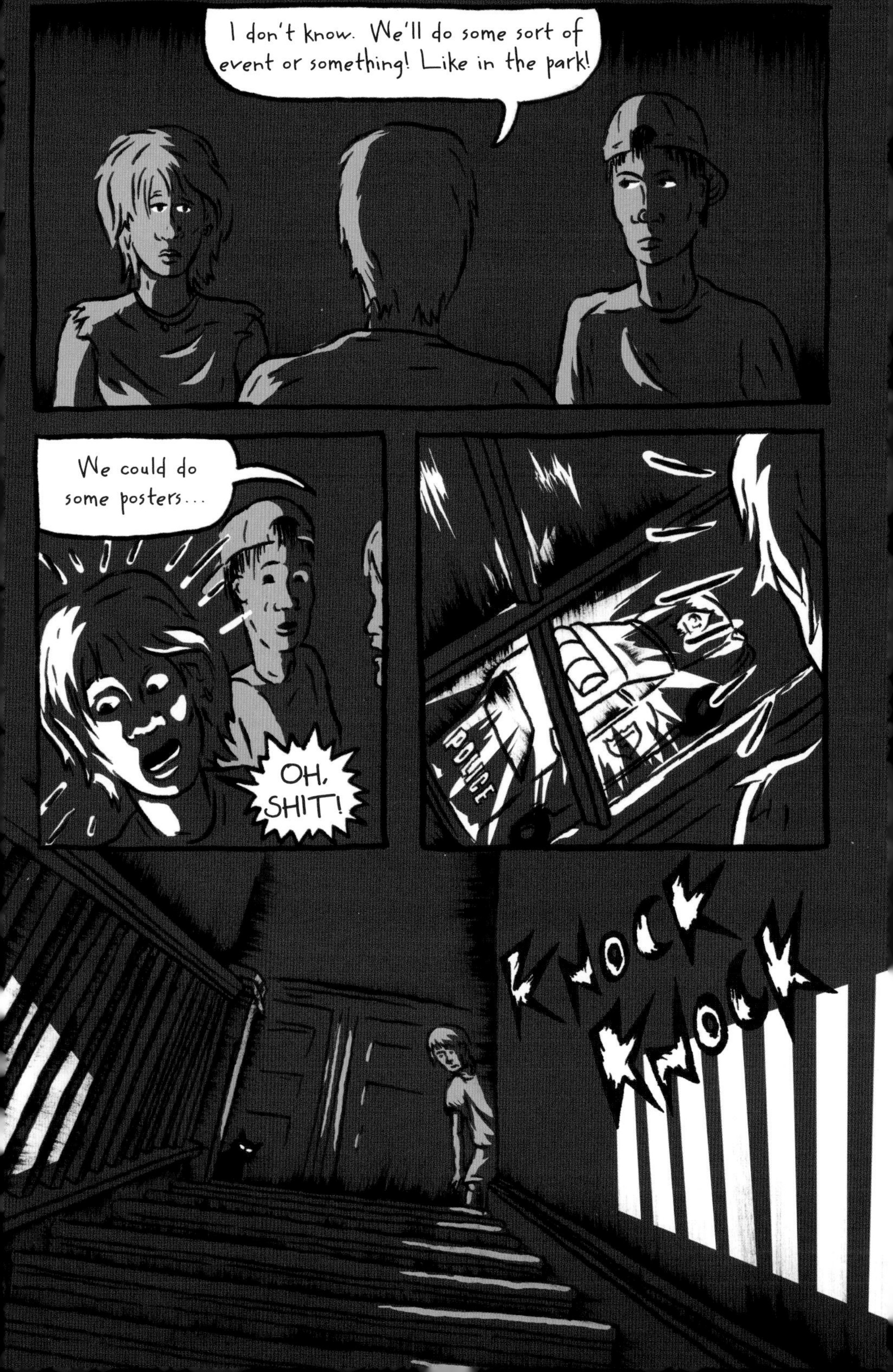

I don't know. We'll do some sort of event or something! Like in the park!
We could do some posters...
OH, SHIT!
POLICE
KNOCK KNOCK

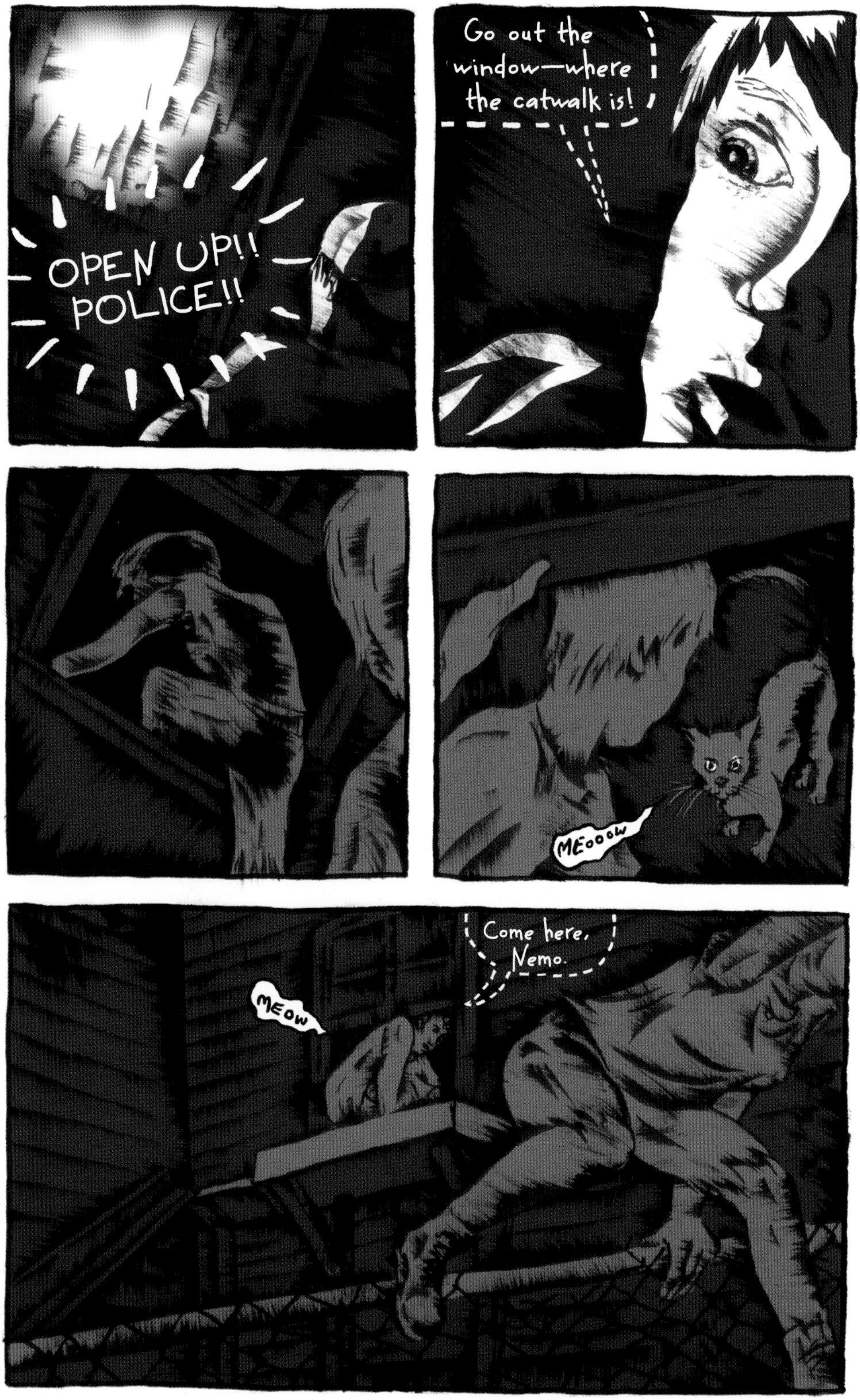
OPEN UP!!
POLICE!!
Go out the window—where the catwalk is!
MEooow
MEOW
Come here, Nemo.

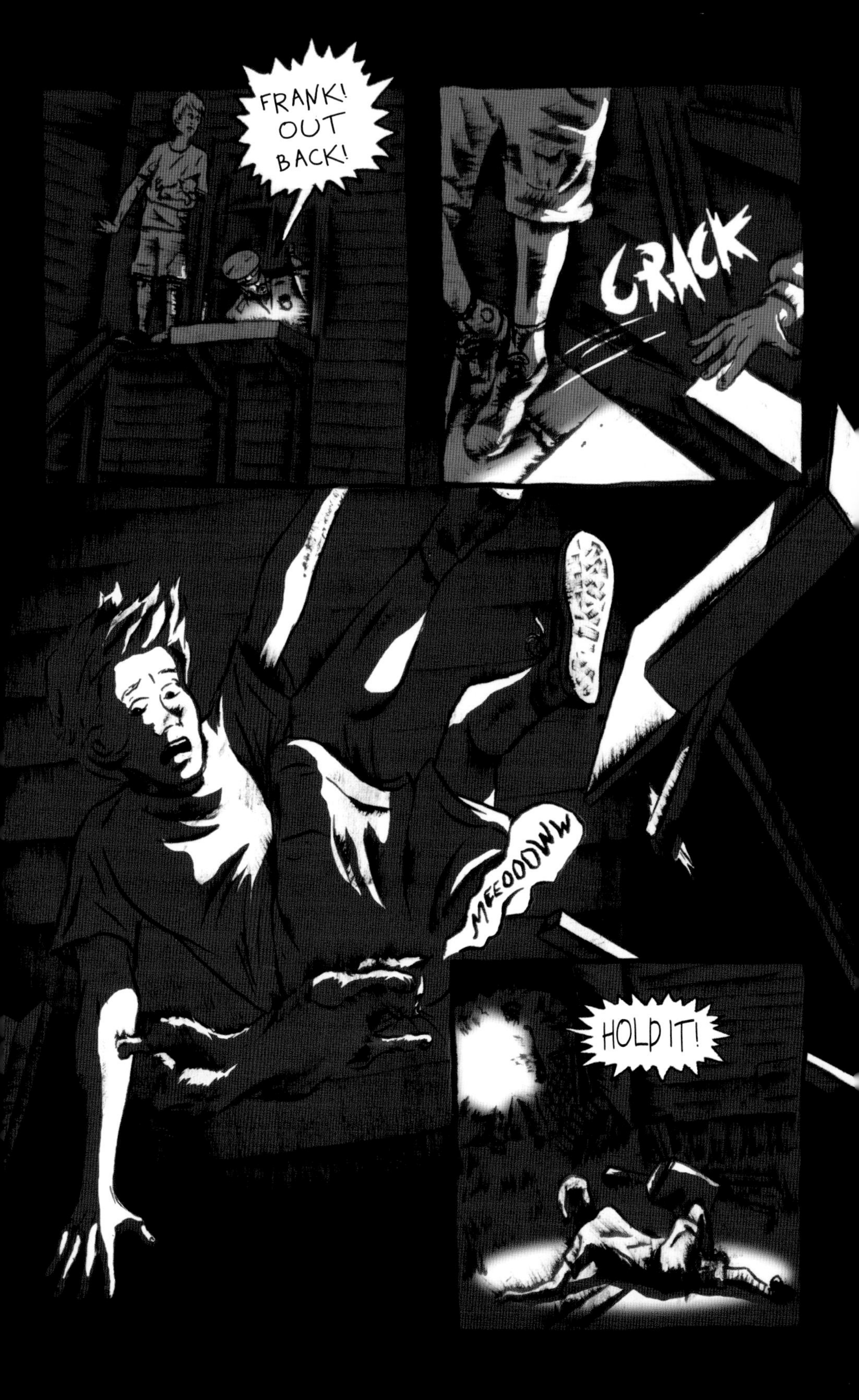
FRANK! OUT BACK!
CRACK
MEEOOOWW
HOLD IT!

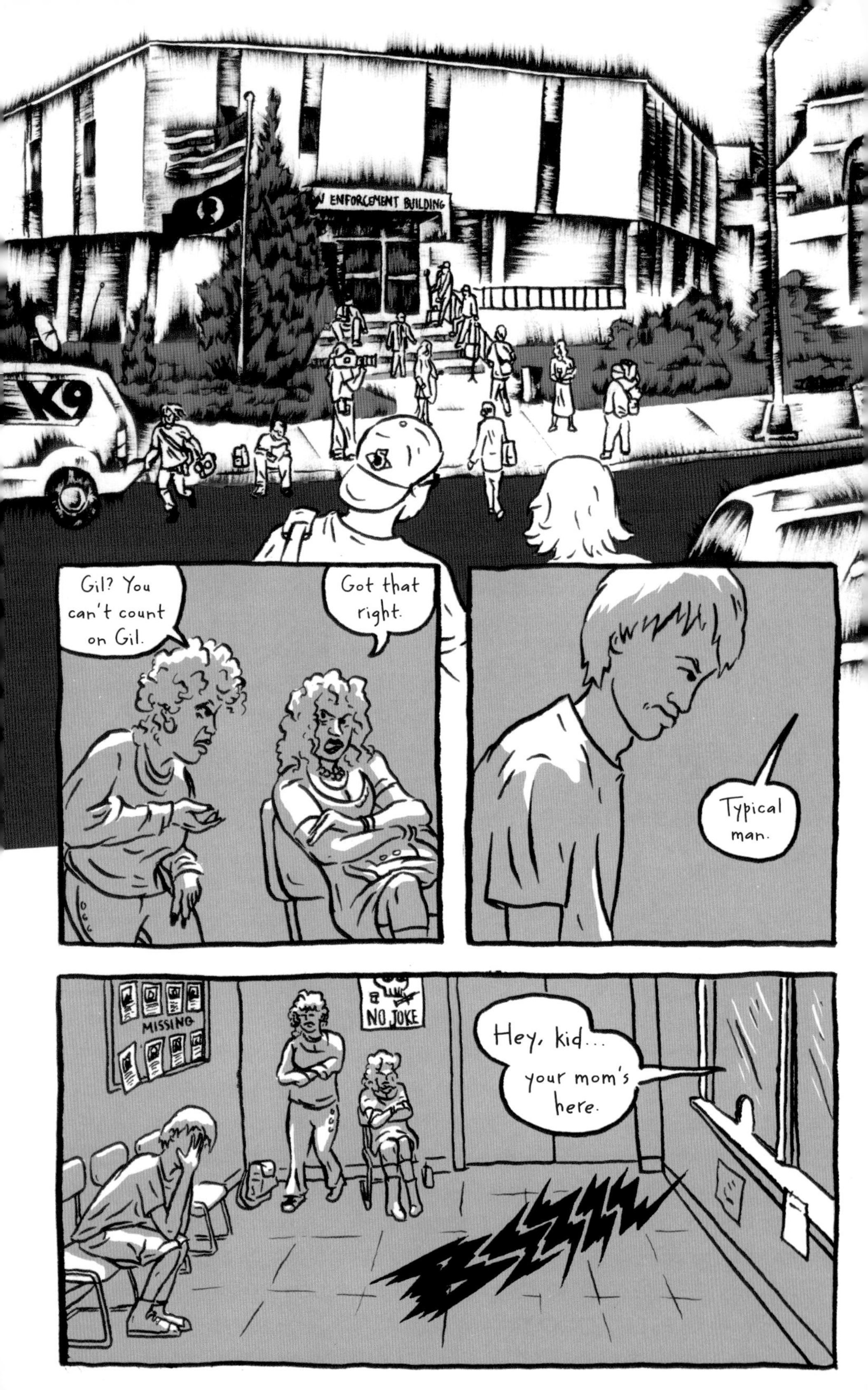

N ENFORCEMENT BUILDING
K9
Gil? You can't count on Gil.
Got that right.
Typical man.
MISSING
NO JOKE
Hey, kid... your mom's here.
BZZZZ

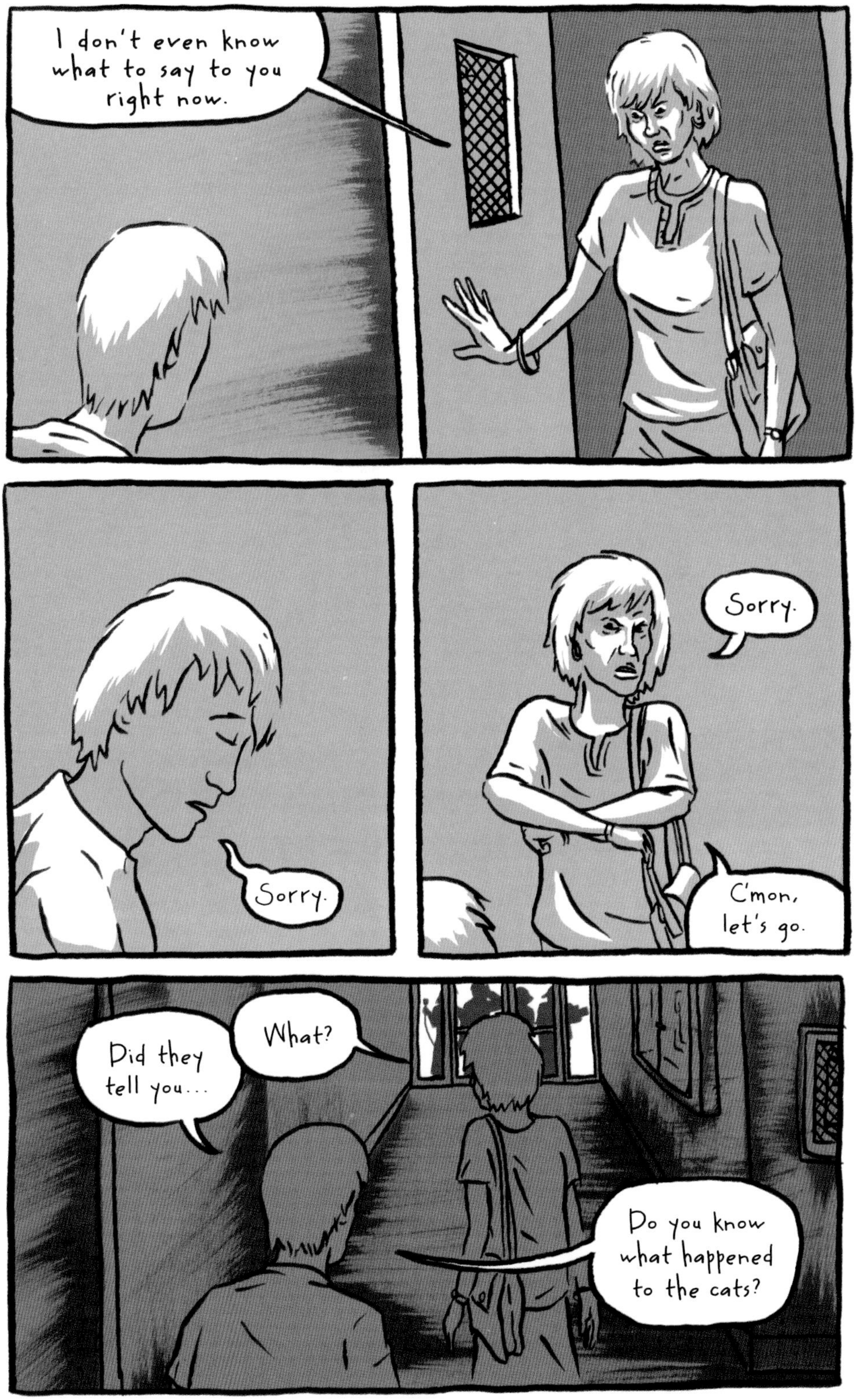
I don't even know what to say to you right now.
Sorry.
Sorry.
C'mon, let's go.
Did they tell you...
What?
Do you know what happened to the cats?

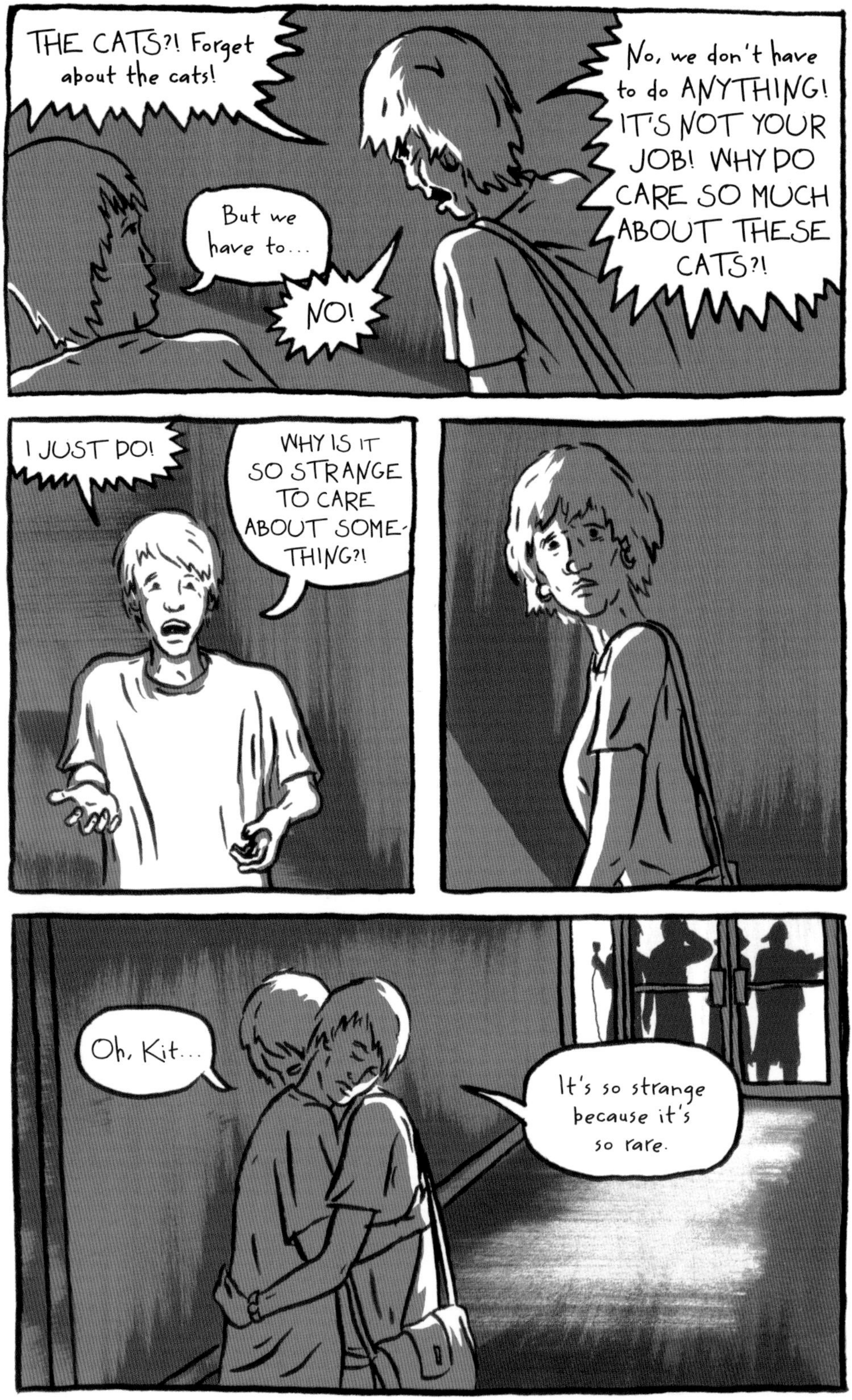
THE CATS?! Forget about the cats!
But we have to...
NO!
No, we don't have to do ANYTHING! IT'S NOT YOUR JOB! WHY DO CARE SO MUCH ABOUT THESE CATS?!
I JUST DO!
WHY IS IT SO STRANGE TO CARE ABOUT SOME-THING?!
Oh, Kit...
It's so strange because it's so rare.

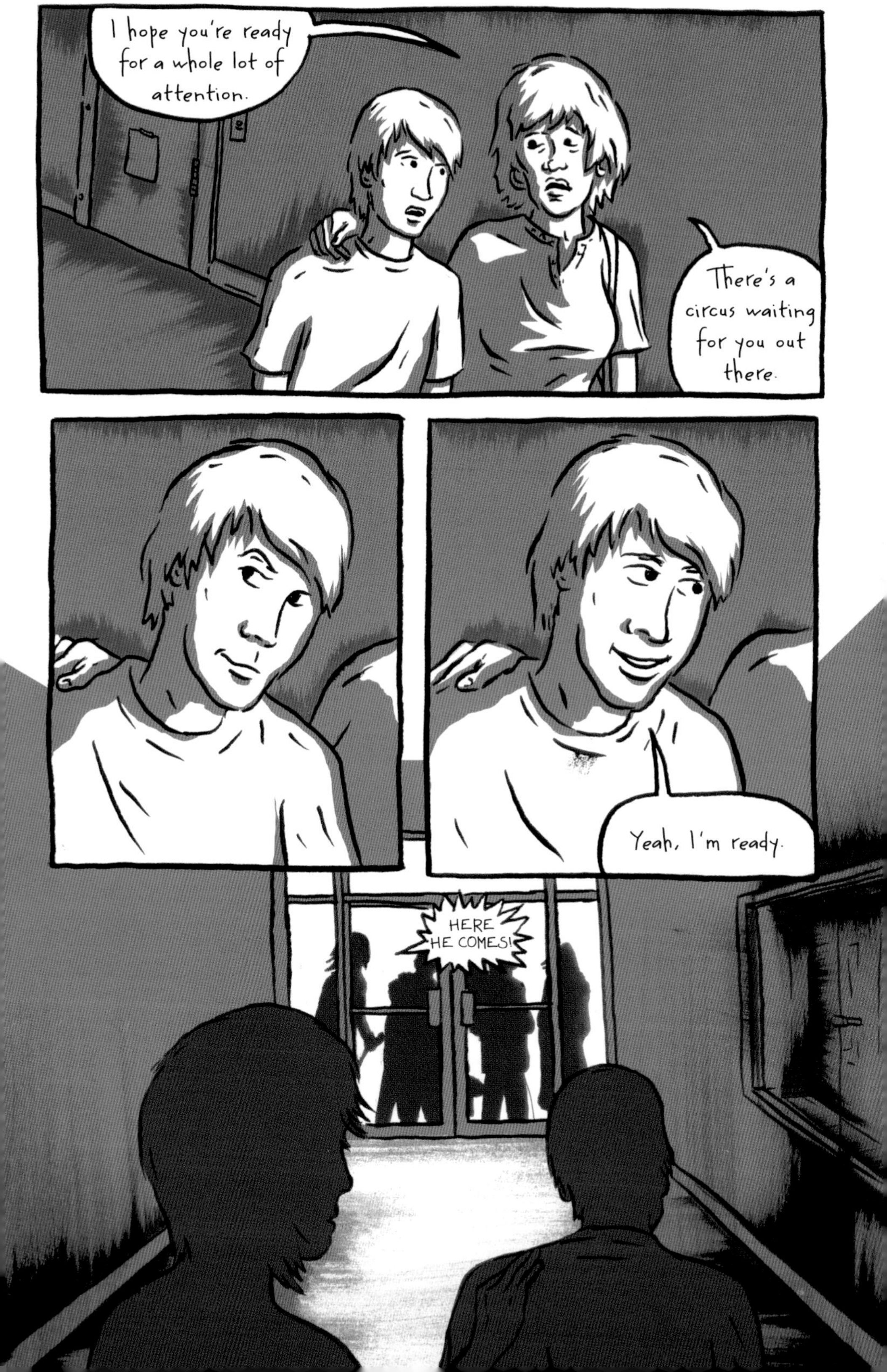
I hope you're ready for a whole lot of attention.
There's a circus waiting for you out there.
Yeah, I'm ready.
HERE HE COMES!

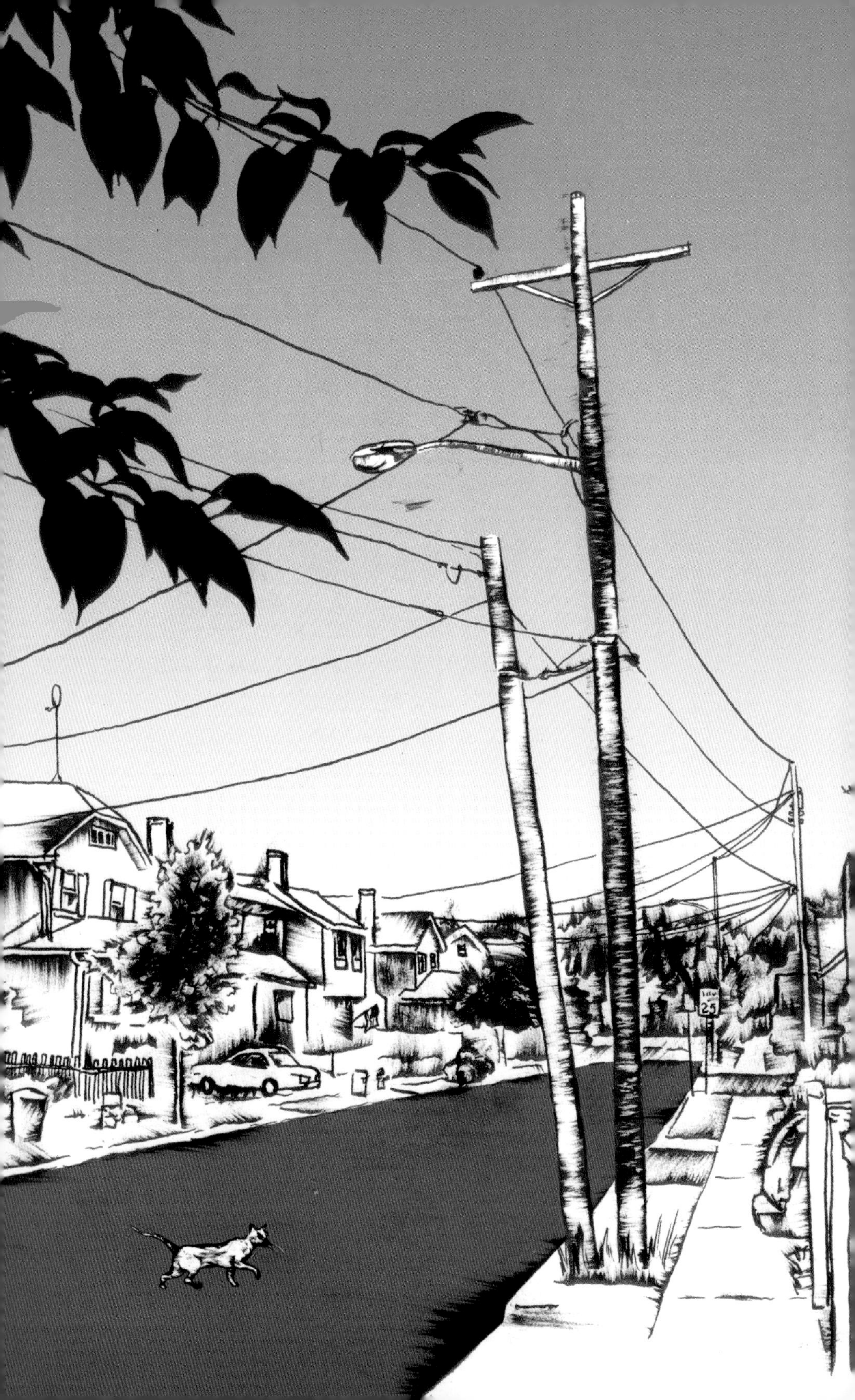
25

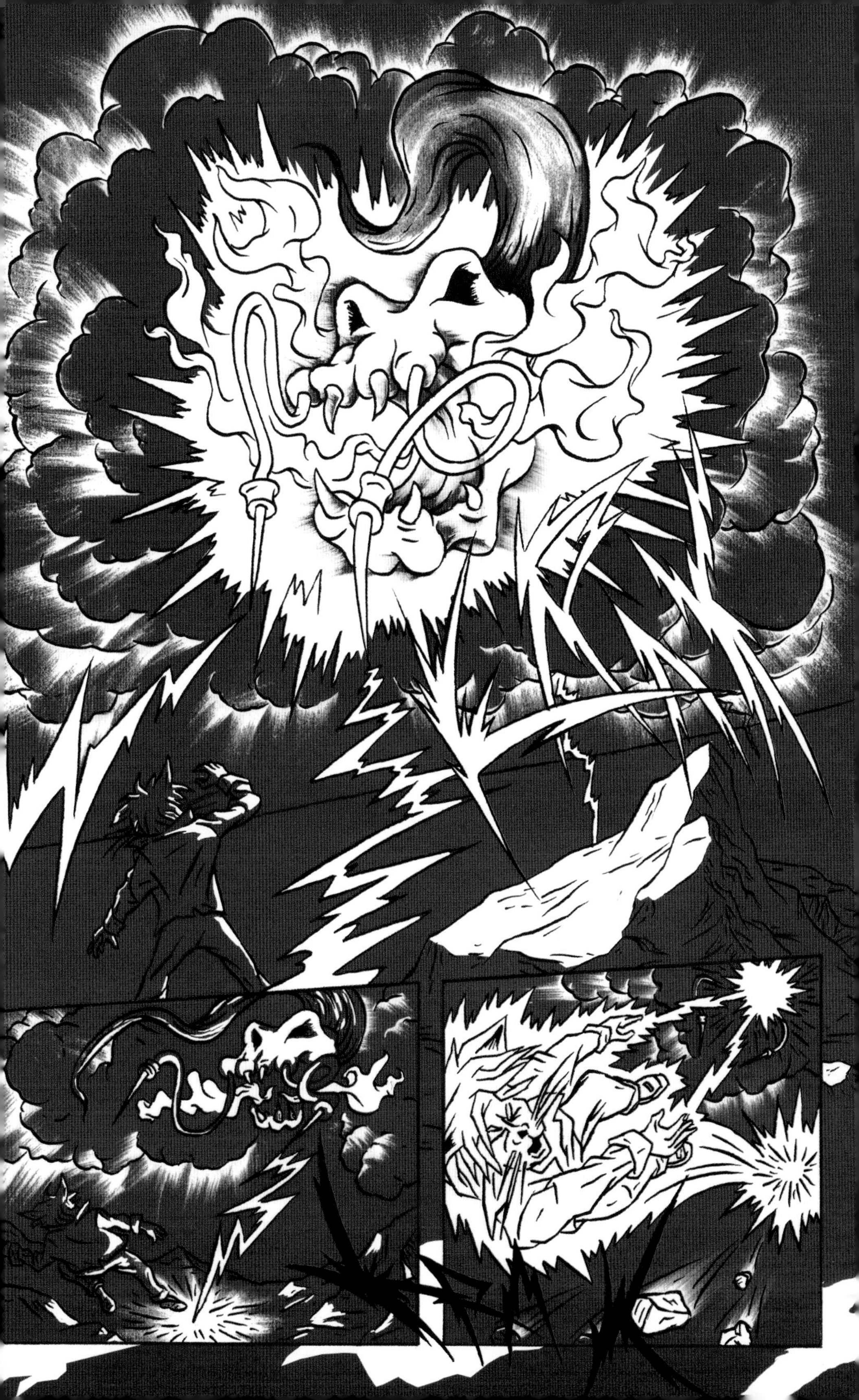

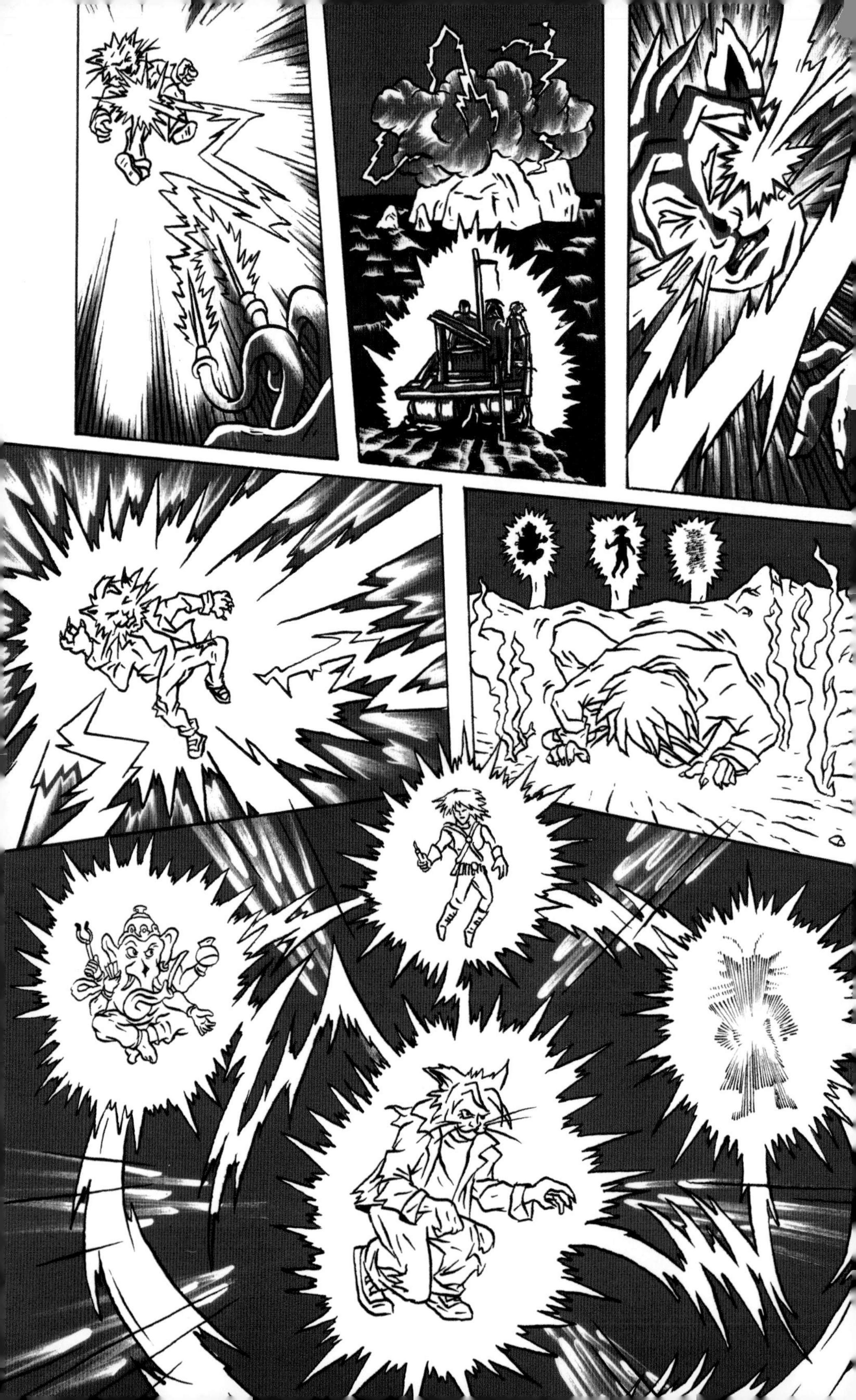

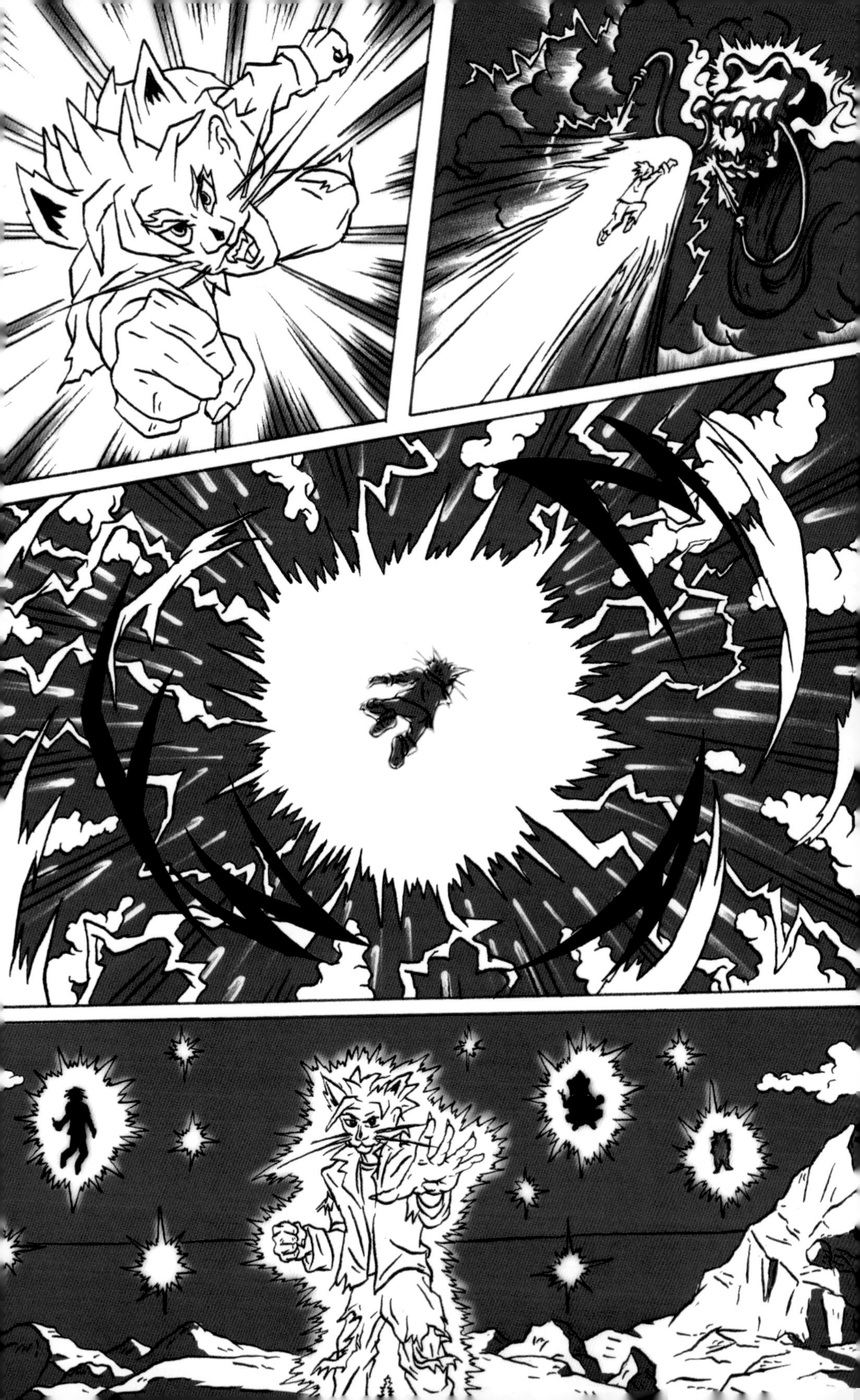

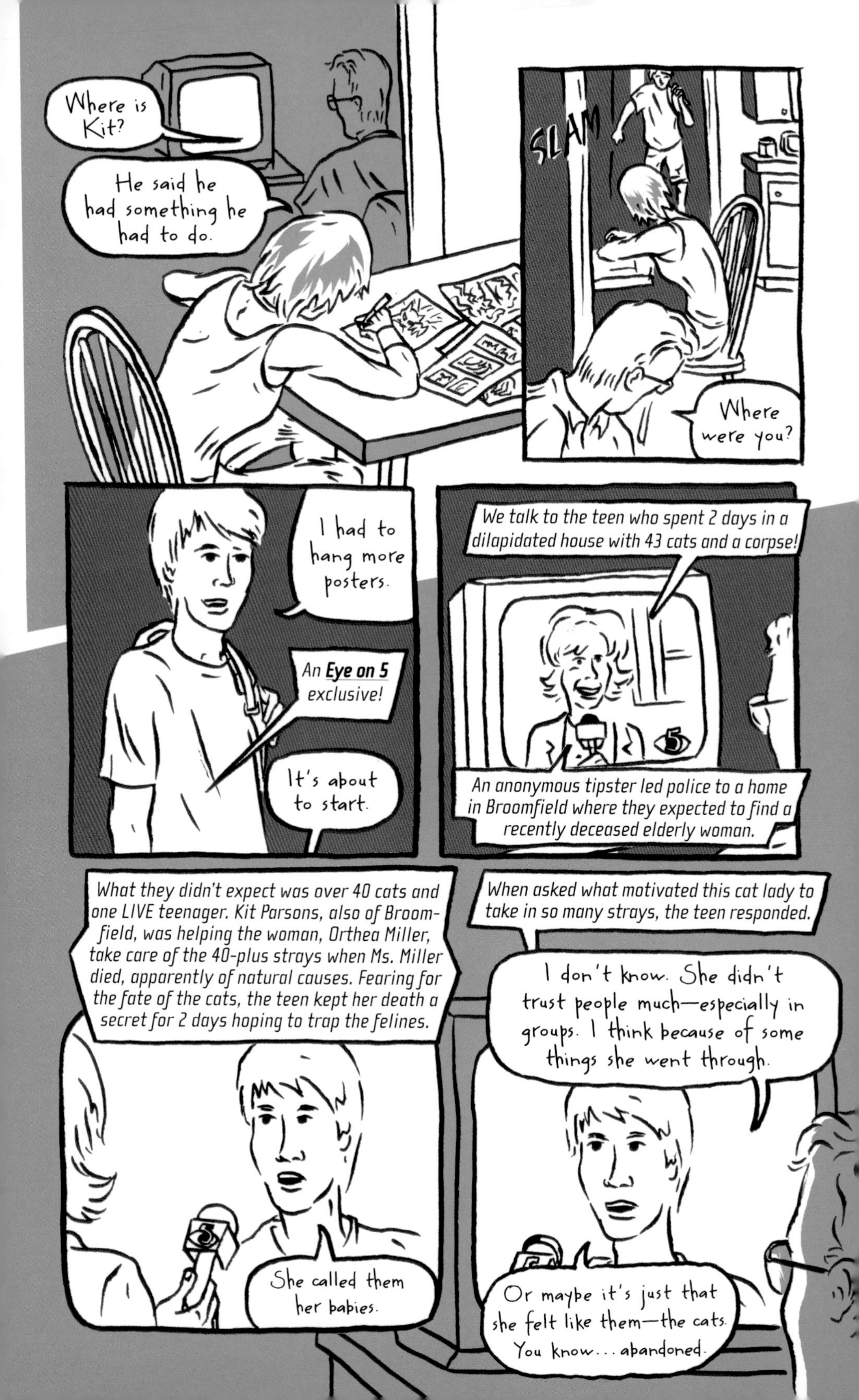
Where is Kit?
He said he had something he had to do.
SLAM
Where were you?
I had to hang more posters.
An Eye on 5 exclusive!
It's about to start.
We talk to the teen who spent 2 days in a dilapidated house with 43 cats and a corpse!
An anonymous tipster led police to a home in Broomfield where they expected to find a recently deceased elderly woman.
What they didn't expect was over 40 cats and one LIVE teenager. Kit Parsons, also of Broomfield, was helping the woman, Orthea Miller, take care of the 40-plus strays when Ms. Miller died, apparently of natural causes. Fearing for the fate of the cats, the teen kept her death a secret for 2 days hoping to trap the felines.
She called them her babies.
When asked what motivated this cat lady to take in so many strays, the teen responded.
I don't know. She didn't trust people much—especially in groups. I think because of some things she went through.
Or maybe it's just that she felt like them—the cats. You know... abandoned.

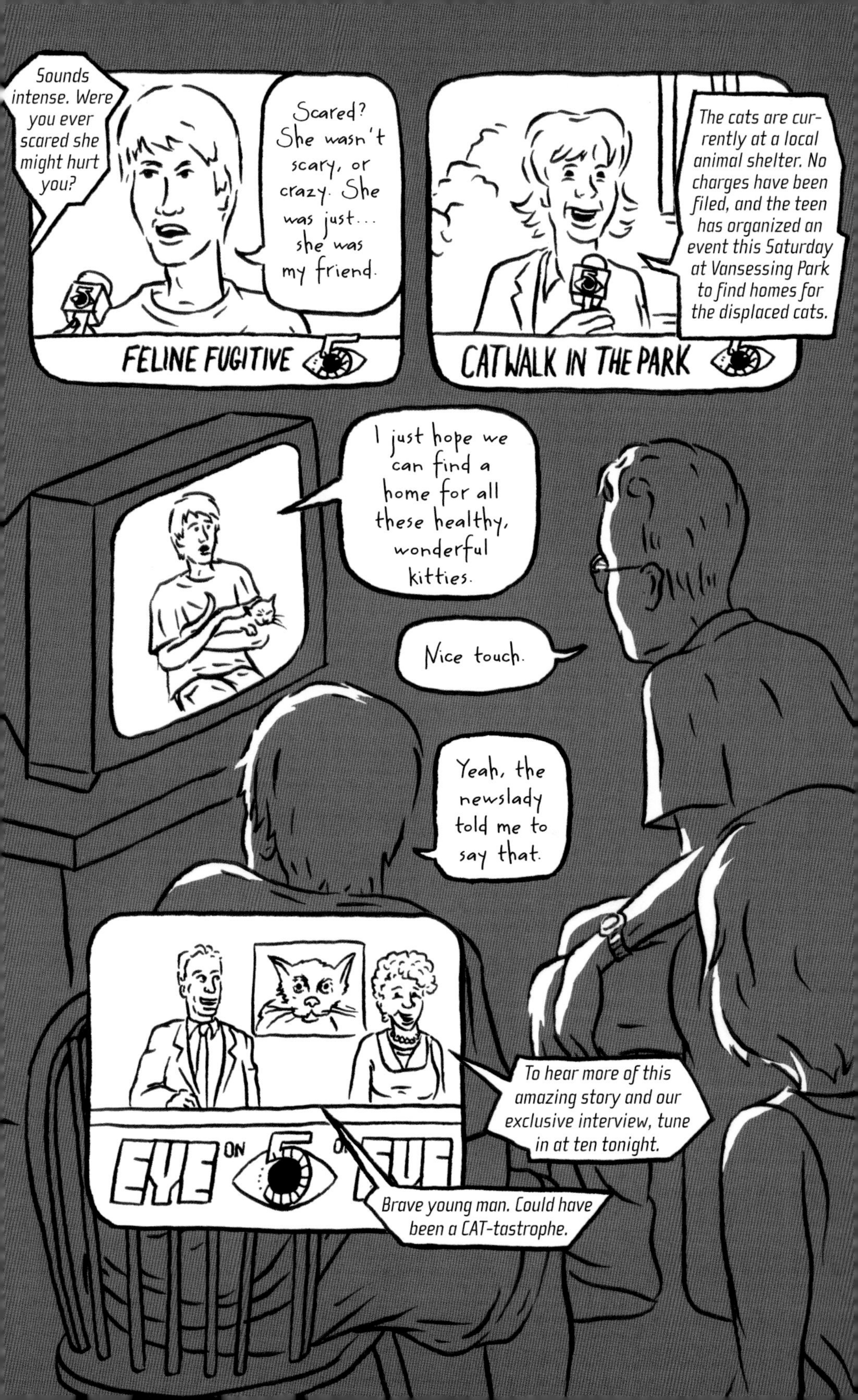
Sounds intense. Were you ever scared she might hurt you?
Scared? She wasn't scary, or crazy. She was just... she was my friend.
FELINE FUGITIVE
The cats are currently at a local animal shelter. No charges have been filed, and the teen has organized an event this Saturday at Vansessing Park to find homes for the displaced cats.
CATWALK IN THE PARK
I just hope we can find a home for all these healthy, wonderful kitties.
Nice touch.
Yeah, the newslady told me to say that.
To hear more of this amazing story and our exclusive interview, tune in at ten tonight.
Brave young man. Could have been a CAT-tastrophe.
EYE ON

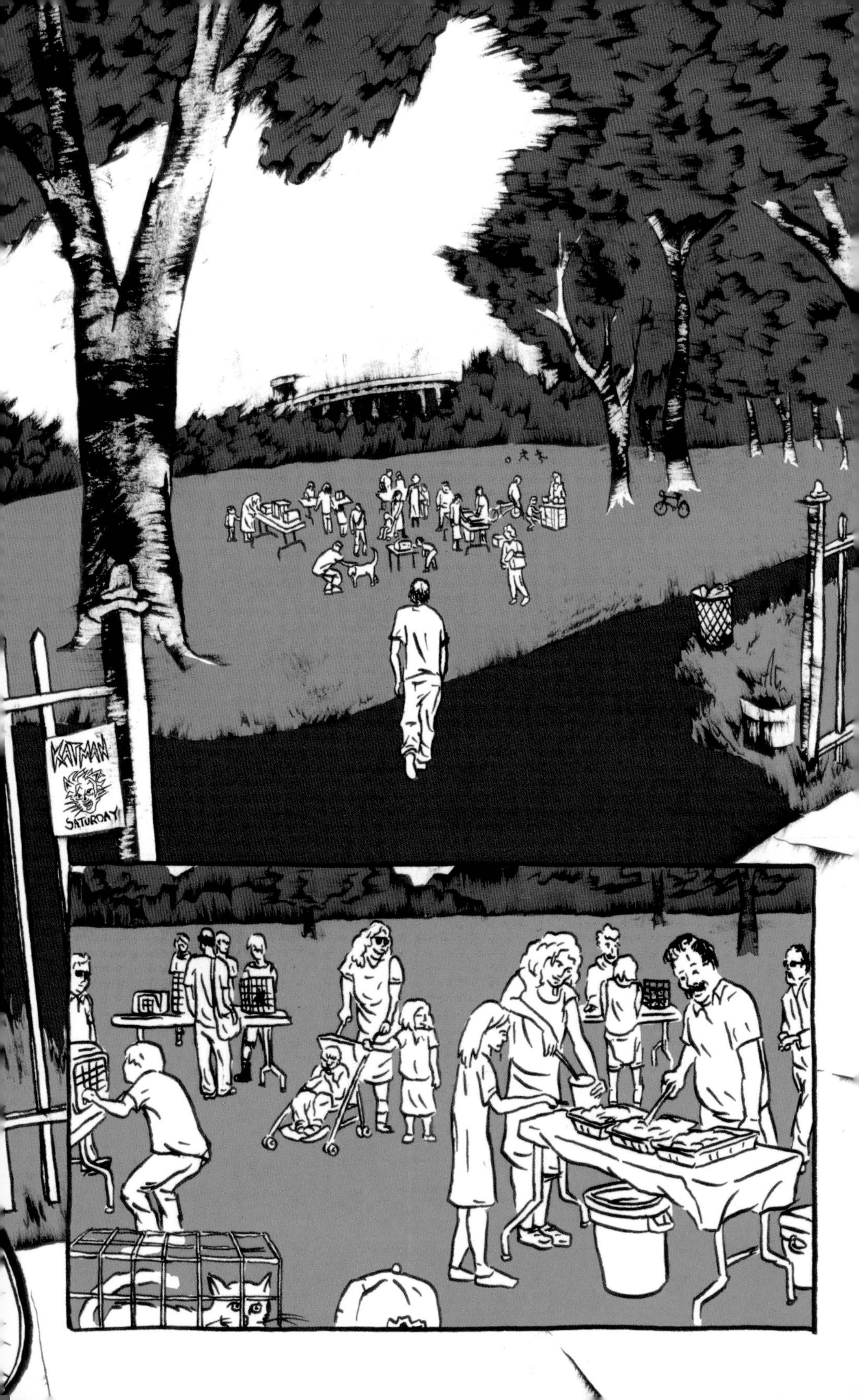
KATMAN
SATURDAY!

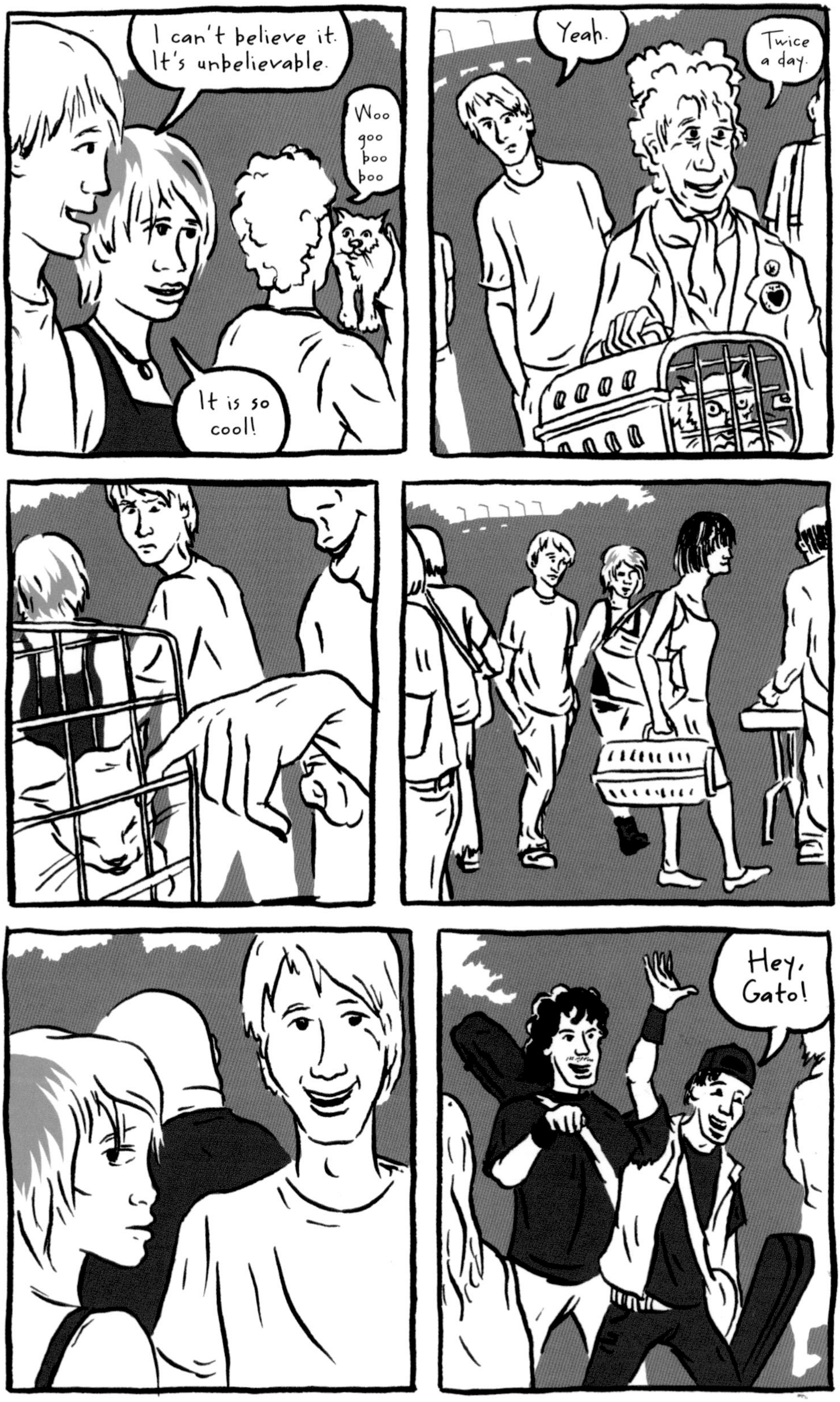
I can't believe it. It's unbelievable.
Woo goo boo boo
It is so cool!
Yeah.
Twice a day.
Hey, Gato!

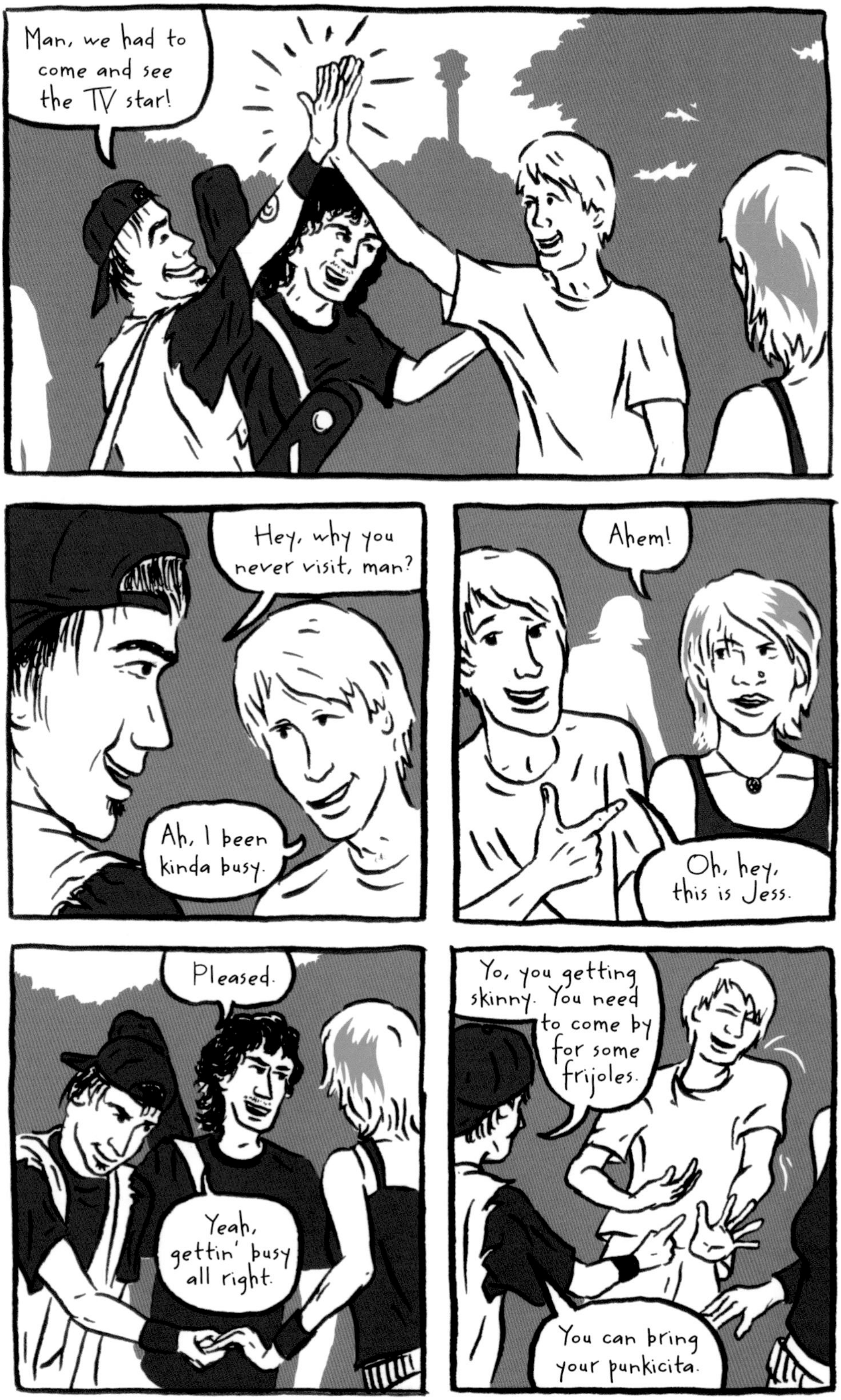
Man, we had to come and see the TV star!
Hey, why you never visit, man?
Ah, I been kinda busy.
Ahem!
Oh, hey, this is Jess.
Pleased.
Yeah, gettin' busy all right.
Yo, you getting skinny. You need to come by for some frijoles.
You can bring your punkicita.

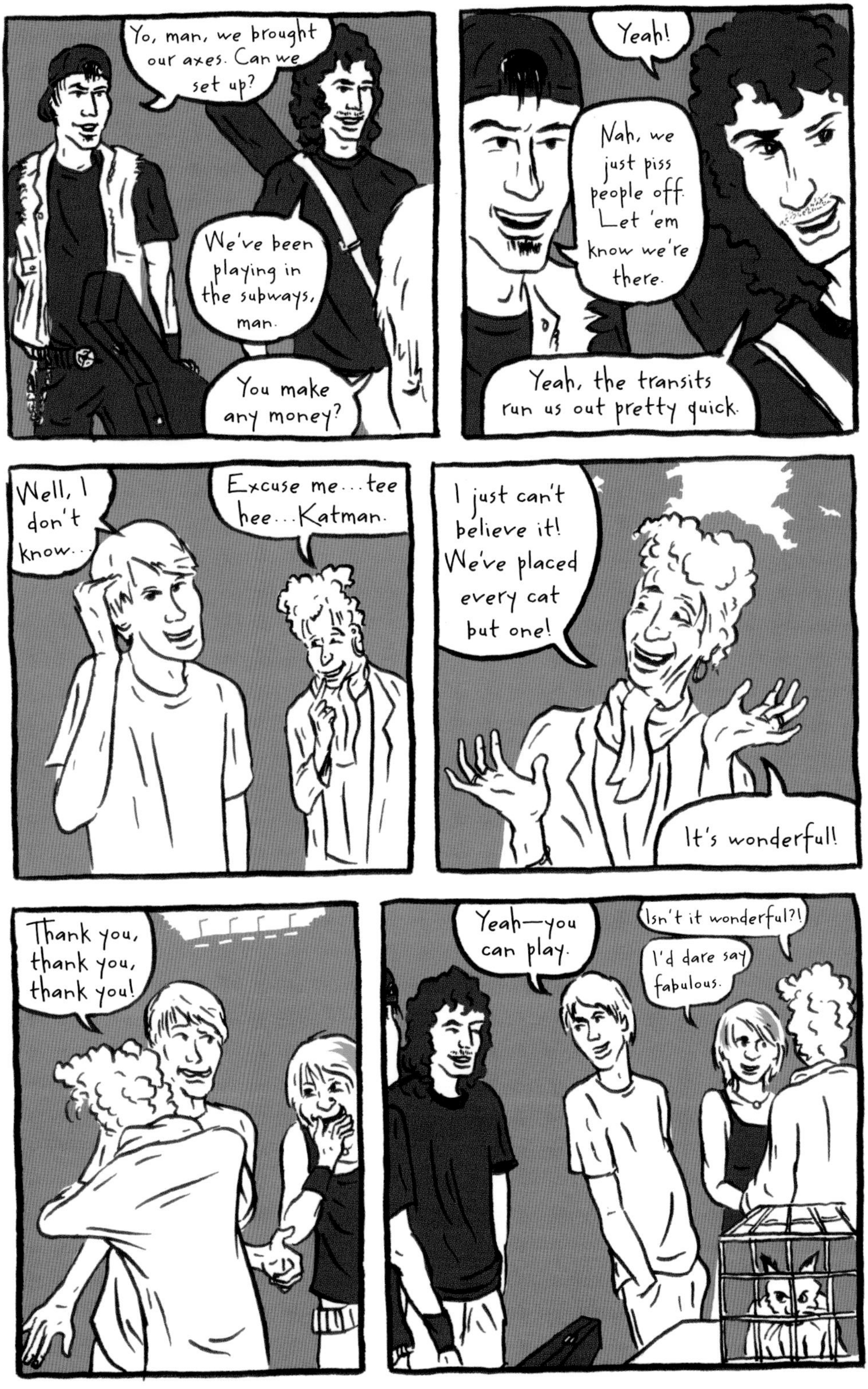
Yo, man, we brought our axes. Can we set up?
We've been playing in the subways, man.
You make any money?
Yeah!
Nah, we just piss people off. Let 'em know we're there.
Yeah, the transits run us out pretty quick.
Well, I don't know...
Excuse me... tee hee... Katman.
I just can't believe it! We've placed every cat but one!
It's wonderful!
Thank you, thank you, thank you!
Yeah—you can play.
Isn't it wonderful?!
I'd dare say fabulous.

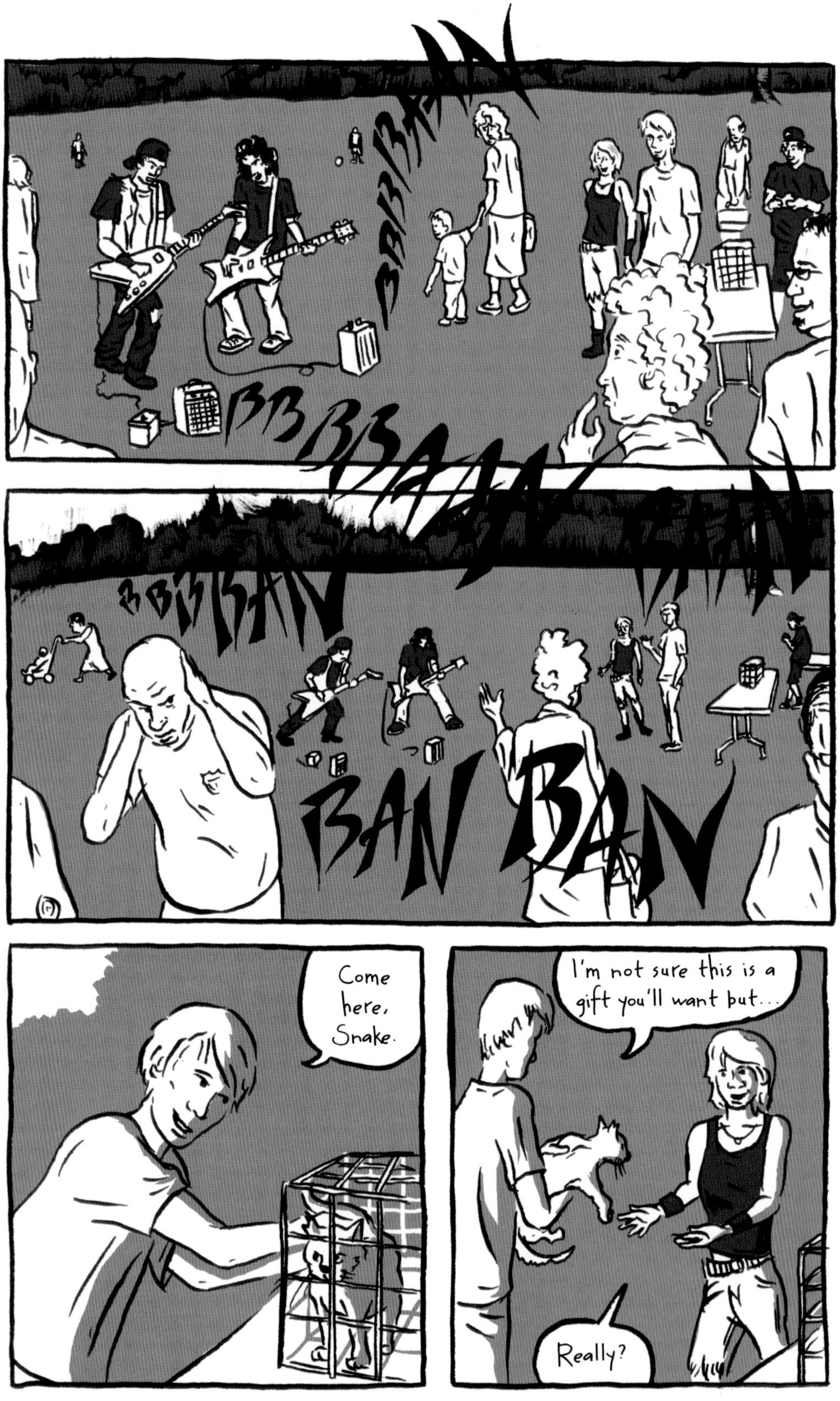
BAN BAN
Come here, Snake.
I'm not sure this is a gift you'll want but...
Really?

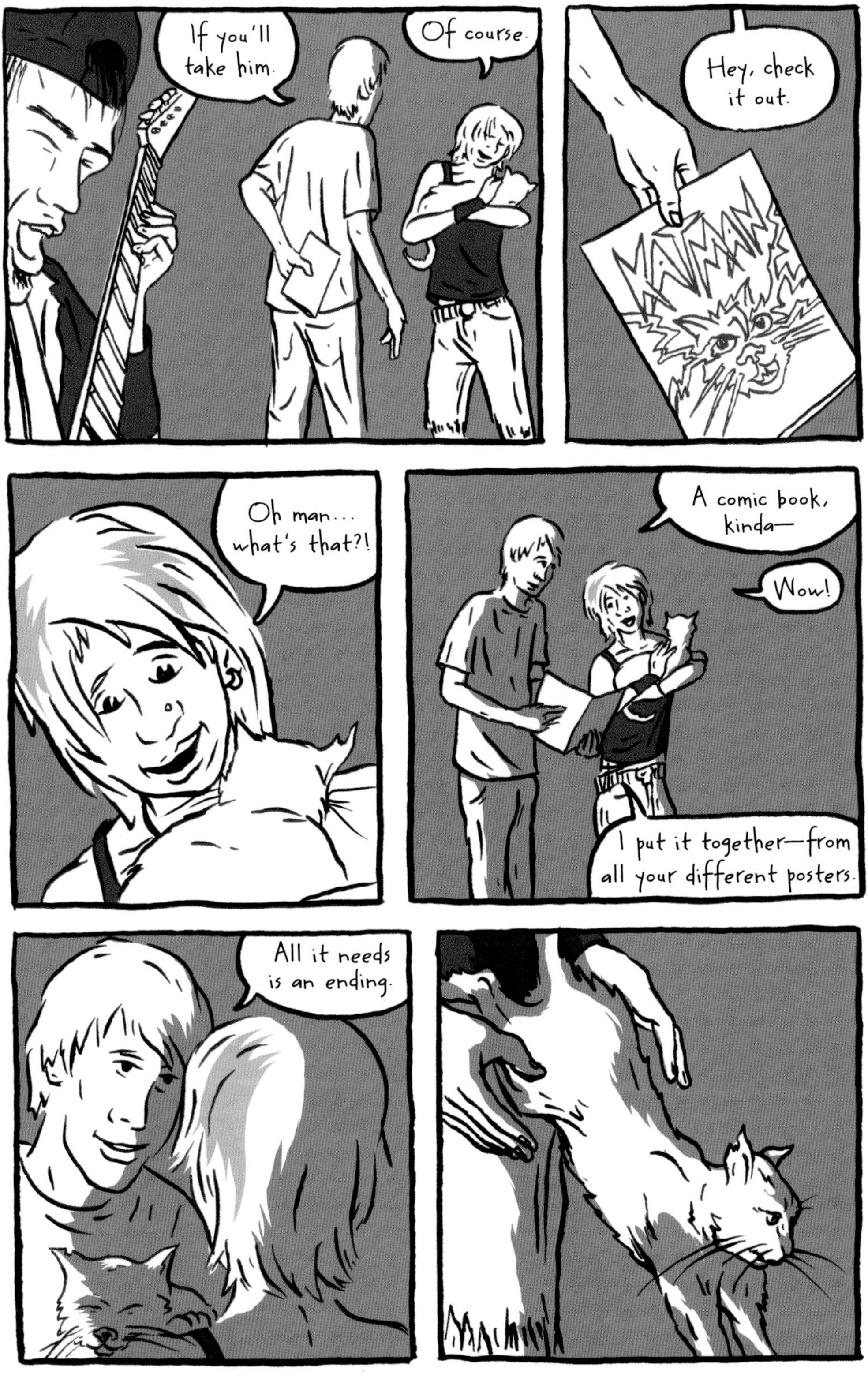
If you'll take him.
Of course.
Hey, check it out.
Oh man... what's that?!
A comic book, kinda—
Wow!
I put it together—from all your different posters.
All it needs is an ending.

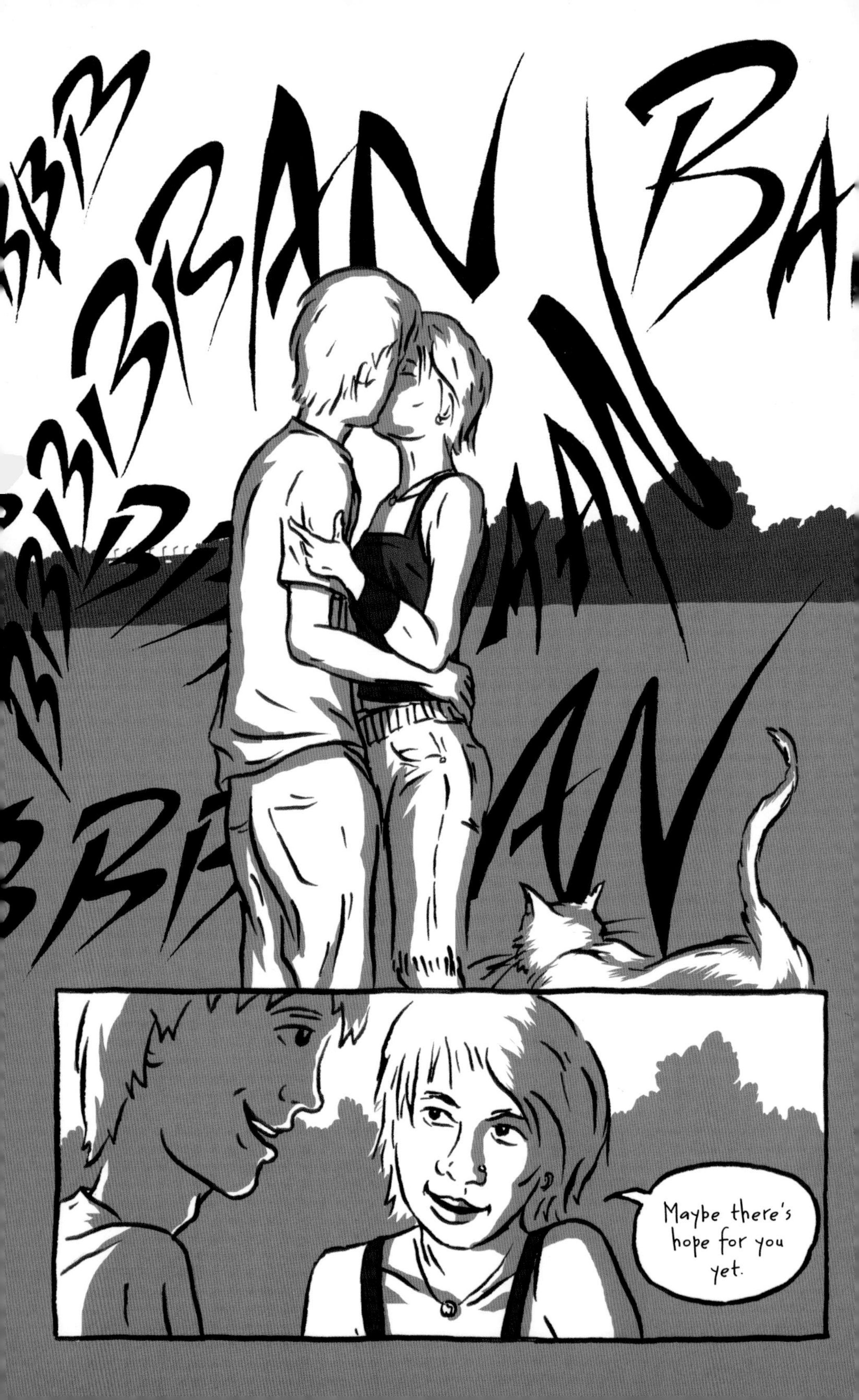
Maybe there's hope for you yet.

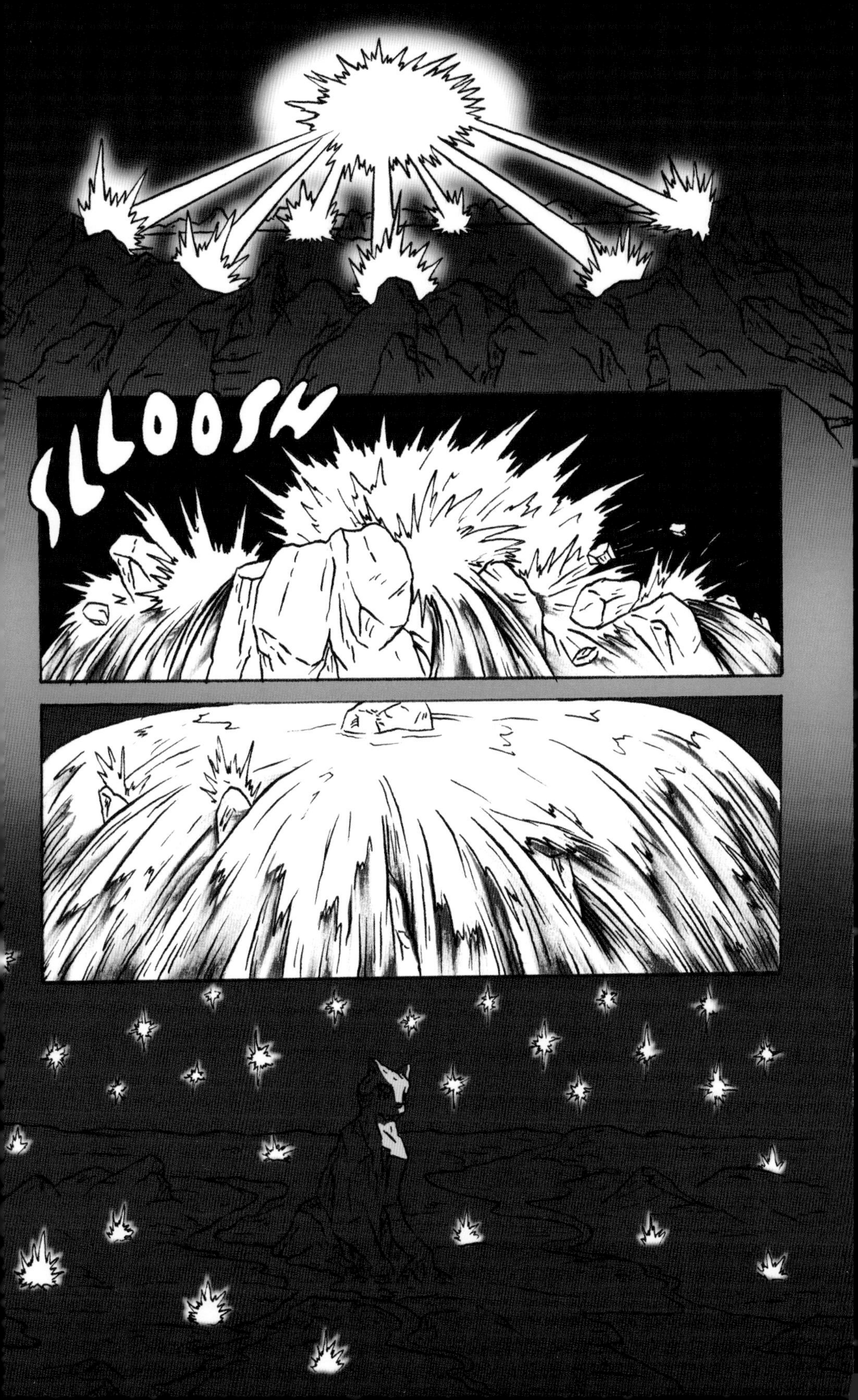
SLLOOSH

I WAS THINKING ABOUT WHAT JESS SAID...

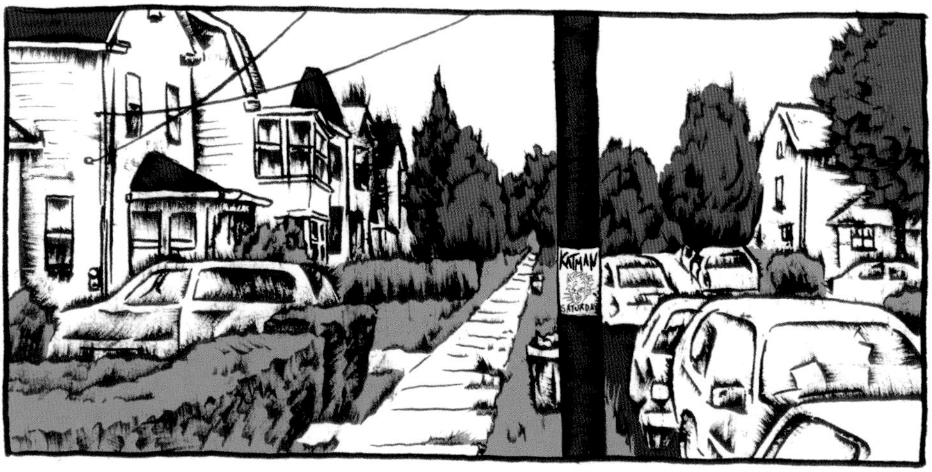
KATMAN
SATURDAY

ABOUT HOW GIVING THE CATS NAMES MADE THEM MORE LIKE PEOPLE.

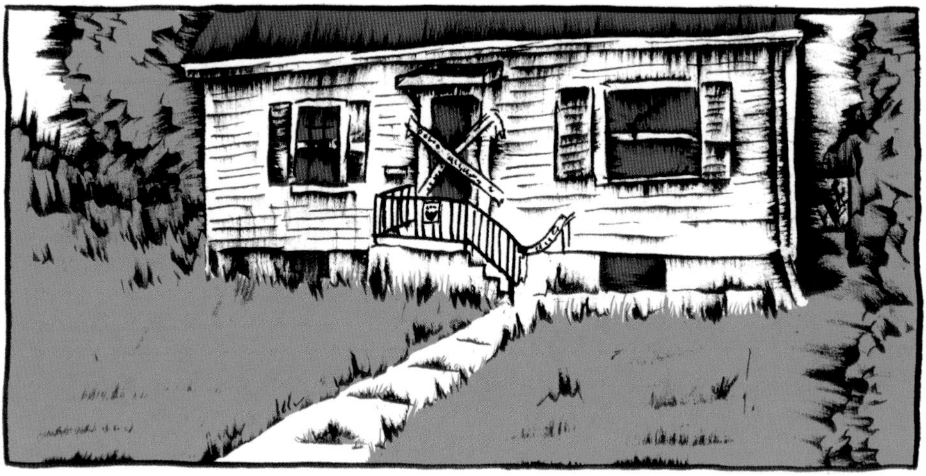

IT'S LIKE NAMING THEM TRANSFORMED THEM OR GAVE THEM SOME SORT OF POWER.

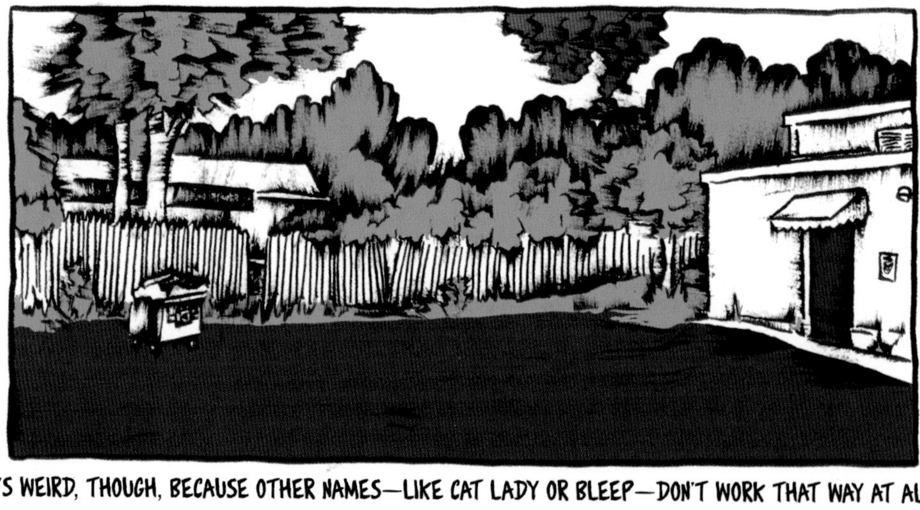

IT'S WEIRD, THOUGH, BECAUSE OTHER NAMES—LIKE CAT LADY OR BLEEP—DON'T WORK THAT WAY AT ALL.

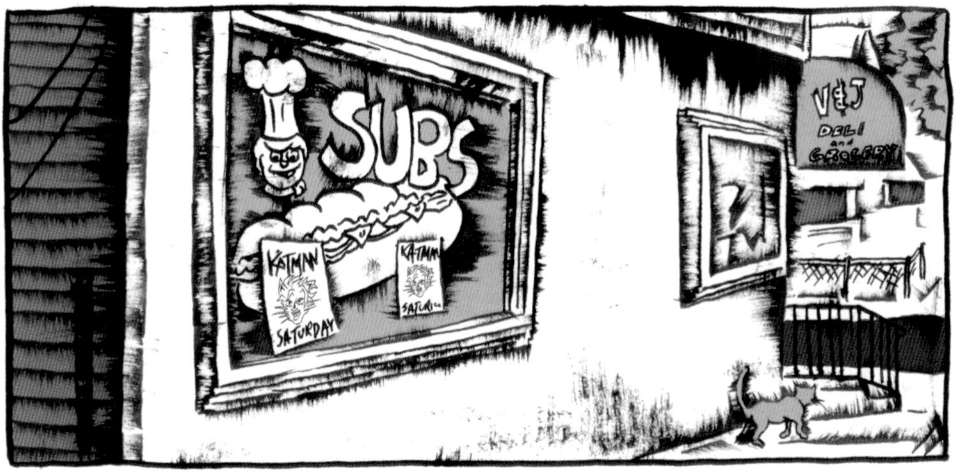
SUBS
KATMAN
SATURDAY
V&J
DELI
and
GROCERY

SO I'M THINKING MAYBE IT'S NOT SO MUCH WHAT YOUR NAME IS...

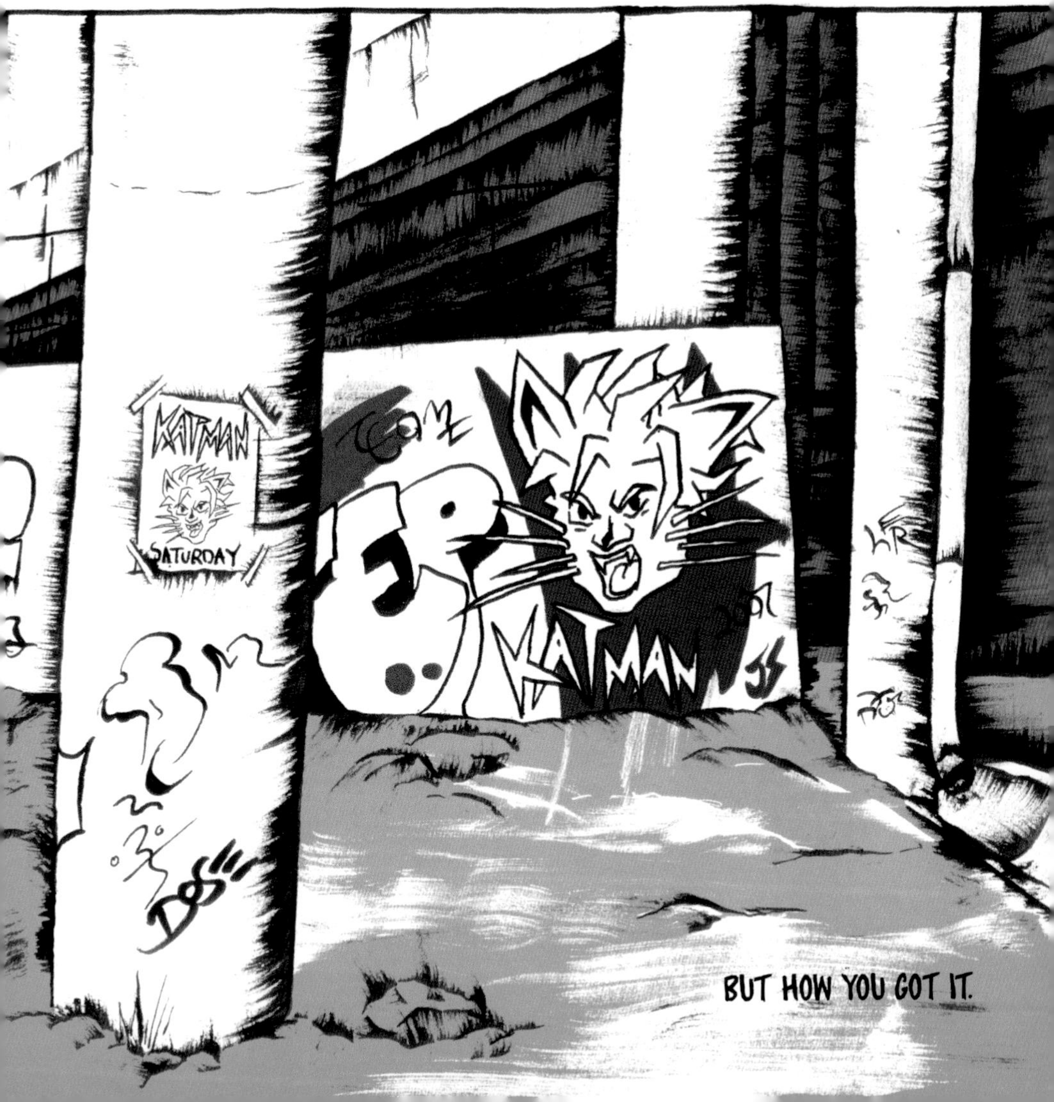
KATMAN
SATURDAY
KATMAN
BUT HOW YOU GOT IT.

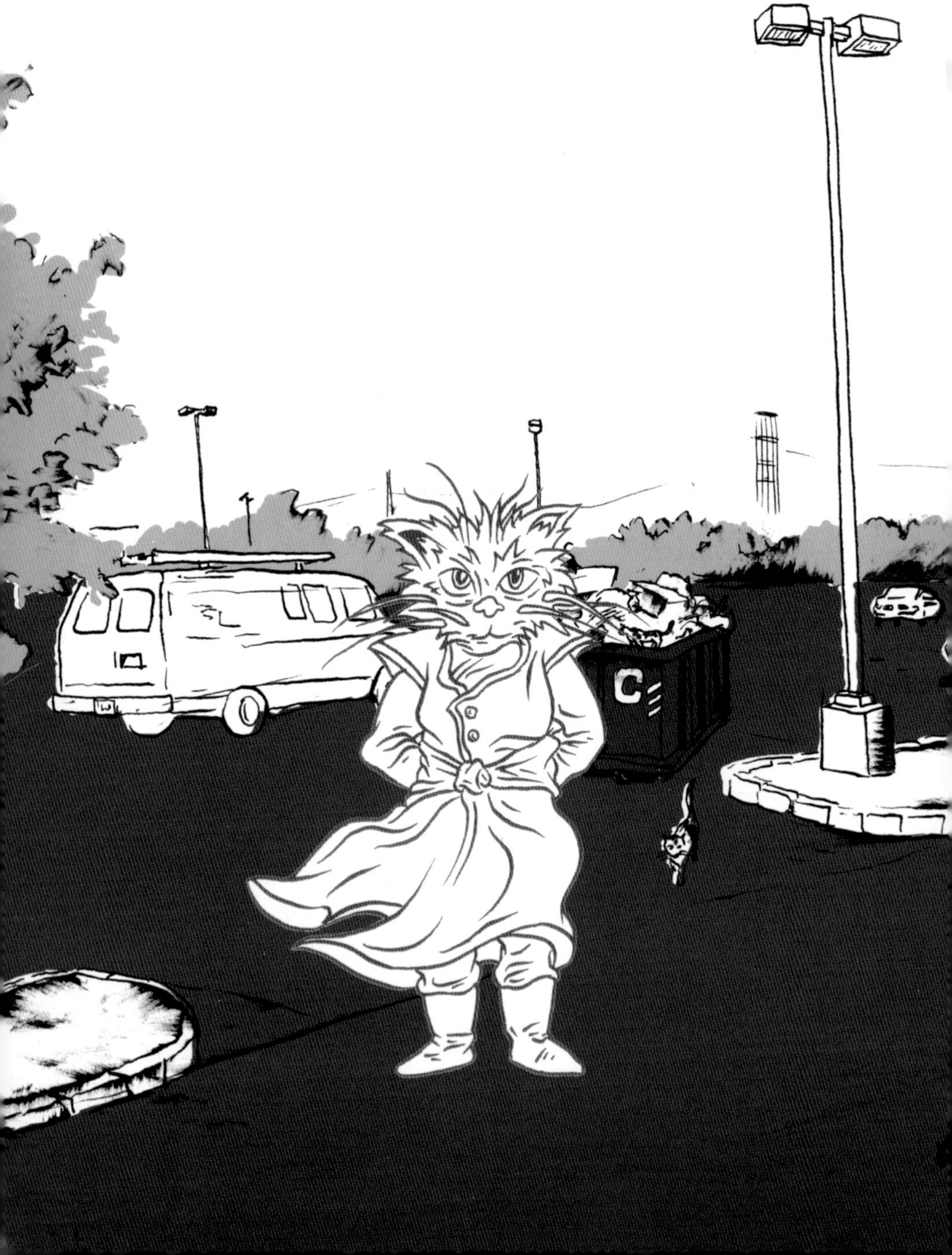
C